Da

'Thrilling and twisty – get 1...

J.P. ....N

'Absolutely terrifying! I turned every page with my heart in my mouth, utterly hooked by this explosive thriller. Ashley Kalagian Blunt taps into the dangers we face online every day and the monsters in our midst.'

PETRONELLA McGOVERN, AUTHOR OF *THE LIARS*

'With *Dark Mode*, Ashley Kalagian Blunt has turned her love of true crime and passion for suspense fiction into a fierce wake-up call of a thriller, one that looks unflinchingly at the horrors of the dark web and sheds light on the unimaginable. Riveting, tense and supremely chilling, this is an eye-opening must-read for crime fiction fans everywhere.'

ANNA DOWNES, AUTHOR OF *THE SHADOW HOUSE*

'Wow. Page turning, chilling dread that kept me guessing until the end. Ashley Kalagian Blunt hits it out of the park, creating a dark world where your worst fears aren't the worst thing to fear – not even close.'

R.W.R. McDONALD, AUTHOR OF *NANCY BUSINESS*

'*Dark Mode*'s greatest achievement is that, as the pieces fall into place, it's not just Reagan Carsen's world that's turned upside down – it's ours . . . there are some realities most of us would sooner pretend are impossible than acknowledge are already here. Kalagian Blunt forces our gaze upon them in this compulsive and breathless thriller.'

JAMES McKENZIE WATSON, AUTHOR OF *DENIZEN*

'If you think that what happens on the dark web will never affect you, this book begs the question: are you sure about that? Like, *sure-sure*? A twisty, terrifying thriller, *Dark Mode* will have you buying a flip phone and moving off the grid the second you turn the final page, just so you can breathe again. I loved it.'

PIP DRYSDALE, AUTHOR OF *THE NEXT GIRL*

'Ashley Kalagian Blunt plunges the reader into the darkest corners of the internet and it could not be more terrifying! A superb thriller that will keep you riveted to the page and dial up your tech anxieties to eleven.'

DINUKA McKENZIE, AUTHOR OF *THE TORRENT*

'*Dark Mode*'s tension is visceral from the first page . . . terrifying and timely.'

AMY LOVAT, SECRET BOOK STUFF

'Hold on tight because this heart-stopping page-turner will shake you to your core. With its bizarre crimes, explosive revelations, and unbearable tension, *Dark Mode* shatters our blithe acceptance of the online world in a nail-biting thriller that is unforgettable. Ashley Kalagian Blunt is a masterful storyteller who has ingeniously twisted fact with fiction to deliver an absolute cracker of a read. Honestly, you won't be able to put it down until you know who, when, where, how and why. Leave the light on, lock your door, and for god's sake, check your privacy settings.'

LYN YEOWART, AUTHOR OF *THE SILENT LISTENER*

'Masterfully crafted and addictive, *Dark Mode* will keep you on edge to the last page . . . I know I'll be thinking about it, and the perverse reality it reveals, for a long long time.'

LEE KOFMAN, AUTHOR OF *THE WRITER LAID BARE*

DARK MODE

ASHLEY KALAGIAN BLUNT

ultimo
press

Originally published in 2023 by Ultimo Press,
an imprint of Hardie Grant Publishing.
This edition published in 2024.

Ultimo Press
Gadigal Country
7, 45 Jones Street
Ultimo, NSW 2007
ultimopress.com.au

   ultimopress

 A catalogue record for this
book is available from the
National Library of Australia

Dark Mode
ISBN 978 1 76115 236 8 (paperback)

Cover design George Saad
Botanical illustrations Cheryl Hodges
Author photograph Courtesy of Marnya Rothe
Text design Simon Paterson, Bookhouse
Typesetting Bookhouse, Sydney | Minion Pro
Copyeditor Deonie Fiford
Proofreader Rebecca Hamilton

10 9 8 7 6 5 4 3 2

Printed in Australia by Opus Group Pty Ltd, an Accredited ISO AS/NZS 14001
Environmental Management System printer.

 The paper this book is printed on is certified against the
Forest Stewardship Council® Standards.
Griffin Press – a member of the Opus Group – holds
chain of custody certification SCS-COC-001185. FSC®
promotes environmentally responsible, socially beneficial
and economically viable management of the world's forests.

Ultimo Press acknowledges the Traditional Owners of the Country on which we work,
the Gadigal People of the Eora Nation and the Wurundjeri People of the Kulin Nation,
and recognises their continuing connection to the land, waters and culture. We pay our
respects to their Elders past and present.

For my parents,
whose love and support make everything possible.

While the characters and their precise circumstances are fictitious, the crimes described in this book are drawn from real events. The attitudes that drive these crimes are also real. And they're everywhere.

PART 1

NATURE/FANTASY

Prologue

Sunday, 15 January 2017

A spider web caught at Reagan's face as she turned the corner, its invisible strands trailing across her cheeks. Busy rubbing the web from her eyes, she got closer than she otherwise might have. Close enough for the early morning sun to catch the wet inner cavity of the naked, pale-skinned torso on the concrete.

A mannequin. It had to be. Human bodies didn't come apart like that.

She edged forward. Gipps Lane was tidy, all bitumen and graffitied concrete, brick walls, and two commercial dumpsters. Nothing alive, not a dandelion or a tuft of moss. Her Timex read 5.57 am. The sun had barely cracked the horizon and already Sydney's mid-January heat was clinging to her skin.

The body lay in a patch of light, its two severed pieces a half-metre apart, off-centre.

A mannequin wouldn't have a wet body cavity, and now that Reagan was closer, she could see flies crawling over the flesh.

A metallic whiff of organ meat caught in her nostrils, jarring loose a memory of a night her mother had cooked liver for dinner.

It's a body. Reagan stood frozen, the knuckles of both hands pressing into her lips. Above, masked lapwings broke the hush, their sharp *kri-kri-kri* like an alarm.

There was no blood. None on the concrete, none on the body.

And for someone to die like that, there should have been a lot of blood.

The smell hit her again – *amorphophallus titanum. Corpse flower.* The plant's giant blossoms gave off a rotting, sweaty, mothball smell to attract carnivorous insects.

The woman's right breast was gone, leaving a rough-edged circle of pinkish-red flesh. A strip of her left thigh was missing. A grotesque joker smile marred her face. Her arms were flung above her head, and her spread legs lay to the right of the torso, as if they could be part of another person. She looked younger than Reagan, twenty or so, no lines framing her eyes. Her skin was chalky. A rash of red bumps ran along the crease of her legs, and chipped turquoise polish covered her toenails. She had no clothes, tattoos or jewellery, no handbag. Her face tilted eastward. *Like a sunflower.*

It was her hair that made Reagan gasp. The dark mess of it fanned around her head, quivering in the breeze.

She straightened, head flicking right and left. No people, and along the bricked back walls and metal roller doors lining the

4

laneway, no windows. On weekdays there were more people about, but at dawn on Sunday, the streets looked abandoned.

A fly crawled along the dead woman's lip, disappearing into her mouth.

Someone needed to call the cops.

And there was no way it would be Reagan.

A flap of wings startled her. An ibis, black-eyed and skulking, stalked toward the body.

Reagan stamped her foot. The bird ignored her, its long black toes curling around the pale skin of the woman's wrist.

'Get away!' Reagan kicked, coming close, and the ibis hopped down, rearing and ruffling its wings as it scuttled away.

Her mobile was in her pocket. But that was traceable, even if she blocked her number.

She needed to get out of there.

She scanned the buildings. No white configurations aimed like oversized guns, no bulbous dark glass. How could there be no cameras? Someone had to be seeing this. The cops must be on their way.

The gamey, butcher-shop smell hung in the air.

A couple emerged from the park at the laneway's end, two silhouettes dwarfed by fig trees, a dog racing ahead. If they saw Reagan sprinting away, it would be worse than if they met her standing over the body, holding out empty hands and saying, *I just found her, call triple zero.*

But if she stayed, the police would want her name, her real birthdate, her actual address, not her postbox. They'd ask a hundred questions, then they'd ask again, their voices flinty, eyes like eels.

Two more ibises snuck toward the body. *Shit.* Where were the couple with the dog? They should be around the corner, with a mobile each, hopefully with the dog leashed.

An ibis pecked at the woman's foot.

With a grimace, Reagan flung one awkward foot out, her back to the ibises, finding her stride.

There was a payphone on Enmore Road. *You can call anonymously.*

But nothing was anonymous these days. If the police wanted her name, they'd get it.

The concrete building on the corner cast the street into shadow. Reagan didn't see the cyclist, hunched over his curled handlebars, a blur of sky-blue spandex and sweat, until she was right in front of him.

He swerved, the swoosh of air from the bike riffling her tank top. A warning rippled through her guts. *His helmet.* It'd been ungainly, protruding. She twisted back. The cyclist continued along the side street. That was definitely a camera on his head.

Above, a raven groaned. She thought of the ibis stepping on the body and quickened her pace.

She hadn't used a payphone since she was a teen. The half booth sheltering this one smelled like urine, and the handset was grimy. Her pulse bashed at her ears. *Report it and hang up.*

She couldn't force herself to dial.

Her Timex read 6.03. Someone else would see the woman. This was a busy neighbourhood, only a few stops from Central Station.

When the woman's death made the news, when he realised how close he'd come to her, the cyclist would review his footage, hand it over to the police. Would it be days before they identified Reagan, or hours?

Unless he hadn't been recording.

She dropped the receiver, wishing she'd run past the woman, blinking sweat and spider web out of her eyes.

'I'm sorry. I can't.' It came out under her breath, unexpected.

She ran, too fast, fighting to calm her pace.

Sydney red gums lined her street. Neighbours grew gerberas and coleus alongside strips of patchy, browning grass. They'd gone thirty-four days without rain in the roiling summer heat. Scientists had discovered that plants in need of water produced a high frequency distress sound, an ultrasonic scream far outside the range of human hearing. Reagan couldn't hear the plants screaming, but she swore she could feel it.

She'd put on her running gear with a tentative smile that morning, admiring the new peach tank she'd received for Christmas, and tugging on her favourite cap, the colours of the Sydney Olympics logo faded with age. Thinking today could be the day things turned around.

Now the dead woman's face stayed with her. Pale and oval-shaped with a broad forehead, defined lips, thin straight eyebrows, a cherubic nose. And those loose, wild black curls.

She could have been Reagan's twin.

It could be a coincidence. A gigantic fucking coincidence.

But there was another possibility.

Him.

15 January 2017

After years of planning, the day has finally arrived. By
now you've seen the news. I could tell you about it in
electrifying detail, but I know we share a preference for
the visual.

02-1024x685hax.jpg
07-830x719hax.jpg
11-577x900hax.jpg

More to come.

1

Tuesday, 17 January 2017

Reagan stepped blearily into the dull light of her apartment corridor, rummaging in her bag for her keys.

She'd fumbled through Sunday, making it to the garden centre minutes before opening, struggling to focus, the woman's body tumbling through her thoughts. She'd jumped at the ringing phone, the door chime, sucking in knife-sharp breaths. What were the odds? How many women were petite with hard cheekbones and big dark curls? Probably lots.

But that woman looked almost identical to her. It was like seeing her own dead body.

By Monday, she'd talked herself down. The dead woman had nothing to do with her. They happened to look alike, that was all.

She was running late and the keys had lodged at the bottom of her bag. She yanked them free, turning to lock the door – and choked.

A white lace negligee lay on the stained olive carpet.

Reagan threw herself back into her apartment, slamming the door and flipping the three deadbolts.

He's back.

She checked the peephole, hoping she'd imagined it. She hadn't. The single piece of lingerie was in the corridor, rumpled but unmistakeable, its two thin shoulder straps splayed above the bra. An oversized bow hung between the cups, as if women should be gift-wrapped.

Was he waiting in the hallway? The peephole didn't let her see more than a few metres beyond her door. *Shit.* She pressed her ear to the heavy wood, but she couldn't hear over her own rapid breath.

She kept one eye against the peephole while fumbling her tiny mobile from her handbag, glancing down just long enough to find Min's name and bash the call button.

'You've reached Min-lee Chasse, leave a message.'

'Min.' Her voice pitched high, the fear piercing. *He's back he's back he's back he's back.* 'Call me.'

She stood against the door, squeezing her mobile, unable to move. Down the hall, a door slammed shut. Reagan braced. No one appeared.

Minutes ticked past, Reagan barely moving. She pressed redial, got voicemail.

He could be waiting outside the apartment, pressed against the pock-marked eggshell paint, just out of sight. Or he could be around the corner, on the stairs. If he'd claimed to be checking the gas meters or dropping off a package, any neighbour would have buzzed him in. No one was cautious enough. No one was afraid.

She wished she could call the police.

Outside, kids squabbled, their voices rising. Reagan kept vigilant against the door. She'd thought the negligee was white, but squinting, she could see it was a weak latte shade. What did that mean?

Footsteps came down the hall. She braced, holding her breath. He couldn't get through this door without a battering ram. Still, she considered shoving the sofa against it, dragging the desk from across the room –

A woman carried an empty plastic laundry basket against her hip, sauntering, her other hand busy with her phone. She was about to trip on the negligee when she stopped, scooped it up and swivelled back toward the stairs.

Toward the ground floor laundry room.

Reagan leaned against the door and sank into a crouch, head in her hands. She was being ridiculous. *Fucking ridiculous.*

It had been five years. She couldn't live like that again, every outing a gauntlet, her life suppressed.

And she didn't need to. It wasn't him. A piece of off-beige lingerie dropped in the hallway had nothing to do with her.

And neither did the body in the laneway.

—

'Did you hear about the woman they found butchered over in Enmore?'

Reagan's Tuesday wasn't improving. She stood at the garden centre's front counter, her lips squeezed into a tight line. The less

11

she engaged Ed, the sooner he'd finish boxing the unsold onion bulbs and leave. The way he said *butchered*, leaning into its hard edges, made her uneasy. She kept her head down, shuffling through overdue invoices.

'It's all over the news.' He didn't need a response to keep a conversation going. She thought about dumb cane. The tropical plant's poisonous sap made the tongue and throat swell, causing speechlessness. 'This old guy found her, on his way to get his morning egg roll or whatever. Cops ended up calling the ambos for him, thought he was having a heart attack.'

She knew. She'd read every article. The call about the woman in the laneway came into the police at 6.22, according to the news. Twenty long minutes after Reagan had been there.

Ed moved on to the garlic bulbs, piling the mesh bags into a cardboard box as sweat patches seeped from his armpits. 'I was over that way, on Sunday. Between the media people and the rubbernecks trying to get in there, traffic snarled up to Redfern. I got stuck on Cleveland, and the aircon in the van is busted. I had a sweat on like a lamb on a spit.'

The city had surpassed the forecasted high again, hitting 37 degrees for the third day in a row. Tuesdays were quiet, and in this heat, no one was gardening. Besides Ed, the only person in the shop was a middle-aged guy in a navy jacket, shambling around on crutches, one leg dangling in a cast. He'd been coming in often the past few weeks, and never bought anything.

Her Timex read 4.17. Where was Min? She hadn't returned Reagan's calls. Reagan phoned again. Still no answer. It was unnerving. Min usually kept her mobile glued to her hand.

'They used some word . . .' Ed snuffled, wet and staccato. He crouched on the floor, lifting a meaty arm to wipe his forehead on the sleeve of his golf shirt, a dusty smear obscuring the Ferguson Seeds logo. 'Dismembered. This woman was dismembered and left on the goddamn street.' Even from across the shop, his gravelly voice was too loud.

'The news said that?' It was an inane response, but what was she supposed to say? What would a normal person say, a person who hadn't discovered a body and bolted?

Late afternoon sun slanted through her front display window, reflecting off the polished concrete floor. The black wall paint and the hanging philodendron vines, woven through upcycled wooden ladders secured to the ceiling, gave the shop a jungle vibe. A side door led to a small greenhouse. There were the usuals, nasturtiums and marigolds, daisies, sweet peas and zinnias; a rainbow of bright summer blossoms filling the shop's cascading shelves. But she prided herself on the unusual, her cobra lilies, carnivorous trumpet pitchers, black bat flowers, doll's eyes, and her rare orchids.

Most people, when it came to gardens and houseplants, were highly unoriginal. She'd envisioned her business as boutique, an individualised niche, but she'd had to surrender a disappointing amount of display space to plants even a child could identify, and more to fertilisers, vegetable seeds, and the onion and garlic bulbs that Ed was unhurriedly packing up for the season. Two spinning metal racks stood sentinel next to the front counter, stocked with floral-themed greeting cards. Reagan drew the line at garden knick-knacks. She refused to sell gnomes, plastic butterflies on stakes, concrete mushrooms painted red and white, and – especially – wind chimes.

Ed stood, hitching his baggy shorts. 'You didn't hear about it?'

'I don't follow the news.' Which was normally true. But since Sunday, she'd spent hours in the shop's closet-sized office, searching for updated headlines among the blithering over Trump's upcoming inauguration. The news offered nothing Reagan didn't already know – 'woman found dead in Sydney's inner west, victim of homicide'.

Min might have some actual information, or be able to get some. Like if the police had a suspect.

From behind perforated monstera leaves, the navy-clad man watched Ed. His long-sleeved jacket must be uncomfortable in the heat. Maybe it kept the crutches from chafing.

Ed tossed the last of the garlic into another box, tapped at his iPad, and ambled to the front counter. Sunburnt skin flaked loose on his forehead. His gaze crawled from Reagan's white canvas shoes and black khaki shorts, her Voodoo Lily Garden Centre T-shirt, the smear of potting soil on her forearm, to her mess of shoulder-length curls gone frizz-wild in the humidity.

'Do you have my herb order today?' Reagan said.

Ed snuffled again, the sound hinting at an alarming store of mucous. 'Can't bring it.'

'Come on, Ed.' She tried to sound annoyed rather than dismayed. 'I put the order in three weeks ago.'

'Your account's been suspended. Didn't you get an email? Manager says we can't bring you any stock until you're paid up.' With an extended sniff, Ed held out the iPad for her signature.

She wasn't going to last long if her suppliers cut her off. 'What if – what if you just brought part of the order?'

'Hey, I don't make the decisions. Wish I did.' He clicked his tongue, a noise to signal a horse.

She took the iPad, the returns figures swimming as she swiped her finger beside *Reagan Carsen*.

The bell above the shop door rang. Reagan turned, willing Min to sail through the entrance.

A couple ushered in a ginger-haired boy, three or four years old. His T-shirt sported a shark licking an ice-cream cone. The parents were in the midst of a murmured conversation, the boy wandering ahead. Maybe she'd make one sale today.

'That's all then.' Reagan gestured to Ed's stacks of boxes.

'Hmmm?' He pursed his lips, his unshaven face souring into a vacant pout.

'I really need those boxes out of here.' The worst part of working retail was being held hostage by anyone who wandered in and mistook you for a willing audience, whether that was lonely customers or licentious sales reps.

'No need to be all rushy rushy,' Ed said, a corner of his lip curling.

Reagan turned away, catching the little boy's eye. She gestured to the trailing red-speckled petals of her Dracula simia orchid. The centre of each blossom featured a tiny monkey face, with serious eyebrows and a playful beard. It had taken three years to get the plant to bloom.

Reagan started to lift the monkey orchid down, so the boy could see it up close. But a shelf of succulents distracted him and he stumbled to a stop, turning toward the rows of spiny cacti. He reached up, teetering on tiptoes, stretching chubby fingers.

'Oh hey, don't!' Reagan called.

The boy pressed three fingers against the reddish-orange tufts of a bunny ears cactus. Despite its cutesy name, the plant was insidious. The kid rubbed at his fingertips, uncertainty clouding his face. He'd feel nothing at first, but the hair-like spines would work their way into his skin like tiny shards of glass.

'Connor?' The father's attention skipped from the boy to Reagan. The kid must have caught the concern in his voice. His eyes widened and he swiped his hand against his shirt.

Reagan yanked a drawer open, grabbed tweezers and her magnifying glass, and dashed over. She knelt beside the boy, smiling brightly.

'Those fluffy cactus bits are called glochids. They look fun, but they're not friendly. Can you lift your fingers for me, like this?' She made a stop gesture. He edged away from her, and bumped into his dad's legs.

The dad knelt beside them, holding Connor's hand still. Reagan plucked a tiny spine from the boy's fingertip. She showed it to the pair through the magnifying glass. The mother joined, peering over the man's shoulder.

'See, no big deal,' Reagan said. *No big deal as long as you get them out.* 'Let's find the rest.'

Quick and deft, she tweezed a dozen spines from the boy's skin. 'All done.'

He turned his face into his mother's leg. 'Thank you,' the woman said, hoisting him onto her hip. 'Oh, Connor, look, those flowers have monkey faces.'

He perked up as she brought him closer. 'Monkeys!'

'It's an orchid.' Reagan told them about the name, how *Dracula* came from the Latin word for dragon. 'That's because the petals have these long skinny tails.'

The red of the orchid's petals looked like speckled blood. *Why had there been no blood in the laneway?*

'How much is it?' the woman asked.

'This is display only,' Reagan said. 'They're very rare.'

Ed hauled the last stack of boxes out the door. The bell jingled as the threesome followed. Last week Reagan would have tried talking up other orchids to them, offered them a discount. Today she couldn't focus. She glanced out the shopfront window, scanning the street, trying not to worry about why Min wasn't returning her calls.

—

Minutes before closing, the front counter phone trilled, her friend's name lighting up the caller ID. Reagan was surprised at the depth of her relief.

'The one time I manage a phone-free family day and there's three missed calls from you,' Min said. 'What's happened?'

'Did you get my message?'

'You know I never listen to voicemail.' In the background, a car door slammed. One of the kids started wailing. 'Hang on,' Min said. Then, muffled, 'Mais, I'm talking to Auntie Rae.'

'Everything okay?'

'We're at the zoo and Maisey's having a meltdown because we didn't see the platypus. Tell me, what's going on?'

She was going to have to be careful with Min. In her panic this morning, she would have let everything rush out. 'Wondering if you were free to grab a drink tonight, or maybe pop over?'

The crying reached a crescendo. 'Hon, could you – thanks.' To Reagan: 'Owen's taking her on a little walk to calm down.'

'Don't worry about it, I just –'

'Why don't you swing by for dinner? Owen and I worked all weekend, so we're taking a couple of days off to give my mum a break. And try to, you know, enjoy summer.'

Reagan closed her eyes, saw the woman splayed on the pavement. The corpse-flower scent crowded her nostrils. The last thing she wanted was to cosy up at home with Min's family.

As Reagan's financial situation had worsened over the past year, she'd found herself calling Min less and less. She was busy with the kids anyway. If Reagan couldn't turn Voodoo Lily around, there'd be no way to hide it and Min would drown her in positivity and platitudes. *It's not a failure, Rae, it's a learning experience.* It would be unbearable.

'You guys must be tired,' Reagan said, 'out in the heat all day.'

'Nah, come on. It's been forever since we caught up.'

Min was her only chance to learn if the police knew anything about the murder.

He isn't back. Why would he be, after all this time?

Still, a little reassurance wouldn't hurt.

'Okay, yeah,' she said. 'Thanks.'

—

Two marked police cars sat across from Reagan's apartment building. She clocked them as she pulled into her parking spot, her gut tightening.

Do you really need a shower? You could go straight to Min's.

After working in the heat, she needed to get cleaned up. Sweat had matted her curls to her head, and dried sweat caked her skin.

The police could be on her street for any number of reasons. Domestic violence, burglary, car theft. There were all sorts of ways a neighbour's day could have soured.

She hesitated at the building door, catching her reflection in the glass. *This morning you said you'd stop being ridiculous. Remember?*

Another part of her was insisting she turn around, head straight back to her Holden. She unlocked the door and stepped inside.

They're not here for you. She edged up the creaking stairs, avoiding the patch where the loose carpet threatened to trip anyone not paying attention. *They might not even be* here. *They're across the street. They're halfway up the block.*

As she reached the first floor landing, voices came from the hall above. Men.

There were twenty-six apartments in the building. *Could be anyone.*

She kept heading up, hurrying, eager to get inside her apartment. She stepped onto the second floor as two men approached from the corridor.

Navy uniforms, black belts, holstered guns.

Her instinct was to bolt, to try to make it downstairs and out the door. Maybe to her car, or into her neighbour's garden, to hide in the thick-leaved viburnum hedges. It took everything in her to keep her feet planted. She gripped her handbag.

They're not here for you.

But they weren't walking past her.

They stood shoulder to shoulder, elbows out, blocking the corridor. Their name badges read Ghazali and Caedin. Ghazali's face was round, slightly swollen, his eyes bloodshot like he'd had an allergic reaction. Caedin was all hard angles. His teeth slanted inward, like a shark.

Caedin pointed at her. 'Are you a resident here?'

Reagan's tongue sat heavy in her mouth, a lump of wet muscle disconnected from her brain.

He looked at a small notepad in his hand. 'Apartment 17?'

Shit. They *were* here for her. They knew she'd found the body. *How?* Surveillance cameras? Mobile phone tracking?

The GoPro footage – the cyclist.

'Do you live in apartment 17?' Caedin repeated, louder.

'I . . .' Her mouth opened and closed. Was it a crime to fail to report a dead body? To flee a crime scene? Could they arrest her?

If they knew her name, they'd seen the files.

Ghazali stepped closer. The radio handset on his shoulder crackled. More officers coming up the stairs behind her? Two police cars – at least four cops.

'Were you in the neighbourhood on Sunday morning?' Caedin asked, eyes locked on hers. How did the files describe her? Unstable, probably.

'I don't . . . know.' *I don't know anything.* She couldn't get it out.

'You don't know if you were in the neighbourhood on Sunday? Two days ago?' Ghazali slid a look at Caedin. His hand moved toward his belt.

Her lungs constricted; she couldn't get enough oxygen.

'We're canvassing the neighbourhood, checking if anyone witnessed anything early Sunday morning, or possibly the night before,' Ghazali said.

Reagan nearly collapsed. She reached for the wall, leaned against it. *Canvassing.*

'Done down here?' a female voice asked. Another pair of cops descended from the third floor, stopping short as they caught sight of Reagan.

'I haven't seen anything,' she managed, one hand pressed firm against the drywall.

Caedin extended a business card toward her. 'If you think of anything, you can give us a call.'

Reagan managed to take the card without letting her hand shake.

2

The evening held the day's heat. An orange-pink sunset glowed with neon intensity as Reagan crossed the Harbour Bridge to Balmoral, the houses growing larger with each block.

A polished sandstone wall surrounded the property. She pressed the buzzer, turning toward the camera. The gate opened to an immaculate garden, the red gum blossoms like fireworks.

'Reagan, welcome.' Hyun-sook answered the door, the baby snuggled over her shoulder. Reagan bowed her head, greeting her in Korean and brushing her fingers through Dashiel's bath-dampened hair. Min's mother had warm, inviting eyes, framed by smile lines. A streak of grey ran through inky black hair that glowed with natural vitality or high-end salon treatments. Her wardrobe centred around fitted blouses and the sort of chic scarves that looked casual while signalling both taste and money.

'I'm just about to put Dashiel to bed,' Hyun-sook said. 'Would you like to hold him?'

Reagan would never say no to having a baby nuzzled in her arms. Dashiel blinked at her before winding the tiny fingers of his right hand into her curls, then sighed and let his eyelids flutter closed. What was it about small children that made a house feel so much more like a home?

They chatted about the garden, Hyun-sook's voice low and cosy, before she eased the baby from Reagan's grasp and said goodnight. Rocking gently and humming a lullaby, she carried her grandson upstairs.

The smell of pork loin and roast potatoes pulled Reagan to the kitchen. The house was all open spaces and high ceilings, with floor-to-ceiling windows showcasing the garden. A vase of sunflowers crowned the kitchen table. Min opened the oven, a cloud of steam dissipating around her. The embroidery on her magenta apron read *Delicious! And the food's okay too.*

'You made it.' She dropped her oven mitts to give Reagan an extended hug. Hyun-sook was a calm lake; Min had the energy of a storm-fed waterfall, and the posture of someone who believed all compliments were heartfelt. Along with the glossy hair that hung to her waist, she'd inherited her mother's fashion sense, but it ran to bright colours and heels. Today's manicure matched the jaunty yellow sundress under her apron. At thirty-one, only a few years older than Reagan, Min had her life a hundred times more together.

Even so, when they did manage to get together, her attention was split, fielding baby-centric texts and calls, leaving abruptly, rearranging plans. She'd been flat out for months on her latest project, a long-form magazine series reporting on an international investigation into child pornography, including interviews with the men convicted. Reagan couldn't bear to hear about it. Weeks had passed since they'd exchanged more than brief texts.

Min clamped her hands on Reagan's shoulders. 'Seriously, three calls today? What's up?'

'Can't I just miss you? And my de facto niece – is Mais in bed already?'

'Owen's reading her *Kookoo Kookaburra*. Don't go up there, she'll never get to sleep. Which reminds me, you have to see this.' Min flicked through photos on her mobile. 'Since I have to do this the old-fashioned way with you, Rae.'

She enlarged a shot of Maisey dressed as Spider-Man, leaping off the couch, the eyeholes of her mask askew.

'You need to print me a copy.'

'If you were on Facebook, you could see the whole album,' Min said. 'Or, if you upgraded your phone, I could, you know, *text* it to you.'

'Yeah, yeah.' Reagan was supposed to smile, to accept the teasing. That was her role as the last person on Earth without a smartphone. Tonight her face wouldn't cooperate, and her words came out deflated.

Min paused, slipped her phone in her pocket. 'You okay, doll? You look peaky.'

'Just tired.' Since Sunday, purple-black bags had spread under her eyes. When she did sleep, the dead woman was there, her slashed mouth opening, the ibis gripping her with sharpened talons. 'Food smells great.'

'Owen was in the kitchen prepping dinner before we left this morning. Culinary workshops are his new thing.'

'The loin's done with a bourbon and brown sugar marinade,' Owen said, coming into the kitchen and greeting Reagan. He never hugged her, which she appreciated. He was solid, strong through the shoulders, the sort of man who wore expensive but understated watches. The summer sun had bronzed his skin and lightened his almond hair, which he wore a touch long for a corporate lawyer type. He could have played the father in a commercial for mortgages or family-sized luxury sedans.

'How's Voodoo Lily going?' he asked.

'Fine,' she said. Reagan needed to sidestep the topic. *If you need money, I can help you*, Min would say, eyes syrupy with concern. She'd probably offer to become a part owner in the garden centre, bring in Hyun-sook's business strategy adviser, *Whatever you need, Rae.*

She didn't want to mention the murder too soon either. Instead, she asked about the kids as Min shredded cabbage for a salad and Owen set the table for three. Hyun-sook had eaten earlier with Maisey. Min shared their plans for a family trip to Fiji over Easter as they sat and passed the dishes around.

Reagan's mobile rang. 'Sorry,' she said, digging it out of her handbag. With a glance at the caller ID, she silenced it. Min raised an eyebrow. Reagan pretended not to notice.

'Isn't it limiting, not having a smartphone?' Owen asked, scooping potatoes onto his plate. 'Isn't everyone on Tinder these days?'

'The garden centre keeps me busy.'

'Owen, there must be a few single guys at your work we could introduce Rae to.' Min winked at her.

'Yeah, probably,' he said.

25

'What's that one guy's name?' Min cocked her head as if to loosen the memory. 'You know who I mean, he's into scuba diving?'

'Min,' Reagan cut in before they could start texting Scuba Guy. 'Did you see the news about the woman they found in Enmore on Sunday?'

'I saw the headlines. Haven't delved into it yet.' Min gave her a curious look. 'Why?'

'I thought you might have heard about it,' Reagan said, taking a bite of tangy pork. This wasn't how she'd wanted to bring this up. *Be casual.* 'From that cop you know.'

'I only contact him when I need some intel.'

Damn it, Min. Usually you can't stop talking about gruesome murders. 'I figured you might be interested. Isn't your new book about female murder victims?'

'Not all of them.' Min was already searching on her phone. 'A few local cold cases. How come?'

If Min got a hint that she knew more than she was saying, she'd go into crowbar mode, trying to prise Reagan open. She wouldn't understand why Reagan had fled from the laneway on Sunday, rather than calling the police.

'Oh my god, Rae.' The phone's light illuminated Min's shocked expression.

Electrified with sudden panic, Reagan thought of the cyclist, his helmet camera. His footage would show her coming out of Gipps Lane, running fast, looking horrified. What if, instead of turning it into the cops, he sent it to the media?

'What?' Owen asked.

'You didn't tell me this was right near your place.' Min turned her mobile to show Owen the spot on Google Maps, her eyes on Reagan. 'Four blocks away. You must have seen all the crime scene activity on Sunday.'

'I didn't see anything,' she said, the words coming out too fast. 'I mean, I'm on the other side of Enmore Road.'

Min read a couple of lines aloud from the article, her eyebrows peaking. But she was talking to herself. Reaching for the pork loin, Reagan asked Owen about his culinary course, and the conversation moved on.

A strangled cry came from the baby monitor. Owen and Min swivelled toward it. Another cry came, louder and longer.

'I'll go,' Owen said. Standing, he kissed Min on the forehead, one hand on her shoulder. She slid her fingers under his, leaning into him and closing her eyes.

Reagan looked past them, to the pile of tiny shoes stacked by the patio door. For a while after they'd met in Korea, she'd been the closest person to Min. She hadn't expected that to last back in Sydney, but still, Owen made her feel . . . displaced.

When he headed upstairs, Reagan stacked his empty plate on hers, fiddling the knives and forks into a tidy row. 'I should go too, I –'

'Whoa, whoa.' Min put her hand on Reagan's wrist. *Shit*. She must have been delusional to mention the murder to Min. 'What's up with you? You never want to talk crime.'

Reagan had struggled through their conversations when Min had been writing her first book, the story of a shocking murder from twenty years ago. She'd learned about the cold case while working on the *Sydney Morning Herald* crime beat, and managed to discover new evidence that uncovered the killer. Her reporting on his arrest and trial had led to an international book deal. The book sat on Reagan's desk, unopened, *Min-lee Chasse* adorning the cover in scarlet font.

'It happened . . .' Reagan took the napkin from her lap, refolding it, 'in my neighbourhood.'

'Yeah.' Min gave her an uncertain, concentrated look. 'That would freak me out too.'

—

Reagan had left her fourth-hand Holden, a snub-nosed beige Barina, parked under a flame tree. Wilted blossoms lay scattered across the windscreen, like blood splatter. Heading for the car, she refused to scan the street. She kept her neck rigid, not checking the back seat. She didn't need to. She was safe.

Inside her handbag, her phone buzzed, insistent. She couldn't keep putting it off. Leaning against the driver's-side door, she sucked in the heavy evening air and pressed the answer button, bracing.

'Reagan.' Cynthia's curt voice made her cringe. 'We were expecting you for dinner. The roast has gone cold.'

'Mum, we said Wednesday. That's tomorrow.'

'Wednesday! Why would you come on Wednesday?'

This was her mother's latest thing, getting their plans wrong. Cynthia had asked her to come for dinner on Wednesday, and Reagan had written it in her diary. The first time her mum rang her to tell her she had the wrong date, Reagan assumed the mistake was hers. The next few times, she'd suspected early onset dementia.

But it was just more Cynthia being Cynthia. There was no point arguing, or getting angry. It would only make things worse.

'You think I'd bother cooking a whole roast for just Terry and me? It's *your* favourite. I don't even like roast.'

Reagan wondered what sort of person she'd be if she'd had a mother like Hyun-sook – smart, ambitious and nurturing.

Tell her to fuck off, Min would say. They'd had many long talks about Cynthia. *Tell her you're done.*

'I can still come tomorrow.' Reagan could hear the defeat in her voice.

Cynthia huffed. 'If you're late, don't expect us to wait for you.'

3

Wednesday, 18 January 2017

Emil Wojciech ushered Reagan into the padded visitor's chair across from his desk at 9.01 am. He was a middle-aged man with waxy skin and wire-rimmed glasses. From a forehead that took up half his face, his hairline stretched back in two wide Vs. She'd met Emil enough times to know that the best way to prepare – other than up-to-date balance sheets – was a scoop-neck dress, push-up bra, and the Yves Saint Laurent matte lipstick Min had gifted her, an understated taupe.

'These statements aren't showing signs of improvement,' Emil said, one hand clamped to his chin. 'At this point, we don't have a realistic strategy for repayment. I can't see how we can defer any longer.'

Even Yves Saint Laurent might not be enough to help today.

Normally their meetings started off with small talk, a flurry of compliments. Today he'd skipped right to the paperwork. It wasn't going to be the quick sign-off on another three-month repayment deferral she'd hoped for.

'I really think things are going to turn around,' she said. Earnest optimism had worked in the past. 'Soon, I mean.'

Emil didn't return her smile. He shuffled the pages, running his index finger down a column of figures. 'I'm not seeing evidence of that.'

The false smile strained her cheeks. 'I'd be really grateful for any advice.' Emil loved to dole out advice.

'Have we talked about marketing?'

She'd meant financial advice. Reagan had chosen the small, independent bank near the garden centre thinking she'd prefer the personal touch it offered. Now she wasn't so sure. 'We haven't.'

'You're in luck. It's one of my little areas of interest.' Emil rubbed his hands together, his tone more jovial, then rotated his computer screen toward her. 'For starters, you have a website with nothing but your contact details. And if I search *Annandale garden centre*, it doesn't appear in the results.'

He wasn't the first person to suggest Reagan could do more online. When she'd opened Voodoo Lily in 2014, it had seemed reasonable to run a local brick-and-mortar business with a minimal web presence and a business email address. Now if you weren't everywhere online all the time, you didn't exist.

Emil talked through digital marketing ideas, speaking slowly, like English wasn't Reagan's first language. She was a twenty-six-year-old dinosaur. Not a woman who might have good reasons for her choices. Who might be trying to protect herself.

She nodded, pretending to take notes. When he grew too tedious, she brushed her hair behind her shoulder, letting her fingers trail along her neck, watching Emil watching her.

'That gives me a lot to think about.' And for once she was actually thinking about it, desperation and dread frothing in her guts. Because if he insisted she start making repayments, she'd be done. She'd default, and she'd lose the garden centre within months.

And then what would she do? Voodoo Lily was her entire life.

'Thinking about it isn't going to be enough,' Emil said, a paternal sternness in his voice.

She flushed. 'I mean, I'm going to pursue these ideas and put a strategy in place.' Whatever that meant.

Emil took off his glasses, folded them and set them on the desk, fiddling until they were parallel to his keyboard. 'I wouldn't do this for just any client, you know.'

His tone offered a hint of good news. She squeezed her hands in her lap. If she left in the next minute and sprinted up the block, she could get to the garden centre and open on time.

'Look,' Emil said, voice brightening, 'why don't you come back with a marketing plan that includes solid web content. And start using our business app. I think you'll really like the features.'

She nodded, leaning forward and digging her nails into the chair's padded edge. There was no way she'd be doing any of that.

4

The first stout raindrops of the summer hit the Holden's windscreen as Reagan sank into the driver's seat. She lowered her window and sucked the cool air into her lungs, wishing she felt more relief. She edged out of the tight parking space behind Voodoo Lily, the rain turning ferocious, pounding the car, and she hurriedly shut the window. Pedestrians scuttled into Ubers in the increasing downpour, slowing the already thick and unruly peak-hour traffic.

The only thing worse than driving across the city in this weather would be calling Cynthia to cancel.

First, she needed to get home to change. It took ten minutes to move two blocks, the lanes merging awkwardly to bypass a stalled bus. A horn blared behind her, others echoing.

A rain-soaked cyclist flew past, pedalling hard through deepening puddles. *The cyclist!* She couldn't ask Min about the footage, which meant there was no way to know if he'd turned it in as evidence.

Fog blurred the car windows. She scrabbled for the defrost settings. If they caught the killer soon, the footage shouldn't matter, but if –

With a crunching metallic bang, the Holden slammed to a stop.

'Shit. *Shit.*' She'd rear-ended a blue-grey Honda Civic.

She dropped her head against the steering wheel. She'd never been involved in a collision before, had certainly never caused one. The Honda looked like a newer model, maybe brand new.

Seemingly satisfied with the havoc it had caused, the rain softened.

There was nowhere to pull over. The Honda's hazard lights came on and the driver's door cracked open.

Reagan couldn't see how much damage she'd done. From the resounding bang of the impact, she wouldn't be surprised if she'd caved in the boot.

Her stomach clenched. She couldn't cope with someone getting shitty. She'd spent the few hours of sleep she'd managed since Sunday flailing at ibises as their long black claws pierced the dead woman's skin.

Of course the Honda's driver was a bloke, dressed in expensive-looking jeans and a white linen shirt, raising an enormous black umbrella that hid his face.

Behind her, a horn blared, followed by several more. Vehicles crept around her car, drivers glaring. The rain slowed to an innocent drizzle. She pulled her registration from the glove compartment and edged the door open, stepping into a puddle that soaked through her canvas shoe.

Reagan pinned her elbows tight against her sides, trying to shore herself up. Her cheeks were burning, shame and embarrassment mixing with trepidation. The driver of a red Audi leaned on the horn, startling her.

'You were driving?' the man with the umbrella called. He stood on the pavement, the umbrella bucking in the wind. Was that an edge in his voice?

'I'm so sorry, my windows started to fog up and –' She flapped a hand toward her Holden.

He tilted the umbrella up. He was probably her age, in moderate shape, maybe a runner. He had the build for it, lanky and lean. Sandy hair swooped across his forehead, brushing the top of heavy framed glasses. A trendy office type, or the owner of a microbrewery. His skin was so smooth and unmarked, it looked like he'd come into the world that day, a fully grown man, untouched by the sun.

His empty expression told her nothing.

'Here, it could open up again any second.' He ushered her under the umbrella. She was close enough to catch hints of cedar and bergamot, and too close to look directly at him. She angled toward the cars, still reeling. She had a clean driving record. What happened now? Would he want to call the police?

The left side of the Honda's bumper was crushed. 'Shit, it looks bad,' Reagan said. Another thing she couldn't afford – an insurance claim.

'Hang on,' he said, and she caught the smoky husk in his voice. 'Can we take a closer look?'

They stepped forward together, huddled beneath the umbrella, and he reached down, running a hand along the concave section of his bumper. 'I think it's pretty minor. And your car looks fine,' he said. 'What do you think?'

One more dent wouldn't make a difference to the Holden. 'Obviously your car is damaged, so I think we should . . .' She reached into her handbag.

'A mate of mine runs an autobody place. He can pop that out no problem.' He hopped onto the pavement, sticking out his palm to test for rain, then lowered the umbrella. The drizzle had relented.

Was this guy seriously not going to ask for her contact details, her driver's licence? Could she be that lucky? 'That's really reasonable of you.'

A beat passed, the traffic choking around their vehicles. Half a block away, the honking started up again. She turned, ignition key in hand.

'Before you go –'

Of course. Who lets someone damage their car and drive away?

'I was supposed to drop that plant off with a colleague, but he's not home.' He gestured to the Honda's rear passenger window. 'Will it be okay if I leave it in my car overnight? It's not going to die?'

A cluster of glossy green and red-orange lanceolate leaves pressed against the glass. Reagan stepped closer. A potted lilly pilly leaned across the back seat.

Another horn blast came from behind their cars, the driver giving them the finger. Reagan pulled her elbows tighter against her sides, desperate to move her car. The Honda driver seemed unperturbed.

'Just – I saw your shirt,' he added.

Reagan glanced down. *Voodoo Lily Garden Centre* stretched across her chest, the shirt's colour the rich purple of the distinctive blossom.

Some people were clueless about plants. 'It'll be fine in the car.' She edged away, wanting to leap into the Holden, but also nervous of appearing ungrateful or rude.

'Great, thanks. I love that name, Voodoo Lily. Might have to drop in sometime.'

He smiled at her, one uneven tooth distracting from an otherwise perfect set. He was almost attractive, though something was a touch off, beyond the tooth. The dimensions of his face, maybe.

Another horn blasted.

'We're open Tuesday through Sunday.' She said it over her shoulder, hurrying away before he changed his mind and asked for her insurance details.

—

There was space in the driveway, but Reagan parked on the street, out of view from the house. She turned off the ignition and sat with the key clasped in her lap.

'You only have one mother,' she said to the empty car. 'Just be nice.'

Rows of red hot pokers bloomed in the garden, surrounded by flowering mountain devil. As Reagan slowed to admire the shrubs' growth, Cynthia pushed the front door open.

'What are you doing hanging around out here?' Cynthia said. 'I've got dinner on.'

Reagan smiled, still relieved that the collision had turned into nothing. 'Hi, Mum.'

Cynthia stood a head shorter than her, a wispy woman with a tight face that never saw the light of day without full makeup. Her peacock-blue linen dress was colour-coordinated with her eyeshadow, and her red resin necklace, chunky bracelet and stud earrings matched her lipstick.

Reagan had planned to give her mother a hug, but it was so outside their normal routine that she pulled back, settling for a hand on Cynthia's upper arm, the type of little squeeze Min gave people she'd just met.

'What have you done to your hair?' Cynthia squinted at her, then turned and headed into the house. Her voice echoed off the high ceiling of the foyer as Reagan followed her inside. 'And why has it taken you so long to get here?'

'It started to pour –'

'You were supposed to be here after New Year's. It's practically February.'

Reagan kept her mouth shut. Refusal to engage was one of the tactics that softened the wasp sting of Cynthia's company.

She struggled to remember what her mother had been like before her dad had come home one night when his wife and ten-year-old daughter were asleep, and, after however many whiskeys was too many, choked to death on his own vomit. Cynthia had found him the next morning.

The balcony offered a distant view of the beach. Tonight, the French doors stood open, letting in the warm breeze and the evening warbles of magpies.

Terry was already seated at the dining table, his head bent over a tablet. A hefty man with tufts of grey hair that stuck out from the sides of his head, he wore his usual collared, button-up shirt like this was a business meeting. Reagan suspected he wore collared shirts to the beach. His skin was the colour of oatmeal, and his personality was just as exciting.

'Lovely to be graced by your presence, Reagan.' Terry often said things that made it sound like he was raised by a thesaurus. His tone was bland; she couldn't tell if the comment was genuine or taking the piss. 'How's the plant business treating you?'

'Good, yeah.' She called to the kitchen, 'Mum, do you need a hand?'

Cynthia bustled from stove to table, cockatoo-print oven mitts on her hands. After years of stretching their grocery budget with rice and lentils, Reagan couldn't blame her mum for wanting to marry a bloke with money. Even if that bloke was Terry.

'Sit down, Reagan, there.' Cynthia centred a single place-setting across from Terry and herself, like it was a job interview, then banged a pan of her trademark béchamel-topped lamb lasagne onto the table. It was one of Reagan's favourites, and Cynthia often cooked it for her. She also gifted Reagan glossy coffee-table books on orchids and succulents, and brought friends to Voodoo Lily, saying, 'You *have* to see the things my daughter grows.'

Cynthia hoisted her phone to take a photo of the dinner table, forcing Reagan into a tense smile, then served the lasagne with salad and garlic bread. 'Terry's company is doing very well. You should ask him about it.'

Reagan went through the charade of pretending to be interested in Terry's business. His work involved phrases like *algorithmic logistics* and *adaptive analytics* that made her want to drop her face onto her plate.

After an anecdote about data migration, Terry managed to transition into Donald Trump's inauguration. 'It's going to be interesting, seeing what happens over the next four years.'

'Interesting?' Reagan said. They didn't usually talk politics, but Trump had become inescapable.

'He's got a lot of supporters.' Terry stuck a finger in his mouth, digging at a back molar. If Reagan had done that as a kid, Cynthia would have put Tabasco sauce on her fingers. Throughout her childhood, their kitchen cupboard had housed a bottle of Tabasco. Reagan never saw it served on food.

She ignored him. 'How have you been, Mum?'

'Did you see those photos of Maisey playing Spider-Girl?' Ever since Cynthia had found Min's Instagram account, she never missed an opportunity to mention Min, her photogenic husband and adorable children. The only thing she never commented on was Min's work.

'I visited her yesterday, actually. She might look into the murder of the woman they found on Sunday.' If Reagan had played the conversation two steps forward in her head, she'd have known it was a mistake.

'That was right in your neighbourhood,' Terry said. 'I hope you're not walking around there after dark.'

'What, women should stay inside after dark?' Reagan said it as a reflex. *Stop. It's not worth it.* She piled her fork with lasagne.

'You know, Reagan, men are murdered more often than women,' Terry said, his mouth full of half-chewed rocket. 'That's just a fact.'

40

And then mutilated and posed naked in public like some sort of porn exhibition?

'Who knows if she was out after dark?' Reagan said. 'The police don't even know who she is yet.'

'Whatever happened, that girl would probably still be alive if she'd been more cautious. Just like when you caused all that . . .' Cynthia paused as if seeking out the right euphemism, 'trouble.'

The shame burned like Tabasco. 'That was over a decade ago, Mum.'

2006. The year everything went wrong.

Cynthia shoved her chair out. 'I have to check on the dessert.'

—

Returning to the dining room with heavy footsteps, Cynthia thudded the pavlova and a ten-inch knife onto the table.

'Reagan, we need to talk about your loan. Terry and I discussed it.'

Her loan? They didn't know about the line of credit at the bank. 'What are you talking about?'

Cynthia's face turned severe.

'Do you mean the money you gave me to open the garden centre?'

'*Gave* you?'

Terry interlocked his fingers and tapped his joined hands on the table, the gesture silenced by the tablecloth. 'Well now, Rae,' – she hated when he called her that – 'I know we didn't establish any formal terms with that down payment.'

After Reagan's two-year English-teaching contract in Korea wrapped up, she'd accepted a similar job in Bulgaria. But she never made it to Sofia. Forty-eight hours after Cynthia's bladder cancer diagnosis, she touched down in Sydney. The opportunity to buy a neighbourhood garden centre came up later that year. When the bank determined she couldn't take on the debt, that should have been the end of things.

Except, from her hospital bed, a gaunt and shaky Cynthia had started going on about wanting to help Reagan. About how it would make her happy to see how her daughter's inheritance would be spent.

Reagan should have asked more questions, should have demanded everything in writing. 'I understood it was part, uh – part of my inheritance.'

'Do I look dead to you?' Cynthia snapped.

Reagan's dinner threatened to retreat up her throat and spew across the table.

'And don't think you'll be getting anything when I do kick the bucket. Children shouldn't treat their parents' deaths like a windfall. It's all going to charity.'

'What we need to do,' Terry smiled, 'is establish a repayment plan.'

'Things are . . . tight,' Reagan said.

Cynthia propped her forearms on the table, spread wide. Terry leaned back, as if needing the distance to take in the full extent of Reagan's injudiciousness.

'If you don't start making repayments by next month, you'll hear from our lawyer.'

'Mum!' A bit of lamb flew out of her mouth and stuck to her water glass.

'It's not fair to us,' Cynthia said. 'It's a lot of money and you're only thinking about yourself.'

The Tabasco burn returned with intensity, flushing Reagan's neck and cheeks. The garden centre was the one thing in the world that brought her comfort.

'Now.' Cynthia took the knife and sliced through the pavlova. 'Are you going to have some dessert like a civilised person?'

5

Thursday, 19 January 2017

On Thursday the heat returned, steam-baking the city. The garden centre was miserably quiet. Dragging herself up and down each cramped aisle of the greenhouse, Reagan deadheaded zinnias, marigolds and violets. Their bright colours failed to shift her mood.

The empty shop gave her time to obsessively refresh the news sites on her office computer. The headlines skewered the lack of police progress in the murder investigation. As far as they'd say publicly, they still had no suspects. Min might have heard differently from that detective mate of hers.

It doesn't matter. The killer couldn't be him. It had been five years since she'd last seen him.

Still, the nameless dead woman jolted into her thoughts, the unnatural halves of her body so still, the breeze ruffling her hair.

Reagan was starting to close up when the shop bell chimed. The man who strolled in wore pressed khakis and a chequered pewter shirt, the dark brown of his belt matched to his dress shoes, straight from the office. He stopped in the doorway, taking in the ceiling vines, the jet-black walls, the cascading shelves of potted flowers.

Catching sight of Reagan, he gave a casual wave, like she was someone he knew.

'Can I help you?' Her voice came out reedy.

'We met yesterday.' He moved toward her with energy. 'You bashed my car, remember?'

Right, the dark-framed glasses, that swoop of sandy hair, their conversation about her Voodoo Lily shirt. If he'd come here to ask for her insurance information, she wasn't sure if her response would be tears or hysterical laughter.

'Was your friend able to fix your car?'

'My mate took a look, said he'll get it as good as new.'

Her knees wobbled with the relief. 'Glad to hear it.'

'Sorry, did you think . . .' he said. 'No, I was in the neighbourhood to drop that plant off for my colleague, and I need a present for my mum. January birthdays, right? You've just wrapped up Christmas, then you turn around and it's straight back to gift shopping. That's when I remembered your garden centre.'

She gestured toward the ghost plants beside him. 'Are you thinking of an indoor plant, or something for her garden?'

'What do you think?' He turned on his heel, stopping abruptly and pointing toward the counter. He strode over and picked up the Dracula simia orchid, examining the tiny monkey faces. 'Actually, what's this?'

'Oh, it's not for –' She stopped herself. Saving her garden centre was going to require sacrifices. 'It's not for the garden. Definitely an indoor plant.'

'Does it grow like this?' He touched one of the petals.

For the first time since Sunday, her smile came easily. 'There's a whole variety of Dracula orchids that have those little faces. They're rare though, because they're tricky to grow.'

'My mum will love it. How much?'

She aimed high. If he baulked, she could bring the price down. 'Three hundred.'

'Can you like . . .' he waved his hands around the plant, 'wrap it up?'

Reagan was sad to see the monkey orchid go, but if she could keep the garden centre open, she could grow another. She crinkled plastic gift wrap as he wandered the shop, bending to touch his finger to the toothy edge of a Venus flytrap.

'So are voodoo lilies a thing, or is that just a name?'

Either this guy was the exceptionally chatty type, or . . . she glanced at his left hand. No wedding ring. Which didn't mean anything. He wouldn't be the first married guy to talk her up.

'They're real. They're also called devil's tongue, but that's not a great name for a business.'

'Depends what kind of business.' He laughed. 'You own this place?'

She nodded.

'I bet it does great on social, with that name and these incredible plants to photograph. I mean, you've got some bizarre stuff in here – people love that.'

Social what? Reagan dug around in a bottom drawer and pulled out two rolls of ribbon. 'Blue or silver?'

He pointed to the silver. 'I work in digital marketing, and so many small businesses struggle for engaging content. If you're a copywriter, you've got to get real creative to keep an Instagram feed interesting. But this place is perfect – endless content.'

She should have guessed. She curled the thick handful of ribbon into tight corkscrews, her thoughts churning.

It couldn't hurt to ask him.

'That looks fantastic. She's going to love it.' He paid, picked up the plant and strode for the door, the bell chiming as he pulled it open.

She dug her nails into her palms and flung the words out. 'Before you go.'

The late afternoon sun poured through the display window, giving him a golden glow. She took a few quick steps so she didn't have to shout, her insides roiling. *What are you doing?*

'I'm about to close up. Would you maybe,' she pointed up the street, as if he might know the pub in that vague direction, 'like to get a drink with me?'

'Uh.' The orchid leaned against his right hip, and he shifted it to his left, the door propped against his foot. Hesitation flicked across his face.

Swimming at Manly as a teen, Reagan had strayed from the flags and the beach had suddenly receded too fast. She'd been foolish, not paying attention, and as the current sucked her away from the shore, she'd thrashed and kicked, choking on the salty water, thinking, *Stupid, stupid.*

Then his expression shifted, his attention focusing on her, a wide grin revealing that one uneven tooth. 'Sure.' He held out his free hand. 'I'm Bryce, by the way.'

The relief hit her, the feeling of her feet digging into the safety of the sand.

'Reagan.'

6

After Bryce dropped the orchid in his car and Reagan locked up, they walked up Johnston street, Annandale's main artery, passing single-storey homes with brick chimneys, their front gardens fenced off. Old-growth trees cast shade over the pavement. Humidity whited out the sky. They sidestepped a trio of kids and their chalk bucket. In bright orange letters, a boy scrawled *Have a GRET day!!*

The pub was mostly empty, the air heavy with hops, the Rolling Stones's 'Start Me Up' on the speakers. The lone bartender pitched his hip against the bar, scrolling on his phone. Reagan ordered a glass of prosecco, not quite the cheapest option. Bryce got a pale ale.

Reagan pulled a twenty from her wallet as the bartender thrust the payWave machine at her. People were using cash less and less. But cards left a trail others could follow, so she carried cash and paid with it whenever she could. The bartender paused, blinking, then set the machine down and took the cash.

'You don't have to –' Bryce started.

'My shout.' Nervousness crackled in her smile. This guy seemed eager to talk. Maybe because he was hitting on her. That didn't matter. All she had to do was get him talking about 'content' so she could figure out a starting place, something to show Emil at the bank. *Look, here, an online marketing plan.* And maybe she could absorb a little of this guy's breezy confidence while she was at it.

Condensation fogged her glass as she carried it to one of the tall tables lining the exposed brick wall, Bryce trailing. He set his schooner down and took the stool across from her. Muted televisions hung in each corner, protests against Trump's inauguration dominating the news.

'So you work in marketing?' Reagan asked.

'Digital marketing, yeah. You know, search engine optimisation, content strategy. It's fun.' He propped an elbow on the table, settling into the conversation. She could see the outline of his mobile in the side pocket of his pants. He hadn't taken it out since he'd come into the shop.

'What would you say,' she ran a finger down the condensation on her glass, hesitating, 'if I told you I don't use social media?'

He flashed an inquisitive smile. 'Like, at all?'

'It gets worse.' She grimaced. 'I don't have a smartphone.'

She'd learned it was easier not to admit this. Everyone's blithe acquiescence to the digitisation of life discomforted her. Min, her mother, her customers, all clutching their phones like they'd be lost if they had to go a minute without them. They barely acknowledged the inherent risks, the complete surrender of their privacy.

'I don't want to ruffle your feathers, but can I ask . . .' Bryce hesitated.

50

Reagan shrugged. 'I've heard it all before.'

'If you don't like technology, why don't you go –'

She cut in. 'Live in the bush?'

'Serious question.' His face had a German shepherd earnestness. 'I read this book recently, *The Stranger in the Woods*, do you know it?'

She shook her head and sipped her wine. It was refreshing to meet a guy who read books.

'True story. This American bloke, from Maine I think. One day he drove into the woods with no plan, and lived there for twenty-seven years, in a national park.'

'Even through the winters?' she asked. 'That part of the US gets a lot of snow, doesn't it?'

'He built some kind of shelter, like a tent, with a gas heater. And he eventually got arrested because he was stealing supplies from cabins in the area. But I'm sure you could figure something out.' Bryce's smile was like the blossoms of *ophrys bombyliflora*, the laughing bumblebee orchid – wide and inviting.

'Reminds me of that Irish journo in the *Guardian*.' The wine was going down too easily. 'He went to live out in the woods with no electricity. He was washing his clothes in a river. It sounded awful.'

'You're not an outdoorsy type?' He twisted his beer glass, centring it on its coaster. He had great hands, nicely shaped with tidy nails. His skin was so unblemished it looked photoshopped.

'Trust me, I've tried.' The conversation was way off track, but it was rare to find someone so easy to talk to. 'After uni, I spent a few years in a little town in Korea, more of a village, really. Met my closest friend there.'

'Village life wasn't your thing?'

Teaching English to primary school kids had been all right, and the nearby mountains featured stunning hiking trails. But if she hadn't met Min, she would have left Gangwon long before her contract was up. As the only fluent English speakers in a forty-kilometre radius, they'd bonded through hectic work weeks and soju-soaked weekends, relieving their hangovers with the Vegemite and Tim Tams Hyun-sook sent. They'd also bonded over deceased fathers – Min's the year prior, Reagan's in her childhood. Min had thought being stuck in a small town would force her to improve her broken Korean, which she'd never managed to learn from her workaholic mother. And it did, somewhat, since she often translated for Reagan. Still, her poor language skills and mixed heritage meant most locals treated her as an outsider. The two women had buoyed each other.

Besides loving city life, she knew her business wouldn't survive in a small town; it was barely surviving in the city. And without her garden centre, she may as well live in Antarctica.

'You know what I discovered in Korea?' Reagan took a sip. 'It's hard to get decent sushi in the woods. Or find a barista who makes your latte just right. Or see the latest visiting exhibition from the Louvre.'

'It didn't end great, that time they set up all those Renaissance paintings in the bush,' Bryce said. 'I think a wombat ended up chewing on a van Eyck.'

People usually interrogated Reagan about how she managed to flounder through life without a smartphone. They didn't make jokes about al fresco art exhibitions.

'I really love the city,' she said. 'Is that where you work?'

'ANZ Tower, near Hyde Park. We face away from the harbour though, not much of a view.'

Too soon, Bryce's schooner was empty, and her glass held one last swig of prosecco. He pointed to it, asking, 'The same?' and was off the stool and striding toward the bar. He carried himself with the same cheery confidence he spoke with. And from certain angles, he was handsome. Reagan caught herself thinking about *orchis italica*. The naked man orchid.

Was she on a date? Bryce didn't seem to be in a hurry to get anywhere, and he hadn't texted anyone to say he'd be late. Did she want this to be a date? It was terrible timing to even contemplate starting a relationship. But maybe it was foolish to keep waiting for the 'right' time. This guy had treated her kindly when she'd damaged his car, and bought a not-inexpensive gift for his mum.

Reagan had a sudden urge to debrief with Min. She was probably at home, coaxing Dashiel to sleep while waiting for Owen to escape the office. Reagan didn't have any illusions about her friend's life. All-nighters with sick babies, the tug-of-war between parenting and work, Maisey's weeks-long refusal to eat anything except raspberry jam. Still, it had to be better than the ache of a too-empty apartment.

Bryce returned with the drinks.

'I need to be honest with you,' Reagan said.

His smile faded. 'Oh?'

She braced, aware she might be about to spoil the evening, maybe offend him. 'I invited you out hoping you could give me some advice, about . . . uh, at the shop, you mentioned using photos of the plants, and I thought –'

He set his hands on the table, his face sombre. 'I had the impression you invited me out because I'm more attractive than Chris Hemsworth.'

'I mean . . .' She bit her lip. A little flirting couldn't hurt. 'I wasn't going to say it in so many words.'

Angling himself away, he leaned against the wall, the easygoing smile back. 'I get it – my dad ran a local hardware shop. It's tough being a small business owner. Tell me what you want to know.'

She glanced at her Timex. 'This place does a good schnitzel. If you've got time?'

—

Reagan got home two hours later, the evening fading to grey, a half-moon brightening the sky. Quiet optimism fizzed inside her. Bryce had given her his number, along with a dozen marketing ideas, and offered to help her try them out. Clearly, he was interested in her. She wasn't sure what she felt about that. But she needed to stop pretending that her financial situation would magically turn around. If she didn't try something different, she was going to lose Voodoo Lily. If someone wanted to help her for free . . .

She relocked the three deadbolts to her apartment, *thunk, thunk, thunk*. The building had no elevator or aircon, and her unit featured one tiny bedroom with stained brown carpet. In summer the apartment trapped the heat, and she spent the nights naked on top of her sheets. But her place was on the second floor, the windows shielded by lemon myrtle trees, and, importantly, the front door was solid wood.

Reagan stripped her sweat-dampened clothes off, tossed them into the laundry basket, and stepped into the shower. She was rinsing the conditioner from her hair when the door buzzed.

Probably a neighbour's Uber Eats, the driver buzzing the wrong apartment. She ignored it.

The buzz came again.

And a third time.

Wrapping a towel around herself, she tracked wet footprints across the scratchy bedroom carpet and along the dark hardwood of the lounge room.

'Let me up.' Min's voice crackled through the intercom, underscored with urgency. Maybe she'd talked to that detective.

She pressed the intercom button. 'It's open.'

A half-minute later, the door handle rattled, followed by an impatient knock. Reagan checked the peephole. Min wore a sleeveless teal shift dress with a white collar, tassel earrings, ruby lipstick, and strappy white heels that showed off her calves. Her hair hung in a loose bun.

As she stepped inside, Reagan said, 'I'm just going to put some clothes on . . .' She trailed off as she caught Min's expression. Her usual bright smile was absent.

'Holy shit, Rae, you need to tell me what's going on.'

Water dripped from Reagan's hair onto her shoulders. 'What?'

'You've been lying to me.'

'Lying?'

'Your acting skills need work.' Min's tone stayed neutral but insistent. 'I saw the crime scene photos. The woman who got killed? She looks exactly like you.'

7

Reagan hugged the towel tight around herself.

'What are you talking about?' She tried to sound confused, but the dread seeped in. Had Min given the police her name? Had she seen their files on her?

'Something's going on, and you need to tell me what it is.' Exasperation edged Min's voice. 'I heard that voicemail, from Tuesday. You sounded terrified.'

'You said you didn't listen to –'

'I had a message I actually needed to hear today. I heard yours in the process. What was going on?'

'I think I, um, got startled. I don't remember.' Reagan curled her fingers into the damp towel, her hands tucked into her armpits. 'It was days ago.'

Min continued as if she hadn't spoken. 'And you came over that evening and asked me about a murder investigation, which you never do. A murder that happened right near your apartment. And *then* I see photos of the victim, and she looks identical to you.'

56

Tapping at her phone, Min pulled up a photo of the woman from the laneway, alive and radiant. It looked like a holiday snap. She stood ankle-deep in a glassy lake, a cheerful blue sky behind her, arms spread as if reaching out to hug the photographer.

'That's her,' Reagan whispered. She shivered, the water dripping from her hair and down her back growing cool. *You abandoned that woman to be picked at by birds like rubbish.*

Fuck. She shouldn't know what the murdered woman looked like. Her name hadn't been released; no photos of her had appeared in the media. Reagan's similarity to the woman should be news to her. She slapped a hand to her mouth, eyes widening. 'Oh my god, that's her? They know her name?'

'She's a tourist, from the US. They flew her mother to Sydney to make the ID, that's why it's taken so long. They're announcing it in the morning.'

Seeing the murdered woman without the slashes and injuries, the resemblance to Reagan was even stronger. 'What's her name?'

'When I first saw the photos, I thought, "That's a bizarre coincidence." I might not have made anything of it if I hadn't heard your freaked out voicemail. What's going on, Rae? What do you know about this?'

'What?' Reagan closed her eyes a second too long. 'Nothing.'

Everything she'd never told Min sat between them. Like what had pushed her to Korea. It had been easier to say, *I just wanted a new experience.*

'Why didn't you phone me instead of driving over here?' Reagan asked.

'I figured I had a better chance of getting the truth from you.'
Min had glimpsed a crack, caught the scent of hidden secrets.

'Let me get dressed.'

—

Reagan emerged from the bedroom in a loose T-shirt and tight shorts, her hair towelled. She hovered near the bedroom door. Min had dropped her bag by the front entrance, like a barricade.

'Tell me what's going on.' She was quiet but firm. 'It's too many coincidences to be a coincidence.'

Reagan pulled her arms tight around her chest. 'Have the police shared anything yet?' For once she wished she could access the news on her phone.

'Why did you call me Tuesday morning? What happened?' This was Min's MO – poking at her, trying to find her weak spots to force her to expose herself. Why did friendship have to be so intrusive? 'You saw something suspicious in the neighbourhood?'

Reagan faltered. 'You didn't give the police my name, did you?'

'There's no point in talking to the police unless you know something.' Min pursed her lips. 'And it sure seems like you do. So why haven't *you* gone to the police?'

Reagan glanced at the front door. This was getting too intense. She needed Min out of her apartment.

'I don't know anything. And I don't want to be part of whatever story you're writing about this, okay?' As soon as she said it, the truth of it struck her. *Of course.* Min was jealous that Reagan appeared to have some connection to the case. 'You probably see this as a career opportunity, but I don't want anything to do with it.'

Min's head snapped back, like she was the one being wronged. 'I'm not even writing about this murder yet. I'm trying to figure out what's going on with you. If you're in danger, Rae, I want to help.'

Reagan squeezed her hands, knuckles cracking. 'I didn't ask for your help.'

'You're the one who called me, and then came to my place and casually brought up the murder of a woman who turns out to look just like you.'

'How was I supposed to know what she looked like? You only just showed me.' Her voice squeaked on the lie. She went to the fridge, Min's eyes tracking her. In the undersized apartment, there was nowhere to hide.

The fridge offered nothing but barbecue sauce and three shrivelled zucchinis. She picked up a dishcloth and scrubbed at an imaginary spot on the kitchen bench.

'There's something going on, Rae. I've never seen you act like this.'

'You need to go.'

'What are you talking about?'

'Leave, please.' She was on the verge of tears, and she wouldn't cry in front of Min, or anyone. The last time she had, Cynthia had slapped her so hard, she'd tasted blood. Reagan quick-stepped across the lounge room, undid the bolts and hauled the door open.

Min planted her hands on the sofa armrest and crossed her ankles. Now what? It wasn't like she could grab Min and push her out. Min had six inches and ten kilos on her. Reagan stood rigid, too distraught to be angry, unnerved by the open door. She closed it.

'I'm not going anywhere until you tell me what's going on,' Min said. 'You get this pinched look whenever I mention the cops. You're acting like I've come here to attack you. And you're the only person I know with three deadbolts on her door.'

Slits in the blinds let in the black night sky as it slipped over the city. A floor lamp glowed behind Min, casting her face in shadow.

'I'd really like you to leave,' Reagan said, a tremble in her throat.

Min stood, giving her a split-second of hope.

She walked past her bag without picking it up, past the door, and into the kitchen. She pulled two glasses from the cupboard, and ran the cold tap before filling them and taking a drink. She brought the other glass to Reagan.

'I'm sorry you think I only care about this because of my work.' Min slipped her heels off. 'But it's you I care about. I'm worried about *you.*'

She had the stubbornness of a dozen mules. Reagan knew if Owen was working late, Hyun-sook would gladly look after the kids. Min would stay all night to make a point.

Maybe if Reagan told her just enough, she'd back off.

—

'Okay . . . listen.' Reagan relocked the deadbolts and carried her water glass to the faded yellow armchair. 'I can't handle questions.'

Min followed, taking a seat on the mismatched leather sofa. Behind her, the sprawling vines of a string of hearts draped over the rim of its cracked clay pot and down the side of a bookcase. Reagan had potted the plant as a tiny cutting with less than a dozen leaves. It was a survivor, the only one Cynthia hadn't managed to kill during Reagan's years in Korea.

'I had this friend.' The words were like sand in her mouth. 'Brooke. We met in Year Three. Our birthdays were one week apart. It was one of those intense kid friendships – weekend sleepover rituals, matching fancy dress costumes, going on each other's family holidays. Well, I went with Brooke's family. Cynthia couldn't afford holidays. And she didn't like Brooke, said she was spoiled. Which was true.'

Reagan pulled her legs up, hugging her knees against her chest. She waited for Min to break in. For once, she didn't.

'When we were fifteen, Brooke got a brand-new computer and soon I was at her house every day after school, on MSN Messenger. We'd take turns logging in and cajoling each other into different chat rooms. It became our whole social life. I was –' Reagan picked up her glass, turned it, and put it back down. 'I was the one pushing it. And I was the one who said we should pretend we were seventeen, because it felt so much more mature. Fifteen felt like a joke, like we were still little kids. But seventeen was practically an adult.

'We had different boys we flirted with. Then this one guy started talking to me. His screen name was BrownSteel, because his eyes were brown, not blue. Stupid. I thought it was clever. He said he was eighteen, and I believed him because he sent pictures of himself – playing volleyball at Manly, with his red Ford Falcon, on holiday in Bali. We talked for months. I lived for that chime MSN made when someone came online. I got moody on days I couldn't go to Brooke's, or if she wanted to do something else. When I slept over at her place, I'd stay up chatting with him the whole night.'

Reagan pinched the bridge of her nose. *Just get it out*. Outside, a cat yowled.

'He wasn't a teenager,' Min said, her voice like cotton. She'd dropped the crowbar tactics.

A breeze from an open window ruffled the string of hearts. All those delicate mottled leaves, dangling on wispy vines. *You can do this*.

'He said his name was AJ, but I think he chose it because my favourite band was the Backstreet Boys.' The shame pulsed in her chest. 'He started asking me to meet up with him in person. I didn't want to. I'd turned sixteen, but he would have been nineteen. I figured he'd realise I'd lied about my age and think I was some bratty kid. And I knew I shouldn't be chatting to him. If Cynthia found out, I don't know what she would have done.'

Min gave a small nod, her face pursed. Waiting.

'Brooke wanted AJ to drive us around in his Falcon, take us to the beach and the movies. She got it in her head that, with the right makeup, I could pass for seventeen. She thought I should meet him and see what happened. I kept saying no. She got impatient.'

If it had ended there, would she be living a different life? Dating someone who respected her career ambitions, who took cooking classes and hoped to read their children bedtime stories one day?

Reagan wished she was doing this over the phone. There was no way she could look Min, or anyone, in the eyes and relive the next part. The shame had seared her, and now it swelled, an overwhelming desire to atomise into dust.

'It rained every day that winter. Just rain, rain, rain. Brooke was grounded, so I couldn't go to her place. It was a Tuesday, and

Cynthia worked late on Tuesdays. Except she'd stayed home that night, with a headache or something.'

The cat's yowling outside continued, rising into a scream. A second joined in, louder. Reagan squeezed her thumbs inside her fists.

'The knock came late, around eight thirty. This was when we lived in the Hurlstone Park apartment. The main entrance door didn't latch properly, so anyone could come into the building. There'd been some issue with my dad's life insurance and we couldn't afford a better place. I was watching a rerun of *NYPD Blue*. Cynthia came into the lounge room and sort of looked at me, like, who had I invited over? Someone called my name through the door.'

'You hadn't invited anyone,' Min said.

'And I told Cynthia that.' The story was like an avalanche, gaining speed. 'I looked through the peephole, and there was this guy I'd never seen. Cynthia and I were staring at each other, and *NYPD Blue* was on the TV across the room. He kept knocking and calling my name. Not mad or anything – just, *Reagan, Reagan, are you there?* Then he tried the doorknob. It was locked and he started rattling it, getting agitated. I was trying to figure out what to do when the door frame gave and the door hurled open.'

8

A tree branch scratched against the apartment window, lemon myrtle leaves pressing against the glass like voyeurs. The knuckle of Reagan's thumb popped with a twinge of pain.

'The guy standing there was in his thirties, so he seemed old to me. His jeans looked ironed. He had receding hair, close-cropped and clean-shaven, like a businessman. Some sort of cologne. A lot of teeth. He was fit, but not attractive, ears sticking out, beady eyes. And he goes, *Reagan, hi, I'm AJ*, like he hadn't just burst through the door. He was so much older, nothing like the photos of AJ. I started backing away while he's going on about how I'm even prettier than in my photos. I tell him I'm going to call the cops and he looks at me all confused. Cynthia is still standing there like a statue, and I manage to get the phone and start calling triple zero. By the time I do, he's gone.'

It was Min's turn to sigh, long and knowing, like she'd seen this coming. 'Rae, I'm so –'

'That's not –' she jerked her head, gave a bitter huff. 'That's just the *start* of it. Cynthia flipped out, accusing me of inviting him over. Two cops came, two men, and basically implied that the guy had done nothing wrong because we had a shitty door. They wanted to know how he had my name, said I must have given him my address. Cynthia called a locksmith, but he couldn't fix the door that night because the wood around the frame was rotted. Cynthia made me pay for a hotel room out of my birthday money.' That was the last time Reagan cried in front of Cynthia, or anyone.

'I tried to explain that I hadn't shared our address, that Brooke must have done it. I thought Cynthia would believe me, since she'd never liked Brooke. But she wouldn't listen. Kept shouting about how I had to pay for the door repair. She called Brooke's mum and said I wasn't allowed to see Brooke anymore because she was a bad influence. At first I was so upset with Brooke, I didn't care.' Upset with Brooke, and heartbroken over a boy who'd never really existed. Reagan had spent hundreds of hours chatting with him about everything – her father's sudden death, her teenage dream of visiting Osaka's Ramen Museum, and the way Cynthia treated her.

The shakiness left her voice, and she sat straighter, feet on the floor, leaning forward. The cats outside had quieted, the hush of night settling in.

'Even with a new lock, Cynthia didn't feel safe in that apartment. The entrance door lock was still busted and some of the neighbours were a bit rough. She couldn't afford anything better in the inner west, so we moved ages away, to Terrey Hills.' It was thirty kilometres north, streets and streets of leafy suburban nothing. 'I had to change schools in the middle of Year Eleven.'

The only good thing about the new place was the garden. A concrete wall and tall eucalypts enclosed the space. Cynthia didn't care what Reagan did back there. She'd tried to remember where that first package of sweet peas had come from – a gift from a teacher, maybe? She doubted she'd bought the seeds, since she'd never planted anything before. It was heartening, the way the green shoots pushed through the soil, their tiny leaves unfurling, angling toward the sun.

'A few months later, the first package showed up.'

Min's mouth opened, the shape of *what*. She stopped herself. Reagan's gaze roamed, settling on a mosquito bite on her arm. She scratched at it, blood welling under her nail.

'It was sitting on the doorstep when I got home from school, with my name on it, nothing else. It hadn't come through the post. It was –' she faltered, grimacing. *Spit it out. You've made it this far.* 'It was this white lace bra set. It sounds obvious now, telling it all at once. At the time, it never occurred to me it might be him. We'd moved so far away, it felt like a different city. And I hadn't heard from . . . from AJ in months. I figured he'd realised I was still a kid and moved on.'

She'd almost slipped. *AJ. Call him AJ.*

Or don't call him anything.

'When I got that first package, I thought it must have been from these girls at the new school. They'd thrown Wite-Out on my clothes and put some nasty notes in my locker. The bra set seemed weird though. It wasn't like they'd grabbed the first thing off the rack, or the cheapest. It was my exact size, and silky. I threw it out before Cynthia could see, and no one at school mentioned it.

'The packages kept coming. Bra sets, a couple of teddies, always white. Tame stuff. I had a job at McDonald's by then and one of the guys there was a creep, so I thought it might be him. But someone was phoning and hanging up, only when I was home alone, never when Cynthia was home. Which meant he was watching the house.'

'AJ had found you in Terrey Hills?' Min sounded surprised.

'A few months later I saw him sitting on a bench I passed on the way to school. At first I thought it was a coincidence, until I saw him again, watching me. Soon it was every few days. It felt like he owned me. He'd be hanging around reading the newspaper on a bench, or sitting at a cafe. Always neatly dressed, and fit, like he worked out.'

'Did Cynthia know?'

'I figured if I told her, she'd rip me out of school and haul me out to Broken Hill. I tried to go to the police –'

'But they didn't help you.'

'One time I was sitting there crying, snot running into my mouth, and this bored cop is telling me I didn't have sufficient evidence, that it's not illegal for this guy to walk his dog past my house or sit at a cafe near my school. And when I told him about meeting AJ on MSN, he said, "If you don't want stuff like this to happen, you're just gonna have to stay off the internet."'

Min gave a slow, sighing nod. 'And you listened.'

'I didn't make any friends in high school. I felt like everyone was watching me all the time, like they knew. I quit the Macca's job, got hired at a different one. It didn't matter. He turned up wherever I was. I'd go two weeks without seeing him, and then he'd be there three days in a row. And the packages kept coming. I think he'd been watching me for months.'

'Did he talk to you?'

'Sometimes he'd say hi, ask how I was, like we were neighbours. He'd ask if I liked his gifts. I didn't respond, didn't tell anyone. The calls had stopped, but he started sending emails, stupid love letters, about how he was waiting for me, and one day I'd realise we were soul mates.'

'How long did this go on?'

Min was starting up the questions, ready to dig in, dissect every angle. Reagan raised her hands, *stop, slow down*.

'When I moved into a share house at the end of high school, I thought it would end. He found me within weeks. Started hanging around the neighbourhood, like before.' Reagan rubbed the back of her hand under her nose. 'One night I went to a bar with a guy from my ecology class, and AJ flipped, sent me this angry rant about how he'd seen me with this guy, and how could I hurt him like that after everything he'd done for me. That was the only time he got mad, if he saw me with a guy. So I didn't date.'

'He threatened you?'

Reagan faltered, the truth growing slippery.

'Not directly. It felt threatening, like *how dare you*.' That part was true. 'I was petrified that he'd bust in to my house again. I had nightmares about him coming through the door with an axe.

'And then it got worse. I came home and found my underwear drawer open. All my bras – the ones I'd bought myself – were gone. I *knew* it was him. I could feel him there, this itchiness in the air.'

'Did you try going back to the police?'

For a moment, a future opened where Reagan didn't have to hide, to pretend. She could tell Min the whole truth, get it all out and over with.

But Min knew her, and she knew Min. If she shared everything, there were two possible outcomes. Either Min wouldn't believe her, because the truth was so ugly and corrosive, it would be easier to deny.

Or Min would go to war.

Reagan dropped her head, twisting her fingers into her curls. 'I moved again. And he found me.' Sydney was a sprawling patchwork city, with endless nooks to burrow into. One time she cancelled her uni classes three weeks into the semester and transferred universities. It had been a paperwork nightmare, and costly, but had bought her three months of freedom.

'This is why I don't give my address to anyone, why I don't want my photo online. One time I found out he *paid* one of my ex-housemates for my new address.' That was the house where he'd crept into her bedroom the night her housemates were away, and she'd woken to find him watching her sleep. She'd blinked awake at 2 am, reached for the lamp switch, and seen him, still as a statue, hands gloved though the night wasn't cold. He was out the first floor window and off the roof in seconds. She should have left the city then. She'd settled for wedging the window shut and padlocking her room from the inside to get through her final exams. 'I didn't know who I could trust.'

'Fuck, Rae, why have you never told me any of this?'

'I've never told anyone.' Her shame was fetid and alive. 'I knew I shouldn't have been chatting up strangers online. I'd lied and said

I was seventeen. I talked to AJ online for months. I brought it on myself.' She'd filled years wondering what she'd done to trigger him. Something she'd said on MSN, the way she'd reacted when he came to the apartment?

Min leaned across the gulf between the sofa and the chair, and put her hand on top of Reagan's. If she were on the sofa, Min would have mashed her into a hug.

'None of it was your fault.' Min was emphatic. 'You understand that, right?'

Reagan could feel the split inside herself. She knew rationally that what had happened wasn't her fault. But in the deepest parts of herself, facts dissolved, meaningless.

'This is why I moved overseas. I took that job in Korea because it was the first one offered to me. All I wanted was to be free of him, to walk down the street without checking over my shoulder.'

'I get it.' Min squeezed her hand. 'I do.'

But she couldn't. Not really.

She didn't know the rest.

9

The kitchen's overhead fixture filled the room with a rude, too-yellow light. Reagan pulled out a bottle of bottom-shelf gin. 'I don't have anything to go with it, other than ice.'

'Ice is good,' Min said.

Reagan cracked ice into two glasses and carried them and the bottle to the coffee table. She submerged the cubes in one glass and handed the bottle over.

Min poured a puddle of gin. 'When was the last time you encountered this guy?'

'Not since I came home from Gangwon.' Curling into the armchair, she sipped the gin, the taste making her scowl. 'I was staying at Cynthia and Terry's place in Mona Vale, remember, when she was in and out of hospital, and I kept expecting him to appear any day, like a ghoul. When that happened, I was going to leave again. I figured I'd reapply at the school in Sofia, and if that didn't work out, I'd try for Seoul or maybe Osaka.'

71

'I forgot you had that job offer in Bulgaria.' Min sat with her feet planted, elbows on her knees, fingers knotted. 'So you haven't seen him since?'

'That's the only reason I've been able to stay in Sydney. I never wanted to live anywhere else, but I would have. And I've looked for him, trust me.' She assumed he'd moved on to another woman, and felt ashamed taking comfort in that. Someone else's torment was her relief.

'Okay.' Min tugged on one of the white silk tassels dangling from her ears, thinking. 'The detective in charge of the case is Imogen Lonski. Absolutely no sense of humour, and I suspect she hasn't smiled in the past decade. But she's an excellent investigator, tough as a chainsaw. She'd be the best person to talk to.'

Reagan's arm jerked, gin slopping into her lap. 'What?'

'Did you ever learn this guy's real name?'

'I'm not talking to the cops.'

'Rae. Seriously.' Min's head dropped to the side. 'The victim looks just like you *and* was left near you. The fact that you've had such an intense stalking experience is a decent lead. They need to hear about this.'

'It's not any kind of lead. It's nothing.' She was adamant. 'I've been back in Sydney for over three years, I've lived in the same apartment, I had to put my name in the fucking business registry. If he was still around, he would have found me.'

'I want you to really listen to what I'm about to tell you,' Min said. 'Some stalkers follow patterns, and there've been lots of studies on different types of stalking. The most typical scenario is men in their thirties stalking women in their late teens or early twenties, exactly like you experienced.'

Reagan tried to interrupt, but Min kept talking.

'But there's no way to predict any individual stalker's trajectory. We don't know what this guy is capable of. And the thing you said that really worried me is that he broke into your room. That's a big escalation in behaviour, a huge red flag. And yeah, not all stalkers become murderers, but most murders involve stalking.' Min raised her hands in emphasis. 'What I'm saying is, you could be in real danger.'

'If he was back, I'd know.' Reagan shook her head hard, eyes closed to block out the intensity of Min's expression. 'I got a little panicked on Tuesday, okay? I saw some lingerie in the corridor but it just turned out to be someone's laundry. And then I thought about it more, and there's no way he could have hidden from me for this long.'

'At least talk to Lonski.'

Reagan huffed, frustration screwing up her face. 'I'm done with the cops, Min – and don't you go giving them my name. Their files probably have me labelled as hysterical.'

'Times have changed, Rae. I'm sure it was awful, being ignored when you needed help, but they're going to be much more receptive now.'

'I will *not* speak to the cops. End of discussion.'

Min flopped against the sofa. 'Then come and stay with me. If that woman's body was left in Enmore to threaten you –'

'Why wasn't she left outside my apartment?' Reagan flung her arm toward the rear of the building. 'There's a laneway right there.'

'Maybe there's too many surveillance cameras, I don't know. Look, this murder was incredibly violent, the things that were done to this woman, I can't even –' she stopped herself, taking a deep breath. 'Her name was Krystal Almeida. American, from Chicago. The police are announcing it at a press conference at eight tomorrow morning.'

Krystal. Reagan felt a surge of protectiveness. When her mother was pregnant, her first ultrasound had revealed twins, and her parents had started preparing for two babies. It turned out to be an equipment glitch. Reagan was alone in the womb.

'You could come,' Min said. 'Hear what they have to say.'

'I told you –'

'I won't give your name to anyone. I promise. But maybe hearing some details of this investigation will make you change your mind.'

'It won't.' Reagan stood, the gin wobbling her legs. She scratched the blood-crusted mosquito bite, her voice quiet. 'Thanks for looking out for me.'

'I'm going to be all over this case, trust me. It just became number one on my priority list. Plus, I've got an inside line – they're putting together a strike force, and my contact is on it.'

'Strike force?'

'NSW Police term for task force.' Min hugged her like a strangler fig. 'Please think about what I said.'

But Reagan was thinking about Krystal, overwhelmed by an urge to learn who she was. The last time she'd wanted to be on the internet this much, she'd been fifteen years old.

10

The city called the stretch of grass near Sydney Police Centre a park, and that's where the press conference was happening, probably as part of some community relations or transparency initiative. Folding chairs fanned out in tidy rows from a black podium, mics sprouting from it like mushrooms. A few dozen people filled the chairs, mostly journos from the looks of their handheld recorders and notepads. A cluster of bulky TV cameras perched on tripods.

Reagan arrived just as a square-faced cop stepped to the podium. He held himself with seniority, the sun glinting off the gold emblem of his hat. She hung back, scanning the crowd from the thick shade of an acacia, black ball cap pulled low over her face, feeling a kinship with *Rhizanthella gardneri*. The western underground orchid produced pulpy seeds like pomegranate pips, giving its blossoms a ripe beauty. Its potential appeal to predators might explain why the plant spent its entire lifecycle underground, reproducing asexually. She'd never visited Western Australia, where the underground orchid grew, but she loved the thought of it flowering in secret below the soil's surface.

Min's jade blazer made her easy to spot, the sleeves rolled to her elbows, revealing cheetah-print lining. Despite the heat, she looked fresh. The only time Reagan had ever seen Min sweat was in a sauna. The people surrounding her wore black and grey and beige, their clothes rumpled, shoulders slumped. It wasn't just Min's jacket that made her stand out like a jewel. She was sitting up the front, had probably arrived early. She liked to be in the fray.

When she noticed Reagan approaching, Min pulled her bag off the seat next to her. 'I didn't expect to see you,' she whispered.

'I can't stop thinking about Krystal.' Reagan had been at the garden centre at 5 am, googling Krystal's name on the office computer. It was incredible how much you could learn about a person in a couple of hours online. Krystal's Instagram account alone went back four years, to her high school graduation, #Sagittarius scattered through her posts. She'd grown up in Bismarck, North Dakota, gone to university in Chicago and worked part-time as a receptionist at a concrete flooring company. She baked pumpkin pies for Thanksgiving and topped them with some American concoction called Cool Whip, built towering carrot-nosed snowmen at Christmas, and had spent the past three months backpacking through Southeast Asia with a friend. The friend had returned to the US after New Year's, and Krystal had arrived in Sydney alone. Her last post was a Bondi selfie, the sun sparkling off the water behind her. Taking an Insta break! Stay beautiful, my loves! It was dated 5 January. Seeing it, Reagan had cried until her eyes burned.

'Doll, you look exhausted,' Min said.

'Too hot to sleep.'

The senior officer at the podium introduced Detective Inspector Lonski, a chalky-skinned woman with a pointed nose, her thin lips pressed in a downturned line, underscoring a stony expression. Reagan wondered if it had developed alongside her career.

Min swivelled forward, notebook open, pen ready, the diamonds in her stacked wedding bands catching the sun.

'We've identified the woman found on Sunday as 22-year-old Krystal Almeida, a US citizen whose last place of residence was Chicago.' Lonski's voice was hard and grinding. 'She arrived in Sydney on flight JQ38 at 7.55 am on 3 January, travelling from Bali. She checked into the Sunrise Hostel in Bondi at 3 pm that afternoon, paying for two nights, and checked out as scheduled on 5 January at approximately 10.30 am. So far, we have no record of her after that date.'

It was plausible she'd crossed paths with *him*, caught his eye. Krystal could have reminded him of Reagan, reignited the worst part of him.

'We're asking the public for help in determining Krystal's movements between her arrival in Australia on 3 January and the recovery of her body on 15 January,' Lonski continued. 'We've found no record of her registering for accommodation after those first two nights in Bondi. She was not reported missing in the United States. In speaking to her family, we understand she had been backpacking for several months, and only had sporadic communication with them.'

Behind the podium, the knobby, contorted branches of a tree stretched skyward. It was a *Salix matsudana Tortuosa*. A tortured willow.

Lonski described Krystal's clothes and army green Kathmandu backpack, details drawn from her Instagram posts. She'd checked out of the hostel with her things, and so far none of them had been found. 'If you saw someone matching Krystal's description on or after Thursday 5 January, or you have information about the whereabouts of her belongings, you can report those details via our tip line.'

The second Lonski invited questions, Min's hand shot up. 'Detective,' she called, 'do you have any suspects?'

'We're pursuing a number of leads.'

The heat pressed in, making Reagan sweat.

'Detective,' a reporter called, his face and arms sun-reddened. 'This crime has some similarities to the unsolved murder of Elizabeth Short in Los Angeles in 1947, the Black Dahlia case. Are you pursuing that angle in your investigation?'

'I have no comment on past cases. Especially not ones from overseas.'

Min cocked her head, frowning, and scribbled *Black Dahlia??*

At 8.31 am, Lonski ended the press conference. People got to their feet, forming clutches of conversation in shady patches. Camera operators disconnected cables and looped cords around their elbows. Someone folded and stacked chairs.

As Reagan stood, a flash of movement near her foot caught her attention. An ibis, something red held in its beak, skulked toward her. She jumped, stifling a gasp.

Min grabbed her arm, steadying her. 'You okay, Rae?'

She gave a jerky nod. Sweat soaked through her bra.

'So, get this.' Min lowered her voice. 'The body was cut in half and left posed in the laneway, no blood. Like, not a drop. This wasn't some random act of violence. It was planned, meticulously. I thought Lonski might mention it, but they must be holding back the details.'

Reagan dropped her gaze. The grass camouflaged Min's jade wedge pumps. 'How do you know that?'

'Talked to my guy. And Lonski wouldn't admit it, but they're nowhere on suspects. They haven't seen anything like this before.' She put a hand on Reagan's arm. 'Are you sure you won't come stay with us?'

'Krystal didn't even live in Sydney. It's not like anyone could have been stalking her.'

Min arched one of her exceptional eyebrows. 'There's a thousand ways he could have catfished her online. It could be the reason she came to Sydney alone. To meet up with him.'

But if that was true . . . 'Have the police found out if she was in contact with anyone here in Sydney?'

'They'll go through her texts and emails, find her online accounts, but that kind of digital forensic work takes time.'

'It's not him, Min.'

11

The investigation went nowhere. Reagan followed the non-stop news about the case, waiting for the cops to knock on her door about the GoPro footage. The lack of police progress became news itself, both locally and in America.

The weekend after their pub drinks, Bryce visited Voodoo Lily and brainstormed a list of marketing ideas with Reagan. He returned after closing a few evenings that week. They ate takeaway while they worked on her website and set up her business profile on Google Maps. A lot of his ideas involved social media. 'There's only so much you can do without it,' he said. 'And it's a lot easier with a smartphone. You can't post to Instagram from a desktop. I'm not trying to convince you of anything, it's just the truth.'

They looked at gardening accounts on Instagram, and she was surprised by the interest they garnered. Some had hundreds of thousands of followers. And reliable information on interesting plants. 'Would I have to use my actual name?'

'Nah,' Bryce said.

She mulled it over for another week. She'd had the computer in the office since the garden centre opened, had a Voodoo Lily email account, and nothing had happened. *He's gone. He's not coming back.*

Saturday passed without a single customer coming through the door. That had never happened before. Bristling with anxiety, Reagan closed early and went to Broadway Shopping Centre. She maxed out her credit card buying an Android, not quite the cheapest smartphone available. Holding the device, she felt the pull of a black hole.

Once she had the phone, Bryce helped her set up Instagram and Facebook accounts, and they started discussing content plans. A sickly electric stress filled her. She forced it back, smiling and joking with Bryce, enjoying his company. His attention was flattering, and after so long running the business by herself, it was refreshing to have help. The next evening, he taught her about hashtags. She'd been aware of them, but much like catheters, had hoped to get through life without having to use them.

'Okay, let me take some photos to get started.' He held the phone up, aiming it at her.

'Not me!' She blocked her face with both hands. 'Just the plants.'

'You'd get more engagement if you posted some pictures of yourself.'

She waved him off. 'I'd prefer not to.'

'Trust me, people will follow you because you're attractive.'

She flushed, feeling the heat in her neck and cheeks. 'Maybe some time when I'm not dripping with sweat?'

He winked at her. 'I'm not a fan of having my photo taken either. Somehow in 2D I come out looking like a horse.'

They wandered through the shop and the greenhouse, talking about her beehive ginger, her prayer plants, and her lithops. 'They're called living stones because people think they're coloured rocks. They're actually succulents.' Bryce took photos, giving her tips on lighting, filters and captions.

'Wow, what's this?' He reached for a dried seed pod on display beside the cash register. The pods looked like tiny grey skulls, their mouths open as if screaming.

'Snapdragons,' she said. 'They dry that way.'

—

A few days later, Reagan was checking her Instagram likes, already feeling their addictive sway, when the bell above the door jingled and Bryce came in.

'I didn't know you were coming by today,' she said. 'What's that?'

'I saw these and had to get them for you.' He held out an odd bouquet, a bundle of wooden skewers tied with curls of black ribbon, topped with cellophane-wrapped lilies. The gold dust on the chocolates resembled pollen. 'I didn't think you needed flowers. I hope you like salted caramel?'

'Happens to be my favourite.'

She'd been trying to tune out her increasing attraction toward Bryce. He was friendly but rarely flirtatious, and she'd become convinced she'd misread the situation. If he wanted to hang out at the garden centre and give her free advice, that was great. She didn't need to go messing things up by pushing for more.

'I thought maybe I should ask you out on an actual date,' he said.

'Oh . . .' She pressed two knuckles to her lips. So he'd just taken his time. Which, she had to admit, made her like him that much more.

'I mean, I'm assuming you're not seeing anyone,' he said. 'I guess I never – oh, shit.'

'Oh, no! I mean, yes, I'm single.' Reagan finger-brushed her hair, self-conscious of her sweat-drenched tee, the topsoil smears on her hands, the scent of chicken manure lingering. But Bryce was used to her looking – and smelling – like this. And he was still asking her out. 'I'm surprised *you're* single.'

He scratched the back of his neck. 'I was seeing someone, pretty seriously. But she got a research position in Greenland, and I wasn't –'

'I didn't mean to pry.' Reagan felt her cheeks redden.

'It's fine. It was a few months ago.' Bryce flashed his smile. She was already accustomed to the off-kilter tooth, hardly noticing it.

They made dinner plans, Reagan still holding the chocolate bouquet, an odd mix of hope and trepidation building. Maybe this was more than a chance to save her garden centre. Maybe it was her chance to have what Min had.

12

Saturday, 11 February 2017

On Saturday evening, Reagan caught the train from Newtown Station, riding the few stops into Central and making the short walk up Devonshire, into the weekend bustle of Surry Hills. She checked herself in the restaurant's window glass, happy with the olive green sleeveless jumpsuit, silver droplet earrings and matching pendant, and the pair of nude heels she'd bought for Min's wedding and hadn't worn since. She'd even managed to wrestle her curls into a semblance of a human hairstyle.

Reagan arrived first. The restaurant's polished wood floors reflected the soft lighting, giving it a warm glow. When Bryce spotted her from the entrance, her heart gave a stupid little flutter. *Don't mess this up.*

She stood as he pushed through the door, in navy shorts and a short-sleeved button-up with a faint pattern of tiny tigers. She appreciated his smart-casual look, the slight effort beyond the default T-shirt standard. Though it would be nice if he switched his thick-framed glasses for contacts on occasion.

They ordered brut cuvée with their curries and naan, Bryce leaning back in his chair, at ease. Because he kept asking, Reagan kept talking about the places she dreamed of travelling. Namibia, to see the *Welwitschia*, a plant that lives up to 1500 years. Madagascar for its suicide palm, a tree that dies after blooming. And Mexico, home to *Stenocereus eruca*, a cactus that 'moves' like a caterpillar by growing at the top and dying at the bottom.

'It's called the creeping devil.' She searched online for a photo, turning the screen to him as her phone chimed with a message from Min. 'Sorry, let me put this away.'

She was already becoming one of those people who couldn't put their phone down. Switching it to silent, she slipped the phone into her pocket as their food arrived.

'Are you finding the phone a big change?' he asked.

'I can feel it shifting my thought patterns. This morning I caught myself opening an email while I was driving to work.'

Bryce wiped a drop of curry off his lower lip, licked his finger. Reagan caught herself thinking about his hands.

'Anyway, I've been doing all the talking,' she said. 'Tell me more about you.'

'What do you want to know?'

'What about, uh . . . your childhood?'

His eyebrows knotted. 'Yeah, it was fine. Grew up near Collaroy, no siblings, just me. Went to Sydney Uni. What about you?'

'We're talking about you. What else?' She was so bad at this. The conversation had gone from flowing to nosediving. She ordered another glass of sparkling wine from a passing server, her mind whirring. 'Did you hear about that murder in Enmore recently?'

Why had she said that? Krystal lurched into her thoughts, her last sunrise selfie at Bondi, the utter aloneness of her body in the laneway, the Joker slash marring her face, *the ibis* –

'I don't understand the true crime obsession people have these days,' Bryce said.

'Me neither.' Reagan leaned forward, tapping a finger against the table. 'I have a friend who wrote a book about a woman who was murdered and buried in the concrete foundation of a house, and then the killer lived there with his wife and kids for years. It was a huge bestseller.'

'Really?'

'She lives and breathes that stuff. She listened to nothing but true crime podcasts while she was pregnant, and I know it couldn't literally affect the growth of the baby, but I still found it creepy.'

'She sounds . . . I don't know, morbid,' Bryce said.

'When we lived in Korea she was a lot of fun, and rarely talked about grisly murders. But after she moved back to Sydney she got really into it.' Reagan took a sip of wine. 'And now it's her career.'

—

She'd promised herself she'd go home after dinner, but there was a gelato place nearby, and she couldn't say no to a scoop of salted caramel. Bryce ordered chocolate and blood orange.

They wandered up Crown Street, the neighbourhood alive with music and laughter, people everywhere. The streetlights filtered through a gumtree canopy. Bats squabbled in the branches, wings whooshing as they flew off. They stopped at a park bench, and Reagan nibbled on her waffle cone. 'Perfect summer night,' she said.

Bryce leaned toward her. She wasn't sure if he intended to kiss her, or if he hadn't quite heard. Deciding it didn't matter, she pressed her lips against his, the frame of his glasses hard against her cheek. She caught a hint of chocolate. She'd dated a Canadian guy in Seoul for a few months, and hated how he'd tried to suck her lips off, unaware of his teeth. Bryce kissed her back, a soft, sweet, perfect kiss that sent a shiver of anticipation through her.

'It's still early,' he said. 'Want to get a drink?'

'Unless . . .' Euphoria raced through her, tinged with the sparkling zest of the wine. Maybe for once, things could be easy. Joyful, even. 'Do you want to go to your place?'

—

Reagan noted the newly repaired bumper on Bryce's Honda. Like the collision had never happened. They wove along the curves of New South Head Road, past the bobbing forest of sailboat masts at Rose Bay, and toward the headland, the city skyline glowing against the night sky, reflecting off the black expanse of harbour. At Watsons Bay, they turned down a leafy side street. Bryce's right hand slid along the steering wheel; his left gripped the manual gearshift. A warm ache spread through Reagan.

She felt like she'd stepped out of her normal life of hypervigilance and self-preservation and into a parallel universe, the universe Min inhabited, where women were bold and life was fun and there were rarely consequences. Reagan had wanted that all along, and never allowed herself to admit it.

A hot flash rippled in her guts. She was alive while Krystal's body lay in pieces, frozen in a morgue.

They parked near a Weetbix-plain apartment building, seven or eight storeys. A blood sun frangipani towered beside the entrance, the faintly sweet scent of its red and yellow blossoms drifting on the thick night air.

In the elevator, Reagan leaned against the mirrored wall, waiting for Bryce to touch her. That's what they were doing, right? Teetering on the stupid heels, she snagged an arm around him. Caught off balance, he fell into her, his chest and hips pressing her against the wall as she kissed him.

The elevator doors slid open, revealing a middle-aged woman with distinctive freckles in a wheelchair, a cardboard box piled with recyclables on her lap. The woman narrowed her eyes as Bryce and Reagan stepped aside, her hands clamped playfully around his wrist.

When she was gone, Reagan leaned in, whispering near his ear. 'Your neighbour isn't very friendly.'

'Never seen her before.'

They stopped in front of a yellow door labelled 17. The same apartment number as hers. Bryce fumbled with his keys for a moment before fitting the right one into the lock. Maybe the wine was catching up with him.

Inside, Reagan stepped out of her heels and onto cool tile. The place surprised her. She'd pictured Bryce living in an undecorated apartment with mismatched IKEA furniture and a wall-sized flatscreen. This place was a miniature palace. A row of folding glass doors at the far side of the apartment opened onto a spacious balcony, a view of the inky harbour and the city beyond, the Opera House and the Harbour Bridge lit in night-time splendour. A full moon rippled on the water. There wasn't a dirty dish anywhere. Not in the open kitchen, with its sleek appliances and rows of hanging wine glasses, not on the jarrah-wood table, not in the lounge room with its charcoal rug and tangerine sofas, matched to a piece of modern art on the wall, a canvas streaked in that same shade of orange. She'd walked into a magazine spread, one that smelled like sandalwood and vanilla.

So this is who you are.

'You like the place?'

She lifted a palm. 'It could do with a couple of succulents. Maybe a potted ficus.'

'You look surprised.'

She shook her head, embarrassed. 'I didn't mean –'

He gestured toward the kitchen. A glass-fronted cabinet held dozens of bottles of spirits, with track lighting and a mirrored back wall, like an upscale bar. 'Can I get you a drink?'

'Maybe . . . later?' Slipping two fingers in between the buttons of his shirt, she kissed him. Hesitation edged her desire. She wanted to see him again, so she could make herself want this. She *did* want this.

He pulled her in to him, his fingers tracing her shoulders, down her arm. Without the heels, she had to stand on tiptoe and tilt her face to meet his lips. As he pressed against her, she slid a hand down his lower back, running her fingers along his waistband, his mouth on her neck, her whole body tingling.

They stepped onto the tufted rug that filled the lounge room, her feet delighting in its softness. Why bother going all the way to the bedroom, when this rug felt like heaven? She swivelled against him, and he fell onto the sofa, pulling her onto his lap.

In her pocket, her phone vibrated against her leg.

'Here, let me –' She shifted, one hand on his shoulder, and pulled the phone out, intending to toss it on the sofa with her clutch. Her eyes flicked to the too-bright screen, catching the first few words of a new email.

From: Reagan Carsen

You fucking bitch i will –

Her hand spasmed, lobbing the phone like it was a live scorpion. It crashed into the glass coffee table.

'Whoa.' Bryce reached for her phone and examined the tabletop for cracks. 'What happened?'

She took the phone mechanically, shoving it into her pocket without a glance as she stood, her body rigid, veins icy, the room contracting.

Bryce stood too, his face a bewildered frown. 'Reagan?' He placed his fingertips on her hip, an intimate touch.

He's found me.

13

'Reagan?' Bryce's voice sounded distant. He said her name twice more.

He stood a few feet from her, watching with concern. His shirt was twisted, his belt buckle hung loose. The idea of taking her clothes off, all that skin, brought Krystal's naked body rushing back, her legs spread wide, arms splayed above her head.

'Are you okay?'

She pressed her wrist against her forehead. The cold had seeped through her, into her bones, but she was sweating and shaking like she had a fever.

'Reagan, what's happened?' Bryce's eyes were wide, his mouth hanging open. He reached an uncertain hand toward her.

Bending over, her hands on her knees, she tried to catch her breath. She could feel herself turning red.

Bryce took a few steps, his belt buckle rattling. He stopped to refasten it.

She wanted to go home, to dismantle the phone into tiny pieces and smash the pieces with a sledgehammer. But it would never be enough. He'd always find her.

Bryce was standing in front of her, holding a glass of water. Where had that come from? She'd wanted to be bold. She'd wanted to have fun. And now she was in some stranger's place, way out in the eastern suburbs, an area she didn't know.

'Can you breathe?'

He's back.

'Reagan, say something!'

Her hands were at her throat. She was going to die here on this beautiful soft rug, in a room with no plants.

Bryce had an arm around her, and suddenly her feet were in the air, her body tucked against his. Her heart was pounding so fast she felt nauseous. The elevator dinged. *What was happening?*

They were outside, salt-water air rushing over her face, and suddenly she was Krystal, lying in the street, every inch of her exposed. Headlights flashed, and Bryce pressed her into a car. *Why was there no blood in the laneway?*

Lights streaked past like asteroids. The car swerved.

The buildings shifted, growing familiar. Sydney Tower slipped into the skyline, orienting her. Chilled air blasted from the Honda's vents, and she breathed it into her lungs, her heart slowing. Her shoes, the ridiculous heels, lay upside-down in the footwell. Bryce must have grabbed them. She edged her feet into them.

'Bryce, I'm so sorry.'

'I'm taking you to emergency.'

She put a hand on his arm. 'It's okay, I think it was a panic attack.'

They stopped at a red light, and he twisted, scrutinising her. 'You kept saying you were having a heart attack.'

Had she said that? Tiredness crested over her. The effort of holding her head up was suddenly unbearable. She sank lower in her seat.

'I just need to go home, thanks.'

The traffic in front of them began to move. He turned forward, giving her a sideways glance. 'Are you sure?'

She nodded.

'If you say so. What's your address?'

The panic spiked.

'Reagan?'

'You can just drop me at Central Station, or whatever's convenient. Edgecliff?' She didn't know this area.

'I'm not dropping you at a train station after you had a meltdown.'

That wasn't the word she would have used, but it was beside the point. It was perfectly normal to share your address after two dates, even one date. Min used to invite home guys she'd just met.

'I'm fine. I'm sorry, I wrecked our night, but I'm exhausted.'

'So let me take you to your place.' He sounded annoyed.

The streets were rushing past again, the Honda racing. Had Krystal willingly gone somewhere with her killer, feeling that same giddy optimism? When had the first flare of uncertainty hit her?

'It's not you, it's – I've had problems in the past. Please just drop me at the nearest station.'

He lifted his hands off the wheel, a frustrated gesture of surrender. 'Fine, whatever you want.'

They drove in thick silence until Bryce pulled over. Further up the block, a sign glowed with the orange train logo.

She pushed the door open. 'Sorry, again –'

'I'm stopped in a bus zone.' His voice was curt.

Reagan scurried out of the car, her left heel wobbling, nausea swelling. The Honda took off, vanishing into traffic. She yanked the pumps off, pinning them between her crooked arm and her ribs as she walked barefoot to the station entrance.

Waiting on the platform, she texted him. Thanks for dropping me off.

Bryce didn't reply. Not that night, not the next day.

By Monday, there was still no reply.

14

The blue and white police tape stretched the width of the side street, blocking it off. A crowd had gathered along the tape, watched by a half-dozen uniformed officers. Reagan drove past, searching for parking. She ended up blocks away, thongs slapping as she retraced the route to Oceanview Avenue.

The morning light had been glorious when she'd rushed out of her apartment, phone in one hand, car keys in the other, alert to every shadow. Forty minutes later, the sun had turned vicious. Peak hour had started, traffic clogging the streets. Oceanview featured plain houses with big garages pressed against the pavement rather than up a driveway, and a few squat brick apartment buildings. Uninspired gardens offered squared hedges and patches of skunk vine. At the end of the street, the rising sun cast a river of gold across the rippling ocean.

She couldn't see Min. This was her idea, and she wasn't even here yet.

'Everyone has to stay back,' one of the officers shouted, a hand cupped around his mouth. A few dozen people clustered along the tape, most with notebooks or recorders. Across the street, television crews unpacked bulky cameras.

Standing away from the crowd, she did as Min had suggested and scanned the men. A guy with a bushy moustache and cheeks like a Kent pumpkin. Another lankily tall and bald, a suit jacket folded over his arm. Two guys across the street, walking a spitz on a leash. After five years, could his appearance have changed so much that she wouldn't recognise him? He'd have the same measured gait, the same wide, square shoulders. But so much could be different, especially if he didn't want to be spotted.

It's not him. The email had been three lines of swearing and threats, random capitalisation, no full stops. That wasn't his style, even when he'd pulsed with anger. And he'd always signed off 'your true love'. Saturday's email had no sign-off. And it listed Reagan's name as the sender, the email address created in her name, r3agan_cars3n@gmail.com. Also not his style.

She'd panicked, just like with the ridiculous negligee in her apartment corridor. Once she'd calmed down, reality had crystallised around her.

A hand touched her shoulder and she flinched. Min had sidled beside her, wearing a zippered playsuit with white and navy stripes, matching navy heels, and silver hoop earrings that swung as she tried to get a better view.

'Spot him?' Min asked.

96

'Why do you think he'll be here?'

'Some criminals are drawn back to the scene. And your guy seems the type.'

'He's not here, because it's not him,' Reagan said.

'So why did you come?'

'To prove to you he's not here.' Reagan pulled the brim of her hat lower. 'Besides, Dover Heights? I never come to this part of town. If it's the same killer, this doesn't have any connection to me.'

'It's definitely the same killer. Get this – remember at the press conference, someone asked about the Black Dahlia?'

'Dahlias don't have black flowers,' Reagan said, scanning the people approaching from up the street. 'Dark purple, but not black.'

'Not flowers. This was a woman, her name was Elizabeth Short. She was twenty-two years old, living in Los Angeles, trying to get into acting. Her body was discovered bisected at the waist.'

That had Reagan's attention. 'In LA? When?'

'January 15, 1947.' Min wasn't smiling, but her voice had a dark sparkle that made Reagan queasy. 'Seventy years *to the day* before Krystal's body was left in Enmore.'

'That's . . .' Reagan didn't know what that was. Definitely not a coincidence.

Min tapped at her phone and turned it toward Reagan. 'Take a look at this.'

Reagan bared her teeth, head flinching away. '*God*, Min! It looks –' She caught herself. It looked like a black-and-white photo from Gipps Lane, two halves of a body pulled apart like a Barbie, the Joker slash of the mouth. But this woman lay nestled in the unkempt grass of an empty lot. 'Is that a crime scene photo?'

Her shock fading, Reagan leaned in to examine the picture. The strange array of wounds looked identical to Krystal's.

'From 1947, yeah. You can find it online in two seconds. According to my guy on the strike force, the Enmore victim was found in the exact same pose as this woman, the Black Dahlia. Her murder was front-page news in the *LA Times* for thirty-one days straight.' She read from an article. '"The body was discovered by a local resident, Betty Bersinger, at approximately 10 am, while out for a walk with her three-year-old daughter."'

Thank god I didn't call the cops. Reagan didn't want her name associated with a murder for decades like poor Betty's had been. It was rattling to realise that, seventy years ago, someone else's day had started just like that Sunday in January had for her.

'The wounds inflicted on both Elizabeth Short and Krystal Almeida – the lacerations to the mouth and thigh, the removed breast – they were post-mortem.' Min must have noted the uncertainty on Reagan's face. 'After death. She died of blunt-force trauma to the head. The mutilation came after. So, as messed up as this is, it's not about torture.'

Reagan fumbled for a response and came up with nothing. 'What did dahlias have to do with it?'

'The victim had pale skin and curly dark hair, so her nickname was the Black Dahlia. There's a photo – hang on.' Min enlarged a black-and-white photo of Elizabeth Short. Loose black curls surrounded a ghostly white face, with eyebrows like hard slashes and dark lipstick over Hollywood-perfect teeth. She carried discomfort in the set of her jaw, and a searching need for approval haunted her eyes. 'Remind you of anyone?'

'I mean, her hairstyle is pretty mid-century . . .'

'She looks exactly like you, Rae.' Min held her phone up beside Reagan's face. 'It's uncanny.'

'So was there another woman murdered in 1947?' She checked her phone for today's date. 'On 13 February?'

'No other murders were connected to the Black Dahlia. But you know what street Elizabeth was found on? South Norton Avenue.' Min pointed to the yellow sign protruding from a wooden telephone pole. The side street the police had cordoned off was Norton Ave. 'The closest he could find, I guess. There's no South Norton in Sydney.'

Reagan pressed her fingertips against her eyes, trying to relieve the pressure there. 'So, clearly, nothing to do with me.'

'You think it's a coincidence you look like this famous murder victim, and now other identical women are getting killed and posed in the same way?'

'How do you know the second woman –'

Someone collided with Reagan, and she stumbled, pitching forward and grabbing Min.

'Let me through.' A fit, silver-haired woman in expensive yoga wear shoved past the crowd. 'I have to see, let me –'

An officer blocked the woman's path as she tried to twist under the plastic tape. 'Stay behind the tape.'

'My daughter's missing!' Her voice was high.

Reagan tensed, her attention riveted to the woman's frantic attempts to get past the cop. Another officer appeared, taking the woman by the shoulders. 'Ma'am, you need to –'

'Shit, I think that's Anna Rhydderch,' Min said.

'Who?'

Frowning at her phone screen, Min twisted away from the sun.

'Tell me if it's her!' The woman's voice descended into a wail. The officers flanked her, gripping her arms, either restraining her or holding her upright.

Min held the phone out to Reagan. A news article photo showed a tan woman in her early twenties, beaming and thrusting a Campari-orange cocktail toward the camera.

University of Sydney student missing, the headline read. Reagan skimmed the article. Erin Rhydderch was a uni student living in a share house in Rozelle. She was last seen on Friday afternoon, three days ago. That evening, her girlfriend received an abrupt text from her saying, Going offline for a few days! Internet break. No one had heard from her since.

'You were asking how I knew what this victim looked like? I'm pretty sure this is her,' Min said. 'She's got those big curls, her face is the same shape – different eyes, but still, she could be your sister. This guy definitely has a type.'

'Why won't you tell me? Why?' The woman repeated the high-pitched question without pause, as if to prevent the officers from delivering bad news.

'This is her, isn't it?' Min scrolled down the article, finding a photo of Erin's mother.

Across the street, a news crew set up a TV camera.

'One more significant link between the cases.' Min lowered her voice, glancing around to check that no one was listening. 'Apparently it requires a certain amount of surgical precision to cleanly sever a human spine. The coroner said that whoever cut Krystal's spine had to have medical training, same as the Black Dahlia's killer. Their spines were cut at the exact same vertebrae.'

Reagan crossed her arms against her shivers. 'It's odd to leave the second victim on a street with a connection to the original case, but not the first one. The name Gipps isn't connected somehow?'

'Look at you, going all true crime junkie,' Min said. 'It's a good question. I've started looking into the Black Dahlia case. As far as I can tell, there's no Gipps connection. But the name might mean something to the killer. These murders are meticulously planned. Which is rare. Despite what pop culture might imply, killers rarely pose their victims. It happens in maybe one per cent of murders. Rodney Alcala, the Dating Game Killer, did it.'

Reagan didn't know how Min could hold so much violence in her head. She cut in before Min launched into details. 'I don't believe this guy was driving around Enmore randomly looking for a spot to leave a body.'

'I agree, he likely scoped out Gipps Lane in advance, and chose it because it had no surveillance cameras.'

'This area is going to be full of cameras,' Reagan said. 'Seems risky to come here.'

'Oh – I meant to tell you, I followed up on whether Krystal had come to Sydney with plans to meet anyone. The digital forensics team hasn't found anything to indicate that.'

'See? It's not him. It's not –' she lowered her voice, the muscles of her jaw like taut wires, 'it's not AJ.'

Just like the email wasn't from him. It was some random troll. Like Bryce had anticipated, Reagan's posts were gaining popularity on Instagram. People were discovering her shop and coming in to take pictures with her cascading rainbow arrangements of blossoms, her doll's eyes and ghost plants. She encouraged photos, reposted them, spent time replying to comments. She'd gained a thousand followers in a week. Her weekend sales had been the best in a year. She'd even started to enjoy it – until that email.

Some jerk had probably stumbled onto her Instagram profile, dug her name out of the business registry, and created an email address to send her the nasty message. End of story. It was just part of being online, and she'd have to live with it. She refused to give up her online marketing now that she was seeing an increase in customers.

'Hello, Earth to Reagan.' Min waved a hand inches from Reagan's face.

'Sorry, what?'

'Are you okay? You seem really tense.'

A third cop joined the ashen-faced woman and the two uniformed cops still holding her arms. She showed no response while he spoke to her, but when he walked away, she followed, the two uniforms flanking her. They disappeared around a corner.

A man walked past carrying a takeaway coffee, its scent trailing. Vehicles and cyclists streamed toward the city. It seemed callous to be so rudely alive on an incandescent summer morning, hovering on the sidelines of a crime scene. Up the street, more people arrived, clustered at the police cordon, some shouting questions to the uniformed cops.

The photo of Erin, vibrant and merry, merged with Reagan's memory of Krystal, cold and still.

'So who killed her? The Black Dahlia?' Reagan asked. 'This can't be the same person from seventy years ago.'

Min squinted into the morning sun. 'The case is still unsolved.'

15

The crowd jostling at the crime scene tape kept growing. Reagan's phone vibrated like a hive of aggravated bees. Turning away from Min, she pulled it out of her pocket, using a hand to shield the screen from the sun.

It's been 4 weeks. When is 1st payment arriving in account??

Cynthia, again. Even though business had picked up, it wasn't enough to start making repayments on what she'd been told was her inheritance.

Min leaned toward her. 'You haven't updated me on your new boy. How was the date?' Her friend could switch gears instantly, from murder to dating. Reagan wasn't sure if that was admirable or unsettling.

'Not great,' she said. 'I haven't spoken to him since.'

'What happened?'

She made a vague gesture. If she told Min about the email, she'd probably insist Reagan report it to the police. And not telling her about the email meant not telling her about the panic attack.

She ought to be upset that Bryce hadn't spoken to her since he'd dropped her off at the bus stop, but mostly she felt shame. Shame at her panic, her abrupt departure, her inability to explain. As a little kid, her reaction to an injury hadn't been to run to her parents but to hide. When she was five, she'd cut her leg on a rock while playing outside. She'd hid in her closet for hours, her calf throbbing, blood caking her tights.

Her phone buzzed. Cynthia wouldn't need to take Reagan to court – she'd harass her to death first. And without Bryce's advice and encouragement, she wasn't sure she could keep her online marketing going. She'd thought she was acclimatising to her new digital presence. But the cold fear in her gut revealed that what she enjoyed about social media was doing it with Bryce, having his support. Alone, she'd flounder, plagued by indecision about comments and hashtags.

'So call him,' Min said. Like it was no big deal.

'What, on the phone?'

'No, on a conch shell.' Min put her hand out for the phone. 'Here, I'll do it.'

Reagan scoffed. 'And say what?'

'That he'll never meet anyone who knows more about plants.'

'Ha, true.'

'I'm serious, Rae. Not about the plant thing. But this is the first guy you've mentioned to me since – hell, since Korea, so there must be something special about him. Don't let him slip away because of one lousy date.'

Reagan tapped the phone against her thigh, ignoring the buzz of another text. It was 8.45 on Monday morning. Early, but not too early. 'Okay, okay. I'll call.'

It wasn't like Bryce was going to answer.

She pivoted and took a few steps up the street. Min cupped a hand to her ear, parodying an eavesdropper.

'Reagan.' That confident, husky voice.

She nearly dropped the phone.

'Oh, Bryce.' Her smile deflated as she groped for what to say, words dissolving into mush. Overhead, a helicopter approached, the roar of the rotor blades blanketing the street. Bryce said something and she missed it. She cupped her hands around the phone. 'Sorry, can you – it's noisy here.'

'I'm heading into a meeting.'

She quick-stepped further from Min. 'I'm, uh, I'm calling to apologise. For . . . everything and, um . . .'

She waited. He didn't fill the silence. Above, the chopper circled.

'Could we meet up? Lunch, maybe?' she asked. It would be so much easier to talk in person. Lunch would have a limited timeframe, ideal if the conversation got awkward. Plus, it was sooner. Get it over with, one way or the other.

'Lunch, today?' Bryce asked.

The storm of emotions his voice was kicking up took her by surprise. Maybe she wasn't ready to share her life with someone. Min snuck up beside her. 'Go for it,' she mouthed. Reagan swatted her away.

'If you're free?' she said.

'Can you meet me near my office?' he said. 'I'll text you an address.'

Reagan ended the call, pocketing the phone and turning her face to hide the smile that stole across it.

Min grabbed her hands. 'What is this, your third date?'

'It's not a date. It's lunch.'

'But this dude's been on the scene a few weeks now,' Min said. 'You know, you haven't shown me a picture of him.'

'I don't have one.'

'Really? You've got Instagram. Send me his profile.'

'It's just architectural shots.' Reagan retrieved her phone – it seemed like she typed in the passcode a thousand times a day – and found Bryce's feed, various angles of buildings, some cast in hard-edged shadow. He had 500 followers. His profile pic was a cross-hatch of the Harbour Bridge.

Min browsed the images, then started typing. 'Bryce Stewart? Are any of these him?'

Reagan scrolled through a couple of dozen Bryce Stewarts on Facebook. 'I don't think so – jeez, there's a lot of guys with that name.'

'There's nothing like the internet to remind you you're not unique. So none of them?' Min took the phone, searched a different site. 'What about here?'

Reagan skimmed a new list of Bryce Stewarts. 'I don't see him. What's this?'

'LinkedIn.'

'He does that stuff for work.' Reagan waved her free hand, dismissive. 'He even has to use that one with the ghost. Napsnap?'

'Snapchat.'

'Right. And I *like* that he's not on his phone every minute of the day, like other people I know.' She gave Min a pointed look. 'It's refreshing.'

Min put her hand on Reagan's upper arm and squeezed. 'Look at that – now you sound happy.'

—

The shop was called Big Sandwich. Judging from the foil-wrapped monstrosities customers were digging into at the handful of laneway tables, it should have been called Unreasonable Sandwich. It wasn't much for atmosphere, between the fluorescent lights and the rabble of customers, but the food must be good, considering the queue out the door and the eight or nine hair-netted staff slapping together sandwiches behind the counter.

The second Reagan spotted Bryce, her heart did a weird swoop thing. *Was that what skipping a beat felt like?*

He exuded easy confidence, one hand pocketed, relaxed posture, an embodied she'll-be-rightness. Everyone else in the queue was scrolling their phones or talking into the headphone cables snaking from their ears. Bryce stood as if at the centre of everything, imperturbable.

'Hey,' she called, joining him in the queue. 'Thanks for meeting me.'

'Sure.' His face remained coolly neutral.

'Look, I wanted to say –' She'd been practising since their call that morning and wanted to get the words out before nerves jumbled them. But the queue surged ahead, the assembly-line staff calling people forward, hustling orders.

'Hang on.' Bryce turned to the counter. 'Yeah, lemon chicken on brown, extra garlic sauce.'

Reagan tried to skim the dozens of options on the menu above the counter. She wasn't hungry. 'The same, thanks.'

When they had their oversized sandwiches, they found a table in the shade. People scraped metal chairs against the concrete, the noise making her wince. The table was so small, their knees touched.

'I'm sorry about Saturday.' If she didn't spit this out, she'd lose her nerve. 'That must have been bizarre for you. One minute I'm fine, the next I'm hyperventilating.'

He thrust a palm up. 'I don't want you to think that's why I haven't been in touch.' He leaned across the tiny table, face close to hers, his sandwich untouched. 'When you insisted I drop you off at the train station, I felt like –'

'I'm sorry about that too.'

'– like you wanted nothing to do with me. When you texted, I figured you were just being polite.'

'No, nothing like that! It's just I've had . . .' she stopped, the words jamming in her throat. She'd planned to tell him, to lay out the bare facts.

Her mother's flinty voice sparked through her. *All that trouble.*

She unwrapped the aluminium foil from her sandwich, folding it and smoothing the creases, buying herself time. She had to use two hands to hoist half of the sandwich, the bread thick, soft and warm.

'You don't have to tell me anything,' Bryce said. 'I only want to ask one question – is everything okay?'

Reagan had a mouthful of sandwich, garlic overpowering her tastebuds. She gestured at her stuffed cheeks while managing to both nod and shake her head.

'Have you received any more of those emails?' He picked up his sandwich. 'It was an email, wasn't it? That upset you. I caught a glimpse when I picked up your phone.'

'Everything's fine.' She said it so fast, she almost believed it. 'And I live in Enmore, in the inner west. Apartment 17 in a run-down building on Chester Street, 52 Chester Street. I'd invite you over, but it's not the cheeriest place.'

She'd done it. She'd given her actual address to someone other than Min and her mother.

Bryce raised an eyebrow, his expression softening. 'You didn't have to do that. I wasn't –'

'I know. Can we forget about Saturday? Maybe try again?'

'Of course.' Under the table, his leg brushed her thigh. 'But do you need any help? Could I look into the email for you?'

'It's fine.' As she said it, she took stock of the shifting crowd around them, checking the shadows. 'But maybe you could come by the garden centre this week? Help me figure out what the hell Insta stories are?'

He leaned in again, his lips close to her ear. On his breath, the garlic smelled sweet. 'Whatever you need.'

16

Wednesday, 22 February 2017

Voodoo Lily bustled with customers taking photos, asking questions, and actually buying plants. Sales were up for the third day in a row. Reagan found herself humming cheerfully, even after a high-ponytailed woman tried to insist on a refund for a dried-out spider plant with a Bunnings sticker.

Reagan missed two calls from Min before she had a chance to phone back.

'I was about to send the police to check you're still alive,' Min said. 'I'm only half-joking.'

'Just busy.' Reagan pinned her mobile with her shoulder as she swept up the potting soil from a knocked-over tray of wolfsbane. 'What's up? I've only got a minute.'

The bell above the door chimed and Ed stepped inside, the sour smell of his Ferguson Seeds polo preceding him. He came to the counter, ignoring the phone at Reagan's ear.

'Got that herb order in the van. Where do you want it set up?'

'Can you hold on?' Reagan said to Min, then muffled her mobile against her shoulder. 'You were supposed to be here yesterday.'

'Well,' Ed smacked his lips, 'I'm here early today.'

Her landline rang.

'You gonna get that?' Ed pointed.

'That open space, left of the begonias.' She pointed, spotting the guy in the navy jacket, his leg still in the cast. How long had he been in the shop? 'Set it up over there.'

Ed crossed his arms, patting one hand against his bicep. 'Not gonna fit there.'

'Just figure it out, Ed.'

He sniffed loudly, wiping his wrist against his nose before turning away. Reagan snatched up the landline, but the caller had hung up.

'You haven't seen the news?' Min spoke in a rush. 'The killer sent photos of both crime scenes to Channel 6, along with photos of Krystal and Erin in what looks like some kind of DIY operating room. Channel 6 released them two hours ago and the internet exploded. The web sleuth community immediately picked up on the connection to the Black Dahlia. CNN has already dubbed them the Sydney Dahlia murders.'

Reagan was struggling to follow. 'There are web sleuths?'

'Can you come over tonight? After the kids are in bed? I have something to show you.'

'Sure, yeah,' Reagan said, grimacing as Ed bashed together wire display racks. 'See you then.'

—

Min wrapped her arms around Reagan before she was through the front door. 'Thanks for making the journey over the bridge, doll.' It was a Sydney joke, the two sides of the harbour worlds apart. 'And you're glowing! Last night's date was good?'

Bryce had come to the garden centre on Tuesday after work, and they'd spent time there before going for dinner, then drinks. This time, Reagan had turned her phone off so nothing could interrupt them. A smile snuck across her face with the memory of Bryce's hands, the weight of his body, the lavender smell of his sheets. 'I stayed over at his place.'

'Oh my god, who are you?' Min beamed as she padded upstairs, Reagan following.

'I met him a month ago and I stayed at his place for the first time last night. That's not moving too fast, is it?'

Min lowered her voice as they passed the kids' bedrooms, speaking with a huge smile. 'I'm so fucking delighted for you.'

The office was more spacious than Reagan's bedroom. She loved this room, with its stately oak desk, maroon leather wingback chair, and thick-piled rug that Min had shipped home from a trip to Tbilisi. Bookshelves lined the walls, spines organised by colour. It was a challenge gifting Min plants she didn't immediately kill, but she'd managed to keep the trailing Christmas cactus alive, along with the potted snake plant that dominated the far corner.

'Although I'm still shocked that you rushed out and bought a smartphone right after meeting him.' Min kept her voice hushed, to avoid carrying through the wall to Maisey's room.

'Everyone told me to get a smartphone. Even you.'

'True.' Min put her hands up in surrender. 'Sorry, maybe staring at photos of murdered women who look like my closest friend is starting to get to me.'

On a large whiteboard, Min had taped headshots of Krystal Almeida, Erin Rhydderch and the original Black Dahlia, Elizabeth Short.

Reagan approached the photo spread. 'It's like in the movies.'

'Like in a police incident room,' Min said. 'So, the killer posted four Polaroids, two of Erin and two of Krystal, taken from identical angles.'

Min pulled a couple of pages from her desk printer and handed them to Reagan, scans of the original Polaroids. 'Brace yourself.'

The photo of Krystal in Gipps Lane brought back the corpse-flower smell, the thick heat of the January morning, the long, black talons of the ibis. *Act like you've never seen this before*. 'This is awful, Min. Why are you showing me this?'

'What if this is your stalker, Rae? What if he comes after you?'

In the crime scene photo from Norton Avenue, Erin had the same horrendous pose, her legs wide, arms tossed open, the missing breast, the slashed face. A second photo captured her from the waist up in a white-walled room, positioned on a stainless steel table. It was a careful shot, showing nothing except the woman, the wall, and part of the metal table.

'The police still don't have any suspects?' Reagan asked, putting the photos facedown on the desk.

'Nothing.' Min shook her head, strands of hair falling loose from her messy bun. 'They haven't even been able to determine an approximate time of death for Krystal. They're officially consulting with the FBI's LA office, looking at possible connections to the Black Dahlia case.'

'This guy sent Polaroids?' Reagan said. 'Who uses those anymore?'

Min held up a finger. 'I thought that too. Why not print them on photo paper at home? So I did some digging. It turns out most modern colour laser printers include tracking information – they print microdots, like a fingerprint. So this guy isn't just smart, he also knows technology.'

'How did you get copies of the photos?'

'Friend at Channel 6.'

'Not your detective friend?'

'Who said he's a detective?' Min said it so drily, Reagan couldn't tell if she was sincere.

'Is this what you wanted to show me?'

'Getting to it.' Min approached the whiteboard, focused. 'Okay, looking at these two crime scenes, what's your first question?'

Reagan tried to picture the killer as a person, a man who had to reset forgotten passwords, who shopped for toilet paper and got holes in his socks. 'What sort of sick fuck could do this?'

'That's easy,' Min said. 'Someone with no empathy or capacity to experience human emotions. This is clearly a psychopath. My first question – why these women? Did he know them somehow?'

'It seems like he couldn't have known Krystal. She'd flown in from Bali a few days before, and you said there was no evidence she'd been talking to anyone online in Sydney.'

'That could be true for Erin too,' Min said. 'According to her flatmates, she went to Callan Park on Friday afternoon and never came home. Her family reported her missing on Saturday after she didn't reply to texts and calls. One theory is that she could have gone to the park to meet someone she knew online. But she also could have met someone there who either charmed her into going with him, or threatened her.'

'Krystal and Erin seem very different.' Reagan had spent hours reading about Erin online. She was studious, a computer science major who'd worn a homemade C-3PO costume to a fancy dress party the weekend before she died. She and her girlfriend often posted selfies from bushwalking daytrips to the Blue Mountains. If Reagan had met her at uni, they might have been friends. Erin's family was furious that the police hadn't begun looking for her immediately when they reported her missing. The police had told them that, as an adult with no history of mental illness, she had a right to turn her phone off and not come home for the weekend. If the police had started looking for her sooner, her family argued, she might still be alive. 'Has the strike force found any connections between the two women?'

'Not so far. Krystal didn't seem to know anyone in Australia.' Min scratched her fingers along her scalp, further mussing her hair. 'So let's assume they didn't know each other, and he didn't know them. He chose them randomly, based on their looks and their context.'

'Their context?'

'Where and when he met them, how vulnerable they seemed. If it's true that he had no personal motivation for killing these women, we have to assume he believes his motives are the same as the Black Dahlia killer's.' Min tapped a finger beside the black-and-white glamour shot of Elizabeth Short.

Reagan turned from the photos to look at Min. 'I thought her murder was unsolved.'

'Technically,' Min said. 'There's a former LA homicide detective who's pretty sure he solved the case.'

'Really?' The eagerness in her voice surprised her.

'It's a fascinating story. This retired detective happened to be talking to someone about the Black Dahlia case – this was decades later, Elizabeth Short died when he was a kid.' Min's voice had that dark sparkle again. 'So this person says, "You know your father was a suspect in the Black Dahlia murder?" He was floored by that, and decided to look into this cold case to prove his dad's innocence. His father was dead by that time.'

'And he figured out who the killer was?'

'Yeah. His father. Dr George Hodel.'

Min's intensity caused Reagan to take a step back as her brain clicked pieces of information into place. The coroner had said the killer would have needed medical training to be able to bisect a spine so cleanly. 'His *father*?'

'The son makes a strong case,' Min said. 'And he should know. He was a veteran homicide detective.'

Medical training. Though Min had mentioned it, Reagan hadn't fully considered that detail before. Because she knew where *he* worked, what he did for a living.

And he definitely wasn't a doctor.

She'd searched online for any scrap of information about where he might be. But he had less of an internet presence than she did. And like her, he had a good reason for that.

17

'Take a look at this.' Min grabbed a coffee table book from the desk and held it open.

A rough ink sketch filled a white page, the outline of a woman's naked body, the face a mess of squiggles. Her arms lolled, hands not quite above her head, bent at the elbows. An aged piece of green paper currency stuck to the page across her pelvis. The money looked European, maybe Italian. One of the figure's legs stuck out beneath the note, and the other protruded from its centre, as if the woman was doing the splits.

The note bisected the body.

Reagan's heart thumped. The sketch's title was *Tire Lire*. 'Did the killer draw this?'

'It's by Man Ray.'

The name sounded vaguely familiar, but Reagan couldn't place it. 'Who was he?'

'Surrealist painter and photographer, well known in his time. Here's the thing – he lived in LA through the 1940s. And, crucially, he was friends with Hodel.'

'So he could have been involved with the murder?'

'There's no suspicion of that. But it turns out Dr Hodel had ambitions of being an artist, had made an attempt at it when he was younger, and failed. The son's theory is that Hodel was hanging out with these surrealists and decided to prove he was willing to take greater artistic risks than all of them.'

'By *killing* someone? You're saying Elizabeth Short died for . . . some twisted art project?'

Min waved a hand, a lowering motion. 'Shhh, don't wake Maisey.'

Reagan pressed her fingertips to her lips. 'Sorry.' She looked from the strange sketch to the whiteboard photos of the three murdered women. How did Min think about this stuff every day, under the same roof as her tiny children? Maybe it was like the fungi discovered growing on the ruins of the Chernobyl nuclear reactor. They grew not toward the sun, but toward radiation, absorbing it.

'Does that explain the drained blood? There's Reddit posts talking about vampire bullshit.'

'You're a Redditor now?' Min turned to the whiteboard photos. 'I think it was practical. Blood's messy. If you're creating a work of art, you don't dump paint over it, Jackson Pollock aside. And I think the artwork theory has potential. I mean, living women are expected to treat their bodies like artworks, to constantly put them-selves on display. Maybe this is why we're so culturally obsessed with pretty dead women. It's a dark insight into our society, the most extreme example of how men use women's bodies to their own ends.'

'This killer is making some kind of statement about . . . women in society?'

'I think he's expressing his personal feelings about our value. Why else send photos to the media, to make sure everyone sees exactly what he did to Krystal and Erin? The wounds are post-mortem, remember. He's not interested in physical pain. He just needs a body to . . . work with. As awful as that is to say.'

'Wait, hold on,' Reagan said. 'This guy, Hodel. He had a son? Who grew up with him?'

'That's its own strange story. The reason LA police had Dr Hodel on their radar was because he went to trial for impregnating his teenage daughter in 1949.'

In the chill of the aircon, Reagan's skin goosepimpled. 'How was this guy not in prison? And how did his son not know about this?'

'The defence labelled his daughter an unstable, unreliable girl, and Hodel was acquitted. The son was a lot younger, and the kids had different mothers.' She gestured to the whiteboard. 'We're getting off track. Hodel is the most viable suspect in the 1947 murder. His son has published several books laying out the evidence. We have to assume the killer knows all this.'

Reagan crossed her arms, tucking her hands away and digging her toes into the rug's thick pile. 'So you think the Sydney killer is, what, a failed art student?'

'Was your stalker an art student?'

'I asked you to not bring that up.' She leaned toward the snake plant, sticking her fingertips into the potting soil. A little dry. 'Has your mum watered this lately?'

'Reagan.'

'I don't *know*. He told me he was a high school student, so your guess is as good as mine.' She brushed the soil from her fingers. 'You really think the Sydney killer's motive is the same?'

'Probably not.' Putting the open art book on the table, Min gestured to the sketch. 'This killer has recreated the Black Dahlia crime scene twice. He's not innovating. It's like he's . . . recreating a masterwork.'

'Oh god, Min.' Reagan winced.

'I'm just trying to get in his head. Elizabeth Short's murder is meaningful to him. If this theory is right, it would be worth getting familiar with Man Ray's art. It spoke to the original killer, so it might give us some insight into what the current one is thinking.' She pointed to a stack of oversized art books. 'So, want to help?'

Grabbing two of the books, Reagan headed for the armchair. A squawk came from the baby monitor, and Min stepped out. By the time she returned, Reagan was absorbed in the images.

At first there were a few connections. A photograph called *Tears*, circa 1930, showed a close-up of a woman's heavily mascaraed eyes, cast upward as if in appeal, clear droplets of glass or plastic set on her skin. An untitled piece, also from 1930, featured two women's naked torsos, portioned by jagged light streaks. A piece from 1944, *Enough Rope*, displayed only frayed strands of rope, crisscrossing the page like lightning strikes. In *Woman with Mask and Handcuffs*, a photo from 1929, two men in suits stared sourly into the camera, an oddly angled image of a woman's head tacked on the wall behind them.

There was more. Knotted ropes around a woman's headless, limbless bust. Dozens of nude women, and nude women's torsos, their arms raised or thrown above their heads. A sketch of a man dragging a naked woman, a rope knotted around her neck. A photo of a naked woman, arms raised, a spider web etched over her body.

And a black-and-white photo of yet another naked woman with dark curls lying on the floor, her arms and legs tied down, a collar around her neck, whip and handcuffs strewn in the background. Two figures bent over the woman, one with a knife, the other with pliers clamped to her nipple. A dark rope lay across her hips, as if bisecting her. It was part of a series called *The Fantasies of Mr Seabrook*, from 1930.

Reagan showed the image to Min. 'How is this even art? It looks like a crime scene photo.'

'Wow, that's straight out of RedTube.'

Reagan frowned, missing the reference.

They worked through the art books, the evening slipping into night, Reagan's exhaustion building to a physical ache.

'Are you hungry?' Min asked.

Glancing at her Timex, Reagan closed the book on her lap. 'I should probably get home.'

'I've got japchae in the fridge.'

She jumped up. 'We could've been eating japchae this whole time?'

—

ASHLEY KALAGIAN BLUNT

Inset cabinet lights gave the kitchen a quiet glow. Min heated two bowls in the microwave while Reagan pulled chopsticks from the cutlery drawer.

'Your mum made this?'

The microwave beeped. Min handed her a warm bowl. 'The woman is a saint. There's no way I could write a word without her. And you should hear Maisey's Korean, it's adorable.'

The japchae was a perfect blend of sweet and savoury, with soft crunchy veggies and a chewy bounce to the glass noodles.

The backdoor squealed and Owen came in, clothes rumpled, leather satchel over his shoulder. Reagan figured Min had married a fellow workaholic so her own all-nighters seemed reasonable by comparison.

'Is that japchae?' He kissed Min on the cheek, greeted Reagan.

Min said *mfph*, her mouth full, noodles dangling from her chopsticks. 'There's more in the fridge,' she managed, but he shook his head, rubbing his palm against the hint of stubble on his cheek. The black bags under his eyes added a decade to his face.

'Long day, Owen?' Reagan asked. It was after eleven.

'About usual.'

'He's been working crazy hours lately, Rae.' Min handed her bowl to Owen, then went to the fridge to heat the rest for herself.

'You're lucky Min puts up with you.' Reagan said it as a joke.

'Because I'm such a good provider?'

His lightness matched hers, a smile in his voice. Still, Reagan took private offence on her friend's behalf when Owen made stupid quips. *As if Min needs anyone to provide for her.* Min never seemed to mind though.

124

He pulled out a kitchen chair to join them, lifting a folded newspaper off it. 'Shit, Reagan. Min said the victims looked like you, but this girl – wow.'

A headshot dominated the front page. Erin Rhydderch, six weeks before her death, her smile tremendous as she pointed to the party tiara on her head, *Happy New Year 2017!* spelled in glittery silver plastic. She radiated optimism.

Owen looked from the oversized photo to Reagan, making the same side-by-side comparison Min had. Then he tossed the paper onto a pile, near a highchair covered in Cheerio detritus.

'Before I forget, are you coming to Dashiel's birthday?' Min asked. 'I texted you about it.'

Reagan pulled her diary from her handbag and flipped through the pages.

'Next weekend,' Min said. 'We're starting at two, but it's a barbecue, so come by after work.'

'I'll see if I can make it.' Reagan grabbed a pen from the table, noting the date. Min had done this for Maisey's birthdays too, inviting friends like the party was for her.

'You *can*. It'll make Maisey's day, and hopefully distract her from the misery of not being the centre of attention.' Min yawned. 'Why don't you stay in the guest room tonight?'

'I'm fine.' She wanted the comfort of her own bed, her plants, her deadbolts. 'I'll text you when I get there.'

'Are you sure?' Min raised an eyebrow, glancing at Owen.

Owen pushed himself up, yawning. 'Let me walk you to your car.'

'Really,' Reagan said, wedging the diary into her handbag. 'My car's right outside.'

—

It was close to midnight when she left, the sky moonless and inky. Reagan paused on the front steps, scrutinising the shadows. Gripping her keys, she slipped down the driveway, past the matching silver Lexuses, an SUV and a sports coupe that Owen and Min drove interchangeably depending on who had the kids.

She checked the back seat before she got in the Holden, and locked the doors as soon as she was in the driver's seat. From the safety of the car, she squinted into the shadows.

In Enmore, instead of parking in her assigned spot, she found one around the corner, a block away from her building. *Make yourself unpredictable.* Old habits creeping back.

The mistake she made, kicking off her thongs and lying on the sofa, was checking her unread emails after she texted Min. There was no reason to open the app, but a kernel of uncertainty gnawed at her, even as she thought, *Anything there can wait till morning.*

She shot upright, rigid.

From: Reagan Carsen

i hope you get every cancer you filthy man-hating skank if i had –

18

Thursday, 23 February 2017

The next morning Reagan left the apartment at dawn. She wore a plain black cap, her hair pinned in a tight bun.

With all the surveillance cameras, the cops could follow her licence plate anywhere in the city. She'd contemplated switching vehicles with Min or Bryce, but that would come with a whole lot of questions.

Instead, she caught the train into the city and arrived at the Avis office a few minutes before it opened. Standing outside the door, jiggling her foot, she tried to figure out an option that wouldn't cost her $117.36. There were local cars you could hire by the hour, but that required creating an online account.

Avis had a car available, a Suzuki Swift, at the price their website had quoted. She'd be returning it before Voodoo Lily opened.

'What colour is it?'

'Let me check,' the employee said, turning to his computer. 'I've got red or . . . red.'

'No, I need something,' Reagan struggled to phrase it, 'less showy.'

The request didn't faze him. 'If you'd like a larger vehicle, I've got a Toyota Corolla sedan in grey.'

It was twenty-five dollars more. She paid it.

Driving against traffic, she returned the way she'd come on the train, the roads busier now, the city waking up under a flat grey sky. She'd brought her dog-eared Sydney street atlas, its coiled plastic spine warping, and had it open to Ashbury, another inner west suburb huddled along the Cooks River. There was no way she was using Google Maps for this.

Even if it hadn't been so significant, she couldn't forget the name Crieff Street, how it sounded like a combination of *cringe* and *grief*. If she could have casually driven past, she might have risked coming in her beat-up Holden. But Crieff dead-ended at the Canterbury Park Racecourse. There was no way back without the attention-drawing awkwardness of a U-turn.

The first time she'd come here, she was eighteen, fed-up and furious. She'd bought her first car, a boxy black Mazda with 117,000 kilometres on it and the lingering smell of wet dog. It had given her a narrow window of opportunity, and she'd taken it.

Crieff Street featured modest homes, forgettable single-storey brick places with clay tile roofs, tidy lawns and concrete driveways. The lots offered more elbow room than those in her neighbourhood.

If she told Min about the emails, Min would insist she go to the cops and explain the whole saga. Which was pointless. Someone else was sending the emails. It wasn't him.

But it wouldn't hurt to check up on him. Providing he didn't spot her.

Number 79 sat second from the end. Her hired Corolla approached the last intersection. She could turn off, speed away from Crieff Street, forget it.

She continued straight, the house numbers ticking up, 53, 67, 71. Two women jogged down the pavement, one pushing a pram. She fought the urge to stop and warn them.

There it was, number 79. At least, that's what the metal digits screwed into the front door read. It had the same bay window and squat chimney. But the last time she'd been here, flakes of cream paint had littered the dying lawn, and an unruly boxwood hedge stretched along the pavement. Now the hedge was gone, replaced by a low brick fence. The muted grey trim gave the house a more mature look. The lawn was still dying, but everyone's was, between the heat and the water restrictions. Two sunshower hibiscuses framed the front door, dotted with orange and yellow blossoms. A tricycle lay on its side in the driveway, its wheels mud-crusted.

Could he have kids? Maybe that explained why he hadn't found her since she'd moved back to Sydney – he'd started a serious relationship, maybe got married.

Reagan parked across the street and glanced at her Timex: 8.07. She'd give herself three minutes. Her phone was powered off, but she put it to her ear, just a woman finishing a call.

The first time, after saving enough of her Macca's pay to buy the dog-smelling Mazda, she'd kept it parked blocks away from her apartment. If he didn't know she had the car, she could turn his tactics against him. And if she found him, she could give the police his address, and maybe they would finally help her. She waited until she caught him walking his ratty hairless dog past her place. When he was out of sight, she'd scrambled to her car, scarf wrapped around her face, hoodie up. She'd followed, two blocks to his Jeep and through the mess of morning traffic to Crieff Street.

But the next day, when she went to the police station to make a report, things hadn't gone how she'd expected.

Across Crieff Street, the front door opened and a woman walked out, maybe Reagan's age. A boy scrambled behind her, leaping down the steps and climbing onto the trike.

Maybe this was his wife, his son?

A man in a suit and a paisley tie came outside, a laptop case slung from his shoulder. He helped the boy manoeuvre the trike into the garage. It definitely wasn't *him* – this guy was Black.

Reagan dropped the phone on the passenger seat and pulled off the sunglasses. Now that she was here, she wasn't sure why she'd come. She was getting desperate.

Even if there had been any indication he was still here, it wouldn't have been much help. It wouldn't have confirmed the emails weren't from him, or whether or not he might be killing women who looked like her. She wasn't likely to catch him dragging a five-foot-four brunette into the house.

Maybe she'd just wanted to make use of the tiny bit of power she'd had.

And now it was gone. He didn't live at 79 Crieff Street. He could be anywhere.

He could be living across the street from her.

19

Saturday, 25 February 2017

By Saturday, Reagan's optimism had returned. Bryce was taking her out for a special dinner that evening, and the day crackled with the joy of anticipation. She was up early, the sun turning her apartment golden, the morning air mild and fragrant. With extra time before she needed to leave for the garden centre, she walked up Enmore Road, passing a couple with three cavoodles in tow, each a distinct shade of brown, and an elderly man feeding crackers to a harness-clad ferret huddled on his shoulder. She turned in to her favourite cafe, a rare treat. Most mornings she drank instant coffee on her drive to work.

She ordered a flat white and was waiting, scrolling an article about the risk of mummified wasps in figs, when she heard her name. She turned, expecting the barista to pass her coffee. Instead, Emil Wojciech stood beside her.

It took her a second to place him, though she'd seen him earlier that week for her follow-up meeting at the bank.

'Emil, hi,' she said. He wore a white golf shirt, blue shorts and thongs. The look didn't suit him. She forced a polite smile. Their meeting had gone well. He'd been impressed by her online marketing plan, added a few suggestions, and signed off on another three-month repayment deferral. 'I didn't know you lived in this area.'

'Oh, I don't.'

The barista called her name, and she retrieved her coffee, thankful for the distraction.

'You live near here?' Emil asked.

She took a sip, nodding. 'It's a colourful place. I just saw a guy with a ferret on his shoulder.'

'Uh-huh.'

'Well, I'll see you . . . at the bank.' Reagan stepped backward, giving an awkward wave.

'Have a good day,' he called.

—

Reagan had suggested a more affordable restaurant, much like she'd offered to pay her share of their last dinner out. But Bryce had insisted on treating her to O Bar, the revolving restaurant at Australia Square. Reagan's dad had taken her up Sydney Tower for her tenth birthday, but as an adult she'd never bothered with the city's tourist attractions. Which, she could see now, over a dinner of swordfish and stuffed zucchini flowers, was a mistake. From forty-seven storeys up, with the sunset casting a rose-gold hue over the skyline as they rotated past Darling Harbour and the Finger Wharves, it was easy to pretend life was beautiful and safe.

For dessert, she ordered a salted caramel martini. She'd taken her first sip when Bryce asked if she was okay.

'Do I not look okay?' She'd thought she was pulling it off, despite the latest nasty email. Sitting at Bryce's side, the sunset laid out before them, she felt more relaxed than she had in weeks. She reached for his hand.

'You seem on edge.' A fake candle on the table reflected in the lenses of his glasses.

'A lot of women are on edge right now.' There were articles about women who hadn't left their homes since the second murder, about the boom in security system installations, about Krav Maga courses booking out months ahead. The lack of police progress in the Sydney Dahlia investigation continued to make daily headlines.

Bryce circled his thumb against her palm. 'Do you feel like you're in danger?'

Below, the Opera House glowed against the darkening harbour. 'Sometimes I think that's just what it is to be a woman in the world.'

Later, curled into him in bed, sweat on her lips, Bryce's snores like tiny sighs, she did feel safe. For the first time since Krystal's murder, she didn't dream about the ibis, or the body.

—

Her phone alarm chirped her awake. Eyes closed, Reagan fumbled on the nightstand for the cool smoothness of the screen.

'Stay in bed,' Bryce mumbled into her neck.

'Mmm.' She pursed her lips, holding the phone above her face while she scrolled through Instagram. Yesterday's photo of cobra lilies already had a few hundred likes. Most people thought the only carnivorous plant was the Venus flytrap, but there were lots of plants that feasted on insects, and some even on frogs, lizards and rodents. 'I've got to be at work before ten.'

'It's Sunday.' Bryce propped himself on an elbow beside her. 'Spend the day with me.'

She dropped the phone into the sheets and kissed him, trailing a fingertip over his shoulder and down his arm. 'Sounds fun.'

'So post online that the garden centre's closed today.'

Sure, if I wasn't on the verge of turning a profit this month. And barely holding off my own mother from suing me.

'I've got a cousin who's been trying to get me out on his sail-boat for ages,' Bryce said. 'He'd love to meet you. And it looks like a great day.'

It did. Bright sky, neon sun, a feathery hint of clouds. Taking the ferry across to Manly, the way it arced around the Opera House and past Fort Denison, had been one of her favourite weekend activities with her dad. Now she couldn't remember her last time on the harbour.

And a private boat would be one place she wouldn't have to watch over her shoulder, which she'd caught herself doing more and more lately. She could turn off her phone, leave it behind. It would be a holiday.

'Or we could spend the day in bed,' Bryce added, nuzzling into her neck.

'Sorry.' She gave him a nudge, extracting herself. 'But maybe if you keep teaching me your online marketing wizardry, I can hire someone to work the occasional weekend.'

'Damn,' Bryce said, smiling as he reached toward the nightstand for his glasses. 'I thought I'd convinced you.'

She took his T-shirt from the floor, slid into it. She'd never understood women who wore their boyfriend's ill-fitting clothes. But maybe her cynicism was a self-defence tactic. Maybe she'd been jealous of those women. She pressed the shirt to her nose.

Bryce lay against a stack of pillows, one hand running through the mop of his hair, the other wrapped around his phone, thumb-tapping. The expansive bedroom windows showcased everything she would miss that day. Boats drifting on the harbour, tiny people queuing along the pier for the Watsons Bay ferry, dogs racing across the sand of Marine Parade.

She pawed through her handbag for her toothbrush. She hadn't felt presumptuous enough to leave one here, and he hadn't suggested it. In the bathroom, toothpaste foaming in her mouth, she winced at her reflection. 'You know I'd rather spend the day with you, right?' she called.

'How about I take Monday off instead?'

She was about to tell him that was unnecessary, that he shouldn't have to fit himself around her schedule.

'Sure,' she said. 'I'd love that.'

25 February 2017

The cops have asked the FBI for help. I'm taking that as a sign my recreation was faithful to Hodel's vision.

So many men don't take action beyond their endless online bitching. To really leave a mark requires a profound statement. That's what Hodel did. He saw females for what they really are — raw materials waiting to be transformed. Beyond providing sexual gratification and childbirth, their lives only acquire meaning when a Man chooses to elevate them to art. And one chunk of clay is no more special than any other.

Of course, with their smaller, less functional brains, they have no way of perceiving that.

What's most impressive about Hodel is that, despite the grandiosity of his work, he felt no desire for fame. He walked away, let the work stand on its own. He was constantly reinventing himself, like Picasso. Yet he did the work and never took credit for it. That is the definition of a Supreme Man.

Further, his work made evident his Manifesto. He took his secrets to his illustrious grave, but gifted us with all the clues necessary to uncover his legacy. He showed his power not by shooting a gun into a yoga studio, not by driving a car into random pedestrians, but by creating True Terror through the highest form of Art that Mankind has ever conceived.

This is how a Real Statement is made, a Statement about the rightful position of females in society, a Statement that will have resonance, a Statement that is layered and refined and grandiose in its planning and execution.

20

'I'm sorry,' Reagan said into the phone. 'You're the fifth person who's asked about dahlias today. We're sold out.'

With the Sydney Dahlia case still making international news despite the lack of police progress, everyone suddenly wanted dahlias. The craze seemed morbid, but it had been good for business. She'd stocked a few dozen blossoming dahlia varieties in fuchsia, cream, raspberry and coral, and had sold the last that morning. Stepping away from the counter, she checked that the door to her tiny office was shut. She could probably charge a ridiculous price for the one dahlia she'd squirrelled away there.

Bryce had taken Monday off. They'd hired kayaks and taken a picnic to tiny, secluded Store Beach, off the harbour's North Head. They swam and lay in the sun and drank Brick Lane craft beers from sweating cans. For most of the day, they had the tiny beach to themselves. Lying in the sand while Bryce swam, she tried out the sound of *Reagan Stewart*.

Still, she'd monitored the other people coming and going from the beach, and squinted, trying to make out faces on passing boats. More old habits.

'Can I say something?'

She was bent, retrieving gardenias from the base of a trolley. Hearing the gruff voice, she righted herself, a pot in each hand. It was the guy with the leg cast, leaning on his crutches, still in that navy jacket. The voice had surprised her, sounding like it belonged to an older man. This guy was in his late twenties, tops.

'Can I help you?'

'I wanted to tell you how happy you look today.' He'd gone from no eye contact to an excessive amount, his stare drilling into her. His hands gripped the crutches, his elbows sticking out. He'd be unnerving, if it weren't for the foot-to-knee cast.

'Uh, thanks.'

He continued to stand on the other side of the trolley, blank-faced and unblinking.

She set the plants down and stepped back. 'Can I help you find anything?'

'Most days you look hard. It's not a good look.'

Injured or not, she was searching for a polite way to tell him to fuck off when her phone buzzed. 'Excuse me.'

The text was from Bryce, but Reagan walked away, speaking to an imaginary caller. She retreated to the counter, flipping through invoices, watching and pretending not to watch.

The bell above the door chimed as Min strode inside, mobile clutched in one hand. She was dressed in workout gear, a turquoise T-shirt and shorts with stylish white sneakers, hair swinging in a high ponytail.

As Min hugged her, the man tottered on his crutches, inching in their direction.

'What are you doing here?' Reagan asked as Min approached, keeping her voice down.

'I've got a piece on the Dahlia murders coming out in *The Atlantic* soon, so I stopped by Gipps Lane to do some research.'

'Research? At Gipps Lane?'

'Checking out the scene for myself. I lay down in the spot where Krystal's body was left – don't look at me like that. It's part of my thinking process.'

Is this some kind of coded message? Could she know you were there that morning? That didn't make sense. The stress of the emails, of everything, was starting to unravel her thinking. This is what he'd done to her, through high school and university. She couldn't trust her reality. She couldn't trust herself.

'Any – uh, any insights?'

'We know they weren't killed at the dump sites.'

The term made Reagan wince. She turned to a table of seedlings in various stages of repotting, taking in the earthy smell of the potting soil.

'I've been thinking about the vehicle,' Min continued, 'about how long he would have to spend in the laneway – pull in, keep the vehicle running, slide the two parts of the body out on sheets of plastic, maybe. So a ute or a van? It would be harder to dead lift them from a boot.'

'They still don't have any suspects?'

She shook her head. 'I talked to my guy this morning. The tip line is getting two thousand calls a day. Lots of leads that have gone nowhere, mostly people who think their neighbour is a bit off, or who had a dream about the killer, or who claim they saw Krystal in Dubbo last week.'

The man in the cast had manoeuvred behind a display of blood leaf, partially hidden but close enough to eavesdrop. Reagan reached under the counter and turned the stereo up as the first notes of Miles Davis's 'So What' played.

'And no connections between Erin and Krystal,' Min continued. 'They've gone through Erin's devices and social media accounts. There's also no indication she was meeting someone that day, no one she was chatting up online. She went to the park and vanished.'

The navy-jacketed man was reading the blood leaf care instructions. Reagan angled so she had a clear view. Min caught the motion and turned, raising an eyebrow.

'Is he a problem?' she whispered.

'Just a nuisance.' Still, Reagan lowered her voice. 'And there's no surveillance cameras there?'

'Have you been to Callan Park? It's mostly boarded-up buildings with graffiti and smashed windows. The place looks like the zombie apocalypse.'

'I thought part of the Sydney Uni campus was there?'

'The College of the Arts, yeah. It has cameras, but the campus is mostly inside the sandstone walls that surround the former asylum – Callan Park Hospital for the Insane, I think it was originally called. There's a lot more park beyond that. The strike force did find surveillance camera footage from a couple of places on Balmain Road, showing Erin heading into the park. But none captured her leaving.'

'So what's the theory?' Reagan asked. 'She walked to the park, then left in a vehicle?'

'That seems likely.'

'I don't understand, isn't the city full of surveillance cameras these days? Can't the police figure out what vehicles were there at that time?'

'It's not that straightforward. They've collected a huge amount of surveillance footage,' Min said. 'This is confidential, but apparently the strike force is looking into a few potential vehicles.'

'So that means they run the licence plates and they'll find their suspect, right?'

'They're trying, but there's an issue with the plates,' Min said. 'One set turned out to be stolen.'

i hope you get every cancer you –

If Krystal and Erin had received similar emails, they could be a significant clue – no, that wasn't the right term. *Lead*.

Reagan forced the question out before she could change her mind.

'Do you know if Krystal or Erin got any strange emails before they died?'

'What do you mean?' Min gave her a curious look.

'I don't know.' Reagan picked up a cloth and gently wiped the curving leaves of a moth orchid. 'Like, threatening ones?'

'Not that I've heard. I'm sure the strike force is across their emails. I'll ask.' She typed a note into her phone. 'What made you think of that?'

If Krystal and Erin hadn't received similar emails, that was good. Another sign that whoever was sending the emails to Reagan had nothing to do with the murders. 'Nothing in particular.'

'But you said email – not messages, not phone calls. Email specifically.'

'I don't *know*, Min.' *Shit, that came out too defensive.* 'Probably because I spent half the afternoon answering customer emails about bloody dahlias.'

Min's phone chimed. 'That's Owen, I've gotta go. He's going to be home in time for dinner for once.' Her arms snaked around Reagan's shoulders, pulling her close. 'Tell me the truth. Are you getting strange emails?'

'It was just a question.'

'I'm worried about you,' Min said. 'You live alone, you work alone, and you've got this nut job in your past who could have turned violent.'

Reagan edged herself free. Even though Min couldn't stop bringing it up, she was surprised by how much relief came from having one other person who knew what she'd gone through – and believed her.

Despite having his back to them, the navy-jacketed man's attention still seemed focused in their direction. Or maybe Reagan was making something of nothing. She couldn't tell.

'I'm serious, come stay with us,' Min said. 'Mum said she'll move into the guest bedroom and you can use her flat.'

'I'm really fine, Min.'

And if someone is after me, I don't want him anywhere near your kids. Or you.

21

Thursday, 2 March 2017

The neighbours whose yard butted along Reagan's apartment building had left their garden to die. The leaves of the plants curled in, the tips browning. As Reagan slowed the Holden, searching for a parking spot, the screaming of the plants vibrated along her skin. The scorching summer's restrictions still allowed watering in the early morning and evenings. You didn't have to stand aside while the plants cooked to death.

After another sweltering day at the garden centre, she thought she might collapse on the floor as soon as she got home. But she drove past her building and around the block twice, peering into shadows, between vehicles and behind trees. She had her keys in hand before she got out of the car, alert to the crunch of gravel, the creak of a car door. When she was younger, she'd developed a sixth sense for him, a feeling that would creep over her skin when he was around. She didn't feel that now. She forced herself to walk slowly, observing the cluster of teens on their skateboards up the street, the elderly woman with her two hunched greyhounds, the magpie striding over the patchy grass, its beak clamped around the tail of a dead mouse. She checked every window and vehicle. Stopping, she turned a full circle on her heel.

If someone was watching her, they were invisible.

In the time it had taken her to get home, new emails had accumulated. She dropped her handbag on the kitchen bench and braced herself as she opened the app. A week had passed since the last email, and each day she'd hoped maybe that was the end of it. Some random arsehole blowing off steam by abusing a stranger.

The first few emails were customer enquiries sent through her website, desperately seeking dahlias. The third was a supplier. The last unopened email had no subject.

The sender's name was hers.

times up whore

That was it, three cryptic words, no capitals, no punctuation. Clenching her teeth, Reagan squeezed the phone as if to crush it. Then she triple-checked the deadbolts.

She couldn't call the cops. And she couldn't call Min, because she'd demand Reagan call the cops.

Before she could talk herself out of it, she phoned Bryce, dialling his number from memory. It had a singsong quality she enjoyed. She knew two other numbers, her mother's and Min's. It was a small, silly thing, but having a third number in her head made her feel like her world had the capacity to expand.

He didn't answer. She was relieved. Telling him could only sour things.

A minute later, he called back. 'Sorry, just wrapped up a meeting.' People were chatting in the background. Another phone rang. 'What's up?'

'It's nothing. Let's talk later.'

He must have picked up on her tone, because his voice shifted. 'What's wrong?'

She placed the tip of her thumb between her front teeth, bit hard into it. 'Can you come over?'

'Are you okay?'

'I'm getting these . . .' The shame burned. You fucking bitch i will – 'Is it possible to find out where emails are coming from?'

'Maybe?' Bryce said. 'Sometimes you can figure out the IP, though it's possible to lay a flash trail.'

She had no idea what that meant.

'It might help if you told me what's going on,' he said.

The shame felt close to bursting, and she pressed her fist into her breastbone. If she showed Bryce the emails, she wouldn't be surprised if he – *what was the word?* – ghosted her. Who'd want to get involved with this mess?

The kitchen tap dripped into the metal sink. The sound caught her ear, huge, cavernous.

'Reagan?'

'Someone's sending these stupid emails.' It wasn't the right word.

'That's it?' Bryce said. 'Just delete them. Block the sender.'

Blocking the sender hadn't helped. Each one came from a new email address.

'They're – I was hoping to find out if they're coming from a specific place, like a house or an office? Or the suburb, if that's

147

possible?' Maybe whoever was sending them wasn't even in Sydney. It was the internet. Vitriol could come from anywhere on the planet.

'You sound really worried,' he said. 'Let me come over. I'll leave now.'

—

Bryce arrived half an hour later. Though Reagan was expecting it, the intercom surprised her. She buzzed him up, then circled the lounge room, snapping on lamps to make the place look cosier.

Inside, he pulled her against him, holding her shoulders, her waist. The heat of the day radiated from his skin. His hands slid down her arms, fingers slipping into hers. Worry crowded his face.

'You need to tell me what's going on.'

She didn't know how. He took in the apartment, her overflowing bookcases and shelves of seedlings, the worn couch hidden under a striped blanket, the uneven humps in the kitchen linoleum. Whatever he thought of the place, he kept it to himself. She gestured at the expansive view of the brick wall out her windows, the lemon myrtle branches stretching between the two buildings. 'My view isn't quite on par with yours.'

'Reagan, come on.' He squeezed her hands. 'What's happened?'

She tugged him toward the sofa, pulling her legs up as they sat together, one knee resting in his lap. Bryce should know what he was getting into. She didn't know what to think anymore. Maybe she'd been wrong.

Maybe it *was* him.

'I'm getting these vile emails, and there's a chance . . . I mean, I don't know, but . . . ' She threw her head back, overwhelm building

148

inside her ribs and behind her eyes. Maybe this was a huge mistake, but she needed help. 'There's a guy who used to – I guess he was stalking me. Years ago.'

Bryce's face hardened, his eyes narrowing. 'What do you mean? Like, following you?'

She gave him a condensed version, leaving out Brooke and the chat room, skipping over the night he'd busted into their apartment and Cynthia stood there, frozen, while Reagan called triple zero.

As she talked, she rubbed her thigh, driving the heel of her hand down hard, pain flaring under it. Bryce touched her wrist.

'Nobody knew the whole time this was going on?'

'My mother did. I was living with her when it started.' Across the room, the refrigerator rumbled to life, filling the apartment with its rattle. 'I'm sorry. I thought this was all in the past. I hate to burden you with it.'

His jaw tensed. 'What are you talking about?'

She fluttered a hand. 'You didn't ask for any of this.'

Bryce took his glasses off, setting them on the coffee table and pinching the bridge of his nose. 'You,' his lips shifted soundlessly, as if he was struggling for the right words, 'didn't *ask* for any of this either.'

She let her head rest against his shoulder, taking in the smell of his skin. The last time she'd felt this secure, her dad had been alive.

'Thanks for being here,' she said.

Bryce stroked her hair, and for a while they sat like that, the light at the edges of the blinds greying. 'So this guy, he's the one sending the emails?'

'I don't think so. They're nothing like the ones he used to send. I just wanted to explain why I'm getting . . . rattled.' It was more than that. Her reality was gaslighting her, certainties collapsing into question marks. 'And maybe if you can find out if they're coming from, like, Queensland or Russia, then I don't need to worry.'

'Did you call the police?'

'Of course not.'

Bryce raised his eyebrows. 'Reagan, you need to call. They can come and arrest the guy.'

'Ha.' It came out as a bark. 'I've been down that road before. Trust me. There's no point.'

Bryce rubbed a spot at the top of his jaw with two fingertips. 'Okay. What do we do? Do you want me to find him and beat the shit out of him?'

It was a joke. She didn't believe Bryce had beat the shit out of anyone in his life. His hands were soft and slender, unmarred, and while he was fit, he wasn't muscular. She put a hand on his chest, absorbing the slow rhythm of his heart.

After a while, he said, 'I still think you should report him to the police.'

The comment clattered around in her head, long after they'd eaten takeaway curries on the couch, and continued after they'd gone to bed, Bryce snoring in soft staccato bursts while Reagan lay grimly awake.

22

Friday, 3 March 2017

Reagan startled, the night deep around her, a tree branch tapping against the window. She reached across the bed and found the sheets cool.

'Bryce?' She sat up, her head foggy with bad dreams and cheap wine. Her pillow was damp. She'd gone to bed with wet hair after a late shower. The sheets under her were damp too, slickened with sweat.

A noise came from the lounge room, the scrape of wood on wood. Was that what had woken her?

The bedside clock read 2.39. She reached for the nightstand lamp. The bedroom door was shut. Hoping for a breeze, she'd propped it open with the doorstop before they went to sleep. Or had she?

Stepping out of bed, she called louder, the cheap plasticky carpet scratching at her feet, the branches rapping, like something wanted in. The late summer night chilled her skin and she pulled on a tank top.

The noise came, a muffled bang.

The thought that Bryce was in trouble, that someone was out there with him, electrified her. But how? Her second-floor apartment was flanked by branches too flimsy to climb. There was no way in but the front door. And she'd definitely deadbolted the apartment door.

Grabbing the doorknob, she yanked the bedroom door open.

The lounge room was dark, the streetlamp outside splaying shadows across the rug.

Bryce was around the corner, in the kitchen, backlit by the stovetop lights. He stabbed a fork into the remains of their duck curry.

'You okay?' he asked.

She walked over and took the fork, digging out a piece of duck and letting the spice bite into her tongue. 'Thought I heard something.'

'Sorry, I was trying to be quiet.'

Reagan stretched up, kissing his cheek. 'All good.'

Before returning to bed, she ran her hands over the hard, cool steel of the deadbolts.

—

In the morning, Bryce walked Reagan to her Holden. On her drive to the garden centre, she detoured through Petersham, searching for a payphone. When she found one, she parked nearby, pulling her black cap low. Her hand quivered as she dialled.

'I think the Sydney Dahlia killer could be Gordon Purdie, P-U-R-D-I-E. He's got a thing for women who look like –' *Fuck*. She'd already said too much. This was the riskiest, stupidest thing she'd ever done. 'White guy, mid-forties, balding. He's a cop.'

She hung up before they could ask for her name.

23

Saturday, 4 March 2017

Bryce showed up at Voodoo Lily early on Saturday, texting his arrival from the back entrance. Surprised, Reagan found him with two flat whites and a bag of croissants from her favourite Glebe Point Road cafe.

'You know me too well already,' Reagan said. 'What's this for?'

'Thought I'd help you set up before you get inundated with customers.' He kissed her as she took the smaller coffee.

Above the counter, a banner reading 'Voodoo Lily End-of-Summer Weekend Sale' hung crooked. Reagan had spent a month planning and promoting the sale, with Bryce's help. He pulled over the stepladder and inched the left side of the sign up.

'You shouldn't be spending your Saturday morning working.'

'I hadn't thought of it that way,' Bryce said. 'I guess I'll head off then.'

She laughed, in love with the sunshine and the smell of the coffee and the pleasure of his company.

'I've got to run some errands this arvo, but I thought we could go to that sushi place on Devonshire for dinner?' He slipped his phone from his pocket. 'I should see if we can get a reso.'

'Hang on,' Reagan said. 'I forgot, I've got this thing I'm supposed to be at tonight. Barbecue at a friend's place. I'd invite you, but . . .'

'What?'

'It's a birthday party for my friend's kid. He's turning one. It's mostly going to be other couples with kids there.' She shrugged.

'So you're worried if I see you around a bunch of kids, I'll start thinking about what our kids might look like, yeah?'

A hot flush raced up her neck. 'I meant you probably didn't want to spend your Saturday evening hanging out with a horde of germy, shrieking children.'

He handed her a croissant. 'Okay.'

She took a bite, chewed. Took another. 'Do you want to come?'

'Is your friend cool with a stranger hanging around her germy, shrieking children?'

'I could check.'

'If our kids had my hair and your cheekbones, they'd be supermodels.'

She rolled her eyes, thinking her heart might explode from happiness.

—

When the shop opened, Bryce kissed her and headed off. She texted Min.

155

Okay to bring Bryce tonight?

She was expecting a quick yes. Instead, Min phoned, her voice laced with surprise bordering on suspicion. 'Was this his idea or yours?'

'Wow, never mind then.'

'You've known this guy, what, barely a month?'

'It's fine,' Reagan said. 'I'll meet up with him after.'

'No, bring him along.' Her usual cheeriness returned. 'I'm surprised, that's all. You've barely been on a date in years, and now you're bringing some guy around after four weeks.'

'Five weeks.' *Five and a half.* She sounded like a teenager.

'It'll be good to meet him,' Min said. 'What does he like to drink?'

—

By the time Reagan made the drive over the Harbour Bridge to Balmoral, it was almost six. Bryce had errands to run nearby, so planned to meet her there.

A rainbow bundle of helium balloons tangled in the breeze above Min and Owen's mailbox. Hundreds more balloons arranged into arcing rainbows filled the garden, and the smell of barbecue drifted from the patio. Hyun-sook's granny flat, which was larger than Reagan's apartment, sat at the back of the property, under the shade of a sprawling Moreton Bay fig. Unlike so many lawns that summer, this one was lushly green.

A dozen adults clumped around the lawn furniture, eating sausages and salad over paper plates, beers and wine glasses within arms' reach. Reagan recognised a handful of Min's friends from the wedding. A few had babies strapped to their chests or snuggled in their laps. A blonde woman perched on her partner's knee waved at Reagan. She smiled, uncertain whether they'd met before.

When Bryce showed up, she could ask Min to introduce them. They could make small talk over drinks, his arm around her waist, his easygoing charm illuminating them both. She should have waited in the Holden so they could have arrived together.

Maisey spotted her and tottered across the lawn, her tiny arms stretched wide. 'Auntie Rae!'

'There's my favourite angel!' Reagan scooped her up, twirling until Maisey squealed with laughter. 'You enjoying your brother's birthday?'

'We got cake!' Maisey's tiny fingernails were each a different colour, matching the rainbow balloons. 'Hide and sneak?'

'We'll play in a bit. Do you know where your mum is?'

Maisey slapped her hands to her cheeks, squishing her mouth into fish lips, and shook her head.

'We haven't seen you this much in ages, Reagan.' Owen came over, Dashiel strapped to his chest, a stegosaurus-themed party hat on his head.

'Nice hat, Owen.' She tickled Dashiel's foot and he smiled, burying his head against Owen's chest.

'Grandma's taking the birthday boy up to bed soon. Where's your bloke? I heard he was coming tonight.'

'On his way.' Reagan set Maisey down and checked her phone. Bryce hadn't replied to her last text. He should have arrived by now.

'Sounds like you're pretty into this guy.'

'He's not unbearable.'

He gave a little laugh. 'What's his name again?'

'Bryce.'

Maisey raced off and returned, holding a party hat with a jungle fern out to Reagan. 'Good choice, Mais,' Owen said. 'It's got a plant on it.'

Would Bryce be this good with kids? It was way too early to be thinking that. Reagan popped the hat on, snapping its elastic string and crouching to show off for Maisey.

'So how'd you meet him?'

This was starting to feel like an interrogation. *Normal people ask their partners' friends about their lives. It's called a conversation.* 'I had some car trouble. He helped me out.'

'It'd be good to see you settled down.'

Reagan bristled.

'Rae, hey!' Min waved from the veranda. Nodding to Owen, Reagan went to join Min, Maisey trailing. Min had a matching rainbow manicure. 'You made it. Where's Bryce?'

'Should be here any minute.'

'I got that beer you mentioned. Your boy has expensive tastes.'

'Oh, you didn't have to – he'd be happy with whatever.'

Min waved a hand toward a row of eskies. 'It's in there when he arrives.'

Bryce did have expensive tastes – his sleek apartment with its harbour view, the restaurants he chose, the handcrafted chocolates he'd given her. Even the monkey orchid he'd bought for his mum. He seemed to have money and enjoyed spending it.

'Have you tried Owen's latest masterpiece? He bought another pig, so we've been eating nothing but ham, pork and bacon.

I shouldn't complain. The sausages with golden syrup and pistachio taste unbelievable.'

Maisey clamped her arms around Reagan's leg.

'We'll play after,' Reagan said, mussing Maisey's hair. 'Let me talk to your mum.'

Maisey stamped her foot.

Hyun-sook came outside, and seeing Reagan, stopped to chat. The minutes ticked by. Her phone hadn't buzzed, and still Reagan fought the urge to check it.

She stepped aside to call. He didn't answer. Min's eyes were on her.

Hyun-sook went to collect Dashiel, and Min handed Maisey a jar of onion relish. 'Take that to Dad.' Maisey teetered away. Min stepped closer to Reagan, lowering her voice. 'Okay, remember how they couldn't determine Krystal's time of death?'

'You really want to talk about this here?'

'Just quickly, before your bloke shows up.' Min pulled a bottle of prosecco from one of the eskies and poured two glasses. 'Still no suspects?'

Reagan didn't believe Gordon was the Dahlia killer. But she also was increasingly unsure if she could trust her own mind. Who better than a cop to know how to murder someone and stage a crime scene without leaving any evidence? Or to potentially tamper with evidence. Gordon could be involved in the Dahlia investigation. She'd searched his name in the news and found nothing. But there would be lots of unnamed cops working the Dahlia murders. On the slim, ridiculous chance that he was somehow involved, she'd had to let the police know. Assuming he wasn't on the strike force, they could investigate and definitively rule him out.

There was no way she could tell Min. She'd want Gordon investigated for the stalking, to get him off the force, if not in jail. She'd dredge up all kinds of misery. And probably put herself at risk.

'Focus, Rae – Krystal's time of death. They couldn't determine it because her body had been *frozen*.'

'What?' She ought to tell Min she didn't want to talk about this anymore. Except she desperately wanted the killer caught, the comfort of knowing the police were closing in. The two murdered women lived in her mind, as if she'd played fetch with Krystal and her dog Comet, had hiked the Ruined Castle Track with Erin on a crisp autumn day.

'Frozen and thawed,' Min said. 'Like, in a freezer. The strike force hasn't found any evidence of her anywhere after 5 January, when she checked out of her hostel, so it's most likely he took her then. We thought he'd kept her somewhere until he killed her late on 14 January or in the early hours of 15 January, to mark the anniversary of the original Black Dahlia murder. But he could have killed her any time and kept her body frozen until 15 January. It's no surprise he wanted her found on the anniversary of Elizabeth Short's murder, but still. The freezing is a strange detail.'

'Was Erin frozen?'

'Nope. So far, it's the only significant difference between the two murders. And that Erin was a local and Krystal wasn't, but that could be incidental.'

Other than the blows to the head that killed Krystal and Erin, neither had any pre-mortem injuries, and no evidence of sexual assault.

'So maybe he's trying to confuse investigators by leaving a gap between when he takes the women and when he leaves their bodies to be found,' Reagan said. 'Can you think of any other reason he'd take Erin and keep her alive more than a day, only to kill her?'

They kept their voices low. On the lawn, two kindy-age kids played tag, running circles around Maisey.

'A few. Have you heard of Leonard Lake?'

'If he's some serial killer, you know I haven't. And please don't tell me anything disturbing.'

'Lake would kidnap women and film them, photograph them,' Min said. 'That was sexually motivated though, which doesn't seem to be a factor here. At least, not in terms of sexual assault.'

Min had an odd concept of what was and wasn't disturbing.

A thought jolted Reagan. 'What if he's short on time? Like, he only had small windows of time, so he had to take them one day, and kill them a day or two later?'

'Auntie Rae!' Maisey was on the lawn, waving and shouting. When she had Reagan's attention, she tumbled into a clumsy somersault and jumped up, beaming.

'Great job, Mais!' Reagan's pocket buzzed. 'Hey, I think Bryce is here.'

Really sorry, not going to make it. Think I'm coming down with something.

'What's that face?' Min narrowed her eyes. 'He's cancelled, hasn't he?'

Reagan's shoulders sank. 'He's not feeling well.'

'Uh-huh.' She tipped back the last of her wine.

'What's the tone for?'

'C'mon, Rae. He didn't want to get thrown into the fire.'

'What fire?'

Min gestured at herself, at the clusters of people chatting across the lawn and around the barbecue. 'Meeting your friends so soon.'

'It was his idea.'

Min arched an eyebrow, her voice teasing. 'But was it?'

'Yes!' Reagan replayed the conversation. She'd told Bryce she didn't expect him to come. She set her still-full glass on the patio table.

'Don't you dare leave.' Min's voice flipped to properly cross. 'Maisey will have a fucking meltdown if you go.'

'I'll play with her for a few minutes.'

'Then what? Don't say you're going to go see Bryce.'

'He's sick, Min.'

'You're sure you want to test that theory?' Min's expression was piercing.

Reagan shook her head, her curls swirling. 'He's not like that.'

'She says, after knowing him five whole weeks.'

'Five and a half.'

An auburn-bobbed woman came onto the veranda and put a gold-bangled arm around Min's waist, her face flushed with either alcohol or sunburn, an outrageous diamond glittering on her ring finger.

'Reagan, hi.' She stayed wrapped around Min like a bejewelled sloth. 'It's so funny, I was telling Matt and Elle about Min's friend who grows strange plants, and like, two minutes later, you arrived.'

Min's smile was terse. 'Rae, when was the last time you saw Yolanda?'

Yolanda, right. She supposed this was another reason social media could be useful – a constant reminder of names and faces.

'Auntie Raeeee!' Maisey called from the lawn.

That's my girl. 'Sorry, Yolanda, I'm late for an important game of hide and sneak.'

24

Of course Bryce wasn't lying. If he hadn't wanted to come to Min's, he wouldn't have offered in the first place. *Right?*

Reagan drove without noticing the flowering banksia and crepe myrtle of Balmoral's well-tended gardens. At Organic Spark, an upmarket takeaway place, she got an extra-large container of cage-free chicken soup with fresh ginger and turmeric. The Holden was curling along New South Head Road, the windows down, the evening heat dissolving in the breeze. Her fingernails dug into the steering wheel.

At his apartment block, a white paper takeaway bag clutched in one hand, she buzzed unit 17.

No answer.

She pressed the buzzer harder.

He was probably in bed, possibly asleep. She hesitated, then called. It rang three, four, five times. Right before his voicemail came on, he answered.

'Rae, hey.'

'I'm downstairs, can you let me up?'

'Downstairs?' His voice was uncertain. Tinny music played in the background.

She tapped her foot against the building's tiled front entrance. Blood sun frangipani blossoms littered the ground. 'I brought you some soup.'

'Oh wow, um, thank you. I'm . . .' a gap stretched out, long enough for a bar of 'Hotel California' to come through the phone. 'Sorry, I'm at the chemist. I'll be home in ten or so.'

The chemist.

That made sense.

There was nowhere to wait on the step without looking like a lost Uber Eats driver. Reagan sat in her car, marinating in sweat, her hands around the fridge-cold soup container. She'd trusted him. She'd sent him the emails. She'd told him about Gordon.

Bryce arrived fifteen minutes later with his own white paper bag, this one with a chemist's logo on it. She met him at the front door. Other than a flush brightening his cheeks, he exuded good health.

Which didn't necessarily mean anything.

'Brought you chicken soup for a hot summer's evening.' She hoisted the bag.

He kissed her forehead, winding his fingers into her curls. 'That's really thoughtful.'

'How are you?' She wasn't ready to let it go. Why was it so difficult to spot a lie?

'Tired. And my throat's scratchy.' He tilted his chin, massaging his glands.

'Right.' The wind ruffled the frangipani. A blood sun blossom tumbled on the breeze, landing on her shoe.

'It hit me like a brick wall,' he continued. 'Sorry I didn't let you know sooner, I went to lay down for five minutes and was out cold.'

It didn't matter. So what if he hadn't wanted to come to a kid's birthday party?

Bryce's hand stayed at his throat. 'Do you want to come up?'

'Not if you might be contagious. Summer bugs can be nasty.' She handed him the soup. 'Sorry, I shouldn't have bothered you.'

'Thanks for this.' He gestured to the soup. 'I'm sure it'll help.'

She kissed her fingertips and pressed them to his cheek.

http://sanct626kufc4mhn92bb03.onion

Hey Ry291, welcome.

Thanks for joining us. I think you're going to find this
group really empowering.

I look for people with special skills and, importantly,
a true red pill understanding of the world. There's a lot
of guys spouting slogans and threats, mindlessly parroting
others. Not you - you see through the rubbish.

You see things how they really are.

And I couldn't do what I do without you.

25

Sunday, 5 March 2017

Min texted. Call me. News.

The first day of the end-of-summer sale had gone better than Reagan could have hoped. If Sunday was the same, she'd make more in this one weekend than she had in the past month. She'd been an idiot for waiting so long to promote her business online. Now she was seeing more customers than since she first opened.

She was so busy restocking display shelves, watering in the shop and greenhouse, and sweeping up from yesterday's surge, she didn't see the text. Or the next three.

Then Min phoned. 'Are you okay?'

'Crazy busy, I'm about to open.' But she'd caught the gravity in Min's voice. Min could be calling for a lot of reasons. Maybe the police had a suspect. Maybe they'd made an arrest. The tightening in her gut, like the crush of a strangler fig, told her otherwise. 'What's happened?'

'There's been a third murder. A woman's been found in Lindfield. I just heard.'

The shop blurred around her. Reagan reached a hand for the front counter, steadying herself. It was less than a month since Erin's death. Another woman, another family – Reagan felt heavy with it.

'Do they know who . . . ?'

'Not yet. But from what I've heard, she looks the same as Krystal and Erin. On the smaller side, fine features, those same dark curls. And the same injuries, sliced through – well, you know.'

'I thought no one who . . . looked like the others had been reported missing.'

'No, no one. But Krystal was never reported missing either.'

'You said Lindfield?' It was a residential suburb on the north shore, nowhere near Enmore. Reagan had driven through it, but couldn't remember ever stopping there.

'It might have some connection to the original Black Dahlia case, like with Erin and Norton Ave,' Min said. 'Or the killer might be purposefully using different parts of the city. Makes him less predictable.'

Make yourself unpredictable. She hated to think she had anything in common with the killer.

'I'm on my way there,' Min said. 'Can you meet me? Scope out the crowd again?'

'No.' Reagan said it automatically, the answer resonating bodily. She couldn't keep doing this. She was emotionally exhausted, and needed all her energy to focus on Voodoo Lily, and making things work with Bryce. 'Sorry, I'm way too busy.'

'Are you sure? Because –'

'This is a big weekend for me.'

'Right, the sale.' Min was perfunctory, down to business. 'If I see any suspicious characters hanging about, I'll try to sneak a photo.'

The heaviness pulled at Reagan, threatening to sink her through the floor and into the sand and clay beneath. Min said the women's wounds were made after they died, but the viciousness of those wounds were still an insight into the killer. He must have hated these women to not only murder them but mutilate their bodies and leave them publicly exposed.

'Oh, hey, did you end up seeing Bryce last night?' Min asked.

'He isn't going to stop, is he?' Reagan said. 'The killer.'

'There's a huge investigative team working on this, Rae. He only has to slip up once.'

But he hasn't so far.

—

Half an hour after closing, while Reagan was tallying the day's sales, Min knocked on the front door, waving through the glass.

'I need your help,' she said.

'I've got a huge mess here, Min.'

'I need you to come to Coogee.'

It was like Min hadn't heard her. 'Can't you see it looks like a mob of roos came through here?' There were huge gaps in the display shelves, signs hanging askew and plants knocked over, soil spilling out of their pots.

'Your former stalker could be a strong lead.'

'For the hundredth time, please don't bring that up.' Reagan turned to a shelf of lifesaver cacti, their red bulbous flowers like alien lips, and inched each pot into a precise line. 'I can't do this anymore. All this gruesomeness is your world, not mine.'

'Her name's Willow Signato. She's nineteen, from Perth, on a big trip around the country. She arrived in Sydney four days ago, after three weeks doing farm stay work in Kangaroo Valley.' Min held out her phone. 'Here, take a look.'

A photo of a young woman filled the screen. Unable to stop herself, Reagan reached for the phone. 'This is her?'

'She doesn't look so much like you and the others, does she?'

She had the cherubic nose and the thin eyebrows. But her face was a different shape, more round, her eyes closer together. And her hair was bright red.

'Notice anything?' Min asked.

'You mean the red hair?' Reagan was still looking at Willow. 'Or the big owl tattoo on her shoulder?'

'Yeah, the hair. Get this, he dyed it black, to match the others.'

The thought of a man forcibly dying her curls – whether she was alive when it happened or not – made Reagan's mouth curdle. Touching another person's hair was intimate.

'It seems like he was searching for a woman who looked like Elizabeth Short, and maybe couldn't find one. So he snatched Willow and tried to make the resemblance stronger. He's starting to unravel, Rae.'

Reagan handed the phone back.

'Another point to consider – it's only been three weeks since the last murder. And Lindfield seems random too, no connection to the Black Dahlia case that I can find – no dates or street names or anything. He's losing control, getting desperate. He's more likely to have made a mistake.' Min kept talking, about how the police had confirmed Willow's identity through the fingerprints and the owl tattoo. Her contact had spoken to Willow's father that afternoon, while Reagan was selling discounted banksia seedlings. Willow had been on a year-long trip. She'd checked in irregularly. It wasn't strange that her parents hadn't heard from her since she'd arrived in Sydney. 'And there's more. On Wednesday, Willow paid for three nights at the Coogee Budget Hostel. She should have checked out Saturday, but she didn't. My contact went by there an hour ago and picked up her luggage. I really think you should come to Coogee and talk to a few people at the hostel.'

'The police will already be doing that.' Reagan kept her back turned, fussing with the plants.

'You'll be asking specifically about someone who looks like AJ. That might trigger a memory they might otherwise overlook. Most of their clientele are probably young. A middle-aged guy might stand out, especially if he's hanging around by himself, or chatting up nineteen-year-olds.'

'I *can't*, okay? You can obsess about this stuff and somehow go on with your life, not looking over your shoulder and worrying you'll never see your kids again. I don't know how you do it. I don't even know why people read true crime! What, they want to feel scared from the comfort of their lounge rooms?'

'I don't think so,' Min said, her calm offsetting Reagan's torrent. 'Investigations are a fascinating, high-stakes puzzle. Think about it, there's always an answer – who the killer is, how they did it, what circumstances led up to the crime. The question is whether investigators can find enough pieces, and interpret them accurately, without bias.'

Reagan moved further away, crouching to pick up a black devil pansy. Pansies were a misunderstood flower. Far from being weak, they could survive water deprivation and freezing temperatures.

'I've got a lot of work to do here.'

'Random thing my guy mentioned,' Min said. 'The last time Willow spoke to her dad, she said there was a place in Sydney that served deep-fried Snickers bars. That's the last thing they talked about. Her plan to try a deep-fried Snickers bar.'

'Fuck, Min.' On their first visit to Seoul, they'd ended up in an American-themed bar in Itaewon, the expat district, dancing to an all-Korean Spice Girls cover band under a giant US flag pinned to the ceiling. The bar played 'The Star-Spangled Banner' at midnight, with off-duty US soldiers singing drunkenly, hands slapped over their hearts. Reagan and Min filled the night with soju bombs, shots dropped into pints of Hite beer, and topped it off at 3 am with the bar's speciality, deep-fried Snickers. Their private term for a great night was a deep-fried Snickers night. 'That's emotional blackmail.'

'So you'll come?'

Reagan stood, wiping the dirt from her hands. 'If no one has seen a guy that looks like him, then that's it. You never bring him up, or anything to do with him, or my past, ever again.'

'Deal.'

'I mean it.'

'I can tell,' Min said, pulling the Lexus keys from her pocket.

—

A beach suburb south of Bondi, Coogee sloped east toward the water, its uninspired houses and apartment blocks spanning the brick colour spectrum – browns, reds, beiges, the purple of a bruise. Scrappy Norfolk Island pines poked above rooftops, their shadows stretching in the early evening sun. The Coogee Budget Hostel featured three storeys of curtained windows, peeling off-white paint, and a patchy garden overgrown with panic veldt grass, an aggressive weed.

The lone guy staffing the hostel that Sunday evening wore a name-tag that read *Kirk*. They found him outside, the glass door to the cramped reception area propped open.

'The police were already here.' Kirk had a stubble beard, rough hands with fingernails wider than they were long, and sleepless eyes. He twisted his head and blew cigarette smoke out the side of his mouth. 'And I barely saw the chick. She got here on my day off. I only saw her once, coming down the stairs on Thursday morning, and I only remember because she had that big ugly bird tatt.'

'We're interested in who might have been hanging around her. Specifically an older white guy, mid-forties.' Min turned to Reagan.

'Uh, yeah, probably mid-forties. Kind of tall, but not really tall. Maybe your height? And dark hair on his forearms. His eyes are small, a bit too far apart. Balding.'

Two barefoot women came up the pavement, wearing bright sundresses and carrying sand-crusted towels. Instead of manoeuvring around Min and Reagan to head inside or continue on, they hung back, whispering on the edge of the hostel property.

'Anything else?' Min gestured at Reagan to say more.

'Sometimes he had a moustache.' She could see him clearly, but her description was coming out as mush. 'Neatly dressed, ironed pants, shined dress shoes. Calm, in control, a measured pace.'

Kirk exhaled a stream of smoke and dropped the butt. 'No one like that staying here.' He didn't seem interested.

'I doubt he'd be staying here,' Min said. 'But maybe walking past too many times, or standing across the street in the evening, or talking to female guests.'

'Nah,' Kirk said. 'We got a guy who comes by on Saturday nights and drops his daks, likes to moon the chicks coming back from the bars. But he's *old* old. And scrawny. Like one of those hairless cats.'

'What about any vehicles driving past too frequently, or parked nearby?'

'You think I'm keeping a list of rego numbers?' He nudged his toe against a piece of loose concrete, then went into the office and closed the door behind him.

'There you go. We're done,' Reagan said. *He's not back. You don't need to be afraid.*

'You could have tried a little harder on the description, doll.'

'Excuse me.' One of the beach-going duo approached, eyes locked on Min. They looked about Willow's age, nineteen or twenty. Salt water dripped from their hair onto their shoulders, and they smelled of sunscreen and beer. One had a martini glass tattooed under her collarbone. The other, striding forward, asked, 'Are you Min-lee Chasse?'

'Yeah, hi.' Min extended her hand. Reagan hung behind.

'Oh my god, we saw your talk at Melbourne Writers Festival last year. I *love* your book. The way you write about the murder's impact on the whole town, the psychological ripple effect – it's my favourite true crime book. And Trista's reading it for her journalism course this semester.'

Min's fans glowed with the excitement of meeting a celebrity, and a minute later, their phones came out and Reagan was taking photos of the threesome.

When she and Min had lived in Korea, they talked about their teaching work, about their students and colleagues and the forever-broken photocopier. They talked about hiking in the Taebaek mountains, about catching the high-speed KTX-Sancheon train to Busan on the long weekend. They talked about trips to Seoul to see the National Palace Museum and hunt down the Itaewon shop that stocked Iced Vovos. They talked about their mothers, and when they Skyped Hyun-sook, she covered her mouth with her hand, laughing sweetly at Reagan's mangled Korean.

In Sydney, Min talked about serial killers and DNA evidence and court proceedings, and she talked about Owen and wedding plans and her move to the north shore and her babies. Reagan talked about Cynthia's cancer treatments and her garden centre and visiting exhibitions at the Museum of Contemporary Art they never quite managed to see. She'd resisted knowing Min the investigator, the writer, the professional – until she'd found Krystal.

Krystal's death had dragged Reagan into Min's world, giving her the chance to know her in a different way.

Behind them, a pair of rainbow lorikeets landed in the rounded crown of a flowering gum, its foliage dense with wildfire red blossoms. The birds rooted through the blooms for nectar, chittering.

'Can I ask,' Reagan said to the two students, 'why do you read books about crime? I mean, what about them appeals to you?'

They looked at each other, uncertain and curious, like the question had never occurred to them. The one whose name Reagan had missed pursed her lips. 'Human nature can be so extreme. It's like, part of who we are, as a species.'

'But doesn't it make you – I don't know, fearful?'

This time they both shook their heads. 'It reminds me I'm grateful to be alive,' Trista said. 'Anything could happen. So, you know, go jump in the ocean.' And she tousled her wet hair and grinned.

26

Monday, 6 March 2017

The phone rang through the Holden's speakers as Reagan waited in standstill traffic for the Spit Bridge to lower. The Spit wasn't the quickest route, especially with the bridge up, but it was the most scenic. On the seat beside her sat a box of apricot Danish, Cynthia's favourite.

She expected the caller to be Bryce, since she'd texted him before leaving, but it was Min, inviting her for dinner.

'Not today. I'm on my way to my mum's.' Reagan had spent the morning curled on the couch, staring into her phone. She'd reread the news articles about Willow's murder, scrolled her friends' Facebook tributes, and absorbed her travel vlogs. Willow had plans for a career as a wildlife handler, and had spent several months as a volunteer, treating wombats for mange. When she spoke about how the disease was threatening the wombat population, Reagan wanted to reach into the phone and hug her. After scrolling Reddit threads on the Dahlia murders and watching YouTube web sleuth videos, she'd forced herself out the door. Cynthia had agreed to accept half her requested payment for March, provided Reagan visited twice a week.

'Oh, she's apologised for being a narcissistic control freak?' Min said.

'Drop it.'

'You don't need her, Rae. My mum will adopt you. Probably legally, if you want. I don't know how that works with adults, but I can find out.'

Ahead, the traffic inched forward. Reagan restarted her car. 'Yeah, thanks.'

'Did you ever read about these experiments done with infant rhesus monkeys?' Min said. 'The researcher kept them in individual cages with two fake monkey mothers, one made of cloth and one made of wire. Even though the babies got their food from the wire mothers, they would snuggle with the cloth ones. So the researcher turned the cloth monkeys into "evil mothers". They would shoot spikes and shake, and some were spring-loaded and would fling the babies across the cage. And you know what? The baby monkeys kept going back to them. They wanted the evil mums to love them.'

Reagan flicked her turn signal on. 'Stay away from cloth monkeys, got it.'

'Rae, I'm serious.'

'I'm sure Cynthia will mellow as she gets older. She already has, a bit.' Was that true? Maybe some days. What did Min know, anyway? Reagan's mother was her sole living relative. For years, she'd felt like she was floating off into space; her mother was the only tether to her childhood, to the grainy memories of her father.

And there was the money Reagan owed.

'Anyway,' she put a hard edge in the word, 'the promo weekend at the garden centre went really well. I tallied the sales after I got home last night.'

'Uh-huh,' Min said, her tone making it clear she'd be returning to the topic of Cynthia. 'Your new boy's really helped you out, has he?'

'I had a heap of sign-ups for the new email list.' She drove across the bridge, the turquoise waters of the Spit glittering in the early afternoon, a trio of tall-masted boats gliding like swans toward the harbour mouth.

'So when do I finally get to meet Bryce? We'd love to have you two over.'

'This weekend?'

They talked dinner plans until Reagan arrived in Mona Vale. She parked in Cynthia and Terry's driveway, taking a deep breath as she turned off the ignition. 'It's just gardening with your mum,' she said to her reflection in the wing mirror. 'It'll be a nice afternoon. *Make* it a nice afternoon.'

She popped the boot and started unloading plants, a collection from the greenhouse chosen with Cynthia's tastes in mind, butterfly ginger lily, Malibu lemon chrysanthemums, and, as a private joke, impatiens. She lined plants, pots and bags of soil and fertiliser along the driveway's edge.

The front door opened, and Reagan's resolve took a horse-sized kick. Instead of being dressed for gardening, Cynthia wore a coral-coloured silk blouse, a white skirt with a smattering of gold sequins, and coral lipstick.

'Today isn't great,' Cynthia said, walking across the driveway with exaggerated slowness. Reagan caught the lilac and juniper mingled in her perfume. She'd never worn perfume when Reagan was growing up. She hadn't gone to the hairdresser three times a week either, instead cutting her hair and Reagan's over the kitchen bin.

Reagan stopped, hands around a large ceramic pot. 'Two hours ago you said today was fine.'

'I think the sushi I had for lunch was off.' Cynthia pressed a hand against her stomach.

'I can't leave these plants sitting around, Mum.'

'Come tomorrow then.'

There it was – her mother's tactical move. If they didn't do the planting today, Reagan would have to come back. 'I work tomorrow.'

Cynthia sniffed, bending to shift one of the pots, a subtle comment on Reagan's inability to form a straight line. 'I should call the restaurant to complain.'

Reagan closed her eyes, pining for a sibling to commiserate with.

An obnoxious guitar riff played at full volume from Cynthia's phone. 'I have to answer this, it's an email from our travel agent. Did I tell you we're going to Bora Bora in June?' She turned her attention to her screen while Reagan propped the gate open and began hauling everything into the garden. It would take twice as long by herself.

Cynthia eventually joined her, crankily positioning a lawn chair in the shade, pointing out where she wanted each plant, then changing her mind.

In the middle of the night, lying awake and thinking of dead women, things seemed simple – if she wanted to have a better relationship with her mother, she had to make more of an effort. Ring her up, offer to bring some plants, spend an afternoon gardening together, rinse and repeat. Alone, in the warped perspective of 2 am, she could exaggerate certain parts of Cynthia's character, downplay others, shape her into a reasonable human being. Now, in the stark reality of the afternoon sun, faced with a mother who would fake food poisoning so she didn't have the inconvenience of changing outfits, the situation looked different. She thought about baby monkeys getting hurled across cages.

'Well, hello there.' Terry sauntered off the veranda. When he reached them, he rocked on his heels and slotted his hands into his pockets.

Reagan said hello, not bothering to get up.

'Doing some gardening, I see.'

'A well-kept garden ups the capital value of any property, Terry.' Maybe she could convince them to accept part of her repayment in plants and labour. They had a beach house north of the city, at Broken Bay, and the gardens were a mess. It wouldn't be so bad to drive out there a few times, especially if she had the place to herself.

'Reagan, it's rude not to ask how Terry is. He came out here specifically to see you.'

All the way from inside the house.

'How're you travelling, Terry?'

'Busy, busy. Expanding the company into some new areas.'

The only way the afternoon could get worse was if Terry started droning on about algorithms or servers, or whatever it was he did. Even Cynthia didn't understand what his business was about, which didn't seem to bother either of them.

'Since you're both here.' Reagan stopped digging and clapped the soil from her gardening gloves. 'I've got some news. I've started seeing someone.'

'Really?' Cynthia said, her disbelief thick. 'What does he do?'

She told them as little about Bryce as possible while Cynthia fired off questions.

'That's nice, Reagan.' Terry said this in the same tone he might use to describe a shade of brown paint. 'We should have him over.'

Right.

'Tell him to come tonight,' Cynthia said. 'We're having prawn linguini. He's not one of those gluten-phobes, is he?'

From her pocket, Reagan's phone chimed. She pulled off a glove, dropping it on the ground.

It was an email. The sender's name was her name.

A chill prickled up her spine.

The subject read, An important message from Voodoo Lily Garden Centre. She hadn't written that.

Gritting her teeth, she tapped open the message. The sender's email address was hers. Not a different account set up in her name, but her actual email address, info@voodoolily.com.

The only text read, There's more where this came from!

As she scrolled down, the video embedded beneath the message began to play.

A woman lay on a bed, glistening skin and taut muscles, every inch of her exposed, legs spread, and an equally naked man, shot from behind and to the side, only his back and neck visible.

The woman was Reagan.

A feminine moan came from the video. Panicking, Reagan fumbled, scrambling to turn off the sound.

Cynthia's guitar riff played.

A horrible thought struck her. *It couldn't be.* Reagan stabbed at her phone screen, revealing the list of addresses copied into the email.

It hadn't only gone to her.

Every contact in her address book was there, including the dozens of new customer emails she'd collected over the weekend.

Cynthia's phone lay facedown on her lap. She stretched a hand toward it. Reflexively Reagan reached for it too.

'What are you *doing*?' With a ferocious frown, Cynthia snatched the phone away.

'There's an email here from you, Reagan.' Terry had his phone out as well.

'Delete it!'

'What has gotten into you?' Cynthia said, annoyance building with each word.

'Don't open that –'

'Oh my *god*, Reagan.' Her face and neck flushed, and she waved the phone away, holding it at arm's length. The same moan came from Cynthia's phone, loud enough for the neighbours to hear.

'It's not me.' Reagan started to back away, out of the garden soil and onto the lawn, stumbling on the uneven ground.

The moan came from Terry's phone too. The video was still playing on Cynthia's phone.

'Fuck me like a beast!' the woman in the video howled. The voice sounded like Reagan's, but she'd never said that – anything like that – in her life.

Reagan grabbed Cynthia's phone, wrenching it loose, hit delete on the email and dropped it to the ground.

Terry turned to her, his eyes still blank, the only change in his demeanour a slight downshift in tone. 'Reagan, this is . . .'

'You sent this to *Terry*?' Cynthia's voice rose to a screech. Her arms flapped and she half-lifted herself, the lawn chair rocking as she collapsed back into it. Her eyes rolled, like a spooked horse. 'This is why you came here today, to wound us with this – this *filth*?'

Reagan backed away faster, her hands out as if to defend herself, one still gripping her phone, her feet moving without conscious direction. Cynthia glared, her face contorted.

As soon as Reagan was around the corner of the house, her mother out of sight, she ran.

PART 2

ALTERNATE/SIMULTANEOUS

27

Reagan hurled her phone onto the passenger seat, where it bounced and landed in the footwell. She got the Holden in motion within seconds, backing down the driveway without checking for traffic on the tree-shaded street. The need to physically distance herself from Cynthia pulsed through her.

In the quiet of the car, her spiralling thoughts crashed into each other. Everyone she'd ever emailed was copied into that video – her suppliers, her regulars, all those new customers. The email sat in hundreds of inboxes, a bomb that would detonate her business, her life. The life she had begun to – her heart seized. *Bryce!*

He'd think she was cheating. The woman in the video wasn't Reagan, but there was no way to prove that. It looked and sounded exactly like her.

She drove without direction, her breath coming too fast and her palms too sweat-soaked to attempt the freeway home. Taking a few random turns, she found herself on a residential street and parked.

She scrabbled on the floor for the phone. Touching it, a fresh wave of nausea overtook her.

She called Bryce.

It rang six times, then voicemail.

'There's an email from me, please don't open it, it's not really from me, it's –' She hung up. It was Monday, 3.37 pm. Maybe he was in a meeting. Maybe he hadn't seen it.

DOnt open emuil frm me!! I ddnt send!! pls call

Looking around, Reagan tried to figure out where she was. How long had she been driving? She'd fled Cynthia without thinking. What else could she have done? As a teenager, she'd had enough screaming matches with her mother to know the woman would believe whatever she wanted, despite any evidence.

Reagan still had the phone clutched in her hands when it started ringing.

Min.

Oh god, the email had gone to Min, and to Owen, and to Min's friends, that smarmy Yolanda and so many others. She'd never be able to look at Min or Owen again. She'd never be able to look at anyone.

She should drive to the nearest cemetery and get them to dig a grave for her to crawl into.

Muting the phone, she dropped it facedown on the passenger seat. It buzzed, a message. She wanted to smash the stupid thing, as if the device itself was the source of her misery, and not the kilobytes of digitised information hurtling through cables – or, rather, the people behind that info.

Where the fuck had the video come from? She wanted to examine it but she couldn't bear to see it again. The face in the video looked like hers, and maybe somehow it was. But the woman's body couldn't be hers. She'd never taken nude pictures. And even if she'd been secretly recorded, she'd never acted like the woman in the video, never said anything like that. Everyone talked about images being photoshopped. Maybe Photoshop worked on video too?

It *must* be Gordon. The video was way too personal to be some random hacker. Had he killed those women as well? She couldn't bring herself to believe it. Or maybe . . . with Krystal's face all over the news, then Erin and Willow, the three of them looking like Reagan, maybe that had triggered him. Maybe he didn't live in Sydney anymore, so that was why he was attacking her through emails. And why she hadn't seen him.

The phone vibrated on the seat. Min. She'd want Reagan to go to the police. And the police would 'need' to see the video. They'd write a tedious report, then never do a thing about it, except share the file among themselves.

Shakily, she put the Holden in gear and started driving, unsure where she was but unwilling to fuck around with the phone to connect the GPS. She tried to remember which random turns she'd taken to get here, but like all of Sydney, the streets were a rabbit warren.

From the passenger seat, her phone rang. *Please be Bryce.* She reached over to turn it screen-side up as a flash of movement played out in a corner of the windscreen.

A girl on a bike, her hair in two long pigtails, darted from between parked cars.

Reagan saw her at the last second, the bike dead-centre with the hood of the car, the kid's eyes owl-wide, her head reeling, scrawny body bracing.

Yanking the steering wheel and slamming the brakes, Reagan narrowly missed her. The car smashed into a cluster of wheelie bins. They scattered, one popping into the air, its lid flung open, wine bottles and crushed egg cartons flying.

The Holden came to a stop on a lawn. In the wing mirror, the kid on the bike vanished down the road, legs pumping the pedals.

The phone buzzed, demanding attention. Reagan gripped the steering wheel. An unwashed yogurt container sat on the hood of her car, globs of yogurt smeared under it. She couldn't remember how it got there, and that thought brought her tears in a sudden, shuddering downpour.

'Hey, what the fuck!'

Reagan's head jerked from side to side until she spotted a barefoot, bare-chested man coming through a side gate of the property her front tyre sat on. Streams of water ran from his swim shorts.

'What do you think you're doing?' His meaty face twisted like Cynthia's. He came toward the car, still yelling.

She'd been steadying herself to get out, right the bins, gather the rubbish, offer to pay for any damage.

Instead, white-hot panic spiked. With no time to pull a U-turn, she reversed down the block and around a corner, spinning the wheel and squealing away.

—

Despite the stress of the peak-hour traffic, Reagan managed to get to Enmore and into her apartment. As she rebolted the door, her phone buzzed, Bryce's name lighting up the screen.

She answered, clenching the mobile, as desperate to talk to him as she was to hurl the phone into the harbour. 'Tell me you haven't opened that email.'

'The garden centre one? Sorry, I've been in back-to-back meetings. Is that what your text was about?'

The day had one tiny mercy.

'You sound really upset,' Bryce said. 'What's happened?'

She opened her mouth. Cynthia's shocked expression, her accusatory, demanding tone filled Reagan's head. She wanted rage, but it lay frozen under thick layers of shame and distress. 'I barely made it home.'

'What? From where?' The concern made his voice ragged.

A butcherbird landed on the windowsill, tapping its hooked beak against the glass.

'Reagan? Are you at your apartment? I'll come over.'

'Don't open that email.'

Her phone showed seven missed calls and fifteen new emails, plus more messages. She shoved it under a sheaf of papers on the desk.

—

When Bryce arrived, she pressed her face into the warmth of his shoulder, breathing in the lemony scent of his thin cotton shirt. They stood like that, the sounds of peak-hour traffic and trilling magpies drifting through the window, the floorboards creaking as she shifted her weight, letting him hold her.

In the kitchen, she took the box of pinot gris from the fridge and filled two glasses.

'What's happened?' he asked.

There was a chance he wouldn't believe the video was fake. That maybe she was showing it to him in an effort to convince him that she hadn't cheated on him, or – she didn't know what. Reagan drank most of her wine in one long gulp.

'Whoa, Rae.' He leaned across the island and touched her hand. 'Seriously, what's up?'

She had no idea how she could go on with her life. She couldn't face her customers or her suppliers. She should probably send some sort of explanation, an apology. Even if they kept doing business with her, she knew they'd be thinking about the video whenever they looked at her.

But maybe Bryce never had to see it. Maybe he could be the one person in her life who didn't know. They could move overseas together. She could change her name, go back to the tedium of teaching grammar to uninterested students in Hanoi or Abu Dhabi or Sarajevo.

'You may as well open the email.'

28

'The garden centre email?' Bryce said. 'I deleted it.'

Reagan could open it on her phone, but that would mean retrieving the monstrous device from where she'd hidden it. 'Won't it be in your rubbish file?'

'Oh, sure.' He started tapping on his phone.

'Wait, wait –' Panic leaping like flames. 'Keep the sound off?'

He nodded, worry deepening around his eyes.

Shame burned in her, as if she were responsible for the whole disaster. 'You have to understand, I didn't send it, and it's not me. Someone broke into – hacked into my email and sent this horrendous – but it's *not* me.'

The video played, its light flickering in his pupils.

'It's fake, okay? It's not me. I would never –' She swept her hands, emphasising *never*, and knocked over her wine glass. It bounced against the counter, pinot gris cascading onto her feet. 'Shit, *shit*.' She grabbed a tea towel and cleaned the wine off her legs with angry swipes.

Bryce bent to help her. 'Rae, is this some sort of revenge porn thing?'

'I don't know what that means.' Her voice cracked.

'The guy you told me about, is he your ex? Did he send this?'

She left the wet tea towel on the floor, the smell of the wine heavy around her. 'He's not my ex. And the video *isn't* me. Nobody ever filmed me, or, or –'

'Is it okay if I take another look?'

Reagan gave a tiny nod, wincing as the video flashed on the screen. 'Can Photoshop do that? Or . . . ?'

Bryce squinted, leaning in to examine the screen.

The video played for twenty seconds, then restarted itself. Bryce zoomed in, watching it through twice more. Reagan squeezed her thumbs inside tight fists.

'Bryce?'

'It's a deepfake.' He turned the screen to her, zooming in on her face. 'See, your hair is too perfect at the edges. And when you turn your head, here –' he paused as the woman in the video tossed her head to the side, 'the proportions of your face are off. If we put this on a bigger screen, it would be even more obvious. When you open your mouth, there won't be individual teeth.'

'Please don't put it on any other screens.'

'Sorry, I just meant – do you want me to delete it? Here. I'll delete it from my rubbish too.'

She took a few long breaths. His clinical analysis was reassuring. A different sort of guy wouldn't have reacted so reasonably.

'I was at my mum's place. When the email arrived. It went to them too.' She told him about the afternoon, leaving out the part about the girl on the bike and the rubbish bins, the pool-soaked man shouting in his swimmers.

'I'm so sorry, Rae. That's awful.'

'How difficult is it to make one of those?'

'A deepfake? Getting easier, but still, not just anybody could do it.'

If Gordon didn't have the skills, he probably knew someone who did.

'Can you tell who sent it?'

'Not from my phone. I could dig around on my computer, but I'm sure it's from a private VPN.' Bryce's voice was gentle, almost apologetic. 'Which means it's probably untraceable.'

'So what can I do?'

He leaned his elbows on the island, lips pressed in a flat line. 'You can report it to the police, but they won't do anything.'

'Not even about the email hacking?' She had no plans to speak to the police. It would be high school all over again, the cops implying it was her fault for using the internet. She doubted things had changed much. She assumed email hacking was a crime though, and a crime against a business might actually matter.

'Unless whoever did this is a complete idiot, it's impossible to track. And the cybercrime people have bigger cyber fish to fry. Or whatever they do with cyber fish.' He rapped his fingernails against the base of his wine glass. 'I can take a look at the computer at the garden centre, see if I can figure anything out. Do you want to go over there tonight?'

'I'm exhausted,' she said. 'But tomorrow, maybe? Only if you have time.'

He clasped her hands. 'Why would someone do this to you? It's a bit . . . vicious.'

Shaking her head, she went to the fridge to refill her glass. 'It must be the guy who was stalking me. But I have no idea why he would do this.'

They settled on the couch, Bryce's arm around her. Folding her legs up, she fitted herself against him.

'Could it be someone else?' he asked. 'Do you know anyone that could hack into emails? Any computer-obsessed types?'

Terry ran that algorithmic logistics company, or whatever it was. And he'd wandered outside to join them in the garden right before the email arrived. The look on Terry's face as the video played hadn't been shock, but a sense of not knowing what to do, what the right response was. Had he known the email was coming? *Could Oatmeal Terry have done this?* Had he harboured some kind of sick fantasy about her, made it real on his computer, and then needed more from it – needed her to see it?

'Or I guess it could be random,' Bryce said, talking to the open room as much as to her. 'Maybe some kind of cyber scam. Some Russian teen trying to extort small business owners. Have you had any emails like that?'

'Not that I've seen.' Reagan pinched the bridge of her nose. It was a terrifying world, where anyone with a few skills and the right app could create a fake sex video of you and distribute it to everyone you knew.

Her brain kept spiralling. *Gordon.* Nothing else made any sense.

Tomorrow, Bryce could help her figure out what to do. Right now, she wanted to collapse into the comfort of his presence. 'Can we stop talking about this?'

'Yeah, of course.' Bryce pressed his face into her curls. 'Do you feel safe here tonight?'

'Can you stay?'

'I'm here for you as long as you want me.' He kissed her head. 'And I promise to keep you safe.'

—

They drank more wine, ordered udon from a place on south King Street and Bryce showed her YouTube videos of unlikely animal friendships on his phone. A giraffe nuzzled an ostrich, licking its face, and the two creatures settled into the grass side by side, gazing into a green lake.

When Bryce was in the bathroom, she unburied her mobile from the mess on the desk. The missed calls were from Min, along with a string of messages asking if she was okay, and what was going on. Min would want her to go to the police, to hire a private investigator, to launch World War III against whoever had done this. It made Reagan weary. Min believed things like justice were more than just words.

Several of the emails were replies from customers who assumed she'd intentionally sent the video, calling her disgusting and demanding to be removed from her mailing list, swearing to never shop there again. One woman wrote that she hoped the garden centre burned to the ground. Ed, the Ferguson Seeds rep, seemed to think the email had gone only to him, and replied with his home address, inviting her over for a re-enactment. Recoiling, the taste of bile in her mouth, she swiped his email into the bin.

A few people had replied to ask if Reagan's email had been hacked, and the reasonableness of their reaction made her face burn.

There was one voicemail. 'I can't believe you haven't called to apologise to Terry and me for your horrendously inappropriate behaviour. If you've decided to become some sort of exhibitionist –'

She deleted it mid-sentence.

29

Tuesday, 7 March 2017

Reagan woke early and, after brewing coffee, settled at her desk. Out the window, the shifting colours of the brick apartment wall were the only hint of sunrise. Bryce emerged from the bedroom in his boxers a while later, yawning and scratching his chest.

Reagan lifted the French press, giving the coffee a swirl. 'Still warm if you want some.'

He kissed her. 'You've started early today.'

She tossed her pen onto the notebook in front of her. 'Trying to figure out what to do. The garden centre's supposed to open at ten, but I can't go into work and pretend it's a normal day.'

Bryce went to the kitchen, opened the wrong cupboard, closed it.

'On the left.'

He found a mug and brought it over to the desk. Reagan filled it, steam rising.

'You sound a lot calmer.' He took a sip and gestured at her notepad. 'What are you thinking?'

'Some sort of apology email? I'll explain the video is fake, and I'm really sorry, and that, I don't know, I'll upgrade my computer security. What else can I do?'

'It doesn't look like it's going so well.'

She'd scribbled out her first dozen attempts. She tore the page loose and balled it up. 'I'm not much for writing at the best of times.'

Bryce scrunched one side of his mouth, an expression somewhere between apology and a smile. 'I wish I could stay to help, but I've got a big morning at work.'

'It's okay, I'm going to ask Min.'

'Listen, I've got a meeting I need to be at, but –'

She stood, waving her hands to dispel his apologetic tone. 'It's fine, you don't need to miss work because of me.'

'I can probably take off early this afternoon.'

'No, really. I'm going to get in touch with Min, get this email sorted, send it out, and then I have to go to Voodoo Lily anyway, do the watering at the least. I can't leave the plants to fend for themselves.'

He put his hands on her shoulders, rubbing circles with his thumbs. 'You're sure?'

She nodded.

'I'll meet you at the garden centre when I leave the office, take a look at your computer. Who knows, maybe we'll be able to track down the fucker who did this.'

Without meaning to, she gave a short, sad laugh.

'What?'

'I wish I'd crashed into your car years ago. I could have really used your help.'

—

Bryce left with enough time to get to Watsons Bay for a change of clothes before heading to the office. In the jarring morning quiet, Reagan unburied her phone from the sheaf of papers and dialled Min's mobile.

She answered halfway through the first ring.

'Oh my god, Reagan, I was about to come over there and bang on your door. I would have yesterday, but Maisey came down with a stomach bug and chundered all night. What's going on? Who sent that video from your email? It wasn't Bryce, was it?'

'Bryce? Why would you think that?'

'But he filmed it?'

'It's not real, Min, it's not me. Bryce looked at it and said it's a . . .' she searched for the term, 'a deepfake.'

'A deepfake?' Through the phone, a car door slammed, and keys jingled.

'He could tell by looking at it closely. There's some telltale signs.'

'Huh.' Min's tone carried a hint of something Reagan couldn't pinpoint. Maybe annoyance that she hadn't caught onto the deepfake herself. 'Are you okay? I mean, I'm sure you're not, but –'

'I was hoping for your help,' Reagan said.

'Whatever you need, you know that.'

'I have to send an email to everyone who received the video.

An apology, and some kind of explanation about it being fake. Everything I write sounds awful.'

'On my way.'

—

She arranged to meet Min at a cafe on Enmore Road, just up the street. It had been easy to be calm when Bryce was with her, but as soon as she was alone, Reagan's unease mushroomed. She left her mobile in one of the desk drawers, shoved her notebook in her handbag, and went up the street. Everyone seemed to be watching her. What if people had shared the video? Anyone could have seen it. She crossed her arms high across her chest, feeling exposed.

The cafe's walled courtyard featured an array of hanging plants, philodendrons and baby's tears. With its high walls, no one could see in, and inside the courtyard there was nowhere to hide. It was as private as a public space could get, and on a Tuesday morning, most of the tables were empty. She opened her notebook.

Voodoo Lily Garden Centre apologises for . . .

We've all been victimised by . . .

I wish I could assure you this would never happen again . . .

She ordered breakfast, and by the time Min arrived the server was bringing out a plate of chilli scrambled eggs with avocado toast. Min ordered a double espresso, sliding her phone onto the table and sitting across from Reagan. Her makeup couldn't hide the bags under her eyes, and her nail polish was chipped.

'Thanks for coming.'

'I'm so, so sorry about that email.' Her voice sounded worn. She must have been awake all night with Maisey. 'So Bryce thinks it's a deepfake?'

The video. Shame ate into her like acid.

'He's going to come by Voodoo Lily later and see if he can learn anything from my computer.' She stuck her fork into the eggs without enthusiasm. The server brought Min's coffee. 'So, I don't know. If Bryce finds any useful information, maybe you could help me figure out what to do next.'

'You need to talk to the police.'

'We both know they're not going to do anything.'

'Not about that. About this.' She tapped at her phone, pulling up a still image of a woman in running gear, her face turned down, a street sign reading Gipps Lane in the background.

Reagan stiffened. *The GoPro footage.* She'd forgotten about it. Almost eight weeks had passed since that morning in the laneway.

Min lowered her voice. An elderly couple sat a few tables away, sharing a muffin. 'You were there.'

'What?'

'At the crime scene.'

'It can't be me.' She said it in a panic, knowing it was stupid.

'C'mon, Rae, you're in the peach tank I gave you for Christmas and your dad's Sydney Olympics cap that you wore everywhere in Korea. You were there! And you've hid it from me this whole time.'

'Do the police know it's me?'

'They'll be working hard to figure it out. They still have zero useful leads. What were you doing in Gipps Lane at 6 am?'

'Going for my run, like every morning.'

'Why didn't you call the police?'

Reagan dropped her head into her hands. 'I know, I should have. But I didn't have my phone.' The lies kept coming. 'I would have had to find a payphone.'

'So you could have waited there, or flagged someone down.' Min frowned. 'Do you run the same route every time?'

'Of course not.' She switched up her routes through the park. But now that she thought about it, she'd started cutting through Gipps Lane to get to the park at least a year ago. That part of her mornings had settled into a pattern. Unpredictability was exhausting.

'You need to talk to the cops, Rae. You might have crucial information.'

'Min, really. I don't have any information.'

'You might have seen something and not realise it's important to the investigation.' She was earnest, determined.

'You didn't give the police my name, did you?'

'Obstructing an investigation is serious shit, Rae.'

'Min!'

'I haven't told them,' she said. 'I wanted to talk to you first. I had to hide my shock when my contact showed me the video and I realised it was you. But you've run out of time. The strike force is going to release this video today.'

'What? *Why?*'

'Why? Because they're short on leads and you were there. The cyclist who filmed this turned it in four days ago when he found it on his camera, and they've already tried facial recognition software.

Because of your hat and how quick the camera was moving, there isn't a clear-enough shot.'

'When did you find out?' She was speaking too loud, the alarm rising in her voice. The muffin couple swivelled in her direction.

'Reagan, listen, they're going to release the video this morning and you're going to have some explaining to do.'

'What, that I didn't call them about the body?'

Min's phone buzzed. 'And you had nearly two months to identify yourself as being at the scene and haven't done it. That's obstructing a fucking major investigation. So when the footage is released, you have to speak to them.'

Reagan shook her head continuously, holding her hands up like she was under attack.

'Somebody's going to recognise you. A neighbour or someone from the garden centre, or, who knows, your mum.'

'I'll deny it. You said they don't have a clear shot of my face.'

'You live right in the area, and if the cops talk to your neighbours, they're going to say you're an avid runner.' Her phone buzzed twice more in quick succession. 'Look, are you going to identify yourself when they release the footage today?'

Reagan stared at her hands.

'They're only going to ask what you saw that morning,' Min said. 'That's it. If you get it over with, they can move on, and so can you.' The elongated hum of a call came from Min's phone.

'Once the footage of me in Gipps Lane is out, the media will want my name –'

'I need to take this.' Min was on her feet, mobile at her ear, raising a hand to get Reagan to pause.

'– and it'll get leaked to them,' Reagan said, talking over her. 'I'll be the only new headline in the Sydney Dahlia case for a week.'

Min pantomimed exasperation, saying into the phone, 'Can you repeat that?' as she walked away.

If Reagan went to the police right now, maybe she could stop the video before it was released to the media, before it ended up on news websites where it would stay forever. But going to the police would be worse, would potentially provoke Gordon.

No matter what she did, she was screwed.

The courtyard began to feel claustrophobic. Min had seemingly left to take her call in private, so Reagan went inside, wallet in hand.

The teenager at the front counter had a tattoo of a smoking koala on her wrist. 'Comes to thirty-five-fifty,' she said, pointing to the payWave machine.

Reagan pulled out her bank card and pressed it to the machine, thinking about who might be able to identify her from the GoPro image. Min was standing on the pavement near the cafe entrance, still on her call. Tucking her card back in her wallet, Reagan turned to leave.

'Um, excuse me, your card was declined.' The teen sounded like she'd been personally put out.

'Oh, sorry.' Reagan retrieved the bank card, touched it to the machine again.

The teen pointed to the display screen and gave an impatient huff. 'Declined.'

There was money in the account. Reagan had checked it yesterday.

'Let me try a different card.'

She tried both her credit cards, twice. A line formed behind her, the muffin couple waiting to pay, people wanting takeaway.

'Maybe the machine's not working?' Reagan tried to keep her voice calm.

The server shook her head, pushing her glasses up her nose. 'You don't have cash?'

'My cards should work.'

Min appeared beside her. 'Here, I've got it.' She pressed her phone to the machine. It ruminated before beeping cheerfully. The server nodded, the frown still wrinkling her face.

'I have cash, Min, here.' Reagan pulled a fifty from her purse as she followed Min onto the street. 'My cards should have worked though.'

Min waved the cash away, slipping her arm through Reagan's, leaning into her as they walked up the street in the direction of the apartment. 'Have things got that bad?'

'My cards must have been magnetised. That messes them up, doesn't it?'

They rounded the corner, where Min had parked her silver Lexus SUV, the apartment half a block further along. She stopped, pushed her sunglasses into her hair, and put her hand on Reagan's elbow. 'It's okay, you can tell me.'

'I *am* telling you.'

'Rae.' Min's face stayed neutral, her eyes full of concern, her voice soft. 'Is this a cry for help?'

30

Reagan stood open-mouthed, trying to process what Min was asking.

Min squeezed Reagan's arm. 'If it was you that sent that email, if you're looking for a way out of your business –'

'What the hell are you talking about?' Reagan pushed Min's hand away. 'Stop touching me, Min, fuck.'

'I don't know what's going on with you.' Min's voice hardened, impatience wearing through. 'You've been lying to me since January and I don't understand why. You're telling me the garden centre is fine when your credit cards were just declined. I don't know what's true and what's another lie. Like with this sex video.'

'The video was *faked*.'

'You know how many individual images it takes to make a deepfake? At least three hundred. Some use up to two thousand. Where would anyone get three hundred photos of you? You, of all the people in the world, who up until a month ago didn't have a smartphone, didn't even have a fucking digital camera.'

Reagan froze. 'Why didn't you tell me that earlier?'

Cynthia loved taking photos, to show off to her friends. Reagan wasn't sure if she'd have three hundred photos of her as an adult. Christmases, Mother's Days, birthdays – maybe there were a few hundred. But no one would have access to them except Cynthia and Terry.

And anyone who could hack into their computer.

Could Gordon have taken photos of her? She'd never seen him with a camera, but he could have one of those telephoto lenses.

'Your voice sounded pretty convincing too,' Min said. 'And it takes hours of recordings for deepfake software to replicate a voice.'

The sun burned like a spotlight, as bright and hot as every day that summer, every day since the rain had broken with a fury during her after-work drive to Mona Vale. The day she'd met Bryce.

'You sounded genuinely upset about the video,' Min said, an undertone of gentleness in her conviction, 'and I thought, "Okay, this doesn't make sense, but there must be something I'm missing."'

Terry. Terry could have her voice. He could have recorded her phone calls, their tedious dinner conversations.

Or someone at the garden centre. Anyone could have put a recording device in there. They were tiny now, weren't they? Impossible to find if you didn't know what to look for.

Or the smartphone. Everything had happened since she'd bought that fucking phone.

'People can,' Reagan stumbled for words, 'can hack into smartphones and record . . . everything, can't they?' Gordon could have done that. If he'd hacked into her phone, he could have used the camera to take photos of her too. The phone made anything possible.

Min took a breath, her palms at chest height. 'That doesn't make sense. What makes a lot more sense is that your business is failing and you want a way out, so you sent this actual sex video, and now you can blame that.'

Reagan twisted, aching to get away. 'My business is going fine, Min.'

'That's why we stopped going out for drinks and meals right after it opened? Why you haven't bought any new clothes in two years? Why you're still driving that old car?'

Reagan thought she'd been hiding her financial struggles. But Min had noticed. Of course she'd noticed. And she'd been considerate enough to never ask.

'You've been under immense strain, keeping your business afloat. And finding Krystal's body would have been traumatic, especially since you've been lying about it for weeks.' Min pressed her palms together. 'I'm asking this as a friend. Are you having some kind of breakdown?'

The question hit Reagan like a bucket of ice water. From the high branches of a weeping fig, a raven called, mournful.

'If you're in trouble, I want to help.'

'For fuck's sake.' Reagan gritted her teeth. Of course Min had come up with her own narrative. 'If I wanted the garden centre to close down, I wouldn't send a sex tape to my *mother*. Someone is targeting me.'

'Then go to the police.'

'I came to *you*, I asked for your help.'

'And my advice is to go to the police.'

A ute passed, brakes shrieking as it approached a stop sign. A few doors down, a chainsaw started. Browning plants bowed, slowly cooking to death. The street began to close in on Reagan, her brain overwhelmed by the noise, the punishing sun. She pressed her fingertips into her temples. 'I can't, okay?'

'No, not okay.' Min's voice was granite. 'Any normal person would have gone to the police as soon as they received that sex tape. Any normal person would have called the police as soon as they found a dead woman in an alley. Why can't you?'

'Everything's so black and white with you! It's like you think you deserve to know everything about everyone. And, look, I admire that in your work. You do things I could never, ever do.' *Like interviewing paedophiles.* 'But can't you trust that I have my reasons for not going to the cops?'

The harshness in Min's expression collapsed, and a look came across her face that reminded Reagan of Maisey, the way the tiny girl puffed out her cheeks right before she burst into tears. Min didn't tear up. Instead, she grabbed Reagan, pulling her into a fierce, painful hug.

'I'm trying to protect you.' She stepped back, still gripping Reagan's shoulders. 'I'm worried because nothing's making sense. It's like you want the police to suspect you of something. It was a crazy random coincidence that you stumbled on Krystal's body. But you refuse to talk to the cops, and that makes it suspicious. You're refusing to go to them now, even when they're explicitly looking for you. You're acting completely paranoid.'

'I'm not paranoid!' It came out as a screech. Min flinched.

'Okay. Okay. Let's go to the station together. You don't need to tell me anything. I know a good criminal lawyer. We can call, ask her to meet us there.'

Reagan bent her face skyward to escape Min's scrutiny. 'I need to go to the bank and find out what's wrong with my cards, and then Bryce is going to try to figure out how my email got hacked –'

Min sighed, a loud, frustrated huff. 'It's obvious I can't help you, Rae. I'm sorry. I should have talked to the strike force earlier. I can let them know you're having mental health issues, if that –'

'You *can't* give them my name, Min.'

'You don't get it. They're critically short on leads. They're going to figure out who you are one way or another. If they release that footage from the laneway and you still don't turn yourself in, they're going to think you're hiding something. You're basically announcing yourself as a suspect.'

'That's not –'

Min wasn't finished. 'And if they start really investigating you, it'll take three seconds on your phone to discover we're friends. My contact is on the strike force. He showed me that video yesterday. He's not going to believe I didn't recognise you.'

Reagan didn't think about Brooke often. But she came to her now, stringy blonde hair that touched her belly button, high-pitched laugh, the pot of cherry glitter lip gloss she habitually dabbed her pinkie finger into. And that day at the waterpark, standing on the edge of the highest slide, a vertical drop, glancing over the edge while Brooke goaded her. *My mum paid for your ticket so you have to go on any slide I want.*

The terror of free falling, as her hands let go of the safety bar and she plunged.

'Fine, all right? I'll talk to the strike force.' *Shit.* She needed time to figure out what to do. 'Just . . . give me one day. I'll go first thing tomorrow.'

'It'll be a lot better if you go today, like, now.' Min flicked her wrist up, her watch face glinting in the sun. 'It's after nine. They'll have released the GoPro footage in this morning's press conference.'

'You have no idea how hard this is for me.'

Min's phone buzzed, a text. Worry creased her forehead. 'Shit, Dashiel's running a fever. I've gotta go.' She shrugged her handbag higher up her shoulder and turned toward the Lexus, calling back, 'Trust me, the sooner you talk to them, the better.'

Reagan stood on the pavement, the word *paranoid* ricocheting in her mind.

31

On the drive to the bank, Reagan replayed the argument on repeat, talking out loud in the car as if Min were with her. She found a parking spot, leaving the Holden askew. The glass doors of a bottle-o slid open as she passed, an air-conditioned blast escaping into the humid morning, and she diverted inside. She picked up her usual boxed pinot gris, put it back. A banner from a local distillery hyped a gin infused with blood lime and pepper leaf. Reagan grabbed a bottle. She could give it to Bryce when he came to the garden centre later, as a thank you for helping her.

'I'm not sure if my bank cards are working. Do you mind if I try them?'

The guy at the counter nodded, looking bored. She hoped the problem might have been the cafe's payWave machine. Reagan tried both credit cards and her debit card. None worked. She handed over her cash, took the brown-bagged bottle, and went next door.

The bank smelled of wet carpet. Reagan fidgeted in the queue as a Billy Joel song played, the volume uncomfortably high.

'My bank cards stopped working this morning,' she said to the teller. 'I think they've been magnetised – or de-magnetised, whichever it is.'

This was a problem she could solve. And once she solved this, she would go to the garden centre and finish writing that damn apology email. *Break things down into small, solvable problems.*

She slid her cards and ID under the plexiglass barrier.

'Let me look up your account.' The teller was an older woman with bluntly cropped hair and puckered wrinkles around her mouth. Her name badge read *Milena*. She turned to her computer, fingertips clacking across the keyboard.

'Reagan Carsen . . .' Milena's smile faded. Pursing her lips, she leaned toward the screen with a squint. The key clacking continued. 'It seems your accounts have been frozen.'

'Frozen?'

Milena gave a sharp nod.

'What does that mean?'

'It means you can't access the funds.'

Reagan wanted to smack her forehead against the plexiglass barricade. 'Why can't I access my own money?'

'We received a report of illegal activity associated with your accounts. It's our policy to freeze them until consultation with law enforcement.'

Consultation with law enforcement. Reagan faltered, her hand on the counter to steady herself.

'There has to be a mistake. I'm not . . . Can I speak with Emil, please?'

'He isn't in today.' Milena remained professionally stern, pushing the bank cards across the counter.

'You can't call him?'

Milena exchanged a look with another teller.

'You must have my accounts mixed up with someone else's. Can you double-check?' Reagan's voice pitched up, pleading.

'I've confirmed the account name and number with your cards.'

'It's a mistake. I haven't done anything. What does it say I've done?' The customer at the window to her left turned to her.

'That's all the information I can provide.'

'It's wrong. You're wrong!' Reagan slapped the counter. Everyone in the bank stopped, watching her. The plunging sensation returned. There was nothing underneath her.

'Ma'am, I'm going to have to ask you to leave.'

Reagan couldn't think of anything to say, but she didn't feel steady enough to step away from the counter. The buzz of the fluorescent lights flooded her brain.

'– asked you twice already –' Milena was still talking, her voice harder.

A security guard appeared beside Reagan, a broad-shouldered woman with her elbows out, hands on her belt.

'I'm going,' she muttered.

—

Outside, Reagan sat in the Holden, the sun slanting through the windshield, roasting her. She should drive to the garden centre, or at least turn the ignition key and lower the windows. Instead she sat motionless, sweat soaking through her T-shirt.

Was this how it happened? The police had released the cyclist's footage, someone had identified her, and now they were closing in.

The bank teller's words tumbled through her mind. *Illegal activity associated with your accounts.* That sounded like a crime to do with money. Which didn't make any sense.

Sweat ran down her neck. Bryce had mentioned that he had a meeting that morning, and Reagan wasn't going to burden him anymore than she already had. She had a fifty in her wallet and a couple more stashed in an emergency envelope at home. Enough cash for a few days, especially since she wasn't opening the garden centre today. She wished she could call her mother.

But that wasn't true. What she wished was that she had a mother who wanted to help her.

Despite everything that morning, her impulse was to call Min. But Min already thought she'd snapped. If she tried to tell her about the frozen bank accounts, she'd probably have her committed to a psych ward.

32

The best wording she could come up with was *Temporarily closed*. She wrote in block letters, and taped the sign to the inside of Voodoo Lily's shopfront door, unsure if only one of the two words was really true.

In her cramped office, she cajoled her browser into loading the news. The GoPro footage was everywhere.

The Sydney Dahlia strike force, led by Detective Inspector Imogen Lonski, is asking for the public's help in identifying a woman who may have information about the murder of Krystal Almeida.

The woman was captured on video running out of Gipps Lane in Sydney's inner west on 15 January approximately twenty minutes before NSW Police received the first call alerting them to Almeida's body.

'If there's a reason this witness hasn't come forward, we want to reassure her we're here to help her,' Detective Lonski said.

Reagan clicked on the video, enlarging it as it played. Like in the screengrab Min had showed her, her face was pixelated, partly hidden by the cap.

Her will to send some sort of conciliatory email to everyone who'd received the video was wilting. She flushed, her stomach clenching. Fake or not, that image of her was implanted in their minds.

As she restacked bags of blood and bone, another thought struck her. If someone had identified her already, the police should be coming to question her. Maybe they were at her apartment right now.

And maybe Gordon Purdie was with them.

—

The afternoon passed in grating stress as she waited for Bryce. The plants kept her busy, and only once did she jump as if electrocuted when someone rapped on the glass door. *Gordon!* But it was just a random trying to get her to open.

Why was she waiting? She should go to the police herself. She lifted the clay pot of a rattlesnake plant, wiping the shelf beneath it. They were coming one way or another, because of her bank accounts or because of the GoPro footage.

Unless Gordon had shut down her bank accounts. The thought made her shiver in the humid air. What was scarier than a rogue cop?

The wall clock read 5.37. Bryce should have been here by now. Wiping dirt off her hands, she hurried to her office, picked up the phone and dialled his mobile number.

A recorded voice answered. 'The number you have dialled is not in service.'

She must have misdialled. No surprise, her hands were shaking. She tried again.

The same message.

She hung up, dialled a third time, and got the same message.

'Fuck!' She slammed the receiver down and forced a slow breath before trying again. She repeated his number out loud as she dialled, focusing on its singsong quality. She was sure she had it right.

'The number you have dialled –'

Reagan pulled the handset away from her face and stared at it. What the hell was going on? *Stress, affecting your memory.*

Bryce should be walking in the door at any minute. But any minute wasn't good enough. She needed to know where he was and precisely how long she'd be cooped up here alone, going crazy. Even her plants weren't bringing her comfort. When Bryce arrived, they could shove the computer in the boot of his Honda and head to his place, where the cops weren't likely to come knocking.

Digging through the paracetamol blister packs and travel-sized tissues in her handbag, she found her diary. She should have written Bryce's number there, but flipping through the pages, she couldn't find it.

He said he'd be here. He's on his way. She killed an hour online, trying to figure out the name of his company. All she remembered was that he worked in ANZ Tower, but that detail turned out to be useless. She paced the greenhouse aisles, unable to do anything useful, trying to come up with plausible reasons why Bryce hadn't shown up at the garden centre.

He could be caught at work, and maybe he'd texted her, instead of thinking to call her at Voodoo Lily.

He could have been in a car accident, or had some kind of medical emergency.

Or . . . he could have seen the GoPro footage in the news and recognised Reagan.

But if that were true, he would have called her. *Wouldn't he?*

She tried calling the number in her head one more time. Same result.

Either Bryce's mobile number was disconnected.

Or she had somehow remembered it wrong.

Of course it was the latter. She'd left her mobile, with Bryce's correct number saved in the contacts, banished from sight in the apartment. She'd have to risk going home.

—

Reagan didn't remember the drive to Enmore, or even turning the ignition. She kept trying to fit the pieces together – the fake sex tape, the frozen bank accounts, and maybe, *maybe*, Krystal's body, left for Reagan to find?

But the other two Dahlia victims, Erin and Willow, were left in suburbs that meant nothing to her. And all three women were victims of vicious, violent murders, whereas what was happening to Reagan was . . . *what?*

Standing in the stairwell, she peeked down her apartment corridor. No cops, or anyone else, waiting outside her door. She hurried inside. Her mobile was buzzing with a phone call, and as soon as she had the deadbolts in place, she sprinted across the room. She hunted through the mess of her desk, certain the caller was Bryce. A stack of books clattered to the floor as she grabbed at the phone.

'Reagan.' Cynthia's voice grated down the line. 'I can't believe you haven't called to apologise for your behaviour. Is that video on the internet? What if Terry's employees see it? Did you think about how that will affect him?'

'How it will affect *him*?'

'What has gotten into you? I thought you'd put all this behind you –'

Reagan thought she'd felt anger before, had probably used the phrase *makes my blood boil*. But now a hot rage churned through her, years of repressed fury erupting.

'I didn't have anything to do with it!' She shouted into the phone, holding it in front of her face, then hung up.

There, Min. I told her to fuck off.

The phone number for Bryce in her contacts had to be correct. She'd received texts and calls from him at that number. But now, when she pressed the tiny phone icon under his name, the same recorded message played. 'The number you have dialled . . .'

Okay. His phone wasn't working. She'd have to reach him another way. *Small, solvable problems.*

—

Driving up New South Head Road, curving past Rose Bay Marina, Reagan hummed to herself. The police hadn't come to her door yet, which implied no one had identified her from the GoPro video. She could arrive at Bryce's apartment and say, *Let's go to Namibia.* And he'd say, *Sure, when?* And she'd say, *Right now, pack a bag.* Standing in the shadow of a 1500-year-old tree seemed a sure way to make her problems seem insignificant. They could fly to Madagascar and search for the suicide palm. They were endangered, but what wasn't these days? If they were lucky, they would find it in bloom, a pyramid of millions of tiny flowers. And they could keep going, to Mexico in search of the creeping devil. There would always be more to see, everywhere. All they had to do was leave their lives behind.

The bottle of native-botanical-infused gin she'd bought for him was still in its brown paper bag on the passenger seat, rolling gently each time the Holden came to a stop.

Reagan found a parking spot a block from his building. It was after 6 pm, so he should be home from work. When he saw her, he would pull her into a tight hug, and everything would be okay. He'd have an explanation for not coming to the garden centre, for his phone number being disconnected, for everything.

As she approached the building's front entrance, a couple were on their way out. The guy hung back, holding the door open for her. His companion narrowed her eyes.

Reagan took the elevator to the first floor. At apartment 17, she raised a hand to knock, then paused, smoothed her hair and tugged at the hem of her shirt, unrumpling it. If Bryce responded the way Min had today – *No. He won't.*

She knocked once, twice.

When nothing happened, she leaned close to the door. No sounds came from inside the apartment.

She knocked once more, half-hearted, already turning away.

The door cracked open.

A woman answered, her look of impatience deepening into a frown as Reagan gaped.

The woman had red-framed glasses, the designer kind that made a statement. Her grey blazer and pencil skirt showed off a lean figure. Sharp collarbones poked through her blouse.

'Can I help you?'

Her tone was short, as if Reagan's appearance was an unreasonable inconvenience. Mind spiralling, her eyes bounced between the woman's uncertain face and the metal apartment number on the open door. Stress might have caused her to screw up Bryce's phone number, but his apartment number was the same as hers – 17. No way she'd forgotten that.

'I'm . . . here for Bryce, is he . . . ?'

'Who?'

'Bryce Stewart.'

'You've got the wrong apartment.' The woman huffed as if Reagan was the latest in the series of idiots she'd had to deal with, and swung the door shut.

You're acting completely paranoid.

The stress of the emails, her frozen bank accounts, Min's accusations – the pressure had built up until Reagan's brain had blown its fuses and stopped functioning. Light-headedness washed over her.

'Wait wait wait.' She stuck a hand out, stopping the door an inch before it hit the frame and forcing it back.

'What are you *doing*?' The woman's face soured.

Reagan kept her palm against the door. 'Do you know Bryce? Maybe he's one of your neighbours?'

The woman held the door firm, blocking Reagan from pushing it open further.

226

'How did you get in the building?' She craned, checking down the hall. As she did, Reagan caught a glimpse into the kitchen, and the bright colours of Bryce's elaborate mirrored alcohol cabinet. 'If you don't leave, I'll call the police.'

Reagan dropped her hand. The door closed hard in her face.

33

Reagan balled her fist, reaching up to bang on the closed door, overwhelmed by an urge to describe the apartment's folding glass door, the tangerine sofas, the tufted charcoal rug, to *prove* to this woman that she'd been there multiple times, had stayed overnight.

But she didn't need to prove it to this stranger – she'd proven it to herself with that glimpse of the kitchen.

She stood in the hallway, a few feet from Bryce's door. The ceiling light above her was dead. The next one flicked on and off.

What she needed was a photo of Bryce. She could have shown it to the woman in apartment 17. But Reagan didn't have any photos. She'd respected that he wasn't one of those people constantly taking pictures of his lunch. In the weeks she'd known Bryce, the only pictures they'd taken had been garden centre shots for Instagram.

Reagan stood in the corridor, frozen with indecision. The door to apartment 17 was going to swing open any minute and Bryce would come out, full of apologies. That was his sister, in town for a visit. *He doesn't have any siblings*. His cousin then. His bitch of a cousin who thought it would be funny to pretend she didn't know Bryce, to send Reagan away.

The light flicked on, off.

Behind her, a door creaked open. Reagan turned, relief already rising in her.

Bryce wasn't there.

The door opposite his hung ajar, and the freckled woman in the wheelchair came out of the apartment.

Reagan was in the middle of the hall, blocking the path to the elevator. She didn't step aside. 'Do you know the man who lives in apartment 17, across from you? He's tall, with sandy blond hair, early thirties?'

Shaking her head, the woman said, 'Excuse me,' trying to manoeuvre around Reagan.

'He's your neighbour? Wears big dark-framed glasses?'

The woman repeated herself, irritation flicking across her face.

'Do you remember me? I was with him on a Saturday evening, about a month ago?'

'Could you *move*.'

'We were in the elevator, and the doors opened and you were there?' Reagan felt like she was going insane. *Completely paranoid*.

'You're making me late.'

'Please, the woman in apartment 17, have you seen *her* before? Does she – does she live there?'

The scowling woman rolled toward her, shoving past to the elevator.

229

—

Reagan stood at the building entrance, the glow of the sunset burning at the end of the street. The blood sun frangipani at the door was still in bloom, its sickly sweet fragrance drifting on the evening air.

Could Bryce have recognised her in the GoPro footage, and decided to . . . what, elaborately ghost her?

Clouds blacked out the stars as Reagan drove home, not knowing what else to do.

—

She eased up the apartment stairs, pausing at the top to peek around the corner. No one in the corridor. But hanging from her door handle was a white paper gift bag, tissue paper spilling over its sides.

She entered the apartment quickly, the bag tucked under her arm. As soon as she had the deadbolts secure, she dumped the bag. A white box fell onto the floor, tied with ribbon. Tearing it open, she found a white silk bra set, 10C bra and size 8 briefs. A small white card read, *your true love*.

He was back. He'd been back all this time.

And now Bryce was missing.

It couldn't be a coincidence. Gordon could have hurt him, or scared him into leaving his apartment or – hell, maybe he'd arrested Bryce on some made-up charge.

She shoved the bra set, tissue paper and box back into the gift bag and dropped it beside the rubbish bin. Moving from window to window, she closed the blinds. Back in the kitchen, she twisted the cap off the botanical-infused gin and poured herself a glass over ice.

The first email had come on Reagan's first visit to Bryce's apartment in Watsons Bay. Gordon must have been watching her even then, and she'd missed it.

What was she supposed to do? She really needed Min, but she could imagine how that conversation would go. Min had called her paranoid before her boyfriend vanished.

Fuck.

The ice rattled in her glass.

Bryce was the best thing in her life, and Gordon was going to destroy that. He probably already had. She felt helpless. She'd have to force herself to call Min. Maybe they could talk to the federal police.

In the morning. She'd figure everything out in the morning.

An email notification pinged, and she picked up her phone.

The sender's name was her name. The message was three words.

I warned you.

Rage burst through her. Her vision turned crimson, like the blood vessels in her eyes had burst. The phone shook in her hand and she screamed. She smashed the phone against the sharp corner of the bench, the screen cracking. She smashed it again, the impact jarring up her arm. A few more smashes and pieces of the glass screen skittered across the room.

She dropped the phone carcass to the floor and crunched over the glass to pour herself another gin.

—

Close to midnight, Reagan pulled off her clothes, double-checked the front door bolts, and curled into bed, expecting to toss through the night. But the long, stress-riddled day and the multiple glasses of gin sank her into a leaden sleep.

At 3.47 am, the front door exploded.

34

Wednesday, 8 March 2017

The door ripped from its hinges and smashed against the floor. Reagan shot out of bed, painfully awake. Shouting and heavy footsteps came from the main room.

'Police! Police! Police!'

Naked except for a pair of black boyleg undies, Reagan stood frozen, the bedsheet tangled around her legs. She grabbed at the sheet, wrenching it up to her armpits. Torchlights appeared in the bedroom doorway. The lounge room lights snapped on, backlighting two men in heavy vests, helmets and face masks, nothing exposed but their eyes. The torches were attached to the largest guns Reagan had ever seen. And they were pointed at her.

'Lie flat on the ground! Hands behind your head!'

The men shouted, chaotic noise, no words she could comprehend. But panic was already dropping her to the floor, curled onto her knees, hands shielding her head, the naked skin of her back exposed. Her face pressed into the plasticky carpet.

I'm going to die I'm going to die I'm going to die –

The commands came several times before Reagan untangled the words, understood they were for her. She wormed onto her stomach, arms bent, her legs still caught in the sheet.

'Don't move!'

Polished boots shuffled around her head, and a gloved hand touched her skin, patting down the sheet before pulling it away. She flinched. The cold metal of handcuffs clamped around her wrists.

From the bathroom, a booming voice called, 'Clear!' More footsteps, drawers yanking open. Her mattress came off its box spring.

'Reagan Carsen?' A female voice, rough, impatient, and slightly familiar.

Reagan craned her head tentatively. A pair of boots were inches from her face, close enough to smell the shoe polish.

The overhead light illuminated the woman above her. She wore no helmet or mask. She stared down, her cheekbones hard, her lips thin and pale. *Lonski.*

'Are you Reagan Carsen?' She repeated the question twice more, louder each time, before Reagan managed to answer.

'Y-yes.'

'Don't move. How many firearms are on the premises?'

Firearms? Reagan faltered. She opened her mouth to respond, but choked on her own saliva, taking rasping breaths between coughs. Two people loomed behind Lonski, guns pointed down at her. Masks hid their faces.

'Speak up.'

'I haven't done anything!'

'Are there any firearms in this apartment?' Lonski repeated.

'None, no. Of course not.'

Lonski stepped away, a rumble of conversation coming from the main room. She returned a minute later with another officer, a woman who'd lowered her face mask.

'We're going to uncuff you.' Lonski stood against the open bedroom door, her hand on a holstered firearm. 'Get up, put some clothes on.'

Reagan started to stand, found herself shaking. Her brain had dissolved, neurons firing meaninglessly. She perched on the box spring, clutching the sheet against her chest.

'We've had multiple reports of gunfire in this location. What's your explanation for that?'

'I don't know what . . .' *you're talking about*, she tried, but a cough rose in her throat.

'We'd like you to come with us to answer some questions.'

'Now?' The bedside clock read 3.55.

'It's that, or we can arrest you. Up to you.'

Reagan stood, her knees weak, the tremble in her hands uncontrollable. Her dresser drawers hung open, their contents strewn across the carpet. She dug a clean bra out of a pile and pulled on the first clothes she saw, jeans and a leaf-patterned shirt.

Lonski escorted her past a half-dozen officers, all in helmets and masks.

Any of them could be Gordon.

In the kitchen, the white gift bag sat beside the rubbish bin, its tissue paper spilling over its sides.

Her front door lay on the floor. They stepped over it. In the corridor, neighbours dressed in pyjamas and Uggs peered through cracked-open doors. Reagan kept her head down.

—

Sydney Police Centre was sixties brutalist architecture at its worst, its concrete exterior now blackened. Inside, Lonski escorted Reagan to a white-walled room with nothing but a table, a two-way mirror, three chairs, a video camera on a stand, and a too-loud wall clock, its *tick tick tick* designed to induce anxiety.

'Wait here.' She closed the door with a thud.

Gordon could be here. He could be watching her right now, through the two-way mirror. She'd seen enough TV to know cops did that. She sat stiffly, angled away from the mirror.

Her temples throbbed and she rubbed them, blood pulsing beneath her fingertips, her thoughts tripping over themselves. They'd asked about gunfire. Maybe Gordon was trying to frame her. Is that what he wanted? To force Reagan to confess to whatever they accused her of and end up in prison?

No wonder Min thinks you're paranoid.

But what else could explain what had happened at her apartment that morning? She'd expected a couple of detectives knocking on her door, demanding she come to the station. Not some sort of SWAT team charging into her bedroom at 4 am.

She dropped her head to the table, the hard plastic chair digging into her. The aircon made the room feel like a fridge. Fluorescent lights hummed angrily above her. A uniformed officer knocked and offered her coffee and she drank it, fearing what she might accidentally say in her exhaustion. How long could they keep her here without charging her? Min would know.

You can get up and leave. You're not under arrest. But Lonski had threatened to arrest her, and she didn't want to find out if she was bluffing.

The *tick tick tick* worked its way into her skin, an itch that popped up at her ankle, on her shoulder, her scalp, her inner thigh. She tried to scratch through her jeans but it persisted, driving her mad, until she slid her hand under her waistline and down her leg to dig her nails into skin. Reagan had read about a Massachusetts woman who'd developed an itch on her upper forehead that was so maddening she scratched right through her skin. Medication didn't help, and she kept scratching, even in her sleep, until one morning she woke up with cerebrospinal fluid leaking from the spot. Her sleeping self had scratched through her own skull, into her brain.

Maybe Reagan would sit in this tiny room for the rest of her life, scratching her way through to her thigh bone.

———

Detective Lonski filled the door frame. She'd put on lipstick, a plum shade that didn't suit her. She sat across from Reagan, her posture like a metre-stick up her spine.

A man followed, and Reagan braced for Gordon's hard smile, one hand tucked in his pocket, his beady eyes. Instead, a pale-faced, scrawny detective in a rumpled golf shirt entered, carrying a cardboard file box with a thin laptop resting on its lid. He set the box and the laptop on the table, then fiddled with the video camera, a red light coming on near its lens. He sat next to Lonski, his posture as rumpled as his shirt, one forearm on the table, leaning hard.

'Reagan Carsen, I'm Detective Inspector Imogen Lonski, and this is Detective Lawrence Ngo. It's 5.52 am on Wednesday, 8 March 2017. This interview is being recorded.' She pointed to the camera.

Reagan should get a lawyer. That would be the smart choice. But a lawyer would charge her thousands of dollars to tell her to keep her mouth shut. She wanted to know what the detectives had to say, what kind of questions they'd ask. She could do this. She just had to appear cooperative, say as little as possible, learn what she could – and use that to get herself out of this situation.

'Do you know why we brought you in?' Ngo asked.

Lonski and Ngo both looked sleep-deprived, but their faces were otherwise unreadable. Ngo opened a spiral-bound notebook, held a pen ready.

'You said people reported, uh, gunfire at my building?' Reagan said.

'In your apartment.' Ngo made a note.

The detectives stayed silent, but they hadn't asked a question, so Reagan pressed her lips together. Though she tried to ignore it, her gaze darted to the two-way mirror. The light shifted behind it. Someone was definitely watching.

'Do you know why anyone would report gunfire in your apartment?' Lonski asked.

She didn't, and said so. They asked more questions about guns, other weapons, disputes with neighbours. A spark of hope flared in her. Maybe, by some miracle, they hadn't connected her to the GoPro footage, and this was only about the insanity at her apartment that morning.

Maybe it was a test. Gordon was watching, waiting for her to tell them about the emails, the lingerie, the years of harassment. *And now he's done something to Bryce.*

The clock *tick-tick-ticked.*

Don't look at the mirror. Look at the table. Look at the stringray-plant print on your shirt.

'Where were you on Sunday, 15 January?' Ngo said.

Though she tried to hold herself still, her shoulders sagged. *Here it comes.* 'At work, then at my apartment.' The lie came as a reflex.

He bobbed his head. 'Did you go anywhere else?'

'It was almost two months ago. I don't remember.'

'You're sure you didn't go anywhere else that morning? Early?'

'I really don't know.' The muscles in her face twitched as she struggled to keep her gaze away from the mirror. She tried to focus on the pattern of creases in Ngo's shirt, a smudge on the white wall. From the corner of her eye, Reagan noted Lonski watching her.

Ngo opened the laptop, turning it and pressing play. The black screen shifted to Moreton Bay figs and the too-bright sunrise. Reagan's neck and shoulders tightened. She'd known they had this, but she wasn't prepared to be shocked back into that horrible morning again. There was no audio. Lampposts flew past soundlessly, the view jerking with each turn of the cyclist's head, left, right, ahead toward Gipps Lane. And there was Reagan, ponytail flailing, sweat stains spreading down her peach tank.

Ngo paused the video. 'Is that you?'

Her impulse was to deny it, but they must know. 'It's me.'

'To confirm, you're coming out of Gipps Lane at 6.02 am on Sunday, 15 January, where the body of Krystal Almeida was reported to police twenty minutes later,' Lonski said. 'We received your name in a tip yesterday morning, after we released this footage, and started looking into you then. So imagine my surprise when I learned the tactical operations team was being called out to 52 Chester Street in Enmore this morning, responding to reports about unit 17.'

'What was your reaction when you encountered her body?' Ngo asked.

He hadn't asked *if* Reagan saw the body. They must have ways of figuring out how long Krystal had been left. *The ibises.*

'I just ran.' Reagan pulled her arms tight against her sides, her hands clutched in her lap. Trying to make herself small. To disappear.

'My question is this: who wanted to bring you to our attention?' Lonski asked.

The black carpet had the same flat, plasticky texture as the carpet in her bedroom. Two tiny circles of paper lay near her feet, hole-punch detritus.

'Reagan?'

She shook her head.

'I need a verbal response.'

'I don't know.'

'Has anyone threatened you?' Ngo kept his tone level. 'Either recently or in the past?'

'No.'

'What were you doing at Gipps Lane?'

'I was out for a run.' She gestured to the screen.

'If you were out for a run and you saw a dead woman's body, why didn't you call the police?'

This is why.

'That's what an innocent bystander would do.' Lonski's voice was calm, overly reasonable. She didn't have to be threatening. The facts were on her side. 'They come across this shocking scene, the first thing they do is call the police. Why didn't you?'

'I didn't have a phone on me.' The lie slipped out before she thought it through.

'Looks like a mobile phone, doesn't it? In the side pocket of your shorts?' She tapped a nail against the image of Reagan on the laptop screen. 'No way to prove that. But –'

Ngo reached into the file box this time, opened a beige folder, and set it on the table, facing Reagan. A photo of her at the payphone on Enmore Road, timestamped 6.04 am. The image was grainy, but her hat and tank identified her.

'Surveillance cameras from the Enmore Hotel show you at a payphone,' Ngo said. 'But there's no record of any call.'

The clock's ticks took on an angry edge. *TICK. TICK.*

'Like you said, it was shocking. I was in shock.'

'So what then?' Lonski, still so calm, like she was coaxing a nervous cat from under a car. 'You went home? You could have called from there.'

Reagan wanted to scream. 'I figured someone else would have called.'

'So you wanted nothing to do with it?' Ngo said.

'It was terrifying. I wanted to forget about it. I wasn't thinking straight.'

'Okay.' Lonski pulled the lid off the cardboard file box, leaning down to wedge it between the table leg and the wall, taking her time as she dug around inside.

Shit, how could they have that much paperwork on her? It was – Reagan had to think carefully – early on Wednesday, and the police had released the GoPro video of her first thing Tuesday, when she was out with Min. Then she'd gone to the bank and discovered her accounts were frozen. Someone had identified her Tuesday morning, and the cops had spent the past day digging up whatever they could find on her.

Had Min given her name to the cops? Or . . . Gordon? Could he have given her name to Lonski? That would mean admitting he knew her, lying about it. Which seemed reckless, even for him.

'What can you tell us about Krystal Almeida?' Lonski asked.

Reagan flinched, a tiny jerk of her head, a tightening across her cheeks. *Krystal was thoughtful, you know, she'd write these really sweet birthday cards with her favourite memories of things we'd done together. She put little drawings in the margins of her college notes, beer-drinking grizzlies, snakes in top hats.* A friend of Krystal's in Chicago, speaking to CNN. Reagan had watched the YouTube clip so many times, she had it memorised.

'She's one of the Sydney Dahlia victims,' Reagan said.

'Did you know her?' Ngo said.

'The news said she was from America.' So far Reagan had said nothing that could be turned against her, no matter what their angle was. And, she hoped, nothing that could upset Gordon. She shifted in her chair, keeping her face turned from the mirror.

'How about the second victim, Erin Rhydderch?' Lonski asked. 'Did you know her?'

'No.'

'Maybe she came into your garden centre some time, looking for plants?' Ngo asked.

Had she? Reagan had spent hours looking at pictures and video of Erin online, and hadn't recognised her. But it was possible. If the police had gone through Erin's credit card statements, they could have found a Voodoo Lily purchase from months ago. Reagan waited for them to spring this on her. Instead, they asked more about each victim. All Reagan knew was what she'd read in the news. The questions were getting easier; maybe they were wrapping up. Maybe she'd passed Gordon's test.

'You said that after you saw the body of Krystal Almeida on Sunday, 15 January, you wanted to forget about what you'd seen, is that correct?' Lonski pulled another folder from the box, this one thick with paper.

'Um, yes.' Uncertainty crept into her. She pushed against the chair, feeling the give of the plastic, trying to distance herself from Lonski.

'Okay.' Lonski pushed the file across the small table.

Before she could stop herself, Reagan checked with Ngo, an irrational impulse to seek reassurance. His face was impassive.

She opened the file. Web addresses in a small font, with time stamps to the left of each, row after row, in reverse order by date. Among the gardening websites and restaurant reviews, there were hundreds of articles about the Sydney Dahlia murders, the original Black Dahlia, and George Hodel. Someone had used a yellow highlighter to mark web address related to the murders. *Who's fucking paranoid now?*

'Don't you need a warrant for this?'

'We have a warrant,' Ngo said.

243

Holy shit. They had a search warrant for her browser history. They were investigating her. She was a *suspect.*

The file lay open, some pages entirely yellow with highlighting. How had they done this? She'd smashed the phone.

Had they gone to Voodoo Lily and seized her office computer? They probably hadn't needed to. That information existed on servers somewhere. They would have gone straight to her internet provider.

'You were interested in the Sydney Dahlia murders,' Ngo said.

'I was following the news.'

'Just this news though. Nothing about the marches against Trump or the floods in WA or' – Lonski shuffled the papers, not really looking at them – 'even any other crime. Just the three Dahlia murders. And their connection to Elizabeth Short in 1947.'

'Is there anything else you'd like to tell us, Reagan?' Ngo asked.

If she asked for a lawyer now, she may as well put up a big banner reading 'Guilty!' *Guilty of what?*

'So after discovering the body of Krystal Almeida while out for a run on the morning of Sunday, 15 January, you followed the story in the news and otherwise went about your life as normal?' Lonski asked.

'Yes.' Caffeine and adrenaline prickled in her veins, turning her skin electric.

Lonski reached into the box and retrieved a stack of photos. She handed them to Reagan.

'How do you explain this?'

Fuck. The press conference with Min – someone had photographed her there. Or, more likely, they'd photographed everyone and picked her out in retrospect. There were photos of her among the crowd in Dover Heights too, the morning Erin was found.

'You were doing more than following the news,' Ngo said.

'But you weren't there the morning Willow Signato's body was discovered,' Lonski asked. 'What happened?'

The clock *tick-tick-ticked*. Reagan set the photos on the table, slowly and gently, and stumbled through a response about her sale weekend. What were they building to?

'It's strange you'd be so invested in this case,' Lonski said, her voice quieter, 'and yet not come to us about finding Krystal's body. You read multiple articles explicitly asking anyone with information to come forward.'

There are things in the world that seem unbelievable. The ghost orchid has no leaves or stem, is nothing more than a root system when it's not flowering. But it does flower, showy white blossoms with distinctive frog-leg petals.

'I was in shock, I don't remember that morning clearly. So I didn't have information worth reporting to you.'

'Two days ago, on Monday, 6 March,' Lonski said, as if Reagan hadn't spoken, 'at approximately 3.47 pm, you drove your car over the pavement and onto the lawn of 255 Waratah Street in Mona Vale, knocking over several bins and damaging one of them before driving off. The homeowner reported your licence plate.'

Shit. She'd forgotten about that.

'Prior to that incident, you had a perfect driving record. So what happened that afternoon, Reagan?' Ngo asked.

'I, uh, don't . . .' What could she say? Driving off was definitely some sort of crime.

'Let's review where we're at so far. We've got you at Gipps Lane the morning Krystal's body was found, and not reporting it to us. You said you wanted to forget about it, but you've clearly had a keen interest in the murders. You've also demonstrated erratic behaviour. And then we get called to your apartment in the middle of the night with reports of gunfire, and can't find any firearms.' Lonski pulled three enlarged photos from the box and spread them on the table, facing Reagan. Krystal standing in Lake Michigan, arms out. Erin in her plastic party tiara, cocktail in hand. Willow bottle-feeding a baby wombat. 'And there's this one other odd detail. The three victims look a lot like you.'

'They look like the Black Dahlia,' Reagan said. 'Elizabeth Short.'

'Who also looks like you.' Lonski tapped the photo of Krystal. 'There's no point denying it. We have reasonable suspicion of your connection to these murders.'

What had Min said? *They're critically short on leads. You're basically announcing yourself as a suspect.*

'That's –' They wouldn't believe her. No matter what she said, they wouldn't believe her. 'I don't know anything.'

Reagan's eyes were hummingbirds, darting to the mirror, to Lonski, to Ngo, back to the mirror. This time, Lonski noticed.

'We can help you,' Lonski said.

'All you need to do,' Ngo said, 'is give us his name.'

They had her trapped.

35

Two quick knocks came at the door. Ngo cracked it open and had a muttered conversation. Reagan shifted, trying to see without being noticed. Ngo turned, the door still partly open, revealing a short, square-faced man. Not Gordon.

'You want some breakfast, Reagan?' Lonski said. 'We can get you a lousy croissant, or a not-bad bacon and egg roll. No? Nothing? Coffee?'

Reagan shook her head.

'Well, I need coffee. Larry?'

Ngo and Lonski followed the third cop into the corridor, leaving her staring at the images of Krystal, Erin and Willow.

Alone, Reagan curled into herself like a dried-out leaf, her forehead on the table. The wall clock said 8.14.

Maybe if she'd read Min's book, or any true crime book, she'd know how things worked. Lonski and Ngo would have to charge her with something, and then they could keep her in jail. She couldn't make bail. And if they were claiming she was connected to the

Dahlia murders, they wouldn't let her walk away. She might not be going home today, or for a long time. Stuck in jail, awaiting a trial, it could be years before she was acquitted. *If* she was acquitted.

The future reached out to her, closing in. The scratchiness of prison clothes, the relentless shouts and clatter and banging, the biting smell of industrial cleaning products, the claustrophobia of never having a moment of privacy.

She could handle anything, if she had her plants.

But there were no plants in prison cells, not that she'd ever heard of.

If she was arrested in connection to the Dahlia murders, Min would write about her, maybe investigate the charges. She might find evidence of Reagan's innocence and lead a campaign to free her. Min would love that role, putting herself at the centre of the story, crusading for justice.

Or maybe Min would fall for whatever story the cops spun. Maybe she'd write about how you could never truly know someone.

Twenty minutes later, Lonski and Ngo returned, coffees in hand. Lonski smelled of cigarettes. She set a bottle of water in front of Reagan.

Ngo pulled more photos from the file box, spreading them on top of the images of Reagan and the web history. Crime scene photos of the three murdered women, splayed like horrid props in their respective streetscapes. His fingertips touched each photo in turn as he spoke. 'We think you know who killed these women.'

She kept denying it. They kept repeating their questions. It didn't matter what she said. She'd never been able to convince her own mother not to blame her; she had little hope with two seasoned detectives. They'd decided on their narrative.

'So there's no one in your life who you think might be involved in these murders?' Lonski asked.

Reagan pressed a hand over her eyes. Could Gordon really have killed three women? *There's no way to predict any individual stalker's trajectory*, Min had said. *We don't know what this guy is capable of.*

And if he was capable of that, what had he done to Bryce? Killed him too? The thought had lingered on the edge of her mind, and now it burst, bloody and riotous. *Bryce could be dead.*

'I don't know what to tell you.' It came out as a mumble.

Ngo looked at Lonski, who gave a firm nod.

'I'm going to play a recording, Reagan,' Ngo said, clicking around on the laptop.

What was this?

He pressed play. A scratchy silence filled the cramped room, followed by an electronic beep. 'I think the Sydney Dahlia killer could be Gordon Purdie, P-U-R-D-I-E. He's got a thing for women who look like . . . White guy, mid-forties, balding. He's a cop.'

'That message was left on the tip line on Friday, 3 March, at 8.07 am.' Lonski tapped her pen on the table in an erratic rhythm. 'Recognise it?'

Shit. She'd made that call Friday. The deepfake video had come on Monday, followed by her frozen bank accounts and Bryce's disappearance the next day. Gordon must have found out about the tip call, must have recognised her voice. Is *that* why he'd done all this?

She gripped the hard plastic arms of her chair. Her eyes skittered around the room. *He's watching. He knows. He's orchestrated everything.*

'Can you confirm that's your voice in the recording?' Ngo asked.

They'd probably tracked down the payphone she'd made the call from, scrounged surveillance footage from the area. If she tried to deny it was her voice, Lonski would stick her arm in the File Box of Doom and pull out photos of Reagan with the grimy payphone receiver to her ear.

'Reagan?' Lonski said.

A thought niggled at her. Something didn't make sense.

'Reagan, is that your voice?'

Would Lonski and Ngo play the recording if Gordon was watching through the glass?

He was only one cop. And Lonski was the head of the Dahlia strike force. Unless Gordon was her superior, how could he be behind all of this?

Maybe Lonski and Ngo needed Reagan to report him. Maybe the call to the tip line hadn't been enough. To investigate another officer, they might need more information, maybe even evidence. Reagan searched Lonski's face for help. She gave away nothing.

Reagan took a shaky breath, steeling herself. If she talked, she might convince them she was being cooperative. But maybe Gordon was on the other side of the mirror, watching her. Maybe she was about to make everything worse for herself.

'Gordon Purdie has been obsessed with me since 2006, when I was fifteen. I couldn't report him because he was a cop. And now these women who look like me are being killed, and Krystal's body was left in my neighbourhood, it's – why aren't you writing this down?'

Lonski's expression remained unchanged. 'We know all about Purdie.'

Reagan gaped. 'Then why haven't you *arrested* him?'

She reached into that damn box again and pulled out another beige folder, flipping through a heavy sheaf of pages. 'On 3 July 2006, officers attend the home of Cynthia and Reagan Carsen, in the suburb of Hurlstone Park.'

Elbows on her knees, Reagan dropped her face into the heels of her hands. She'd never escape that date. Before 3 July, she'd been an average teenager, with a single mum and second-hand clothes, but on the whole, carefree, getting decent grades, taking swimming lessons, chatting up boys online. After that day, the world darkened.

'From that point, multiple complaints against an unnamed male, until they abruptly stop.'

'I don't want to get into this.'

'You're the one who brought him up,' Lonski said.

Reagan lifted her head. Hopelessness was weakening her limbs, making her long to sink into the floor. 'That was years ago. I'm talking about now. He's been to my apartment.'

'Did you see him?' Ngo asked.

She'd seen the silk bra set he'd left for her. 'Yes.'

'You believe Purdie could do this? Kill these women?' Ngo's tone was genuine, and Reagan latched on to that.

'He's a creep. And when I found out he was a cop, he threatened me, told me no one was going to help me.' She stopped. The only time she'd named him was in her call to the strike force tip line. She'd never mentioned him in connection to the stack of stalking reports Lonski was paging through. 'How did you know it was him? Stalking me?'

Ngo set his pen down, parallel to the edge of the file folder.

'You went out of your way to avoid speaking to us about the Dahlia murders, but you're very keen to pin them on Purdie. You've googled his name every day since 15 January.' He flipped a page in his notebook. 'Gordon Purdie, Gordon Purdie Sydney, Gordon Purdie stalking, Gordon Purdie NSW Police.'

Reagan tried to keep her voice neutral, tried to pretend Lonski and Ngo were customers asking about propagating bleeding heart or importing devil's hand trees. 'You asked me who I thought was involved. That's my best guess.'

'When was the last time you said you saw Purdie?' Ngo asked.

'He was hanging around my apartment in Enmore yesterday.' She hadn't seen him, exactly, but he'd definitely been there.

'What time did you see him?'

Trying to explain about the lingerie would get things off track. What time had she gotten home from Watsons Bay? 'About 8 pm. And he might have been sending me threatening emails.'

A subtle look passed between Lonski and Ngo. So they hadn't been through her emails yet.

'Did you report seeing him to the police?' Ngo asked. 'Or report the emails?'

'No.'

'Why not?'

This is why! Reagan wanted to shriek. She pictured *codariocalyx motorius*, native to Southeast Asia. Known as the dancing plant, it moves its leaves when exposed to high frequency sounds. Researchers were unable to explain its behaviour.

'I assumed Purdie could access anything I reported. I didn't want to . . . antagonise him. That's why I tried to give you his name anonymously, through the tip line.'

'And when was the last time you saw Purdie?' Ngo repeated.

Reagan squeezed her hands. 'I told you, he was there yesterday evening.'

'Okay, enough,' Lonski said, suddenly stern. 'Why are you actively trying to interfere with this investigation?'

Reagan struggled to process the word. 'Interfere?'

The two detectives exchanged another look, seemingly able to read each other's minds.

'We know it's not Purdie,' Ngo said.

'We checked.' Lonski's hard gaze fixed on Reagan. 'We took that tip very seriously. And we agreed, he seemed like someone worth looking in to.'

Reagan sat up straighter. Lonski was the first cop to ever acknowledge Purdie as anything other than an ordinary bloke going about his business.

'And after we saw your search history, we concluded he could have been the man stalking you, going back as far as 2006,' she said. 'There were some inconsistencies in the reports, his name appeared as an investigating officer too many times. In 2012, he was let go from the force for inappropriate conduct. Similar allegations, nothing proven.'

He wasn't a cop anymore? She'd searched online, but he still had no presence. He must have taken that habit from police work into civilian life.

'Here's the thing,' Lonski said. 'Gordon Purdie moved to Darwin four years ago.'

Reagan sighed, weary. 'So he –'

'He's dead, Reagan.' Lonski had clearly been waiting to drop this on her.

The words didn't make any sense. 'Dead?'

Ngo nodded. 'He died of a stroke in Royal Darwin Hospital last year. We've checked the medical records.' There was a flicker of sympathy in Ngo's face, like he could imagine how disorienting this must be.

'But he came to my apartment . . .'

'You saw someone who looked like him. Or' – Lonski placed her hands on the table, impatience underscoring her voice – 'you're lying to cover for someone.'

If Gordon was dead, what the hell had happened to Bryce? And where the hell had that gift-wrapped bra set at her door come from?

My boyfriend is missing. She was on the verge of blurting it out. There was no reason not to. Gordon wasn't a threat.

But she held back. Something was deeply wrong, and until she knew what, she couldn't risk saying anything. What had she missed? Maybe Bryce had seen the GoPro footage in the news yesterday morning and recognised her. And then he'd – what, had his phone number disconnected and arranged for a friend to go to his apartment and pretend he didn't live there? Within hours?

The emails, the deepfake video, her frozen bank accounts, the lingerie left at her apartment – someone had orchestrated that, and had likely harmed Bryce.

Terry. He could have made the deepfake video. And maybe he'd go as far as hacking into her email to send it to her contacts. But why would he send it to Cynthia? To throw suspicion off himself?

She was grasping. Terry didn't have any reason to do this. He was just a crusty old guy who licked his teeth too much.

A hard knock interrupted them. Ngo got up, took a second file box from the same square-faced detective, and put it on the floor beside his chair. 'Thanks, Turner.'

Lonski was repeating a question, but Reagan couldn't focus. She'd forgotten the two-way mirror. *Gordon is dead.*

Tracing it back, everything strange had started that morning in the laneway. Two days later . . . she'd met Bryce.

Bryce had been surprisingly forgiving about being rear-ended. He'd had that potted lilly pilly in his back seat. He'd shown up at the garden centre the next day, splashing money around and talking about online marketing. The one thing she desperately needed help with.

Holy shit.

What did she know about Bryce? He'd said his parents had retired to Byron Bay, that he didn't have any siblings, that he worked in digital marketing in the city.

If he didn't live in apartment 17 in Watsons Bay, she knew nothing.

What did Bryce know about her?

Everything.

—

'Let's try this again, Reagan,' Lonski said. 'Start with 3 January. Where were you that day?'

The day Krystal arrived in Sydney. 'At work, then at home.'

'You didn't go anywhere else?'

Ngo dug around in the second box, came up with a plastic evidence bag. They'd collected evidence from her apartment.

'Maybe this will help.' He opened the bag and removed Reagan's diary.

Opening the diary, she found the middle of January, the pages mostly blank. A dentist appointment early on 10 January, and *pub drinks* on 19 January, the first time Bryce had come to Voodoo Lily.

They went through the week methodically, Lonski throwing out questions, Ngo making notes like he planned to follow up every mundane detail.

'And how about Friday, 10 February. Where were you?'

When Erin went missing. 'At work.'

'You didn't go anywhere else?'

They talked through Saturday, then Sunday, Reagan giving the same answers. Saturday, 11 February, was the night of her first proper date with Bryce, the night the first email had shown up and everything had gone south. She didn't mention him. It would muddy things, and they were already muddy in her head.

'What about the morning of Monday, 13 February?'

The day she and Bryce had patched things up over lunch. 'You know where I was.' Reagan tapped her fingertips on the photos taken at Oceanview Avenue, near where Erin was found.

256

'And before that?'

'Before that? What, before 8 am? Asleep at home.'

'Can anyone vouch for that?'

'No.'

'How about Sunday, 5 March?'

Willow.

They talked through Sunday, Reagan waiting for them to ask about her excursion to the Coogee Budget Hostel with Min. They didn't, and she left it out. Lonski already thought she was overly interested in the case. They worked backward, through the days Willow had been in Sydney. She'd checked into the hostel on the Wednesday evening, and paid for three nights. But no one remembered seeing her after Thursday, and her phone activity went dead that afternoon.

Reagan was hardly paying attention. When she'd finished her final year of university, she'd started applying for English-teaching jobs overseas. She'd never travelled, didn't know the first thing about it. She applied for a dozen jobs, including one for a school on a Greek island that didn't require any previous experience. The school responded quickly, the first one to do so, and she tore open their letter, picturing sunset swims in the Mediterranean. The school was impressed by her CV and were eager to have her start for the upcoming term, no interview required. Before her arrival, the letter went on, they had to tailor a uniform for her, so she only had to reply with her measurements along with three photos of herself, naked, from the front and sides.

She hadn't told her mother about the scam. It would have elicited another lecture about how it was selfish to want to move away, topped off with one of Cynthia's favourite sayings. *If it seems too good to be true, don't be stupid enough to believe it.*

Bryce had seemed very, very good.

Bryce's apartment had no plants, but more than that. No photos. No prescription medications in the bathroom. Nothing personal, like an IKEA showroom. If Reagan had snooped through the drawers, would she have found clothes belonging to a tall, stylish woman with a corporate job? His wife, maybe, who'd been away travelling? When Reagan had accidentally bashed into his car, had Bryce then decided to have a fling with her using a fake name?

If so, he'd done a lot of work for a fling, helping her with her online marketing. There were easier ways to have an affair. So maybe the woman in apartment 17 was his crazy ex-wife who still had a key and . . .

'I said, where were you then?' Lonski asked.

Reagan startled. 'Sorry?'

Lonski tapped the table. 'Reagan, are you with us?'

'Do you need a break?' Ngo asked. 'Another coffee?'

'There's something . . .' She should tell them about Bryce. They could help find him.

'What is it?' Lonski leaned forward, hyper focused.

Bryce's phone was disconnected. The woman at his apartment in Watsons Bay had denied he existed. What did she actually have to give them?

They'd already accused her of interfering with the investigation. If she told them Bryce's name, but had no number or reliable address

for him, not even a photo or the name of his employer, she'd sound
– well, crazy.

Like she was making it up.

She slid the photo of Krystal toward her, rubbing her eyes. 'I was
just thinking . . . you know Krystal had a schnauzer named Comet?
He sleeps at the front door of her parents' house, waiting for her
to come home.'

—

The wall clock ticked. Reagan propped her arms on the table to
keep herself upright. They started over, Lonski and Ngo dissecting
details for each of the dates the three victims had vanished.

Reagan's answers felt hollow. They were talking about the
murders, but she was focused on Bryce. If he wasn't at the Watsons Bay apartment, how could she find him? She tried to
dredge up specific details. The unnamed hardware store his
father had run a decade ago. The panelbeater friend who'd fixed
the Honda. A supposed Sydney-based cousin with a sailboat,
also unnamed.

After nearly six hours in the claustrophobic room, she was
getting too hungry to think. She wished she'd said yes to that bacon
and egg roll. She could really go for one with extra –

Extra garlic sauce. What was that oversized sandwich Bryce
had ordered?

Lemon chicken on brown, extra garlic sauce. The way he'd said
it – it wasn't the first time he'd made that order. He'd known exactly
what he wanted.

'And what about 21 February?' Ngo asked. 'When did you arrive at work that day?'

What was the name of that sandwich place? She pictured it, tucked into one of Sydney's few laneways, the hair-netted ladies squeezed behind the counter, the queue out the door.

Lemon chicken on brown, extra garlic sauce.

If she ever got out of here, she was going to track Bryce down. Someone had targeted her. *Someone* had left the gift-wrapped bra set at her apartment yesterday.

Bryce's sudden entry into her life at the same time was starting to feel like an impossible coincidence.

36

The clock read 10.46 am when the door heaved open. Lonski and Ngo had left her again, and now here came Lonski, her face still a mask of professional neutrality. Reagan wanted to slap some emotion into her. She should be out looking for a murderer, and instead she'd wasted all this time on Reagan.

'You're free to go.' Lonski crossed her arms and propped a shoulder against the doorjamb. 'We consider you a person of interest in this case. If you have any plans to leave town, you should reconsider. It wouldn't be a good look.'

Reagan mumbled a response, not fully believing she was going to walk out of here. Was this a trick?

She stumbled from the chair and down the corridor.

On Goulburn Street, she stood blinking against the high sun, the heat of the day welcome after hours in the chilled interview room. She ought to go home and shower – except the police had knocked down her door, and who knew what state they'd left the place in. She didn't have her sunglasses, or much besides her handbag, which held her keys, an SPF15 lip balm, her Opal card, a few twenties and a handful of change.

It was lunchtime, and she was in the city.

They hadn't asked her about the bank accounts. She stopped at a cafe, got herself a flat white with two sugars, and tried her bank cards. Still frozen. She was grateful that she stubbornly kept cash in her wallet, unlike Min and probably most people these days.

Her first thought was to stake out ANZ Tower, but it was a skyscraper with thousands of people working in it, and multiple entrances. A gut feeling told her he might not work there at all. So who knew if he came to the city for lunch, or how often he ordered a lemon chicken sandwich with extra garlic sauce.

But she had nothing else to go on.

She planned to wander around the general area of the sandwich shop, hoping to stumble on it. Passing the gleaming Apple Store on George Street, she had a better idea.

The shop bustled with tourists escaping the midday heat and office worker types on their lunch breaks, blue-shirted Apple staff zipping among them. Reagan found a free MacBook and opened Safari. Her fingers drifted over the keyboard, then she searched giant sandwich Sydney CBD lemon chicken.

It was the first result. A cafe named Big Sandwich, near Hyde Park. Photos showed the cramped shop, staffed by older women in hair-nets crowded behind the counter. The place was hardly larger than the interrogation room.

As she was closing the browser, Reagan saw someone point to her. A few feet away, two people squinted at a lofted phone, then across to Reagan. They were young, early twenties, the woman with mermaid green streaks in her hair and a silver nose ring, the guy in a crop top. Their eyes flicked back and forth, phone, Reagan, phone.

She rocked unsteadily, her stomach roller-coasting. Could the police have released her name to the media? They were desperate to show progress, and the fact they'd questioned someone in connection to the Dahlia case would be big news.

The green-haired woman lowered her phone, still flicking glances her way, talking too quietly for Reagan to hear. She could bolt for the front doors.

No one else in the shop seemed to have noticed her. She turned to the MacBook. Steeling herself, she reopened the browser and searched Sydney Dahlia news.

NSW Police have questioned a person of interest in connection to the Sydney Dahlia murders. The unnamed woman was identified from a cyclist's GoPro footage filmed close to where Krystal Almeida's body was found in January.

The woman was brought in after the NSW Police Tactical Operations Unit were called to an inner west apartment building at approximately 4 am today. Responding to multiple reports of gunfire, they made a forced entry into a Chester Street apartment building.

They've now confirmed the reports were what's known as swatting, when false information is submitted to emergency services in order to elicit a police response. This type of criminal harassment is more common in the United States, where victims of swatting include Tom Cruise and Rihanna.

'We have found no evidence of firearms in the building, or gunfire in the neighbourhood,' NSW Police spokesperson Alyona Soroka stated in a press conference earlier this morning. 'Officers have canvassed neighbours extensively.

'If this was swatting, it was highly coordinated. We received multiple reports within a few minutes.'

Soroka declined to answer questions about the connection between the swatting event and the Sydney Dahlia murder investigation, or reveal the name of the individual questioned.

Reagan skimmed a few similar articles, then risked searching her name. Nothing.

Channel 6 had released footage of the police action at her apartment, shot from her building's car park. The police had shone oversized spotlights into her windows – that had been the glowing light that had leaked around the blind. As the spotlights came on, a dozen helmeted, heavy-vested officers flooded the main entrance, the first carrying a metal battering ram. The footage played twice in the short segment.

How could a TV crew have made it to her apartment that fast? Maybe the police had tipped them off.

'Excuse me.'

Reagan whipped around to face the mermaid-haired woman.

'I wanted to ask if you'd heard about the murders that have happened in the city? You look a lot like the victims and I –'

'Yeah, thanks.' Reagan deleted the browser's search history and left.

—

Big Sandwich was on the other side of Hyde Park. Reagan stopped into a chemist, thankful again for the cash in her wallet. She bought an oversized pair of sunglasses and a floppy hat with a sunflower print. It wasn't much of a disguise, but it might prevent Bryce from spotting her before she could see him.

In the sandwich shop laneway, the smell of fresh bread and roast chicken made her hunger unbearable. The queue to order stretched out the door, and a gaggle of people milled about, heads bowed over their phones, waiting for their food. She got in line, chose an American-style Reuben, corned beef on rye. Leaning against the wall as she sat and ate, she angled herself behind other customers, watching the comings and goings. In the sunglasses and hat, no one paid attention to her. Still, she glanced at her watch every minute or so, as if waiting for an increasingly late friend.

After an hour, the ache returned to her feet and calves, and the toll of the police interrogation began to catch up. The edges of her vision blurred. This was a waste, a stupid idea. Her life was falling apart, and all she could think to do was hang around a sandwich shop, hoping to run into a man who might have only eaten here once. It felt incomprehensible that the last time she'd seen Bryce was yesterday morning, when he'd left her apartment, supposedly to go to work.

With a last look around, Reagan left the laneway, keeping her head low. The corned beef churned in her stomach. She was out of ideas. There was nothing to do but go to the garden centre and look after her plants.

Across the street, a man rode a lawnmower across a tiny park space. It wasn't only dehydration that made plants scream. Scientists had discovered that grass shrieked when cut with a power lawn-mower. It produced a sound at 85,000 hertz, far outside the range of human hearing. Whether that meant grass felt pain remained unknown. But scientists also suggested that the sweet summery scent of fresh-cut grass was the smell of the plant's fear.

That scent wafted across to her. Reagan slowed as the lawnmower circled the park, wondering about the sound of grass screaming.

And Bryce walked right past her.

She sucked in a breath, but his head was down, typing on his phone.

At least, the guy looked like Bryce. But a lot of men looked like Bryce, with his average height and build, generic haircut and unassuming clothes. He didn't have any tattoos or noticeable scars, didn't wear his hair particularly short or long. This guy had on straight-legged jeans and a plain black T-shirt. No one would look twice at him. Reagan wouldn't have, if he hadn't walked in front of her.

He continued up the street, toward Darlinghurst. After a second's hesitation, Reagan followed. Her Timex read 1.43.

She kept following, two blocks, then five, starting to lose her nerve. She was probably following a stranger for no reason. When he stopped at an intersection, waiting for the light to change, she hung back, partly obscured behind a white gum, pretending to paw through her handbag. The guy kept his head down, absorbed in his phone, giving the occasional glance toward traffic lights.

Maybe Min was right. Reagan must be having a breakdown. Could she have *imagined* the bra set? She should turn herself in to a psychiatric ward. It might give her a chance at building an insanity defence to use when Lonski charged her with accessory to murder.

The light turned, the crosswalk signal rapping its mechanical tone. A few of the pedestrians moved to step off the kerb, then froze or jumped back, the screech of brakes grabbing their attention.

The man looked up from his phone, swivelling his face toward the sound.

It was Bryce.

She'd found him.

37

Reagan trailed Bryce further into Darlinghurst. He was fine. Not murdered or kidnapped, but walking around in the early autumn sunshine. Why hadn't he come to the garden centre on Tuesday afternoon? Why wasn't he at his job? Why wasn't he looking for her? She wanted to grab him by the shoulders and shake him while she screamed in his face. How *dare* he. How fucking dare he walk around in the middle of the day like any ordinary person.

He slid his phone into his pocket, never glancing behind him. He was confident. Why would he suspect anyone of following him, especially a woman in a floppy sunflower-print hat?

She slowed, taking the conspicuous hat off while keeping pace a few car lengths behind Bryce, and turned it inside out to show the slate grey lining. With the hat back on, she tucked her curls out of sight.

Bryce turned toward a russet-brick apartment building, pulling keys from his pocket. He trotted up the three entrance steps, and pushed the glass door open as she reached the building's brick walkway. Head down, she dug into her handbag for her own keys, as if she lived there.

As she approached the three steps, she risked glancing up. Inside the foyer, a pair of metal elevator doors slid shut. The elevator's floor display panel, red numerals on black like an alarm clock, switched from G to 1.

A few seconds passed. The display panel stayed at one.

Reagan tugged on the metal door handle. Locked. If she got inside, what was she going to do? Go knocking on every door on level one until she found him?

The building was on a corner. Its layout looked simple, with six apartments on each floor, three in front, three in back. It was built into a slope, so what was the ground floor around the front was a basement level at the rear. This meant level one in the front was only slightly elevated above ground level at the back. Each apartment had a narrow slab of balcony, wide enough for a barbecue and a couple of chairs.

The rear of the apartment faced another residential street. She sat on a bus stop bench, thought about removing the hat. Left it on. How long could she sit, pretending to wait for a bus, before she became conspicuous?

The building's balconies were empty of people. Only one had any plant life, a potted crown of thorns cactus. She felt certain that wasn't Bryce's place. Unless he lived with someone. He might have a girlfriend or a wife. He could even have kids.

She hung around, buoyed that she'd made it this far and clueless about what to do next. Bryce's apartment could be on the front side of the building. A bus came and the driver stopped for her.

She waved it on apologetically. The afternoon sun stretched across the sky. Her Timex read 5.01. There would be daylight until after seven.

Reagan went up the street, found a chemist, and bought a pair of scissors. A block away, she went into a kebab place, ordered a lamb gyro, and went to the toilet. The brand-new scissors weren't meant for hair, and she struggled to cut off her thick curls, impatient with the dull blades. She dropped handfuls into the rubbish bin. She was tired of looking in the mirror and seeing Elizabeth Short.

When she was finished, she had a frightful pixie cut.

She picked up her gyro from the counter and ate it in a park, wary of spending too much time in view of Bryce's apartment building during daylight.

When the sun went down, people would turn on their lights. And if they didn't close their blinds too fast, she'd be able to see straight into those apartments.

Reagan killed time, wandering around Darlinghurst, barely noticing the gardens and old-growth trees. She passed a second-hand bookshop, where she found a dog-eared copy of Annie Proulx's *Barkskins* on a table outside the door. She bought it as a prop.

On the next block, wedged between a cafe and a bottle-o, a sandwich board advertised a tiny florist-slash-garden-centre. Reagan slowed. A collection of potted succulents filled the window display, the clay pots shaped like native animals, the plants growing out of the backs of wombats and the heads of wallabies. She checked her cash, then went into the shop and came out a minute later, settling her purchase into her handbag.

By 5.45 pm, she was on the bus bench, sunglasses off, nose buried in the open book.

The blinds in the cactus apartment, the one on the building's right corner, were already down. The residents seemed aware that people could stare into their windows from across the street.

At 6.12 pm, a light came on in the middle apartment. She could see movement there. The silhouettes looked like two women. They rolled down the blinds soon after.

A few minutes later, a light snapped to life in the leftmost apartment. The blinds hung open. From Reagan's vantage point, the top half of a kitchen was visible, a refrigerator and cupboards, one open.

Someone moved into view – a sandy sweep of hair, black T-shirt. It might be Bryce, but at this angle, it could be a similarly built guy, or a short-haired woman. The figure walked away, came back to the fridge, vanished again.

A swelling fury sat with Reagan. She'd pushed herself to let Bryce into her life. She should have paid closer attention, been more vigilant. There must have been signs she'd missed.

She almost didn't see the person in the leftmost apartment come to the balcony door. She caught the movement and looked up.

It was him.

—

Bryce wore a charcoal cardigan with a square collar, expensive-looking. It wasn't the kind of thing to wear sitting around at home.

He lowered the blinds halfway. The apartment lights blinked off.

Reagan left the book on the bench and quick-stepped to the front corner of the apartment building. A minute later, Bryce strolled out the door. He had suede dress shoes on, not the trainers he'd worn that afternoon.

Was he going on a *date*?

What else could he be dressed up for on a Wednesday evening? He'd met someone new already.

Or he'd been seeing someone else all along. The pain of his deceit was surging. She'd thought they could have a future together. She'd never even known who he was.

She readied herself to duck around the corner if he came her way, to sprint up the street and hide. But he turned in the opposite direction and walked to his Honda, half a block away.

His *licence plate* – that would be evidence of his actual identity. Why had she never thought to take down his licence plate when they first started dating? She could have asked Min if her police contact would check it.

Because that sounded paranoid.

Bryce's car was too far away for her to make out the plates now. It didn't matter. She had a better plan.

Reagan returned to the rear of the apartment building, waiting. Bryce's place stayed dark. The apartment below his looked equally quiet, no lights. A scattering of other neighbours had glowing windows, but no one had come onto their balconies to fire up their barbecues or appreciate the cool March air, the glow of the evening cityscape.

Nearby, the smell of fermenting rubbish lingered around a red-lidded bin, the square type with wheels on one side. Reagan shoved it closer to the balcony. The bin was more than a metre high, and if she could manage to stand on it, she could boost herself the short distance onto the balcony.

Her Timex screen glowed in the dark – 8.19 pm, the sky turning navy, the chirrup of crickets echoing. She took the hat off and tossed it on the ground.

If she could get into that apartment, she could find his real name. A passport, a rental agreement, a piece of mail, anything.

And when she had his name, she could march into the police station and shove it into Lonski's hands. She could explain about the emails, the deepfake video, the lingerie. Bryce had probably been the one to make the fake gunfire reports too. *But why?*

She could figure that out later. Now, she needed to move quickly.

Reagan struggled with the bin. However she tried to position it on the uneven pavement, it sat off-centre, wobbling like a cafe table. When she got it as level as she could, she grasped the top with both hands and hauled one knee onto the lid, then the other. The lid started to buckle under her weight. The bin teetered as she placed her hands on the building wall and shakily tried to move, uncurling a leg to set one foot on the lid, her handbag swaying against her side. It was like the Manly surf school outing that Min had talked her into her first summer back in Sydney.

She lifted herself enough to set her left foot onto the bin. Crouched awkwardly, she began to ease further upright. This was much harder than she'd expected – and slower. Any second, a vehicle could drive down the street and catch her in its headlights.

She managed to get one hand on the balcony rail. As she did, the bin rocked, throwing her off balance. Her weight shifted too fast and the bin flipped. Reagan stifled a shout. Her legs dangled in the air, her free hand floundering for the railing, not fast enough to grab on.

She fell.

Her back hit the side of the bin and she floundered into the pile of spilled rubbish – sticky takeaway containers, a chicken carcass, balled-up tissues. She jumped up, gagging and swearing under her breath. Staying in the shadows at the side of the building, she checked nothing had fallen out of her handbag.

Someone must have heard the commotion. After a few minutes, no one appeared. She ought to get out of here before she got herself in trouble.

But she couldn't force the image of Bryce charming some other woman out of her head. Who the hell was he? And what had he done to her?

Stepping through the rubbish, she righted the bin and wedged it against the apartment wall. She hoisted herself on top, getting her feet on the lid and grabbing for the balcony rails. Kicking up, she hauled herself gracelessly toward the balcony. Her final upward thrust sent the wheelie bin back onto its side.

She climbed over the rail and stood on Bryce's balcony. *You can do this.* A defeated hopelessness had leached into her after the sex video email, but now –

'Hey!'

A beam of light hit her in the face, obscuring her vision. She raised a hand to shield her eyes.

On the next balcony, someone had a flashlight on her.

38

'T ash, there *is* someone out here!' A woman's voice came from behind the flashlight.

'I'm so sorry to bother you.' Reagan spoke in a rush, hoping the waft of rubbish coming off her didn't reach the next balcony. 'I ran out to grab dinner and locked myself out. This is my boyfriend's place – you must be his neighbours?'

Lonski would love it if Reagan got arrested like this. She'd probably leave her to wallow in her rubbishy stink in a holding cell. Then she'd charge her for breaking and entering, and keep her in prison until they could put her on trial as an accessory to the Dahlia murders.

A second figure appeared behind the first. 'What's happening?'

'This mole's sneaking into Adam's place.'

Adam? Was she breaking into the wrong apartment?

No. That had been Bryce in the window, and Bryce who had strolled down the street and into his blue-grey Honda.

'He told you his name was Adam?' She dropped the sweetness, her voice turning bitter. 'Look, I made the mistake of sleeping with this arsehole – he said his name was Bryce – and he made a sex tape and refuses to delete it. I'm trying to get some leverage before he posts it all over the fucking internet.'

There was a pause, a moment as wobbly as standing on the rubbish bin.

The flashlight snapped off. 'Fuck him,' the first woman said. 'He seems like a creep.'

'Good luck,' Tash added.

They went inside.

Reagan was shaking. Other neighbours might be on the watch. They could have already called the police.

She'd hoped the balcony's sliding door would be unlocked, but when she pulled on the handle, it didn't give. The glass was thick, and even if she could have found something to break it with, the noise would have drawn too much attention.

There was only one other possibility. She stood at the edge of the tiny balcony and reached across to pull at the insect screen covering a frosted window, ripping a corner away from the metal frame. The window was open a crack. Standing on her toes, leaning out, she gave it a shove. It slid clunkily, revealing a cream-tiled bathroom.

She felt eyes on her, but glancing around, saw no one.

Gordon is dead. He's been dead all this time. That was going to take some getting used to.

Focus, hurry up. The drop below the window was at least four metres, onto the pavement below. It wouldn't kill her, but she doubted she'd be in any shape to climb onto the balcony again.

She leaned over the railing, trying to look casual as she sized up the window opening. It was going to be tight. Maybe too tight.

She could abandon the plan, climb back over the rail and lower herself enough to drop to the street.

And then what? The deepfake woman's moan filled her head.

When she was a kid, when her father was still alive, a house on the corner of their street had caught fire. Walking to school the next day, her hand snug in her dad's, she'd stopped to stare at the blackened, smoking shell. The day before it had been a home, private. Now it stood exposed, nothing left but the frame.

Hiking her handbag high on her shoulder again, Reagan gripped the balcony rail. She swung her right foot onto it. She gave a tentative hop on her left foot. The window was uncomfortably far. With a deep breath, she launched herself, throwing her hands up and out, aiming for the narrow window frame.

She found herself hanging, half inside the shower, legs kicking into open air. The frame ground into her ribs as she flailed, grabbing the side of the water-speckled tub and pulling herself forward, collapsing into a puddle of shower water.

Anyone walking past couldn't have missed that awkward performance. *Fast, fast, fast.* Scrabbling up, she slipped, stepping onto the bathmat, swearing under her breath. She pulled on the cheap gardening gloves she'd bought at the florist's and wiped the window frame where she might have left prints.

His name. Find his name. The best-case scenario would be finding his wallet, with his driver's licence. Unlikely he'd left that behind, but he must have a birth certificate or bank documents.

The place smelled stale. Squinting in the dark, she flicked on a light switch, revealing an apartment that was smaller than hers, the lounge space demarcated from the kitchen by more cheap office carpet, the same unappealing parmesan colour. She lowered the window blinds to the floor and began a systematic search. In the main room, a tidy stack of delivery boxes stood next to the front door, one stray foam peanut littering the carpet. Plastic-sealed cup noodles formed a line along the benchtop. The bedroom featured a mattress on the floor, a muddle of sheets across it. Bryce – or Adam, or whatever his name was – kept his clothes organised, his shoes on a rack in his closet. Like the Watsons Bay apartment, there were no photos. Nothing hung on the walls. Other than the clothes and a toothbrush resting on the edge of the sink, there was nothing personal.

And there, in the bin, was her beautiful monkey orchid, its leaves yellowed and its blossoms shrivelled, their little faces contorted.

That alone deserved the death penalty.

In place of anything homely, there was computer equipment. A large table in the lounge room featured three monitors hooked up to a laptop. In the bedroom, two more monitors and a second laptop occupied a low desk, a thick bundle of cables snaking across it.

The delivery boxes – the labels would have his name. She ran to grab one. The label read JJ Smiths. The rest were the same.

Footsteps came from the hallway, approaching the door. Her chest tightened, and she squeezed her hands. There was nowhere to hide.

A distant door squeaked opened, followed by the cheery sounds of friends greeting each other in the hall.

No time. Rattling through the kitchen drawers turned up elastic bands, a sole pen, batteries, and a handful of mismatched cutlery.

'Why couldn't you keep your birth certificate in the kitchen?' she muttered.

In the bedroom, she heaved each corner of the mattress up, then went to the bathroom and lifted the lid on the toilet tank because she'd seen a movie where a spy had hidden documents in a ziplock bag that way.

Nothing.

Shit. Bryce could return any minute, and Reagan was standing around, wasting time.

Unless . . . Where did people keep all their information these days, whether they wanted to or not? She grabbed the two laptops, yanking their cables loose. She could figure out what to do with them once she got out of here.

One more thing. Standing over the bed, she carefully lifted her other purchase out of her handbag.

Australia's Gympie-Gympie shrub has a sting so agonising and long-lasting, people have been rumoured to kill themselves to escape it. Stinging hairs cover the plant, each capable of delivering a potent neurotoxin, even after the plant dies. The wounds begin like a wasp sting, then swell and whiten, sometimes weeping. The pain can last for months. If Reagan could have found a Gympie-Gympie, she would have spread handfuls of its stinging hairs through Bryce's sheets. It was what she'd dreamed of doing to Gordon, torturing him where he least suspected it.

Tonight, she had the next best thing. She'd had the florist put her other purchase in a plastic bag and tie it closed. Keeping the gloves on, Reagan retrieved it from her handbag and untied the plastic handles. Soil had slipped in the bag, probably when she fell off the rubbish bin, but the plant and its pot were undamaged.

She tugged Bryce's sheets away and held up the red bunny ears cactus. With a gloved finger, she gently brushed the cactus's fine barbed glochids over the bed. The hair-like spines were invisible against the beige sheets.

She spent a few extra seconds over his pillow, coating it thoroughly. The spines wouldn't drive him to suicide, but they'd be torturous enough, especially when he discovered he couldn't wash them off. Like tiny slivers, they'd work their way under his skin. *And maybe into his eyes.*

Reagan considered leaving the partly denuded cactus on the nightstand, its kangaroo pot watching over the bed. Thinking better, she wrapped it in its plastic bag, fitted it and the two laptops into her handbag and slipped out the front door.

It wasn't like Bryce was going to call the cops about the theft, not if he was guilty of – well, something. It had to be a crime to call in fake gunfire reports to the police. And sending the deepfake to her customers seemed criminal. She had no idea what was on the laptops, but she suspected there'd be enough to have him arrested. A computer expert might be able to prove he'd created the deepfake, that he sent those emails to her, and maybe, now that she thought about it, that he'd been behind the freeze on her bank accounts.

Could he have really done all that? Who the hell was he? And what did he have against her?

She hurried toward the CBD, the laptops bouncing against her hip. On Elizabeth Street, she caught a taxi to Enmore. At her apartment, a plywood board was loosely nailed across her door frame, crime scene tape strung across it. She wedged her fingers underneath the board's edge, prising it away from the frame.

Inside, black fingerprint powder covered door handles, window ledges, the bench and the tabletop. Her bookshelves stood empty, everything scattered. They'd taken her smashed phone, leaving pieces of the screen scattered across the kitchen floor.

She showered the rubbish stench away and changed into clean clothes. Her mattress sat askew, the sheet crumpled on the floor. Despite the mess, the bed looked inviting. She was shaking with exhaustion, a deep ache spreading through her bones and muscles and eyes.

Her few centimetres of remaining hair looked like it'd been cut by a five-year-old. Rubbing in some styling cream, she took twenty seconds to slick it back. The loss of her hair changed her face, made her look harder and weather-worn.

She took the two laptops from the bag and popped them open. Both displayed password screens. She tried *password*, *admin*, *I'mAFuckwit*, got nowhere.

She didn't have time for this. She shoved the laptops back in her bag and walked up the street to the same payphone where she'd stood on a Sunday morning nearly two months ago and failed to call the police about the body in the laneway.

She took a deep breath, picked up the handset, and dialled.

—

Reagan stood facing the street. At 10 pm, few cars drifted up Enmore Road. Nearby, a dog barked, high-pitched and insistent.

The phone rang five times before she answered. 'Min-lee Chasse.'

'Min, it's –'

'I've been trying to reach you all day! Turner – that's my contact – said they released you before lunch. What the fuck is going on?'

Turner. Ngo had said that name this morning, when another detective had come to the door. It would be just like Min to ask her contact to check up on her.

'Did you give the cops my name?'

'I waited, like I said. I was planning to go this morning, but Owen talked me out of it. And then I learned they were already talking to you.' A car door slammed in the background. 'And before you ask, I don't know who gave them your name. Either Turner doesn't know, or he won't tell me.'

There was no way to know if that was the truth, but she'd never known Min to lie, to her or anyone. 'I need to tell you something.'

'A lot of fucking things, and –'

'He was a cop, Min.'

That stopped her.

She gave Min the short version of how she'd discovered Gordon was a cop. 'I figure he wrote in the reports I'd made, about me being attention-seeking, or fabricating things, I don't know. After I saw him at the station, I never went back.'

'And I called you paranoid. I'm sorry, Rae. I was so frustrated, and I'd been up all night, although that's no excuse.'

Reagan was surprised at how easy it was to forgive her. 'It would have helped if I'd told you the whole story. I assumed he still worked there, but Lonski and Ngo told me he died last year.'

'Last year? Are they sure?' Min sounded surprised. 'Hey, are you okay? When Turner told me about the swatting in Enmore and I realised the strike force was interviewing you, I asked him to check in. You might have seen him?'

Suddenly she remembered that Min didn't know anything that had happened with Bryce.

'I asked him about your bank accounts,' Min continued, 'and he told me, confidentially, that they were frozen due to a police-generated request to the bank. But when he looked into it, he couldn't find any information connected to it.'

'What do you mean?'

'Normally the police would have an open investigation tied to the request, and they need a warrant to freeze the accounts. According to Turner, the bank had received the warrant, but when he looked into it, it hadn't come from the police. So he dug deeper. Turns out the warrant information was fake.'

It didn't matter. Time was ticking away.

'Min, listen. I think Bryce has something to do with my accounts being frozen, and the deepfake video. I just stole his laptops.'

39

Reagan paced inside her apartment building foyer, waiting for Min. In the neighbour's garden, the plants had wilted, their leaves brown, their stalks hunched. The longer she stayed in the foyer, the more intolerable the plants' torture became. Finally she strode outside, crossed onto the neighbour's property and grabbed their hose.

She was still watering when Min pulled up. Lugging the two laptops in her handbag, Reagan hurried into the Lexus.

'Holy shit,' Min said, 'what happened to your hair?'

Reagan ran a hand through what was left of her curls. 'Never mind.'

Min reached out to hug her across the armrest. Reagan flinched, then softened and accepted an awkward embrace.

'When I talked to Turner, he said Lonski has gone full tunnel-vision on you. You're the only person they've been able to find with an actual tie to one of the crime scenes, and she's convinced you know something.'

'Yeah, that was clear after six hours stuck in a box with her.'

Min pushed her seat back and twisted to face Reagan. 'So explain why you stole Bryce's laptops?'

Everything had happened so fast.

'Okay. Listen. The last time I saw Bryce was yesterday morning, before I met you in Enmore. He was supposed to come to the garden centre that afternoon, but he didn't show up, and when I tried to contact him, his number was disconnected. So I went to his apartment . . .' The story tumbled out. 'I doubt Bryce is his real name.'

Min had her phone out, taking notes as fast as Reagan was speaking. 'Oh my god, Rae, I'm so sorry. I thought you were having some kind of breakdown.'

Reagan waved the comment away. There were more important things to focus on.

'Look, we need to hurry. I think Bryce is out with another woman right now, and I don't know – I mean, who the fuck even is he? What if he's screwing her around too?' A darker possibility hovered at the edge of her mind, but she held it back. She tapped her handbag, the two laptops sticking out the open flap. 'There must be evidence of what he did to me on these.'

The doubt on Min's face seeped into her voice. 'I know you're upset, and I get it. But I don't think taking those was the best move. We don't know if there's anything on them. And even if there is, it might not be admissible in a trial.'

'Too late, I already took them. I want him exposed. He's destroyed my business, and thanks to the police raid, I'm prob-ably going to get evicted from my apartment.'

Min shifted toward the steering wheel, turning the ignition. 'I'll call Turner, get him to meet us at the station.'

'What?' Reagan grabbed her arm. 'We need to find out what's on them first. And we need his actual name.'

'We don't want to tamper with potential evidence. If there is something incriminating on the laptops, a judge may rule it admissible, if it ever goes to trial. Judges have a lot of discretion.'

'What are you going to say to Turner?' Reagan struggled to rein in her impatience. 'That I broke into someone's apartment and stole his computers, and we have no idea what's on them but they should check them anyway?'

Min dropped her hand from the steering wheel and turned off the Lexus's engine. 'I wasn't planning to use your name. But you're right. Even if you're willing to make a full statement about everything that's happened, I doubt Turner can make the laptops a priority. They could sit around for weeks.'

'That's why I called you,' Reagan said. 'You must know someone who can get into them, and see if there's anything concrete on Bryce that we could give the cops?'

Min rubbed her sleeve over her phone screen. 'Remember that child exploitation group I did that investigative series on?'

'The one I didn't want to hear about.'

'Bingo.' Min was already unlocking her phone, fingers moving fast, a ghostly light on her face. 'I worked with a white-hat hacker on that one.'

Reagan didn't know what that meant, but Min sounded confident. She let her head drop against the seat, closing her eyes.

'One problem. He's in Sweden.'

The phone buzzed. Min kept typing, new messages popping onto the screen.

'There's a guy in North Parramatta he says is really good, he'd trust him with our lives.' She gave a sarcastic laugh. 'He's asking if we want to be put in touch.'

Reagan stiffened, wide awake. 'With a complete stranger? He could report us to the cops. Or . . . or end up hacking *us*.'

Min gestured at the laptops. 'We've got two options, Rae. This or the police.'

40

North Parramatta was a half-hour drive. Min parked in front of a stumpy stucco apartment building, bordered by a tidy hedgerow. Its yellowing lawn glowed under the streetlamp.

'Is this the place?' Reagan's Timex read 10.37 pm. Not the best time to show up at a stranger's home.

'It's the right address.' Min sent a text and got an immediate response. 'He says buzz number 5, he'll let us up.'

Inside, they hurried up the stairs, Reagan lugging her bag. Before they reached apartment 5, the door jerked open, revealing a mid-twenties guy with a pile of dark hair, a rough beard and the thickest eyebrows Reagan had ever seen. He waved them inside.

'Gamo?' Min said.

'That's me.' He had a low, strained voice, no trace of a smile, and an accent, maybe Russian. 'Keep your voices down. My housemate is sleeping.'

They followed him through the lounge. The only sign of plant life was what might have been a patch of mould on the ceiling, and technically that was a fungus. Three enormous monitors across two desks dominated a bedroom-turned-office, a too-bright overhead light fixture at its centre, a lumpy black sofa in the corner. Tacks secured a tricolour flag to the far wall, its horizontal bands red, blue and orange. On the desk, stray pieces of macaroni hardened in a cheese-crusted bowl. An open bag of freeze-dried, chilli-flavoured broccoli and two empty bottles of VB completed the still life.

Gamo pointed at Reagan's bag. 'Those the laptops Cenn mentioned?'

'Yes, they're –'

'Don't tell me how you got them. Just tell me what you need. Wait, hang on.' Gamo left, returning with a dining room chair hoisted in each hand. 'Here.'

Reagan glanced at Min, trying to signal her apprehension. This guy didn't seem pleased with their intrusion into his Wednesday night. Min didn't respond, so Reagan sat in the hard-backed chair. Her body ached for sleep, but she was on edge.

'What's the situation here?' Gamo reached a hand toward the laptops, gesturing. Reagan hesitated. This was starting to feel foolish.

'If you don't have time . . .' she started. Min gave her a searing look.

Gamo dropped into the black leather office chair, his gangly legs bent like a grasshopper's, arms dangling. 'Look, I owe Cenn a favour.'

He was talking to Reagan but looking past her, his mouth a hard line. A little like Lonski. Reagan wanted to leave, to drag Min to the Lexus and figure out a different plan. There had to be other people, people Min actually *knew*, who could do this.

'Cenn told me Gamo's the best in Sydney,' Min said, like she was reading Reagan's mind.

He swivelled his chair toward Min. 'You wrote those articles about that child abuse case out of Adelaide?'

'That was the project Cenn helped with, tracking those guys down.'

His nod, combined with a softened expression, indicated some kind of respect.

A heat spread through Reagan's head, like she was coming down with a sudden flu, but she handed the laptops over. Gamo took them, spun his chair to face the desk, and started pulling cables from drawers, hooking up both laptops in some convoluted ritual.

'We're trying to find out who this guy is, his name. How long do you think it might take you to –'

'No idea.' Gamo had his face to his screens, already typing. His deepening frown filled Reagan with pessimism. 'It would help if I knew what I was looking for.'

'I think he made a deepfake of me, and emailed it from my account to a bunch of people.'

'Could be a while,' Gamo said, as much to himself as to them. 'There's a heap of security on these laptops.'

—

Gamo had a kettle and a bar fridge in the room, so Min made two cups of tea and they settled on the sofa, waiting. Gamo was onto a third beer.

'Are you okay?' Min whispered, handing Reagan a Sailor Moon mug.

Reagan didn't know how to answer. What would Bryce do when he returned to his apartment and discovered the missing laptops?

Her tea had gone cold by the time Gamo said, 'You were right. This guy's involved in something.'

Reagan's Timex read 1.47 am. She must have dropped into the peacefulness of sleep, but within a second, the strange voice and unfamiliar space set her back on edge.

Min hopped up, dragging the dining room chair closer to the desk. 'What have you found?'

'Do you want the bad news,' Gamo said, 'or the really bad news?'

'What is it?' Reagan was on her feet, hovering behind Min.

'I don't know yet, but you should read this.' His voice was grave. 'Your dude runs a dark web forum. Here.'

He set one of the laptops in front of Min. Reagan leaned toward the screen. It was an unfamiliar website with no graphics, white font on a black screen.

http://sanct626kufc4mhn92bb03.onion

The Sanctum public post
11 January 2017, 9.12 pm
Target 09 – Recon Phase
I was feeling uninspired with Target 08. It takes work to find the right Target, especially with the bloody foids getting so goddamn predictable. I wanted to shake things UP.

I discovered Target 09 last year. As you can see in the photo, she's a scrawny white foid with black curls like a fucken bird nest on her head.

She owns some stupid plant business in Sydney's
hipsterville west, so I started by hacking into her
emails. Usual business shit, invoices, deliveries, blah
blah blah, lots of overdue statements (no surprise she's
failing, business was invented by MEN for MEN).

Here's where things start to get interesting. I couldn't
find a personal email – this foid DOESN'T HAVE ONE. Like
she just walked the fuck out of the 1800s. Things got more
compelling from there, because it seems Target 09 barely
uses the surface web. She has no social media accounts,
and there are almost no photos of her anywhere. Like,
anywhere. This foid thinks she's too superior to muddy
her feet in the filth of the internet like the rest of
society. For that she needs to be punished, to be stripped
naked and shoved into the dirt and destroyed.

Normally foids have their entire lives online – pictures
of their homes, their families, their hobbies, their
breakfast. I know everything about them before I ever meet
them. This Target is a complete mystery. She runs a plant
shop, but who the hell is she beyond that?

I'll have to actually get to know her.

Finally I might have a REAL challenge.

I've been tracking her movements for weeks and she's as
predictable as a metronome. Tick fucken tock.

– 107 comments –

PunishedHER: Fuck yeah, we've been waiting ages for this!

BetaKing: Target 08 was awesome, but this sounds fucking classic

WarriorMan: Time to go old school, raze this pretentious bitch to the ground

88_loyal: You are the KING!

41

Thursday, 9 March 2017

Reagan was suddenly wide awake. She wanted to smash the laptops, storm back to Bryce's place and scream until his eardrums burst. The memory of his hands on her was like centipedes crawling under her clothes. She pressed her palms against her stomach, willing herself not to throw up. How was this possible? Bryce had seemed so . . . normal.

'Jesus Christ.' Min looked nauseous too. Reagan had never seen her so rattled, her face pale, her eyes wide. Min turned the laptop screen away. 'You shouldn't read this.'

'Is this your guy?' Gamo asked.

'It's me that he's –' Reagan's mouth turned sour.

'Wait, you're the chick in this? With the plant business?' Gamo reeled, like he'd caught a bad smell. 'Holy shit, yeah, maybe don't read anymore.'

'How much more is there?'

Gamo had the same website open on another screen.

'What website is this?' Min said. 'Can you find out who this guy is?'

'It's a dark web site. You can tell from the dot onion in the URL. And this poster is the site admin – like, he runs it. I'm trying to get into the back end. In the meantime, I'm downloading these posts.'

Reagan grabbed the laptop, turning it to face her.

'Rae, seriously. Your face is like, grey.' Min reached for it, but Reagan held firm.

'I need to know.'

The Sanctum public post
18 January 2017, 11.45 pm
Target 09 – Creeper Phase
Foids know about love-bombing these days, they listen to
each other's stupid podcasts and Instagram videos. That
shit is for amateurs. The best way to give foids a false
sense of security is to insert yourself into their lives in
a way that feels innocuous, and give them a series of cues
(based on careful recon work) that lets them take the lead.
Normally I know a foid's weak spots before meeting them
in person. I've already hacked into their phone, seen the
inside of their house through their webcams, seen the
naked photos they thought they'd deleted. They write
out their secrets in texts and emails like they're
having private conversations. Meeting them is often
anticlimactic. I was bored by the last Target before I
met her IRL.

But with Target 09 there was NONE of that. My recon convinced me she was cautious to the point of paranoia. She doesn't even own a smartphone. She's got some old flip phone like it's fucken 1998! I started to suspect she might not be a real person, but some sort of police honeypot. But if that were true, they would have at least created a fucken Facebook account for her. Target 09 seemed too far-fetched to be fake.

After observing her for several weeks, I put into play one of my most ingenious plans yet. I've gotten lazy with the last few Targets, arranging meet-ups through their online dating profiles. When you can hack into a foid's Tinder account, see their matches, read their chats, it's too fucken easy. And you all deserve better.

To give her the ultimate sense of control, I needed her to take the lead. So I figured, get Target 09 into a vulnerable situation, get her adrenaline going. She's a sloppy driver, like most foids, but to orchestrate an accident so it looked like her fault? That was the challenge.

The simplest play would have been stepping out in front of her car, but there was too much risk of an actual injury. It would be trickier to get her to hit my vehicle. I tried a few times last week and had a lot of near-misses.

I have to admit, I was having fun.

The rain gave me the perfect opportunity. I found the ideal spot on her commute from work — she drives the same route every time, like a homing pigeon. I got myself in front of her, hit the brakes, and WHAM! Stupid fucken foid drivers.

Target 09 was exactly as pathetic as I figured she would be. Pig-ugly face, but a decent enough body that I won't have to chunder after fucking her.

I'd visited her shitty little plant shop a couple of times last year, watched her talk to customers. I knew this foid would be embarrassed and falling over herself to give me her insurance details. I told her it wasn't a big deal, I had a friend who could sort it. Then she noticed the plant in my car.

OF COURSE I had a plant in my car! Get the foid talking about ITSELF, its stupid interests, act like it's really smart, that you're lucky to have the chance to listen to its goddamn blather. I suspected a control freak like her would only feel comfortable around a man who appears gutless, so I acted sweet and unaffected. I've said it before and I'll say it a thousand times – fucking with a foid at this level requires hardcore acting talent.

The trap is set. She just has to walk into it.

The Sanctum public post
20 January 2017, 1.07 am
Target 09 – Creeper Phase
An easier Target would have gone out with 'Bryce' right after the car incident. But Target 09 is skittish. She

needed more motivation. And you know me - I've always got a plan.

So I went to the stupid plant shop. Target 09 goes on and on about some dumb flower (that's the other thing, you have to have the patience of a SAINT) and I'm nodding and smiling and complimenting the foid's knowledge instead of her body (foids are getting stupider about when and how men are 'allowed' to compliment them, more fucken hoops to make us jump through because we can never be good enough for them) and meanwhile dropping hints about how much I can help her promote her stupid business online.

You would not BELIEVE how much useless marketing garbage I had to teach myself for this Target. The identity I created this time is simple. 'Bryce' is an easygoing marketing bloke, born and raised in Sydney (not even close to the truth).

She fell for it, of course. Fucken foids can't help themselves. They're so desperate for little scraps of approval and affection, so pathetic you can play them like a piano. And they love to believe they're in charge. They're so fragile, physically and psychologically. (As a society we waste so much money on their neediness, their nonsense health conditions and moodiness - one day broader society will recognise the need for culling them and keeping only the most genetically pure as breeders. In the poultry industry, male chicks are tossed into a shredder after hatching. The same should be done with infant foids.)

Target 09 invites me for a drink. I can see she's fucken salivating for me. This dumb foid would have sucked me off right there in the pub if I'd told her to.

For our Sanctum noobs, pay careful attention to this part. Targeting protocol for the first encounter is to act disinterested. If you show any interest, the Target will sense it and conclude she's superior. That's how their pathetic brains work. Polite neutrality will wound their pride, and they'll get desperate for you.

Target 09 was dying to drink, of course. Alcohol is probably the only thing that gives her self-confidence. So we're at the pub, the foid yakking the whole time. (Why has no one invented a foid muzzle?) I tell her about some stupid shit books I pretended to read — foids love that rubbish.

So there am I with Target 09, having a drink and wondering if she's going to make this harder than it needs to be, when finally she suggests dinner and I know I'm in.

Time to ratchet up Creeper Phase.

— 183 comments —

GeneralMayhem: fucking GENIUS as usual WOW
88_loyal: mind blown, man, this is what we show up for!
BetaKing: You're right, the police would probably give you a citizen's award. Look at how Trump treats foids, and he's about to be fucking president

PunishedHER: It's so good to finally have someone brave
enough to talk like a real MAN instead of pandering to
foids for votes. Do you operate in the US? So far we've only
seen Aus/NZ??

At the phrase *pig-ugly face*, Reagan let out a muffled yelp. He'd
spent weeks on this, maybe months. How could someone so twisted
have convinced her he was normal? And desirable. She'd considered
Bryce good-looking. Now his face grew puggish and asymmetrical
in her memory, his worst features exaggerated.

'You couldn't tell he was whacko?' Gamo said, working across
two other monitors.

'I –'

'He's obviously a con artist,' Min cut in, a warning snap in her
voice. 'And a psychopath. You couldn't have known, Rae. This is
so fucked up.'

Reagan pointed to the screen. 'They keep using this word, *foid*.'

'Short for female humanoid. It's a way of dehumanising women,'
Gamo said. 'It's come out of the Men's Rights community. You know,
Men Going Their Own Way, PUAs, incels. This is some kind of
splinter group.'

'I have no idea . . .' Reagan faltered. She thought the dark web
was for buying drugs and hiring hitmen.

'They're online communities of dudes,' Gamo said. 'None of
them are good news. Men Going Their Own Way claim they're
living without women but spend all their time online talking about
women. Incels are involuntary celibates. They think women owe
them sex, and have some strange ideas about how the world works.

PUAs are pickup artists, which doesn't sound as bad, but they basically teach guys to abuse women and call it seduction.'

Reagan had worked hard to insulate herself from the toxic cesspool of the internet, but its violence was there, festering, leaching into the rest of the world. She'd thought she could turn away from it, protect herself. Just like the cops had told her to do.

'These groups all spout hateful nonsense,' Min said. 'And they're on the surface web, not the dark web. They're bigger than you'd think. Hundreds of thousands of members.' She turned to Gamo. 'Any idea how big this one is?'

'It looks small. Like, less than a hundred? If you skim through the comments, it's the same user names. But they're really active on the site, logging on daily, posting heaps of comments.' Gamo gestured toward Min. 'See if you find anything useful there. I'm still trying to get into the admin account. Let's see if we can find out who this fucker is.'

Min put a hand on Reagan's shoulder. She wanted to shrug it off.

The Sanctum public post
1 February 2017, 2.33 am
Target 09 - Creeper Phase
It's time to do what you do best! Let's dig into this
bitch and see what we can find — all help appreciated!
Reagan Carsen, dob 22/05/1990, current address 17/52
Chester St, Enmore, past addresses . . .

'How did he get all this information on me?' The dismay cracked Reagan's voice.

'He's gotta be a hacker,' Gamo said. 'And these guys seem really organised. Probably most of this group are skilled hackers.'

```
The Sanctum public post
4 February 2017, 1.17 am
Target 09 - Creeper Phase
```
Turns out one of our newest brethren, BetaKing, has put the rest of you to shame! He's a fucken real-life COP!!1! And he did us the service of looking up Reagan Carsen in the old school NSW police PAPER files, where he uncovered ... wait for it ... some random stalker!

You can read through the attached docs yourself, but the short version is: Target 09 gets doxxed when she's 16, some bloke shows up at her apartment, DOESN'T DO ANYTHING (I mean, c'mon mate, the only reason not to rape a foid is for the long con! If I wasn't doing this, I'd be raping foids every night) and she falls apart for her entire fucken life, going to the cops whenever she sees a shadow – until the police reports suddenly stop. No wonder she's such an unhinged whacko.

I'm thinking we can have fun with this, start hinting that this dude might be back. Everything he did is there in the files. We start with a few emails, leave it ambiguous – we don't want her skipping town too fast! – and build from there. Let's see if we can get this foid to fucken unravel.

He'd known. He'd known everything.

'Holy shit, one of these guys is a cop?' Min said. 'Gamo, is there any way to find out who all these commenters are? We've got to track them down, especially this guy.'

'Probably. Depends how good they are at covering their tracks.'

The men who'd been watching her could be anyone. She was right back to being sixteen, her address and phone number floating around the internet, a man at her door, and the glance of every stranger a threat.

```
The Sanctum public post
10 February 2017, 1.17 am
Target 09 - Creeper Phase
This is the trickiest phase, when so much can go wrong. At
least Target 09 wasn't lining up other men to manipulate
on dating apps, like so many foids do.

And get this!! Target 09 shelled out for a brand-new
smartphone to be in touch with 'Bryce'. She's hooked like
the big stupid fish she is.

In a way I'm disappointed. She's making it too fucken easy.

Show begins at 7 pm AEDT tomorrow. No replays so be sure
to join LIVE.
```

'What does this mean, no replays?' Reagan asked. She ran a hand through her cropped hair; there was barely enough to grip.

'This dude wore glasses?' Gamo's voice was grim.

Reagan nodded, remembering how Bryce would set them on the nightstand at night before falling into bed with her.

'Looks like they were equipped with a camera, so he could broadcast when he was with you.'

He broadcast our dates to his sick website. Reagan couldn't bring herself to say it out loud. A group of strangers had been watching her. The grease from the lamb gyro churned in her stomach, and she wished she would throw up to relieve the nausea. The sick feeling sat heavy inside her.

Then she saw a screenshot of the first email she'd received, on the first night she'd visited the Watsons Bay apartment.

```
The Sanctum public post
12 February 2017, 3.38 am
Target 09 - Creeper phase
As you all witnessed on the live stream, Target 09 has
completely fallen for Bryce. She wanted to tear my clothes
off right there on the street. I could have done her in
the alley behind the ice-cream place, but it's better to
make them wait.

I've been running this new deal, doing one-night things
with career foids who think they're too good for
relationships - you get in their place, set up some basic
in-house and digital surveillance, and you've got the run
of their place whenever they're away (fake ID with that
address, get a locksmith to open it up, find the spare
keys, make copies, blah blah blah; it's not easy but so
much more FUN than Airbnb). This bitch in Watsons Bay was
away for a month, some cruise on the Danube. So I cleared
out her photos and foid shit, boxed it up in the closets,
and took Target 09 there. She walked in thinking she'd won
```

the lottery, like, 'Here's this rich guy with this great place, and all I have to do is attach myself to him so I can leech it for myself.' She could barely get in the door before she started pulling my clothes off.

I set up that email in the afternoon, so I knew precisely when it was coming. What I didn't know was that we'd be back at 'Bryce's' place by then, with her sliding her hands into my pants. Ripper timing! I should win an Oscar for not laughing when she chucked the phone. She looked like she'd been slapped by a ghost.

After the email, I thought Target 09 was going to have a heart attack. She's a psychological disaster. Which makes her more fun to mess with.

The Sanctum public post
13 February 2017, 9.39 pm
Target 09 – Creeper Phase
I thought maybe we'd lost this one and were going to have to skip ahead to a very anti-climactic razing, but the FOMO trick always works. Foids are like snot-encrusted toddlers who only want a toy because some other kid has it. Further evidence of how predictably pathetic (and pathetically predictable) they are. So after her little meltdown Saturday night, I didn't respond to her desperate messages. Foids are like dogs. You don't touch them, you wait until they come to you.

She begged to have me back, giving me her home address like some gold-plated olive branch. Like I hadn't already followed her home weeks ago! Target 09 is ON! And trust me, you won't be disappointed.

The Sanctum public post
27 February 2017, 2.13 pm
Target 09 — Creeper Phase
I have a feeling we're going to be moving into the next phase VERY SOON — though this foid is nicely unpredictable, so who knows haha. MAKE SURE YOU JOIN US!

The Sanctum public post
3 March 2017, 11.58 am
Target 09 — Full Penetration
Fuck it was hard not to laugh in her face when she started blathering about getting those emails. The trick is to listen to that rubbish and keep your mouth shut and sometimes ask a question in an 'Oh my gosh that must have been so terrible for you' tone and foids can't stand it. She's probably spent all these years fantasising about him having the balls to break in and rape her, but he let us down.

Anyway, cameras are up!! She's all yours, boys, ENJOY.

— 87 comments —
GeneralMayhem: I don't know how you do it. I'd have socked her in the mouth so hard, her teeth would have come out the back of her head
88_loyal: I hope you fuck her up like that foid they found at the side of the road

Below the post, three photos of Reagan's apartment filled the screen. They showed the bedroom, lounge room and kitchen, shot from a high angle, seemingly from the ceiling.

Reagan leaned in, squinting. In the bottom corner of each image was the current time to the millisecond. And the milliseconds were running up, the seconds ticking over.

'Gamo, are these live video feeds?' Min asked.

He wheeled his chair toward them. 'Looks like it. Must have installed cameras in your place.'

'How's that possible?' Panic rippled through Reagan's voice. 'They'd have to be on the ceiling, I'd have seen them.'

'Do you have light fixtures about where these cameras would be?'

'Oh shit,' Min said. 'There are lightbulbs that work as wifi-enabled security cameras.'

Gamo cupped his hand to his chin, massaging it. 'That's what I was thinking. This guy doesn't fuck around.'

'He *replaced* the lightbulbs?' Reagan said. *When?* Then she remembered one of the few times he'd slept at her place and she'd found him up in the middle of the night in the kitchen, snacking on leftovers. A noise had woken her, wood on wood. Like a chair scraping across hardwood.

On screen, the time illuminated on her kitchen microwave ticked over – 2.37 became 2.38. But Bryce couldn't have replaced the bedroom lightbulb while she was sleeping. Unless . . . *Who knows what he did while you were in the shower.*

The Sanctum public post
4 March 2017, 10.33 pm
Target 09 – Full Penetration
Had to do some fast talking tonight! The stupid foid invited me to some dumb party, so I pulled the *Of course I'd love to, oh no sick at the last minute* routine.

AND SHE SHOWED UP AT MY DOOR.

Not my door, of course — the decoy door. I had to rush
over there and meet her so she didn't get suspicious. This
foid is too fucken feisty for her own good.

'Oh *fuck*,' Min said under her breath. 'Holy fuck.'

The Sanctum public post
5 March 2017, 1.01 am
Target 09 — Full Penetration
I've noticed a few of our new guys talking about killing
the Target, slicing her up like those bitches in the news.
Let's get something clear: the most intimate thing you can
do is make someone fall in love with you and then destroy
them psychologically. Murder, generally speaking, is
boring, and the dead foid isn't around to suffer. Foids are
easy to break. Their psyches are delicate. A hairline crack
causes them to shatter. Mess with them for a month and
they'll have PTSD for years, develop crippling anxiety,
whine and cry and spend all their money on psychiatrists.
There's nothing more pleasurable than destroying a foid so
completely they never feel safe again.

The Sanctum public post
6 March 2017, 10.40 am
Target 09 — THE RAZING, part 1
It's been a fun ride, but it's time we entered end game.
I've dragged this out longer than usual because the whole
protect-me-from-my-imaginary-ex-stalker thing was too
perfect, plus this Target didn't trust the cops farther

than she could spit, so I could fuck with her as much as I wanted. And she was such a whore in bed, always begging for it, I'm almost sad to have to raze her.

But the foid in the decoy apartment is back from fucking around in Europe, and I've got a new Target lined up – Target 10! So let's raze this bitch.

Here's the deepfake! I pulled stills and voice from the broadcasts. It was simpler with earlier Targets to make a covert recording and blur my face, but YOU KNOW ME! I love a challenge. Plus this fucked with her even more – was it that scoundrelly STALKER?!

And now for the thick creamy icing on this goddamn cake – I just found out the Target is visiting her parents this arvo. Fuck I hope they're all together when it arrives in their inboxes. What a cosy family moment. If they had an online security system, I'd hack into it to capture their reactions, but apparently they're not scared enough of the world.

– 219 comments –

Ry291: Honoured to be part of this, man. Can't wait to see how it unfolds

The Sanctum public post
7 March 2017, 10.11 am
Target 09 – THE RAZING, part 2
Tonight is the night! Thank you to the legends who hacked into the bank to trigger a freeze on her accounts,

I couldn't do this without you guys. The freeze is easier
than manipulating the accounts; all it requires is a
certain message that appears to come from law enforcement.
It takes days, sometimes WEEKS, for the banks to sort it
out. It's MEMF, Minimum Effort, Maximum Fuckage!

And it seems like this Target might have secrets even we
didn't know about. One of you legends just sent me the
news about some bitch running away from that crime scene
back in Jan – does that look like her, or what?

For some bonus excitement, make sure you're watching the
live feed later today when I deliver a gift courtesy of
the world's lamest stalker.

Tonight we'll hit the police comms systems with the SWAT
messages at 3.45 am. Some of you are also jumping on
board to tip off media – let's make this big news! Be sure
you're ready to go if you're taking part. Everybody else,
watch here live!

And get ready for Target 10, starting soon!

'I gotta say, this is one of the most messed-up things I've ever
seen,' Gamo said. 'And I've seen some messed-up stuff.'

'Rae, I'm so, so sorry.' Min's voice was a whisper.

Bryce had done all this while pretending to care about her.
And she'd fallen for it. She was so colossally stupid. She squeezed
her thumbs in her fists until pain shot through her knuckles. She
wanted to wail and sob and find Bryce and set him on fire. He
could be out with another woman right now. *Target 10*.

Min squeezed her shoulder. 'How are you?'

Reagan forced an audible breath out her nostrils. 'Terrible. I can't even –' She gestured at the screens, her hands throbbing.

Gamo's office chair squealed as he shifted from one screen to the next. 'I've had a skim through his posts about the other eight women he targeted. He moves around – Melbourne, Auckland, Perth. He's doxxed them just like he did to you, and incited the group to dig up info on them.'

Before Reagan could ask, Min said, 'Doxxing is revealing someone's personal details – address, email, phone number.'

'There's heaps more files and shit to go through on these laptops,' Gamo said. 'I'll keep looking.'

Reagan stood, wanting to escape Min's touch, to throw herself through the window, to run away.

'I don't understand . . . he's on there admitting to crimes,' she said. 'Does he think he can't be caught?'

'Most people think everything on the dark web is untraceable. It's not that simple. But if you hadn't taken his laptops, this dude probably could have gotten away with this a lot longer. Especially since he's kept the site's user base so small. He's not stupid. Hang on, hang on.' Gamo interrupted himself. 'Fuck, Min, take a look at this.'

She leaned over his shoulder as he shifted the laptop to give her a better view.

'That looks like one of the photos that's been all over the news, right?' he asked.

Reagan picked up on his shift in tone. 'What is it?'

'I don't – where did you find this?' Min said.

'In some random file.'

'What is it?' Reagan repeated, moving to stand behind them.

On screen, Krystal lay on a metal table, head lolling away from the camera. Blood seeped from a wound to her head, dripping from her hair and onto the floor.

Across the top of the photo was the file name 02-1024x685hax.jpg.

'It's definitely not a photo that's been in the press. They were taken from the other side, you couldn't see the injuries to her head,' Min said. 'And they were Polaroids. This looks like –'

'Looks like a digital photo,' Gamo said.

'Are there any more?'

'I'm looking.'

'What does that mean?' Reagan asked, though she had a terrible feeling she already knew. 'What are you saying?'

'It could mean . . .' Min took a breath. 'Shit, Rae. It could mean Bryce is the Dahlia killer.'

42

'It's a solid lead, but it's not proof,' Min said. The Lexus headlights flashed as she clicked the locks open. The two women got in the car, Reagan holding the laptops against her chest. At 4 am, stillness hung in the night air, broken by the growls of a possum. A bloated moon cast eerie shadows.

'What do you mean?' Reagan said. 'He talks about the deepfake, and the fake reports to the police, everything. And this morning with Lonski and Ngo, we went over the dates of all three murders about a dozen times. Bryce definitely had opportunity in every timeframe.'

Gamo hadn't been able to access the back end of the dark web site. 'Give me a few days and I probably could,' he'd said. But if Bryce was the Dahlia killer, there wasn't time.

Min clutched her car keys, shifting to face Reagan. 'I don't want to downplay what he's done to you, but it isn't making international news. And other than the photo of Krystal, there's nothing that links Bryce to the Dahlia murders. None of the other eight women he targeted look like you, judging from the photos he posted. And he was posting about you while the murders were happening, and the only mention of them is when he argues against murdering women.'

'And you think he's telling the truth? He clearly hates women, and he's not concerned about committing crimes. He's probably keeping it quiet because he's worried about getting caught,' Reagan said. 'I mean, they've got the FBI consulting on the Dahlia murders. Maybe he thought it was too risky to write about.'

'Maybe.' Min scratched her hand through her hair, frowning.

'So let's go.'

'What's your plan, Rae?'

'I'm going to do what you've said all along. Go to the police, give them the laptops.'

Min tapped the key against the steering wheel. 'That's a terrible idea.'

'I need Lonski to know I'm not interfering. I can show her I'm trying to help.'

'And what are you going to say?'

Reagan wanted to grab the key and shove it in the ignition. 'I'll tell Lonski everything.'

'Including that you broke into Bryce's place? No. You can't do that.'

'Why? Because the laptops are stolen?'

'It doesn't matter if they're stolen, the police can still use them as evidence. It's only a problem if *they* obtain evidence illegally.'

'Great, then let's go.'

'I think I should take the laptops in. I can say an anonymous source gave them to me. Then I'll show them the photo of Krystal and give them the Darlinghurst apartment address.'

'And how am I supposed to convince Lonski I'm not hiding information from her?'

'Let me worry about that.' Min held out the key. 'Here, you drive. I'll see if I can reach Turner, have him meet us at the station.'

—

An hour later, Reagan waited in the Lexus outside Sydney Police Centre, her hands tucked tight across her chest. An empty chip packet blew past the windscreen.

Min had decided to go straight to Lonski. She wanted to keep her contact with Turner secret.

'I'll tell Lonski I received the laptops from a confidential source who's scared for her life,' Min had said on the drive into the city. 'She'll spot your name in the files and probably drag you in for another interview. But we're giving them a viable suspect, someone to focus on other than you.'

Back in the passenger seat, Reagan pulled her knees up, hugging them to her chest. She was alone for the first time since calling Min the previous evening.

Scrawny white foid. Stupid plant business. Bird nest on her head. Pig-ugly face. Such a whore. Hooked like a big stupid fish.

A rubbish truck rattled past, its engine high-pitched, like a scream. Min bustled up the street.

'Are they going to arrest him?' Reagan started talking before Min was in the car. 'You gave Lonski his address? What do they need, a warrant? How long does that take?'

Min turned the ignition and lowered her window. Cool air rushed in. 'I made it clear he could have another woman already.'

There was a tone under her words, and Reagan picked up on it. 'And she didn't listen.'

'She did.'

'But she's not *doing* anything.'

'It's 4.30 am, Rae. It's amazing she was even at her desk. Let's give them a few hours.'

Min offered to take Reagan to her place in Balmoral, but until the police arrested Bryce, Reagan didn't want to go anywhere near Min's house, or her family. They got a room on the 27th floor of the Darling Harbour Sofitel. Reagan was too tired to argue when Min paid. She couldn't have afforded it anyway.

'I'm going to crash here for a few hours with you,' Min said, handing Reagan the room key and gesturing toward the elevators. 'I'll let Owen know. No point driving home and waking everyone.'

She was asleep on top of the doona before Min finished texting.

—

Reagan startled awake, disoriented by the unfamiliar lavender scent of the doona cover, the white noise of the aircon, and the wall of sun hitting her like a spotlight. She untangled herself from the blanket Min must have thrown over her, and pushed onto her forearms. Through the floor-to-ceiling windows, the morning sun burst in with force.

Beyond the harbour, the city's skyscrapers stood clustered, the windows of office towers, apartments and hotels like a million watchful eyes.

Min appeared, mobile in hand, wet hair pulled into a tight bun. It was 7.30 am, and she was already up and showered, looking grim but awake. Standing at the Nespresso machine, she fiddled with the metallic capsules.

'Any news?' Reagan sat up, angling away from the sun. She ran her fingers through her hair, felt its absence. 'Have you talked to what's-his-name? Turner?'

The scent of coffee with a hint of hazelnuts drifted through the room.

'They're not going to arrest Bryce today,' Min said.

'What do you mean?'

'That's what Turner said. The strike force hasn't had their morning briefing yet, but he spoke to Lonski. Even with the photo of Krystal, they want to take some time to analyse the laptops. The photo has no metadata –'

'No what?'

'Normally digital photos have info about what kind of camera they came from, things like that. That data is missing.' Min handed Reagan a coffee mug. 'They're checking to see if the photo is fake. Which . . . it could be. We didn't think about that last night.'

'What about everything else? The posts about everything he did? The cameras in my apartment?'

'None of that has anything to do with the Dahlia murders. So the strike force doesn't see it as a priority. There's a lot of things they can charge him with based on those web posts. It's illegal to record someone in a private place without their consent, and he's admitted to swatting you. They're going to pass it on to other detectives, who'll need to verify things before they make an arrest. Which means interviewing you, too. And there's another issue.'

Min turned her mug in her hands. 'The dark web site, where Gamo found Bryce's posts? It's gone.'

'Gone?'

'Deleted, I guess. Gamo downloaded a copy of the site, and I handed that over on a USB. But the site itself is gone. And with the dark web, there's no trace.'

'Is that good?' If the site was gone, that meant the posts and videos about her, the comments, were gone too. 'He couldn't do this to anyone else?'

Min let out a sigh like a punctured tyre. 'With sites like these, they tend to pop up under a new URL. It's the same issue with child abuse sites. Authorities shut one down, and it's back under a different name within days.'

In the corridor, people rolled suitcases, chatting. A woman laughed. People going about their lives. Reagan didn't know what day of the week it was. Reality felt unstable, like her life had been dumped into the sea, and every time she tried to grab a piece of it, another wave tipped over her.

'You told the police he was out with someone last night?'

Min gave a slow nod. Her tired eyes, the starkness of her face and her flat tone suggested defeat. Reagan had never seen her like this.

'So what can we do?' If the website was gone that must mean Bryce had come home, discovered the missing laptops, and deleted it somehow. It might also mean he would abandon that apartment, with no intention of returning. It'd take less than an hour to pack the few things he had and slip away like an eel.

Min made another coffee and sat on Reagan's bed, both hands tight around the mug. 'Look, I have an idea. But you're going to hate it.'

43

The police would arrest Bryce, based on what he'd done to Reagan, as soon as they looked into it properly. Once they had him locked up, they could take as long as they needed to investigate him for the Sydney Dahlia murders.

'So we need to put pressure on them to arrest Bryce,' Min said.

'You mean I need to go through those awful posts with the police?' Dread knotted her guts. 'I doubt they'll listen to me. They've already pegged me as some kind of lunatic who might be covering for the Dahlia killer.'

'Fuck that. Look, I have a contact at Channel 6. They can set you up with an exclusive interview and air it tonight. It's still early – there's plenty of time to record and promo it for the seven o'clock news.'

'You want me to go on the *news*?'

Min raised a hand, *Hold on, hold on.*

'Haven't I been humiliated enough?' Reagan's voice was piercing, even to her ears. 'You want me to tell the whole country that I was stupid enough to date a guy who turned out to be a complete fraud and sent a fake sex tape of me to everyone I know?'

'I wouldn't suggest this if I didn't believe it would help.'

Fuck. Reagan was on her feet, backing toward the windows, trying to get as far from Min as possible.

'We've got the names of the eight other women Bryce claims to have done this to,' Min added. Bryce's posts about his previous targets included their full names, birthdates, addresses, and in some cases their social media profiles. 'I'm going to go home, hug my kids, and start contacting them. If we can get one other person to share what she went through, it will help legitimise the web posts. There'll be huge public pressure to arrest Bryce.'

If they can even find him. 'So get one of them to do the interview.'

'We need to line this up right away, Reagan. Right now, you're the only person we've got.'

She'd already had her whole life exposed on some creepy sub-corner of the internet. Now Min was asking her to do it again, on national television.

'I get how much you hate the idea.' Min spoke with the level tone of the person who knows they're on the side of reason. 'The bullshit Bryce wrote, everything he did, was horrendous. So you get back at him by putting him in prison.'

Reagan tried to imagine herself speaking to a camera, on a news program that would be broadcast not only on TV, but across the internet, immortalising her misery on YouTube.

'You want to help Krystal?' Min said. 'This is it.'

Reagan turned away, grabbing at the curtains and yanking them closed to block the view. 'Find some other victim.'

—

After Min left, Reagan showered, then ordered avo toast and eggs from room service. When the food arrived, she picked at it. Brown-gold light seeped around the edges of the curtains.

In their village in Korea, everyone had known her. The only white person, she was instantly identifiable and the source of constant speculation. Reagan didn't understand people who wanted to be famous – it meant sacrificing their privacy. But she also didn't understand people who posted photos of their homes and kids and bedrooms online, and that seemed to be everyone these days.

Coiled on the hotel bed, a pillow hugged to her chest, Reagan turned on the TV. Three photos filled the screen – Willow, Erin and Krystal. Another news segment on the Dahlia murders, as if nothing else was happening in the world. She lifted the remote to change the channel, but Krystal's eyes seemed to lock on to hers. Her aging schnauzer would be by the door, waiting for someone who was never coming home.

She envisioned a concrete prison cell, devoid of plant life, cold and discomforting. Instead of herself in it, it was Bryce.

She picked up the hotel phone.

Min answered without saying hello. 'I knew you'd come around.'

—

Three hours later, a stylist hovered beside Reagan, layering foundation onto her cheeks. He wore a toolbelt much like the one she wore at work, except his was filled with dainty brushes and an eyelash crimper, and not speckled with topsoil.

The stylist's eyes had widened when he'd seen Reagan's impromptu haircut, and he'd not so tactfully suggested a wig. But no one had a wig available, and they were already short on time.

Min had arranged for Channel 6 to set up at Voodoo Lily. She'd retrieved Reagan from the hotel, both women on the lookout for Bryce. Most of the plants had survived a couple of days of neglect. The producer seated Reagan in the greenhouse, in front of a row of hooded skullcap, its soft purple blossoms like tiny trumpets.

'I don't like this, Min.' Reagan was wearing her friend's blazer with the cheetah-print lining over a black shift dress, also Min's. 'Have you talked to any of the other women?'

'I've tracked down a few of Bryce's past victims. Some don't seem to be online, which isn't surprising. I've left messages with the ones I found. It's still early. And I've got someone visiting the apartment in Watsons Bay, to try to find the woman who owns the place. The cameras are likely still in her apartment too.'

The TV interviewer, Oliver something, broke away from a hushed conversation with the producer and approached Reagan and Min. He was tall, with greying temples and a too-long nose, and wore a navy suit over a light blue shirt, no tie. He introduced himself, shaking Reagan's hand. There was a flatness in his eyes that made her wary. But if she'd learned anything, it was that her ability to read people was subpar.

'I've reviewed the web posts you sent, Min.' Oliver spoke with the same dark undercurrent of excitement Min was prone to.

Things were spinning out of control. Reagan wanted to retreat, but she had nowhere to go. Even if her apartment was repaired, the cameras had poisoned the place.

'This is quite the story.' Oliver kept talking, either ignoring her unease, or blind to it. 'We're following up with the other women mentioned on the site. It's unfortunate the website was deleted, but the hacker you put us in touch with has corroborated it. We're trying to get a quick interview with him. We're also onto the police about investigating the site administrator.'

Reagan wasn't sure if he was expecting her to say thanks. What sort of men belonged to Bryce's sick web club – or the other groups Gamo had mentioned? How did she know this guy wasn't one of them?

'We're going to show the footage of the SWAT raid, from the lounge room and bedroom cameras. We'll blur your body, of course. And we'll show a still from the deepfake, also blurred.'

Everyone I know has already seen it. The stylist put two fingers on Reagan's chin, turning her head. Fighting a reflex to jerk away, she tucked her hands under her thighs.

The producer, a woman in her twenties who looked six feet tall and still wore high heels, broke away from the cameraman to stand beside Oliver. 'And, really important,' she added, 'we can't say that you suspect this guy of being the Dahlia killer, for legal reasons.'

Reagan wrenched her head away from the stylist to look at Min. 'I thought that was the whole point.'

The producer raised a hand. 'We can talk about the photo you found on his laptop, of the first Sydney Dahlia –'

'Krystal Almeida.'

'That's right,' she said, like Reagan had answered a maths question. 'And the audience will reach the obvious conclusion.'

'That's where the pressure will come from,' Min said. 'Everything else, Bryce has already admitted to in these posts, and the police have a copy of them. They're essentially a detailed confession of everything he did to you. So focus on that.'

The stylist dabbed at Reagan's cheeks for the hundredth time, and suddenly people were hustling around. A spotlight hit her in the eyes. The producer unfolded a chair opposite Reagan, and Oliver positioned himself in it, fiddling with his mic. He gave some preamble, speaking into the camera. Reagan couldn't focus. Her vision blurred.

'Let's start at the beginning,' Oliver said. 'How did you meet Bryce Stewart?'

An icy panic crystallised inside her. Her name and face would be on television, online. Everywhere. Gordon was gone, but now the whole world, through the internet, could peer into her life like they owned it. The threat of Gordon felt tame compared to this.

The lights blinded her. 'It, um, it started –'

'We'll need you to speak up,' a pert voice called.

Stumbling, she explained about rear-ending the Honda, his visit to Voodoo Lily, inviting him to the pub. He'd manipulated everything, right from the start. *What if I hadn't asked him out?*

Bryce – the Bryce that had written those vicious posts – wouldn't have given up that easily.

Oliver kept asking questions, about the dates they went on, the apartment in Watsons Bay, inviting Bryce to her apartment. It was easier if she talked as though it had happened to someone else. She said, 'After about a month, I invited him to stay at my place,' but she pictured Krystal or Erin or Willow, and the words came more easily. She had compassion for those women.

They must be wrapping up soon. She'd told the whole story, and like Lonski and Ngo, Oliver had started asking her versions of the same questions. The thick makeup was melting under the lights, making her skin itch.

Oliver paused, frowning at his notes. 'Reagan,' he said, leaving a weighty pause, 'what do you think made someone like Bryce target you?'

Made him . . . What was this guy implying? Reagan looked for Min, but she was hidden behind one of the spotlights.

'He gets a rush from hurting people and sharing it with others like him, who are so devoid of community in their offline lives, they seek fellow sadists on the internet.'

'Knowing what you know now, what would you do differently?'

'What would *I* do?'

Just like Cynthia, blame, blame, blame. *None of it was my fault.* Reagan had never really believed that, but suddenly the truth of it was more blinding than the spotlights.

'How is this on me? This was a well-planned, coordinated con. What am I supposed to do, get a background check on every person I meet? Hire a private investigator to vet every guy I go for a drink with? This man committed crimes against me, and bragged about it to a bunch of sycophantic degenerates on the dark web – and I should have *known* better? The idea that I could have done something differently to spare myself ignores the fact that he would have done this to whatever woman caught his beady shark eye next.

He did this to eight other women before me, and probably started elsewhere, with less organised but equally destructive behaviour.' She was getting louder, a fire in her throat. Oliver turned toward the producer. Reagan wanted to grab him by the collar, get in his face. 'I used to think I could keep myself safe by staying off the internet. I thought what happened there didn't have anything to do with me. I wasn't aware of all these groups who exist to advocate misogyny, who indoctrinate others into blaming women for everything they perceive to be wrong with their lives. The violence those groups espouse affects people in real life. It impacts all of us.'

Oliver waited, his face blank. A stillness crept into the greenhouse.

'I think that wraps it up,' he said.

44

Reagan closed herself in the garden centre's tiny bathroom while the news crew packed up, scrubbing off the makeup. A crack spread from the mirror's corner, casting an equator across her face. Min's voice came through the thin wall, patches of muffled sound.

A knock rattled the door. 'They're gone,' Min called.

Reagan pushed the door open. 'I can't get this shit off.'

'Hang on.' Min riffled through her handbag, unearthing a package of makeup removal wipes. 'I told Oliver what I thought of those last couple of questions.'

'And?'

'And I told him they better run your response in full.'

Reagan's tears started fast and hard, without warning, and she crumpled onto the toilet lid. Min squeezed into the space beside the sink, and Reagan wrapped her arms around her friend's waist, crying into her abdomen.

In the greenhouse, Min helped with the watering, urging her to stick to what was necessary. 'We don't want to hang around here longer than we need to.'

Reagan pressed her fingertips into the soil of a potted hurricane cactus. 'I don't know when I'll be back.'

'Doll, I can send Owen to do the watering. We'll look after you.'

—

Curled on the plush Sofitel bed, Reagan slept the rest of the afternoon. Min left and returned with a pair of new pyjamas and some clothes for the next day, and her favourite pizza, chicken and mushroom with barbecue sauce, jalapeños and aioli.

Min pulled a bottle of pinot gris from the minibar stock. 'Wine?'

'If Bryce somehow finds us, I'd prefer to be sober.'

They were down to the last slice by the time the interview started. Min hadn't heard back from the four previous victims she'd managed to track down, despite repeated messages. They watched the interview together, seated on the bed against a mountain of pillows. Each time her on-screen self opened her mouth, Reagan cringed.

As the interview wrapped up, there was a shot taken from behind Oliver, looking over his shoulder to Reagan, and his voice saying, 'Do you have any final thoughts?'

She baulked. 'He never said that.'

'Voiceover,' Min said. They aired only a brief excerpt from Reagan's final response, calling Bryce a shark. 'The coward.'

The credits came on. Min muted the TV. 'It was the right thing to do.'

Reagan rubbed her face. Her eyes were tender and puffy. 'Still feels terrible.'

Min wanted to stay the night, but Reagan convinced her to go home. 'I don't want to be the reason your kids develop abandonment issues. Or your husband.'

Min squeezed her into a hug, and Reagan hugged her back, not wanting her to let go.

When she had the room to herself, she pushed the edge of the curtain aside. Across the city, a million windows glowed against the black sky. In how many homes and offices were people online right now, egging each other into violence, dehumanising and abusing women, enjoying the misery of strangers?

When Gordon Purdie had burst into her home, he'd taught her that men were capable of all kinds of things.

Bryce had taught her that even when you tried to avoid those men, they could still find you.

—

Wrapped in the hotel's plush white robe, the curtains closed tight against the night, her skin smelling of cyclamen and rhubarb thanks to the high-end lotion, Reagan felt numb. Everything had been so, so bad, and the interview had been the hardest thing she'd ever done, harder than staring down Lonski and Ngo. In comparison, numbness felt okay.

She picked up the phone and dialled a number she knew by heart. Terry answered.

'Terry, can you put Mum on?'

'Reagan.' His voice turned heavy. 'I don't think your mum wants to talk to you.'

So they'd watched the interview. Of course they had. Cynthia's friends would have seen the promos earlier in the day and let her know, if Cynthia hadn't seen them herself.

'Oh.' Reagan wasn't sure where to go from there. 'I don't have a mobile anymore, and I won't be at my apartment or the garden centre for a while.'

That wasn't why she'd called. She'd planned to tell Cynthia what she should have said to her in 2006.

'About the garden centre,' Terry said.

Shit.

'Look, Terry, I can't repay –'

'I was surprised to learn everything in that news segment. You should have let us know.'

Because his tone was so colourless, she couldn't parse his meaning. *You should have warned us about this bad publicity?*

'You can't run the centre right now. You take as long as you need to pay us back, Reagan. That money will be yours one day anyway.'

A low static hummed through the receiver. She opened her mouth, then closed it, replaying the comment in her mind. She'd never heard him say anything that contradicted Cynthia.

'And if you need any help, you should come to me. Your mum can be a bit . . . rigid.'

Reagan's defences went up, her suspicions wailing.

But she had no real reason to doubt him. Maybe he was just a decent person who, for inexplicable reasons, happened to love her difficult mother.

'Uh, thanks, Terry. Thank you.'

'Do you have my mobile number?'

It was in her diary, which was still in a police evidence bag. Terry recited it, and she copied it onto a hotel notepad.

'I'll talk to your mum. And I mean it. Call me if you need anything.'

—

Reagan was sound asleep when the phone rang at 6.15 the next morning. It was Min, her voice bright and urgent.

'They've got him,' she said. 'They arrested Bryce.'

45

Friday, 10 March 2017

Forty minutes later, Min picked her up from the Sofitel, and they drove back to the concrete police centre on Goulburn Street.

Hours after Reagan's interview had aired, they'd arrested Bryce. Min had been right – the television promos of the interview had put pressure on police to review Bryce's laptops, which had given them more than enough evidence to charge him with multiple crimes. When he'd come home on Wednesday evening to find the laptops gone, he'd packed up his apartment and wiped the place clean of fingerprints. By the time the police showed up late on Thursday to arrest him, the apartment was empty. Bryce would have eluded them if not for the couple next door. When they spotted him packing his car the morning after meeting Reagan across the balcony, the two women had thought to snap a photo of his licence plate. NSW Police arrested Bryce in a motel in Grafton, 600 kilometres up the coast.

The arresting officers had driven Bryce back to Sydney overnight. They were due to arrive any minute.

'His real name is Elias Wiler,' Min said. 'I tried looking him up online, couldn't find anything. He's a ghost.'

Elias. It didn't suit him. Or maybe it did – Reagan really didn't know.

Min wedged the car into a loading zone.

'Are you sure this is a good idea?' Reagan asked.

'It's 7 am on a Saturday, what are they going to do? Tow me?'

'No, I mean –'

Min squeezed her shoulder. 'You're telling me you don't want to see this fucker in handcuffs?'

She pulled her sunhat low across her eyes. They hurried up the street, Reagan struggling to keep pace with Min's long strides.

A crowd had gathered. News crews unfurled cables and hefted cameras onto tripods. Of course the police wanted the press here. The two women manoeuvred along the side of the building, close to a wide set of glass doors guarded by uniformed officers. Reagan kept her head down.

The three or four dozen people in the crowd pressed in as a police van approached and pulled into the driveway, stopping short of the glass doors. Officers piled out of the van, temporarily blocking the view as they shuffled their captive out the back door and toward the throng.

Reagan thought she might keep her head down, not bother to let Bryce – Elias, whatever – see her. But her eyes snapped to him as the officers led him forward, one on either side, his arms pinned behind him.

'Elias, why'd you kill them?' reporters shouted, holding out microphones.

The last time she'd seen him had been in her apartment, before work, the morning sun filtering through the lemon myrtle trees, lorikeets chirping, the coffee from her French press strong and hot. He'd kissed her and said he'd come to the garden centre that afternoon, to try to figure out who had hacked into her emails and sent the deepfake.

Now she expected him to look exhausted, or worried. But his face was hollow, like a plastic mask without a person behind it. He ignored the shouted questions and staccato camera flashes. She recognised the grey linen button-up he wore, one she'd pulled off him and found entwined with her own clothes on the floor of his bedroom – no, some random stranger's bedroom.

She flushed as he turned, his eyes fixing on her. A smirk crept across his face, warping his features.

'You like the cactus spines I left you?' The snarl came from her gut, surprising her.

His smirk vanished. 'Fucking worthless –' Elias started, and the cops grabbed him tighter, one snapping at him to shut up.

'You're going to prison because of me,' Reagan said.

They pulled Bryce through the doors. He was gone.

46

Sunday, 12 March 2017

'I don't understand why you're doing this, Rae. The Channel 6 producer told me they're getting hundreds of enquiries from people who want to support you.'

With Dashiel strapped to her chest, Min followed Reagan as she moved trays of plants from the greenhouse into her car.

'I can't spend my day standing behind the shop counter, wondering about every person who walks through the door, what kind of predator they might be.' Reagan turned away from Min, unfurling a plastic sheet and spreading it across the Holden's back seat, running on autopilot. The past few days had been too much to process. She ought to be upset at clearing out the garden centre, and she would be – the devastation was approaching like a tsunami. 'Or if they saw that deepfake of me.'

'So you're running away.'

'You keep calling it that.'

Brushing her fingers through Dashiel's fine dark hair, Min leaned a hip against the car. 'Bryce is in jail. They're not going to let him out.'

After Bryce's arrest on Friday, the police had held a circus of a press conference, saying the investigation was still ongoing, but there was evidence connecting him to the Dahlia murders. Reagan had spent most of the day in an interrogation room with Lonski and another detective, not Ngo or Turner. This time she had the support of a defence lawyer Min had arranged – and paid for – as she tried to reconstruct every detail of her relationship with Elias Wiler since the day she'd rear-ended his car. Lonski's tone hadn't changed much. As far as she was concerned, Reagan was still a suspect. But her voice no longer had that edge of desperation, and the eight-hour interview had wrapped up without threat of future arrest.

'I wish you'd come stay with me.' Exasperation crept into Min's voice as she followed Reagan into the greenhouse, Dashiel's dangling legs bouncing with each step. 'This is really rash.'

'I'd be in your way.' The Holden looked like a mobile jungle. Plants filled the boot, back seat and passenger seat, a few leaning out open windows. The fuller the car got, the more the decisions weighed on her. She selected two of the three potted beehive gingers, pointing to the third. 'Can you take a few home? Would your mum plant them?'

'I'll put you to work,' Min said. 'Give Mum a few hours off from Maisey.'

'Uh-huh. What about Owen?'

'He loves your company. Come on, stay with us. Bring all the plants.' She waved a hand at the scattering of remaining pots and seedlings.

They'd been through this ten times. Even in a hat and dark glasses, Reagan couldn't walk through the Sofitel lobby without people recognising her, pointing, trying to talk to her. Twice reporters had been waiting, blocking the elevator doors as hotel security escorted Reagan past. When Terry had called to say he knew someone willing to purchase most of Voodoo Lily's plants in bulk, she'd only taken an hour to think it over. The couple had arrived that morning with two trailers.

Now they were gone, and the day's last shadows were fading into dark. Min had driven to Annandale with Dashiel, saying she would 'help out'. Reagan had tried to convince her not to come. According to Lonski, someone would get her bank accounts sorted on Monday, maybe. Along with the lawyer's fees, Min was still paying for the Sofitel room, putting Reagan increasingly in her debt.

Outside, a cool wind swirled fallen leaves across the car park. Summer had withered, and autumn was announcing itself. She wedged a tray of zinnias into the car. 'I need to get away.'

The playfulness left Min's voice. 'You think you're going to have any anonymity in Pearl Beach? It's barely a village. The locals will recognise you, and the press will find you. Your mum's beach house might be private, but that's not going to stop people.'

The sigh Reagan gave was louder and more despairing than she'd intended.

'And what are you going to do out there alone?' Min continued. 'Stay here, let me find you a therapist.'

Reagan rubbed at her eyes, the built-up stress unyielding. 'I'm closing my business. I have no idea what I'm going to do with my life. I'm sorry that I don't feel like hanging out with your family.'

'Rae, be serious. I've been getting heaps of requests for interviews with you. You got dealt a shit hand, but you can turn it into a lucrative platform.' That twinkle slipped back into her voice. 'I already talked to my agent about a potential book, and she's keen. We could co-write it. You broke the Sydney Dahlia killer case, it's huge.'

'Only because he targeted me.' Reagan's tone was cutting. 'There's nothing sexy about this situation.'

Dashiel started to fuss, his little fists thrashing, then burst into screams. Min went to change him, leaving the Lexus keys with Reagan. She packed the remaining plants into the boot.

She was waiting by the Holden when Min returned, Dashiel's face disgruntled and tear-stained.

'I'm leaving tonight. I'll pay you for the hotel when my bank accounts get sorted.'

Min tipped her head with a wince of disappointment. It was rare things didn't go her way.

She took a matchbox-sized package wrapped in cherry red paper out of her pocket. 'Well, I wanted to give you something to mark a new beginning.'

The muscles in Reagan's face strained. 'You always do this, Min, and I never have anything for you.'

The box contained black pearl stud earrings.

'They're not expensive, don't worry. I just thought they'd suit your new hairstyle.'

Reagan put the earring box in her pocket. 'Thanks.'

'Oh come on, Rae, try them on.'

Reagan was too tired to argue. Placing the box on the Holden's roof, she fiddled with the earrings in the wing mirror.

'Simple but elegant,' Min said.

'Thanks.' Reagan tapped her fingers against her thigh. 'Hang on.'

Jangling her keys, she opened the passenger door and rooted around among the plants, pulling out a potted dahlia, its half-dozen blossoms like pom-poms, the petals blood red with white tips.

'It's a Checkers dahlia.' Reagan handed the pot to Min. 'Maybe it will, I don't know, inspire your writing.'

'I thought there were no dahlias left for sale anywhere in the state?'

'I was keeping this one for myself. But it suits you. Anyway, I hope you can bring the kids to visit some weekend.' She pointed to the dahlia. 'And let your mum water that.'

47

Tuesday, 14 March 2017

A ninety-minute drive north of the city, Pearl Beach was a world away. Terry and Cynthia's 'beach house' wasn't on the beach, but it had a slivered view to Broken Bay, between the Sydney red gums and golden wattle that sheltered the property from the road. As Terry had promised, the key was under a rock by the side door. Reagan had the place to herself. Cynthia's knick-knacks cluttered every surface. Reagan paced the empty rooms, collecting the ceramic kookaburras, decorative soaps in the shape of seashells, jars of coloured sand, and souvenir Japanese lucky cats, and shoving them into drawers.

At sunrise, she made the steep walk down to the beach, a floppy-brimmed hat hiding her face. She probably didn't need it. The few dog walkers and joggers kept to themselves. She left her thongs by the pavement and let the rust-yellow sand buff her feet. As the sun splashed neon pink and orange across the water, a pod of dolphins surfed the cresting waves.

'This is okay,' she said out loud to herself, to the dolphins. 'This is okay.'

She repeated it in the overgrown garden later, as she worked on a plan for the car-full of salvaged plants. Terry had bought the property not long after marrying Cynthia. They used it infrequently. 'Stay as long as you like,' he'd said in his usual colourless tone. She'd agreed because she was staying in exchange for landscaping work. 'Fix up the gardens however you think best. It'll be a surprise for your mum.'

His support was especially unexpected, considering Cynthia wasn't speaking to her. She was waiting for Reagan to apologise for shouting at her on their last call. And for the deepfake video, and for embarrassing her on national television, and, and, and.

For the first time, Reagan began to imagine a life estranged from her mother.

After two days without speaking to anyone, with no news and no internet, the piercing buzz in her head faded to a low hum. The Tibetan Buddhists had a practice known as the 'three years, three months, three days' retreat, named for the length of time spent in meditative silence in a temple in the French Alps. Reagan had wondered about the type of people who could isolate themselves so completely for so long. Now she began to see the appeal.

Late Tuesday afternoon, she was in the kitchen spreading butter and Vegemite on sourdough when the phone rang. The landline was unlisted. She'd given the number to precisely two people.

'Reagan,' Lonski said. The clipped, gravelly voice made Reagan tighten her grip on the phone. 'I'll get straight to it. Other than a few photos on his computer, we can't find any evidence that directly ties Elias Wiler to the murders. He has strong alibis for two of the three timeframes in question.'

The stress that had ebbed away since she'd arrived at Broken Bay crashed through her. Her free hand went to her earlobe, twisting one of the black studs. 'I don't understand. You're letting him go?'

'Definitely not,' Lonski said. 'We have enough to convict him on multiple counts of fraud and a variety of other serious charges. It seems his income came from several online scams he was running, mostly ransomware. It's an ongoing investigation, and his bail has been denied.'

'That means . . .' Reagan struggled to deconstruct her understanding of Bryce for the second time. 'You don't know who the Dahlia killer is.'

'That's why I'm calling. Given your high profile in relation to this case, we think it's unlikely the perpetrator would target you at this stage. But it's prudent to be cautious. Do you feel safe, where you are?'

Through the windows, beyond the headland, the sea churned. 'No one knows where I am except you, my stepfather and Min-lee Chasse.'

Lonski offered to send a patrol car past. Reagan declined.

—

She'd only brought one bag, had barely unpacked. *Terry had been quick to offer the beach house. Too quick?*

And even if Terry had nothing to do with it, how hard would it be to discover her mother online, to look up property records?

Reagan dashed around the house, grabbing her clothes, a book, her toothbrush. Once her bag was in the Holden's boot, she stood beside the car, keys in hand. She could start driving, head to Byron or Brisbane, abandon the car outside the airport, catch a flight to Namibia. Her life might be in shambles, but with her credit cards working again, she could at least have the chance to stand in the presence of a 1500-year-old *Welwitschia*.

She was about to leave when she glanced at the garden, at the array of plants she'd grown from seedlings. They were all that was left of Voodoo Lily. They'd bake in their pots, dry out in days. If she could get them into the ground, water them thoroughly, they'd have a chance.

It would only take a few hours. She'd be on the highway before dark.

—

Reagan worked faster than she had even the day before Voodoo Lily opened, when she'd badly underestimated the effort of setting up the shop and the greenhouse. As she dropped her gardening gloves and tools into the wheelbarrow and stepped through the uneven grass, a moonless sky absorbed the last traces of dusk.

She should have quit half an hour ago. It was too dark to bother putting things into the gardening shed, so she manoeuvred the wheelbarrow beside the door and headed for the beach house, wishing she'd left a light on. She'd have a quick shower and get out, drive north, maybe to Coffs. Or turn inland, to Armidale.

'Reagan!' A voice came from near the house. 'Reagan, is that you?'

It was male, and familiar, but in the disorientation of the dark, she couldn't figure out who it was. 'Sorry, who's there?'

'Min's in hospital, she's asking for you.' Owen, his voice ragged, breathy. He must have run from the car.

'What? What's happened?' Her mind spun with gruesome possibilities. 'The killer went after her?'

'I'll explain on the way.' He clamped a hand to her bicep, and she scrambled beside him, toward the front of the house, stumbling on a tree root.

'Does your phone have a flashlight?' Reagan asked. 'I can't see the –'

'I tried to call, on the number you gave Min. No one answered.'

'Is Min okay?' Regret hit like shrapnel. That she'd never told Min how much she loved her, how much she mattered. Instead, she'd stiffened at every hug, every comforting touch.

'Why did you leave her? Is Hyun-sook with her?'

She tripped again, going too fast, and Owen's hand tightened, keeping her upright.

They came around the front of the beach house. The Holden was there, parked beside the garage. The car behind it was black, definitely not a Lexus.

'Where's your car?' An instinctive warning sounded deep in her brain. She'd never seen that car before. She slowed, trying to pull away from him as his fingers dug into her arm. 'Owen?'

'Why would I be driving my own car?' His voice hardened.

Panic crashed through her, muddling her thoughts. She needed to get to Min, needed to help her, but she couldn't think with Owen acting so strange, saying things that didn't make sense.

'Let go, you're hurting –'

Something came at her, fast. She flinched but couldn't evade it. A bomb went off behind her eyes and she pitched forward. The sharp, downward momentum was the last thing she remembered.

48

Reagan woke to a screaming headache. She was on her back, staring up at a row of white-hot lights, a ceiling coated in lumpy yellow foam. The surface beneath her was hard, digging into her shoulder blades and hips.

She tried to sit up, but her limbs weren't responding. No, that wasn't it. Three heavy straps cut into her shoulders, hips and calves, pinning her hands against her thighs.

Her ears rang, the sound fading and rushing in like the tide. The air smelled astringent, like chemical cleaners. She tasted blood. Mixed with the smell, it made her nauseous.

One of her ears cleared. Someone was in the room with her, moving around and muttering.

'. . . and if he talks, if he tries to reveal . . .'

Owen? Reagan tried to speak but her tongue sat sluggish. She turned her head. The movement sent explosions of pain through her temples.

A large metal storage cabinet dominated one of the room's white walls. She didn't recognise the space. Owen was there, pulling open drawers, but this wasn't any part of Min's house that Reagan had ever seen.

A chunky black camera stood on a tripod, and behind it, photos of the Sydney Dahlia victims covered the wall, as if this were an art gallery. In some, the women were strapped to a stainless steel table, with a lip around the edge, a bucket underneath.

Reagan stretched her fingers as far as they'd reach. The smooth metal beneath them angled abruptly upward. The table had a raised lip. For containing fluids.

She choked, a ragged, sharp cough, her head lifting and banging back against the table, her fingers scrabbling to grip onto anything. Owen had moved out of sight.

'Owen?' It came out as a croak.

'Finally awake?' A twist of disgust in his voice.

Her eyelids sank, blinding her. They'd never felt so stubbornly heavy.

The *schint* of scissor blades came with a tug at her shirt. Wrangling her eyes open, she forced her head a centimetre off the table. Owen was cutting off her jeans.

'What . . . ?'

'You're not here to yak.'

'I don't know what you're . . .' The words came out thick and hoarse. Her tongue was swollen, blood trickling through her mouth. She must have bit it when she got hit at the beach house. *Was that what happened?*

She was injured, he was helping her. The straps prevented her from hurting herself further. Her mind grasped for any explanation but the obvious.

He tugged a piece of her jeans away. The cold air on her leg made her more alert.

Owen wasn't here to help.

The scissors sliced through the other leg of her jeans, then through her shirt. They clattered to the polished concrete floor as he grabbed the loose flaps of shirt and ripped them apart, the material tearing with a sickening sound. His eyes rolled around the room as he yanked at her sleeves, trying to pull the shirt off, the fabric cutting into her biceps.

Owen couldn't be doing this. He had a happy marriage, wonderful kids, a successful career.

She strained against the straps, trying to arch and heave her body. They didn't give.

'Stay still!' Owen snapped an arm out, reaching behind him. A short blade glinted as it rushed at her, plunging into her shoulder. The impact came as a heavy punch, chased with an electric burning. She gasped.

Owen leaned over, pressing his face close to hers as he twisted the blade.

'You had to fuck everything up.'

She tried to pull her face away, but he grabbed her chin, crushing his thumb and fingertips against her jaw. He pulled out the knife blade and let it drop to the floor, releasing her face to stroke her hair. He ran a fingertip around the edge of the wound, smearing the blood.

Then he sank it into the hole, wriggling it there.

This time she screamed.

'You're too dangerous to make use of.' He dug his fingertip deeper into the flesh of her shoulder. Her vision swam. 'I thought about gutting you at Pearl Beach and leaving you there.'

A horrible realisation surged through her.

Min. She'd given the beach house address to Min.

And if Owen was doing this . . . Min might be dead. He would have killed her first. She was too much of a risk. Too smart. The pain of picturing her closest friend – the knife wound in her shoulder was easier to cope with. Tears stung her eyes.

But Owen couldn't be the Dahlia murderer. The last time she'd seen him, he was playing with Maisey at Dashiel's birthday party.

'It was me, you know. Who gave your name to Elias.'

The ringing in her ears faded in and out, the pain from the wound disrupting her thoughts, overwhelming everything. Was she hearing him right? Elias was . . . *Bryce*? What did Owen have to do with Bryce?

What about the kids, and Hyun-sook? If he'd killed Min . . . There was a term for that, one of those awful phrases Min tossed around. *Family annihilator.*

'I wanted "Bryce" to fuck you around. Last year, actually. His timing wasn't ideal. Still, it was satisfying. I didn't know you'd turn into such a psycho.'

Owen pulled his bloody finger out of her shoulder and wiped it across her cheek. She snapped at him, catching the edge of his finger with her teeth before they slipped on the blood and jarred together.

He slapped her, the impact whipping her head to the side. The post of her earring cut into her skin, that one tiny pain momentarily outshining the rest.

'You look exactly like her.' Owen stared at her, an unsettled look in his eyes that Reagan had never seen before, anywhere.

Her? Who was he talking about?

Then she saw it, on the wall behind him. A photo of Elizabeth Short. The Black Dahlia.

'I was obsessed with her for years, turning it over in my mind. And then *you* arrived, and it was like she'd walked into my life. That's when I knew. I knew I had to do it.'

The chill of metal touched Reagan's navel.

'As much as I wanted to – and I really wanted to – I couldn't use you. You're too close. It was too big a risk.'

The pain in her shoulder flared white hot. She grit her teeth, refusing to make a sound. She couldn't follow what he was saying.

'So I left the first one for you. I knew you'd come through that alley. I know everything about you.' Owen stood above her, holding what looked like, from Reagan's awkward glimpse, a surgical knife. 'I can keep you alive while I remove the entire length of your large intestine. It's not difficult. I've done it to pigs.'

I'm going to die here.

'You should know I'm not interested in that. I don't get off on it. But you think you're such a smart fucking cunt, I have to make an exception.'

I'm going to be a body someone finds.

'You've forced me to do this. For exposing Elias, destroying everything he accomplished. He was brilliant, and now he's stuck in a jail cell.'

In the jungles of the Philippines, rat-eating pitcher plants secrete sweet syrup to entice mice, frogs and rats. Their prey slide inside the liquid-filled pitcher in hopes of a tasty treat, and find themselves scrabbling to climb the slippery walls. Too late. The acidic liquid has already begun to dissolve the creature alive.

Reagan had read about *Nepenthes attenboroughii* many times. She'd never once thought she might end up being the rat.

'And now I've got to dispose of you somewhere no one will find you. In a tip, I think. Chopped up, sealed in a barrel with concrete. Hell, I could leave you under the house like that. No one will come looking for you here. It's such a fucking waste. You would have made a great canvas.'

Since they'd met, an instinctive twinge had warned her about Owen. She'd thought he just didn't appreciate Min as fully as she deserved. She never could have imagined this.

'Owen?' A faraway voice called, sweetly familiar, over the squeal of a door hinge. 'Reagan?'

She strained her head toward the sound of footsteps.

Min. Min was *alive.* She stepped into focus at the far side of the room, light glinting off a rose-gold handbag. Min would help her, Min would –

A terrible thought exploded through her.

Min had told Owen where to find her.

She wasn't here to save Reagan.

She was part of it.

49

The pain that shot through Reagan at the sight of Min was unlike anything she'd experienced.

She'd trusted Min. And Min had told a sadistic killer where to find her.

No wonder she wanted to stay close to the investigation, to write about it. She must have been protecting Owen. Maybe even helping him.

Min's effort to contain her excitement at the Dover Heights crime scene – *she'd known*. She'd been waiting for it. Is this why she'd been so insistent about Reagan staying with them in Balmoral? She'd been planning this all along.

Reagan's head throbbed, the ringing in her ears swelling. Her will to fight fizzled. She was sinking into thick, black ooze. The room's lights faded. Maybe someone had switched them off.

Waves of extraordinary, searing pain crested and receded. She could trace the pain back from this moment in an unbroken chain, to her best friend's betrayal in Year Ten, the look in Brooke's eyes when she'd laughed at Reagan. *Cut the cry baby act. You were too chicken to give him your address, so I did it for you.* The fierce expression on Cynthia's face as she blamed Reagan. *I've worked myself to the bone to provide for you since your father died, and now look what you've done.* The bored exasperation on the cop's face. *You're just going to have to stay off the internet.* She'd internalised the blame, when she should have been demanding apologies.

And Min. She'd worked so hard to earn Reagan's trust. The more of someone's trust you had, the more you could hurt them. That's why Bryce had weaselled his way into her life, made himself indispensable to her. The more she wrapped herself in his support and companionship, the more she let herself think she might love him – the more he could hurt her.

Owen, with his knives and brutality, all he could cause was physical pain. In that sense he was weaker. Weaker than Bryce and much weaker than Min, who caused an acid-tipped pain that carved through Reagan's chest and into her soul.

Let this end.

There was no point in living in a world where everyone was cruel, where you had to try to hide yourself away, waiting for people you trusted to betray you.

Scuffling roused her. With immense effort, Reagan forced her eyes open to the blaring lights and turned her head. Min and Owen were hugging – or dancing? Her vision was too blurry to tell.

Her ears rang, her thoughts swam. The two of them were *celebrating* Reagan's death.

Min sank to the ground. Red splatter marked the wall behind her, abstract art. Owen towered over her.

Wait.

Had he hurt her? Was he turning on her too?

She tried to call to Min, but her tongue flopped, her mouth unresponsive. The ringing in her ears grew deafening.

Maybe the truth was that everyone eventually betrayed you, no matter what you did or who you were to them.

The blackness washed over her, and Reagan let herself drift into it. The edges of the pain softened.

This is what had happened to Krystal. She'd been right here, on this table. Reagan had found her, and someone would find Reagan too. She hoped that person would stay with her, would shoo away ibises and protect her from dogs. Like she should have done for Krystal.

Something slammed into the table. Adrenaline shot through Reagan. Her ears cleared, the noise of the room fading in with a whine, and her eyes struggled to focus, the light so bright the room seemed to glow.

Min lay slumped on the floor.

Owen stood over Reagan, his face seething. She heaved against the straps. The table wobbled underneath. There was something about the way Min lay, her head and legs at awkward angles.

Something wrong.

A switch flipped, lightning tearing up her spine. Reagan was brutally, horrifically awake.

Owen leaned toward her. Rage pulsed through her blood. She strained, thrashing against the straps, the wild animal in her loosened, adrenaline burning through her limbs.

'This is all your fault,' Owen shouted, and that only made her rock harder, feeling the table move underneath her. She rocked, giving the table momentum, bucking hard into it, and the world shifted, spinning violently as she and the table crashed to the floor.

A blood-wetted knife lay there, on the linoleum, close enough for her to grab for it, fingers wrapping around the hardness of the handle. She flailed for the strap, but she couldn't angle the knife toward it.

Owen was kicking at her arm, screaming incomprehensible expletives.

The kicks felt like nothing. She focused on his other foot, stationary and exposed. She reached out and stabbed the knife through the canvas of his shoe.

He roared and dropped to his knee.

She pulled the knife out and he grabbed for it, leaning too close. She had just enough range to slash at his calf, tearing the knife through his pants and into the flesh of his leg close to his ankle, pulling it toward her through muscle, the blade slicing the meat of his leg but catching in the khaki fabric. Blood raged in her ears like a storm.

Owen grabbed her wrist, squeezing until it gave, a collapsing of sinew and maybe bone. She clung to the knife through the pain, shoving it deeper into him. He had both hands on her wrist, screaming at her. Her fingers went numb as he wrested her arm away.

He wrenched the knife free of his leg. Bright blood gushed, soaking through his pants. Jerking upright, he kicked at her again, but the swing fell short and he collapsed onto his knee, the knife quavering toward her.

'Fucking useless *bitch*.' His voice was a hiss. He thrust his arm at her, the blade bloody.

Reagan grimaced, her whole body recoiling, the table jolting.

There was no way to escape the knife.

This is it.

The truth of it flooded her. There would be a final breath to take, a final thought, and then nothing, not even black but its absence, the absence of everything.

It was her mother that came to mind, her mother's fear. Everything in Cynthia's life had been motivated by fear and smallness. Now, in what Reagan believed was her ultimate breath, she saw her mother as a flawed and injured creature trying to shelter herself and her child from the ruthless furnace of the world, a creature made small by grief at the loss of her first husband, unable to make room for her child's needs.

She would die stripped to her underwear, her mouth full of blood, strapped to a metal table on a concrete floor. She could forgive her mother. And she could forgive herself for trusting Bryce.

The knife came at her.

50

The air shifted and Reagan opened her eyes to a blur of movement behind her.

Owen groaned and tumbled to the floor in a heap, the knife still in his hand.

The blur was Min, wielding a long, cumbersome piece of metal. She brought the object down once more and Owen crumpled. Blood seeped from his leg, spreading toward Reagan. She squirmed against the straps but they held tight to the overturned table.

'Holy shit, Rae.' Blood streaked down Min's face from a slash in her forehead. The other half of her face had begun to swell, including her split lip. Her eyes were wide, mouth slack, her expression shocked and dazed.

If she was acting, she was doing a superb job.

'Help me up,' Reagan said.

Min limped as she came toward Reagan.

She strained to push the table upright, but it was lopsided and heavy. Climbing over it, she tugged at the strap holding Reagan's hands in place. 'Shit, the buckle's wedged under here.'

'I can't move, the straps are too tight.'

'Hang on, hang on – there.'

Reagan's hands fell loose. The pain of returning blood flow prickled through her fingers.

'I can't get at the other buckles.' Panic crackled in Min's voice. 'The table is crushing them.'

'Min, is this – this isn't your house?'

'Owen's mum's. In Croydon. She died last year?' She said it as a question, as in, *Remember that?* Reagan had gone shopping with Min to find shoes for the funeral, rocking Dashiel in his pram while Min tried on black pumps.

Croydon. Reagan stretched her fingers, more prickles of feeling returning. The straps still held her chest and legs to the table, leaving her hips sagging. Her right wrist seared with pain where Owen had crushed it. She stretched her left hand for the knife, the one she'd slashed him with.

'How did he find me?'

'He found you?'

'At the beach house.' Blood dripped into her throat, and she choked, coughing fiercely.

'I told him you were staying at your stepdad's property up the coast.' Min was still pulling at the straps, panting with the effort. 'I don't know how he found it. I'm sorry, I don't understand – he went there?'

'What' – Reagan struggled to hold everything in her mind, feeling details tumble away – 'what are you doing here? How did you –'

'I don't understand,' Min repeated, stuck on the phrase.

'He told me to come with him, that you were in the hospital.'

'What?'

'Croydon . . .' The word bouncing around Reagan's brain suddenly took meaning. Croydon was in the inner west, far from Min's home in Balmoral, over the Harbour Bridge. 'How did you get here? Why . . .'

'What the fuck are you *doing*?' Owen pushed himself to his feet, one hand to his head.

'Owen,' Min said. Reagan couldn't see her behind the table. It sounded like she'd stood up. 'Stay down, stay over there. You're hurt. I'm going to get help.'

What is she thinking? Fuck. Reagan reached up with the knife and tried to cut into the strap holding her shoulders. She struggled to grip the blood-slickened handle. The thick leather resisted the blade.

'You're supposed to help me!' Owen flew toward them. Min came crashing over the table, kicking wildly, her bare foot hitting Reagan in the jaw.

Owen had her by the hair. 'You're supposed to help me!'

Reagan's head was pounding, the room swirling and yawning. Was she hearing him right?

Why would Min have tried to free her if she was involved? *To cover her tracks. She knows how to fool the cops.*

So why not just kill Reagan?

She sawed furiously at the strap, the blade slipping, nicking her knuckles. The leather started to give, the strap tearing under her weight, and her upper body dropped.

'We can fix this.' Owen's voice was ragged. 'No one has to know. We get a couple of barrels, get rid of her tonight. If Elias is smart, if he keeps quiet, there's no link to me.'

He still had Min by the hair, and she writhed on her tiptoes, clawing at his hands. 'Let me – stop! *Stop!*' Fear pierced each word.

Reagan propped herself on her side, lunging for the strap beneath her knees. Owen dragged Min toward Reagan and kicked at her hands, droplets of blood flying from his bloody leg.

His foot crashed into her, and the knife skittered out of reach.

'Do you see what she's doing, Min? She's trying to ruin our family. You insisted on bringing this whore into our life. I'm trying to fix it!'

She had to get her feet free. The strap was tight, flattening her calves against the table, but she could wriggle her legs, twisting, grabbing the metal lip for leverage. She heaved, her hands slipping on warm blood.

Her legs shifted under the strap.

'You need an ambulance!'

'Stop fighting me!'

A bang interrupted the shouting. Reagan pulled her feet free as Owen cracked Min's head against the wall. She collapsed to the floor.

Reagan was still on the floor, perched on her tailbone, her feet numb from restricted blood flow. Owen lunged at her, his shouts incoherent – Min slumped down the wall, her head at such an awkward angle, *could her neck be* – and he crashed into Reagan like a bull, grabbing her by the shoulders.

She went limp, her eyes closed, regret pulsing. Min had offered real love, in her own abrasive way. Reagan had put up walls, keeping her out. Waiting for Min to betray her.

And maybe that was its own betrayal.

Owen was on top of her, hitting her in the face, the pain chaotic. She forced herself to stay limp. He was stronger than her, but he was overconfident. She probably couldn't save herself, but if she could buy Min enough time to get up and out of the room, to call for help . . .

She felt him slacken. *Wait.*

He started to get off her, to stand up. *One more second.*

The knife was under her hand and she grabbed it, moving fast. He was on his knees, still pushing himself up. He didn't see it coming.

The blade went into his side below his rib cage, right to the handle. He screamed, wild, throwing himself sideways with the impact.

Reagan was up, sprinting the few steps toward Min, her foot hitting a slick of blood and sliding the final inches. The blood trickled toward a drain in the floor.

'Min, get up!' Was she breathing? *This isn't going to work.* 'Where's your phone? Your phone!'

At the edge of Reagan's vision, Owen pushed himself to his feet, staggering.

Min made a noise, unintelligible, her eyelids flickering. Reagan had one hand on her shoulder, shaking her. She tried to pat her pockets with the other hand, but it flopped strangely. *Where's the goddamn phone?*

'Up, get up!' she shouted, and Min's eyes snapped open. She jumped to her feet, rocking back against the wall, Reagan clinging to her. Her hand in the pocket of Min's blazer unsteadied them both.

Owen shouted. Blood spluttered from his mouth, dripping on to his chin.

He had a knife, not the short-bladed one protruding from his side, but a much larger one, the clean metal catching the light.

Four steps away and moving fast. Reagan grabbed onto Min, out of ideas, her panic explosive.

Owen hit the slick of blood – his own blood, from the leg wound that continued to seep – and his momentum shifted, his leg sliding, his arms going up, the knife coming free, his body arching.

The noise the table made as the back of his head collided with its upright metal edge was like a cleaver into meat.

The buzzing of the overhead lights rushed into the silence. Reagan and Min stood rigid, uncertain. Owen lay unmoving, his legs wide, one arm pitched above his head and propped against the table.

'Min, where's your –'

Min was in motion, running for Owen, dropping to her knees, hands on his face. 'What have you *done*?' The last word came out as a keening. She bent and pressed her face into his chest.

As Reagan's adrenaline faded, pain set fire to her shoulder. Her breath came in shuddering huffs, and she doubled over, fighting nausea. The fire radiated through her rib cage and into her neck and arm. Wet blood ran from the wound, slow but persistent. She grabbed her torn shirt off the floor, balling it against the cut.

The table lay on its side, blood pooled and smeared around the crumpled straps. Smears of blood marred the white walls. A Polaroid camera sat on the bench.

Min's wailing softened, and Reagan hobbled toward her, wincing and hissing through her teeth. She repeated Min's name quietly, leery that Owen would lurch upright again.

She touched her left hand to Min's shoulder. Her right hung limp and numb.

'Where's your phone?'

'He was renting it. He told me he was renting it.' Min pointed to the ceiling, her words jumbled in a horrified rush. 'He's got this soundproofed. He had these renos done when she died, to rent it out, he said. He must have been planning – how *could* he? *How* could he have done this? When Dashiel was born. He couldn't have. And I didn't – I didn't see . . .'

Right. Owen's mother had died of pneumonia a couple of weeks after Dashiel was born. Reagan had only met her once, at Min's wedding.

She wanted to ask how Min had found her, how she'd come at just the right time. But she looked like she was going into shock, staring slack-jawed at a blood-free spot on the wall. The purple swelling in her face was getting worse, one eye puffing shut.

Gritting her teeth, Reagan reached for Owen's outstretched arm, pressing her fingers to his wrist. No pulse.

Min rocked, his hand sandwiched between hers. Blood speckled the platinum of his wedding band.

'We need –' the pain surged and Reagan's voice crackled, a cry breaking in. 'We need an ambulance.'

Min nodded, staring into a corner of the room. She folded Owen's hand onto his chest and struggled to her feet. She was missing a shoe. Reagan searched but couldn't find it.

'Will you be able to get up the stairs?'

'Stairs?' Min asked.

Reagan had assumed they were in a basement. Elizabeth Short, the Black Dahlia, had almost certainly been killed in the basement of the Hodel house.

Min hobbled across the room and pushed the door open. A seal ran around its edges. A solitary light fixture hung midway down the hall, which opened to a kitchen and lounge room. 'It's a bedroom.'

Reagan grimaced, propping herself against the wall for support, smearing blood. The *clink* of something tiny hitting a dry spot on the concrete floor came from beneath her. One of the black studs had fallen out of her ear. She reached for it, and saw the back was still attached. It had torn through her earlobe.

Min took a few steps and faltered, half-turning, disoriented. 'Oh god, Rae, get rid of those earrings.'

'What?' Reagan tensed, her hand lifting to the other earlobe. She winced with the effort. 'Don't tell me they're from one of the dead women.'

Min looked horrified. Her handbag lay inside the door, and she picked it up, her voice steadying somewhat as she dug through it. 'I had Gamo buy them from some shady site when you told me you were leaving the city. They've got a tracking device in them. A really fucking expensive one.'

Reagan's fingertips caressed the earring.

'I was so worried about you, and I know it seems extreme, but with your name all over the news, which was my fault . . . I realised you might not wear them, but I didn't know what else to do.'

Unexpectedly, Reagan started to cry, overcome by the surprising feeling that she liked Min knowing where she was. She liked Min *knowing* her.

She wiped her nose on her wrist. 'That's how you . . . ?'

'I've been checking the app since you left. I was surprised when I saw you coming back into Sydney tonight, and then you were at this address and I thought, I don't know, maybe you and Owen were having an affair . . .' She put her hands on her knees, a tremble in her shoulders and her voice. 'I mean, not actually, but I couldn't reach Owen, and I had this sick feeling.'

Reagan put her hand on Min's shoulder, holding it there. 'You saved me.' The quiet in the house was unnerving, like the rest of the world had been erased.

Min started to shake violently, hyperventilating, her words jumbled. 'He can't have done this – he can't, our anniversary is next week, we're going to Fiji over Easter.' She dropped to her knees, one hand on the wall.

'Min.' Reagan tried to steady her voice. 'We need an ambulance.'

'My phone's . . .' She pushed the handbag toward Reagan. 'I can't find it.'

With her injured arm still pinning the balled-up T-shirt to her shoulder, Reagan upended the bag onto the floor. The phone bounced, landing facedown.

NSW Police evidence #JY2872901-2
Excerpts from direct messages between Elias Thomas Wiler
(aliases Bryce Stewart, Adam Hull) and Owen Chasse.
Retrieved from a forensic examination of Owen Chasse's
computer hard drive.

http://sanct626kufc4mhn92bb03.onion/DMs

10 May 2015 [From Owen]
Thank you for inviting me into the Sanctum. I'd been
hoping for more from the Rally For Men group, and I'm glad
my posts drew your attention. Your project is brilliant.
The point you made about the men who take a gun and shoot
up crowds — I agree, it's brutish and achieves nothing.
The psychological warfare you're waging against the female
takeover of society is much more strategic. And much more
interesting.

I'm curious, have you heard of George Hodel?

10 May 2015 [From Elias]
Glad to have you here, man. Just looked up Hodel. So they
think he killed a bunch of women in LA and Chicago, then
went to San Fran and became the Zodiac Killer? Pretty
impressive if that's all true.

11 May 2015 [From Owen]
That's what's most astounding about Hodel. He was never
caught, never took credit, at least not publicly. When the
LA cops started to close in on him, he likely bribed them.
(Back when only men were allowed on the police force,

I imagine they were keen to help him.) But Hodel learned
from his early efforts and operated freely after that.
He never spent time in prison, lived a full life, and was
still dedicated to his work in his later years. Something
to aspire to.

—

7 September 2015 [From Owen]
Congrats on your work with Target 06. Your ingenuity is
a pleasure to witness. The group you've curated here
are impressive too. None of that frothing at the mouth
immaturity you find on so many sites.

It's time I told you that I have my own work underway.
It's a slow process of preparation, but I like to make
sure things are done right. If I were a different sort of
person, I might curate a group of like-minded individuals,
the way you've done, to share the triumph with. Instead,
I'm hoping you can be my sole witness.

7 September 2015 [From Elias]
You've got me intrigued, man.

7 September 2015 [From Owen]
Have you read much about Dennis Rader? Naming himself BTK
was melodramatic, but I find him an interesting case. He
killed ten people over a span of decades, all while living
a double life as a dedicated family man, a husband and
father. His downfall was that he wanted a legacy, which
led to him getting caught. If he'd had someone to share
his work with, I wonder if he would have felt the need to
communicate with the police.

The irony is that we wouldn't know about his family life
if he hadn't been caught. How many killers are there
like him, whose family and church lives provide effective
camouflage?

I could spend hours discussing Rader, but I have a
pig carcass to dissect. Did you know their spines are
anatomically similar to human spines?

8 September 2015 [From Elias]
Don't tell me you're thinking of getting MARRIED.
I couldn't stand having some bitch tracking my every move.
The only domestic situation I could tolerate is a harem —
keep a bunch of foids locked up and pushing out kids
except when you want two or three in the bedroom.

8 September 2015 [From Owen]
I'll let you in on my secret — I'm already married.
Unmarried women become whores. You have to do your part to
prevent society from being overrun. It's all part of the
effort to forge a better world for our sons.

9 September 2015 [From Elias]
You have a KID? Man, I hope you're not one of those
brainwashed sub-males who changes nappies and shit.

10 September 2015 [From Owen]
What're a few nappies when you're playing ten-dimensional
chess? Besides, I married well. I have a mother-in-law who
believes in the value of changing nappies. And in leaving
me alone to do my work.

I'll admit that my ultimate fantasy is a son who grows up to one day reveal my legacy to the world, like Hodel's son has. I wonder if Hodel encouraged him to become a police detective, or if that was simply one of life's beautiful coincidences?

10 September 2015 [From Elias]
Big talk! You still haven't told me what you're planning.

10 September 2015 [From Owen]
You'll know it when the time comes.

—

30 April 2016 [From Owen]
I'm wondering if you take suggestions for targets? There's someone who'd make a fascinating challenge for you, and who I suspect is your type. I'd consider using her myself, but the connection to me is slightly too close. She's in Sydney.

1 May 2016 [From Elias]
I haven't taken requests before, but send me her info. I'll have a look. I'd definitely be up for a challenge. It's starting to get too easy. Fucken foids put their whole lives online, they're like ducks in a goddamn barrel.

1 May 2016 [From Owen]
Her name's Reagan Carsen. She runs a garden centre in Sydney's inner west. Here's what's interesting — she only uses the internet for her business. She doesn't even have a smartphone. If friends text her, she PHONES them back.

I want to wrap my hands around her throat and bash her head against a wall.

Here's a photo.
RC.jpg

1 May 2016 [From Elias]
Sounds like a self-important bitch! Single, no kids?

1 May 2016 [From Owen]
Fits all your criteria. Who would marry her?

1 May 2016 [From Elias]
It's outrageous that whores like this are allowed to vote. All she's good for is having babies and she's not even doing that. I can't find anything about her online, except this stupid plant shop. Man, you really brought the hot tip!

—

4 January 2017 [From Owen]
I see myself as the Leonard Lake to your Charles Ng. You might not have considered yourself in those terms before, but I think they're apt. Though in many ways what you do is more malicious.

4 January 2017 [From Elias]
Lake and Ng, what a couple of nutters. Are you telling me you're building a bunker? Haha. I'm still waiting to hear what you're up to, man.

BTW I've got your Target request in play. Looking forward to fucking her up.

—

15 Jan 2017 [From Owen]
After years of planning, the day has finally arrived. By now you've seen the news. I could tell you about it in electrifying detail, but I know we share a preference for the visual.

02-1024x685hax.jpg
07-830x719hax.jpg
11-577x900hax.jpg

More to come.

15 January 2017 [From Elias]
Wow, you weren't fucking around! I don't know, man, you've got some titanium balls, but that kind of shit brings a lot of heat. Most of the foids I've targeted haven't reported my shit to the cops because it makes them look like gigantic idiots. A lot easier to keep out of prison that way.

16 January 2017 [From Owen]
That's all you have to say? You think I'm going to get caught? What kind of hack do you take me for?

16 January 2017 [From Elias]
Target 09 lives pretty fucken close to where you dumped that first body. That better be a major coincidence.

17 January 2017 [From Owen]
Would I let any detail come down to coincidence? I wanted
her to be afraid more than anyone, even if I could never
use her myself. I thought you'd be amused by this secret
connection between our work.

18 January 2017 [From Elias]
You could have fucken warned me about this shit when
you gave me her name! You've got every cop in the state
looking for you.

19 January 2017 [From Owen]
Stop whining, 'Bryce'. I gave you her name a year ago.
I didn't know you'd take so long to act on it. I wasn't
about to wait around to see if you could manage to fit the
perfect target into your schedule.

23 February 2017 [From Elias]
What the fuck, man, you're taking photos, sending them to
me, to TV stations, who knows what else? It's not 1947.
There's DNA and all that CSI shit. Going to be tough to
bribe everyone.

25 February 2017 [From Owen]
The cops have asked the FBI for help. I'm taking that as a
sign my re-creation was faithful to Hodel's vision.

So many men don't take any action beyond their endless
online bitching. To really leave a mark requires a
profound statement. That's what Hodel did. He saw females

for what they really are - raw materials waiting to be transformed. Beyond providing sexual gratification and childbirth, their lives only acquire meaning when a Man chooses to elevate them to art. And one chunk of clay is no more special than any other.

Of course, with their smaller, less functional brains, they have no way of perceiving that.

What's most impressive about Hodel is that, despite the grandiosity of his work, he felt no desire for fame. He walked away, let the work stand on its own. He was constantly reinventing himself, like Picasso. Yet he did the work and never took credit for it. That is the definition of a Supreme Man.

Further, his work made evident his Manifesto. He took his secrets to his illustrious grave, but gifted us with the clues necessary to uncover his legacy. He showed his power not by shooting a gun into a yoga studio, not by driving a car into random pedestrians, but by creating True Terror through the highest form of Art that Mankind has ever conceived.

This is how a Real Statement is made, a Statement about the rightful position of females in society, a Statement that will have resonance, a Statement that is layered and refined and grandiose in its planning and execution.

25 February 2017 [From Elias]
You can make all the fancy proclamations you want, but if you
get caught because of DNA or whatever else Hodel never had to
worry about it, you better not drag me into your mess.

I've put a lot of effort into Target 09 and I've got a
captive, salivating audience to cater to, but I'm thinking
of cutting my losses and getting the fuck out of Sydney.
You're drawing way too much heat. What the fuck else do
you have planned?

25 February 2017 [From Owen]
Nothing. A fallow period. Finish your little game with
Reagan. I thought you were worthy of her. I'm usually not
so wrong.

The FBI isn't doing anything more than reviewing their
ancient files on the Black Dahlia. And I don't think you
have anything to fear from the NSW police.

Look what I've achieved. International headlines.
Feminoids too afraid to go out alone. A definitive
statement about the primacy of men and our role in
the world.

—

5 March 2017 [From Elias]
This is what you call FALLOW? A third body?!? You're
fucken nuts. You better make sure you raze every record of
my site, these messages, everything. I won't go to prison
because you get off chopping people up.

7 March 2017 [From Elias]
THERE'S A VIDEO OF THE BITCH FINDING THAT FUCKEN BODY?!
Why am I learning this shit from the goddamn news?

7 March 2017 [From Owen]
This is the first I'm learning of it myself. What, your
girlfriend never told you I left the body for her? Seems
like you don't know her as well as you thought.

7 March 2017 [From Elias]
I'd turn you into the police myself except you're such a
loose fucken unit, you'll probably go blabbing about my
operations to try to save your own sorry arse. You better
watch your back.

8 March 2017 [From Owen]
Don't you understand?! You inspired me to act on my
ambitions. I'd confess my own actions to the police before
I'd compromise you. I've done this for our cause. I've
done this for YOU.

[Correspondence ends]

51

Friday, 17 March 2017

It was Lonski, smelling of cigarettes and a headachy perfume, who picked Reagan up when she was discharged from the hospital three days later, her wrist itching madly under its cast. She'd already made a statement, Lonski and Ngo sitting beside the hospital bed, notepads open, voice recorder running.

'We found a box full of licence plates in the garage of the house,' Lonski said, her voice as flinty as ever. Tracking those plate numbers, the strike force had found the black Toyota Corolla, belonging to Owen's deceased mother, in the vicinity of each crime scene, with different licence plates each time.

Out the window, the glass and steel of the CBD flashed past on her right, the azure twinkle of Darling Harbour to the left.

'And we've cleared Min-lee Chasse,' Lonski said. 'She has strong alibis for the timeframes in question. She was surprised to learn Owen had quit his job at the start of the year. She's lucky their financial statements support her narrative.' Min and Owen had separate bank accounts, separate banks, and contributed to a common account for household bills. When they got engaged, they'd agreed to financial independence. Min had talked about it a lot, was proud of it.

'You don't need to convince me,' Reagan said. 'I know she couldn't have anything to do with it.'

'Try convincing the public about that. "How could she not have known?" Speculative bullshit.'

What do you know, even Lonski's got some empathy.

Ahead, the traffic came to a standstill, a stream of red brake lights stretching for blocks ahead. They sat, Reagan trying to scratch under the edge of the cast. Her shoulder burned under the stitches. Time for another round of painkillers.

'I suppose you've cleared me too,' Reagan said, half joking.

There was no humour in Lonski's voice. 'As much as possible, yes.'

'It'd be nice to get an apology.' She was still joking, trying to soften the mood. 'You know, for the interrogation. And for busting into my apartment at 4 am.'

The light cycled from green to red with no movement. Lonski kept her eyes on the traffic. 'I'm not going to apologise for doing my job.'

Fair enough.

—

Journos crowded the Four Seasons lobby. Lonski arranged a manager to meet them at a service entrance and escort Reagan to floor 31.

Min opened the door wearing a white hotel robe, her hair wet and tangled, the smell of freesia and ylang-ylang drifting. Her face looked pale, her split lip less swollen but still raw, one purpled eye still partially closed. Reagan expected Min to wrap her in a hug, but her arms hung limp. The hospital had kept her for twenty-four hours, monitoring for concussion and infection. She'd spent the next day with the police, making a detailed statement.

It was midday, but Min had the curtains closed, lamps glowing yellow.

'I convinced Lonski to make a stop so I could get us some duck curry.' Reagan held up the bag.

'I'm not hungry.'

Min had booked a suite so she, Hyun-sook and the kids could stay together. The police were dismantling their house, looking for evidence.

'Your mum's out?'

'Took the kids up to the pool. Maisey keeps asking about Dad,' Min said, her voice flat and quiet. '*Dad, Dad, Dad.* We told her he's away.'

Reagan didn't know what to say to that.

A voice came from the corridor and they both froze, eyes on the door until the sound faded. Reagan sat at the dining table and opened the duck curry, its rich smell filling the room. She pulled chopsticks from the bag and picked out a lychee. It looked like an eyeball.

'I tried to call yesterday. Lonski said you turned your phone off.'

'All my colleagues are in the media, so you can imagine . . .' Min ran a hand down her face, folding herself onto one of the sofas.

Her hairbrush lay on the end table, and she picked it up, staring at it like she couldn't remember what it was for.

'A lot of people asked about you. At the press conference.'

Min turned the brush over. 'I called Yolanda yesterday and asked her to go to the house and pick up a few of the kids' things. The look on her face when she dropped them off . . .'

It was like Min was lost. 'Have you talked to your contact? Detective Turner?' Reagan asked.

'Oh.' A hint of Min's former liveliness flicked across her face. 'You can't mention this, but I found out who identified you. From the GoPro footage.'

'Who?'

'Bloke named Ed Drucker. He wanted to know if there was reward money.'

The Ferguson Seeds rep. He'd spent enough time staring at Reagan's body to recognise it.

She picked at the curry, trying to wait, but couldn't hold back. 'Talk to me, Min. How could Owen have done this?'

'I can't make sense of it. He seemed so . . . normal.'

'So did Bryce.'

'You knew him two months. I've been with Owen five fucking years. Now I have to question everything. Like with his mum . . .'

'What?' Reagan started. 'Did he kill her?'

'She caught a bad flu, and was sick for a while. Who knows? Lonski's checking with the hospital, but of course there was no autopsy, and she was cremated.' A fire replaced her malaise. 'Remember that whole thing about her not liking me because I'm "Asian"? I think he was lying from right when we first met.

380

He didn't want me spending time with anyone who might contradict the story he was spinning.'

A chill crept into Reagan.

'The police are going through his hard drive,' Min said. She gestured to a sheaf of papers on the desk. 'Did they tell you he was part of Bryce's dark web group? Owen *bragged* about the murders in messages to Bryce. He must have thought the dark web site was so secure, his messages would never be exposed.'

Reagan was struggling to keep up. 'Didn't the police say the killer must have had surgical training to cut the women's spines the way he did?'

'He'd been practising on pigs.'

I can keep you alive while I remove the entire length of your large intestine. The memory seized her.

'There's a walk-in freezer in the basement at his mum's place, full of pigs strung up by their hind legs,' Min continued. 'They think that's where he kept Krystal after he killed her. They're checking for DNA.'

A bang echoed from the corridor. They both flinched. Tiny feet came running past the door, little voices giggling.

Reagan waited for her heart to slow. 'So why . . . why would he . . . ?'

'Reading through some of the evidence Lonski's shared, things he wrote, it's all excuses.'

'But why was he obsessed with Elizabeth Short's murder?'

'He never talked about it, and even after the news broke about Krystal, he didn't act particularly interested. But they found an enormous shelf of books on the Black Dahlia at his mum's place, including ones by Steve Hodel . . . And now he's dead, so I can't ask him. He's a stranger to me. And there's so much we don't know.' Min's hands whipped around while she talked, frenetic. 'It's obvious he was egotistical and narcissistic and violent, and in control enough to hide that for years. I thought he respected my career ambitions. But he wanted me wrapped up in my own work and in being a mum so I was too distracted to notice his secret life.'

'So Owen was . . . faking his emotions?'

'I thought the killer was incapable of guilt and empathy, that his actions were for his own amusement. But Owen really loved the kids. That never felt fake. I've been trying to think if there was any sign, any time he was violent or . . . The only thing I can think of is that, after Maisey, he really wanted our second child to be a boy. But so did I – one of each.'

'Is that possible? For him to love them?'

'Some killers separate their home life from their violence.' Still on her feet, Min paced around the table. 'Dennis Rader killed ten people in Kansas while married with kids and was apparently a great dad. He was a church elder, an Eagle Scout leader. Had a normal childhood too, like Owen always said he had. John Edward Robinson murdered eight women brutally, hid their bodies in barrels on his property, and his children and grandchildren couldn't believe what he'd been accused of. They loved him; he babysat and coached little league. And Keith Jesperson. He was a husband and father during his murder spree, and he had seven or eight victims, all women. Though he wasn't as successful at keeping things separate. He killed a bunch of kittens in front of his daughter.'

'Thank god Maisey and Dashiel are too young to remember any of this,' Reagan said, giving into the insistent urge to *look on the bright side*, even in a situation like this.

'But they'll live with it forever. And what am I going to tell them?' Min stopped abruptly, her hands covering her face. 'It's my fault this happened to you, to the kids, I should have seen –'

'Whoa. Stop.' Reagan took Min's arm, easing her onto the sofa.

'I can never go back to our house. When the cops are done with it, I don't know. I might – I don't even want the baby photos. He's in all our family pictures.' Tears ran down her cheeks. 'It's like I killed them myself.'

'Your kids are fine!'

'I mean the women. Krystal and Erin and Willow. I was writing articles about their deaths while living with the man who killed them. Why couldn't I see it? I could have stopped him. I talked to him about the murders every day, and he just nodded along.'

Reagan squeezed her hand. Min could see through Reagan because of her uncertainty, her hesitation. She couldn't see through Owen.

'I feel like they're here,' she said, 'all three of them. Asking how I couldn't have known. He was so *good* with the kids. He made Maisey laugh all the time. How could he –'

She doubled over, crying harder. Reagan folded her arms around Min's shoulders, her whole body rocking.

Reagan didn't feel the need to push away. She could sit here with her friend through to nightfall, and into the next day, and forever. It was a strange feeling.

Min dug her fingers into the sleeve of Reagan's cardigan, holding on. Reagan's stomach turned icy. She was thrust back to Pearl Beach, rushing along in the dark beside Owen, his hand gripping her arm.

Then Min snuffed once, twice, and Reagan felt the warmth of her friend's body against hers, caught the scent of ritzy hotel shampoo and duck curry. Reagan jumped at every shadow, every tiny noise, and in the hospital she'd only been able to sleep with the lights on and the TV turned up.

But she was okay.

She held Min tighter.

https://www.anewplaceformen.com

New post from Ry291
1 March 2018, 11.29

This post is on behalf of Elias Wiler, one of the greatest
martyrs for men's rights of the 21st century. I've visited
him in Long Bay and though he has been denied internet
access, he will continue to communicate through me.

We know the reason Elias is in prison. He was targeted by
Reagan Carsen, a lying cunt who wants him and all men to
suffer.

This whore-mouthed bitch represents everything wrong
in our lives, everything that's holding us back from
achieving our full male potential. She needs to be
stopped.

Find her address, find all her details, flood her with
messages. Make her know we're coming.

We need to destroy her.

– 3,729 comments –

Author's note

I f you asked me, as a lifelong thriller fan, to name the most chilling book I'd read, for many years my answer would have been *Red Dragon* by Thomas Harris.

Then, in 2020, Laura Bates came out with *Men Who Hate Women*. Bates isn't a thriller writer, and *Men Who Hate Women* isn't fiction. It's a deep dive into the growing network of misogynists that thrives online and leeches into all aspects of our lives. Bates interviews former members of extremist groups that plan and commit acts of terrorism against women and society, and that strategise best practices for radicalising and grooming teenage boys through social media. It's a disturbing, urgent book.

Bates's work informed a lot of this novel, as did Steve Hodel's ongoing investigation into the 1947 murder of Elizabeth Short and his father's involvement. Details about the Black Dahlia and George Hodel's friendship with Man Ray come from Steve's website, books and interviews, from the podcast *Root of Evil*, and from Steve himself.

I've also taken inspiration from *Hunting Warhead*, a podcast about the investigation into the world's largest child abuse website; *The Darkest Web* by Australian true-crime author and investigative journalist Eileen Ormsby; and *Rattled* by Ellis Gunn, a memoir of surviving a stalker.

Two books that inspired Reagan's smartphone reluctance are *The Way Home: Tales from a Life Without Technology* by Irish author Mark Boyle, and *The Stranger in the Woods: The Extraordinary Story of the Last True Hermit* by Michael Finkel. Both were published after January 2017, but no other books suited Reagan and Bryce's conversation quite as perfectly. I hope you'll forgive this slight bending of the space-time continuum.

Maisey's favourite book, *Kookoo Kookaburra*, is by First Nations author and illustrator Gregg Dreise.

The researcher who experimented on rhesus monkeys to prove that babies need love was Harry Harlow; I learned about his work in *Stranger Care* by Sarah Sentilles.

I highly recommend all of these resources.

While I've drawn from a lot of true events, and included many true-to-life Sydney details, *Dark Mode* is a work of fiction.

Acknowledgements

I wrote the majority of this book on the lands of the Gadigal People of the Eora Nation. I acknowledge the Traditional Owners of Country across Australia, and recognise their continuing connection to land, waters and culture. I'm grateful to write in a beautiful place with rich storytelling traditions.

An enormous thank you to my readers – thank you for choosing this book, for supporting literary culture, for being your excellent self. It's been a strange journey to get here, but it turns out deep in my soul I'm a crime writer. (I probably could have guessed when my first book opened with an assassination.) I plan on writing many more psychological thrillers, and I hope you'll join me as I keep exploring the chilling aspects of human nature.

The Ultimo Press team swept into my life bearing apricot-almond squares covered in dark chocolate. I still can't believe how lucky I am to be working with James Kellow, Robert Watkins, Alisa Ahmed, Emily Cook, Katherine Rajwar, Brigid Mullane, and especially Alex Craig, who texts me articles about stalkers and really knows how to make a manuscript shine. Thanks also to Copyeditor Supreme Deonie Fiford, plus Rebecca Hamilton, Simon Paterson at Bookhouse, George Saad, and everyone working behind the scenes to bring books to readers.

Pippa Masson is a literary firecracker who sends the best emails a writer could hope to receive. Thanks also Caitlan Cooper-Trent, Dan Lazar, Caitlin Leydon and Kate Cooper for your hard work and utter magnificence.

In March 2020, I was supposed to spend a weekend at Clunes with Anna Downes, R.W.R. McDonald, Petronella McGovern and J.P. Pomare. We met on Zoom instead. Their friendship helped convince me I could wrangle this story into an actual book, and their support has felt like winning the lottery. Special thanks to Anna and Petronella, whose wisdom helped shape an unwieldy early draft.

My immense thanks to James McKenzie Watson for his luminous friendship. I had the privilege of watching James transform from mediocre aspiring writer to exceptionally talented, award-winning debut author within a few short years, and I'm still in awe. I'm also grateful for the years we've spent podcasting together. Chronic illness made my life smaller, but it's also allowed me to connect on a deeper level to others living with ongoing health challenges. To James and all our podcast guests who've shared your experiences, thank you for making the hard days easier.

James gave his usual incisive feedback at several stages of this book. For feedback on early drafts, my deepest thanks to Ren Arcamone, who immediately understood what this novel was really about, and always inspires me to write better; Jacqui Dent, the only person to have read all my manuscripts (except the unreadable ones); utter joy Michele Danno – your sharp feedback is always welcome; Cathy Johnstone, possibly the kindest person on Earth; Amanda Ortlepp, another sharp thinker and plotter; and Sanchana Venkatesh, one of the best people to talk books with. Amy Lovat, your enthusiasm, dedication and joyfulness are an endless inspiration. I'm so glad books brought us together. Thanks enormously also to Pip Drysdale, Dinuka McKenzie, Hayley Scrivenor and Lyn Yeowart.

I'm lucky to have two incredible feedback groups. Huge thanks to Peter Higham (for all the rats and mice), Jay Martin, Jonathon Shannon and Simon Veksner and others already mentioned here – this book is immensely better for all your generous feedback and discussion. Eternal thanks to Michelle Troxler, who started it all.

To Andrew Patterson, fellow crime writer and ex-cop, thanks for sharing your fascinating experiences and casting your forensic eye over the story (and for letting me keep the battering ram). And to the cop who left his business card in that Newtown cafe and then replied to my random email, thanks for the intel.

The extraordinarily excellent people at Writing NSW deserve special mention, especially Jane McCredie, Julia Tsalis, and Claire Thompson. Thanks to everyone I was lucky enough to work with over my years there, including our exceptional tutors. I learned so much from all of you.

I wrote the first words of what would become *Dark Mode* in the Ladder Room at Varuna, the National Writers' House. Create NSW supported the manuscript's development with a Small Project Grant. I also received a fellowship from Katharine Susannah Prichard

Writers' Centre, and was an artist-in-residence at Bundanon Trust. I'm grateful to these institutions and their dedicated staff, who have worked especially hard to continue to support artists through the upheaval of climate crises and the pandemic. Thanks also to fellow artists who shared plant insights, especially Rebecca Mayo, Callum G'Froerer, Aimee Gardyne, Sarah Rayner and Sophie Carnell.

I owe huge thanks to the authors, editors and other professionals who have supported my writing career, many of whom I'm lucky to count as friends. Special mention to Louise Allan, Jean Bedford, Kavita Bedford, Katherine Collette, Pamela Cook, Samuel Elliott, Judyth Emanuel, Candice Fox, Marcelle Freiman, Linda Funnell, Jackie Gent, Nicole Hodgson, Darryl Jones, Toni Jordan, Emily Maguire, Kate Mildenhall, Monique Mulligan, Bronwyn Mehan (who launched my career and remains a strident supporter), L.J.M. Owen, Cathy Perkins, Arna Radovich, Fiona Robertson, Serge Selian, Annabel Smith, Laurie Steed, Rachael Turk and Alex Alexander, and the irrepressible Dani Vee. Cass Moriarty, your joyful enthusiasm was one of the highlights of this whole adventure. Jacinta Dietrich, I hope this doesn't give you nightmares, but you know if it does, I want to hear about them. Walter Mason and Lee Kofman, there's a special place in my heart devoted to you.

Through her skilled mentorship, Sarah Sentilles has impacted this book in profound ways. I'm grateful to her and for the ongoing camaraderie of Authors Anonymous, especially Katherine Tamiko Arguile, Shelley Baird, Robynne Berg, Bronwyn Birdsall, Liza Boston, Jane Briggs, Alison Flett, Noè Harsel, Anne Keely, Melissa Manning, Anne Myers, Rachael Mead, Julie Perrin, Anne Pitt and Sue White.

My lifelong thanks to friends who've supported me in myriad ways – Alexandra Berlioz, Eleanora Bodini, Michelle de Souza, Leo and Marion Dent, Oldooz Dianat, Kate Dilanchian, Adele Dumont, Rosie Evanian, Ani Fabricatorian and the Galoyan family, Robert Fairhead, Scott Gibbons, Fran Giudici, Samia Goudie, Sarah Hodges-Kolisnyk, Fran Jakin, Rhonda Kaidbay, Mark Keenan, Helena Klanjscek, Sherry Landow, Kate Leaver, Sneha Lees, Sharon Livingstone, Dash Maiorova, Alyona Morozava, Arminé Nalbandian, Carol Neuschul, Marije Nieuwenhuis and Richard Heersmink, Sheila Pham, Rachel Ramberran, Ruth Rinot, Ruth Shead, Khyati Sharma (whose boundless love of good books is a joy), Laura Setyo, Cassie Watson and Lindsey Wiebe.

To my parents, I'm grateful for you every day. Thanks also to all my family, especially Pam Blunt and Kerry and Janet McLuhan.

My husband Steve came up with the book's title early one morning while we were swimming at Camp Cove, and shouted it over the waves. Since 2016, Steve has been reheating my hot water bottle, tucking me under my weighted blanket, making my rhubarb stew, and generally caring for me on all the long, hard days I'm unable to care for myself. In return, I promise not to talk about murders at breakfast.

ASHLEY KALAGIAN BLUNT is the author of *How to Be Australian* and *My Name Is Revenge*, which was a finalist in the 2018 Carmel Bird Digital Literary Award. Her writing appears in the *Sydney Morning Herald, Overland, Griffith Review, Sydney Review of Books, Australian Book Review, Kill Your Darlings* and more. Ashley teaches creative writing and co-hosts *James and Ashley Stay at Home*, a podcast about writing, creativity and health. Originally from Canada, she has lived and worked in South Korea, Peru and Mexico. *Dark Mode* is her first psychological thriller.